SHADOWS OF WAR

SHATTERED HONOR

ANNE WHEELER

For Meghan and Hope, who asked for more Chase.

. . . they shall beat their swords into plowshares, and their spears into pruning hooks; nation shall not lift up sword against nation, neither shall they learn war anymore.

ISAIAH 2:4

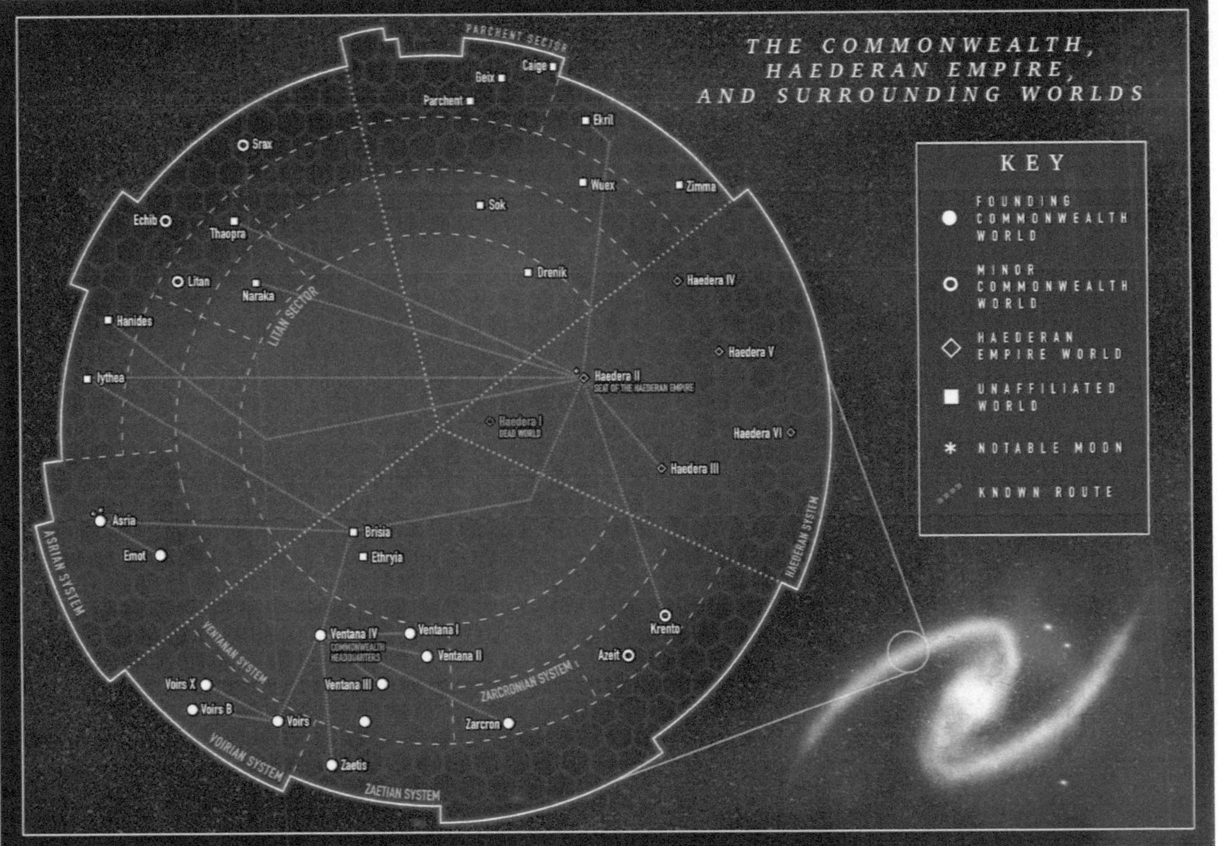

THE COMMONWEALTH,
HAEDERAN EMPIRE,
AND SURROUNDING WORLDS
PARCHENT SECTOR
Caige
Geix
Parchent
Ekril
Srax
Wuex
Zimma
Sok
Echib
Thaopra
Drenik
Haedera IV
Litan
Naraka
Haedera V
Hanides
LITAN SECTOR
Iythea
Haedera II
SEAT OF THE HAEDERAN EMPIRE
Haedera I
DEAD WORLD
Haedera VI
Haedera III
Asria
Brisia
Emot
Ethryia
HAEDERAN SYSTEM
Krento
ASRIAN SYSTEM
Ventana IV
Ventana I
COMMONWEALTH
HEADQUARTERS
Azeit
VENTANAN SYSTEM
Ventana II
Ventana III
ZARCRONIAN SYSTEM
Voirs X
Voirs B
Voirs
Zarcron
VOIRIAN SYSTEM
Zaetis
ZAETIAN SYSTEM
KEY
FOUNDING COMMONWEALTH WORLD
MINOR COMMONWEALTH WORLD
HAEDERAN EMPIRE WORLD
UNAFFILIATED WORLD
NOTABLE MOON
KNOWN ROUTE

CHAPTER ONE

KATRYN BARELY FELT KAZ'S HAND AGAINST HER BACK IN THE CROWD that wound through the main hallway to the lab's greenhouse. It wasn't quite a crush, but it certainly felt like one as the contingent of scientists, engineers, and technicians was herded forward at gunpoint by Imperial Haederan Army troops. Some cried—silently, of course—but most were quiet, overwhelmed by their swift change in fortune. Even on a planet located in the path of the Haederans' ongoing military conquests, the Iythean Research Association had claimed they would be safe. Iythea was a barren planet with no infrastructure to speak of. The Haederans didn't want a scientific station.

They'd been wrong. The age-old cold war between the Interstellar Commonwealth of Autonomous Planets and Modules and the Haederan Empire had turned hot.

There was no doubt the seizure of the Iythea station had been strategic, part of the Haederans' larger annexation plan the Commonwealth had been fearing for the past few years. It'd certainly been straightforward—the Imperial Haederan Navy had swooped down to the sweltering planet hours before, depositing six squads of marines in space suits outside the collection of unarmed domes. They'd rapidly overcome the meager security the Association had provided, and now the Iythean employees waited in line to be processed. *Like meat.*

Kaz coughed, drawing her attention away from the rifles.

"It does them no good to keep us here if they're only after a strategic location," he whispered in her ear. "If they plan to set up a base here, they'll release us. They have to. The Commonwealth won't stand for yet another unprovoked attack on one of our planets."

As if the Commonwealth had stood up to anything so far— they hadn't. In any case, she couldn't respond to him out loud, not without the Haederan corporal ten paces away. She answered Kaz with a quiver of her head, disagreement and a warning at the same time. The Haederans would never repatriate them. Most of the researchers were citizens of Commonwealth worlds and weren't likely to be sent back to their own planets, including her own planet of Zarcron. Her brother, a Commonwealth Navy finance officer, would be horrified when he heard the news—not that there was anything Xan could do about it.

Her head swam as the line advanced until everyone was inside the greenhouse, pushed against the walls by rifle-wielding soldiers. So it was to be a massacre like the Commonwealth had accused the Haederan Empire of carrying out on Drenik just a month ago. It'd been her greatest fear when the first word of the attack had come, and now it was happening. With any luck, it would be fast and painless.

No shots came though, and as her eyes flickered from side to side, a man in a green uniform pressed through the flood of Haederan soldiers in the center of the module. They parted when they recognized him. An important man, then.

Kaz whispered again. "Imperial Haederan Army colonel."

She was grateful for the information, but would he ever learn to shut up?

The colonel eyed them with something that might have been disgust before he spoke.

"This research station now belongs to His Imperial Majesty,

the Emperor of Haedera. If anyone would like to contest that claim, now is the time to speak up."

Feet shuffled all around her, but the unnerving silence continued.

"Good," he said. "That will make everyone's lives quite a bit easier. You're still here to work. Perhaps not the work you signed on for, but work nonetheless—just for a different employer. You'll be treated as humanely as possible"—*in this dump*, Katryn imagined him adding in his mind as he looked around—"but dissent and escape attempts will not be tolerated."

There were murmurs through the crowd at this, and Kaz choked down another cough. Not a massacre, but slave labor instead. Was that better? She wasn't sure.

After a shorter speech than she'd expected, the colonel gestured to a lieutenant with a tablet and walked to the end of the line of prisoners. The two moved from person to person, stopping every so often to talk to a few of her colleagues individually. Random selections, all from different planets with different IRA jobs. It didn't make much sense.

Katryn held her breath as the two Haederans came closer, identifying each person and assigning them a number. One through five, as best she could determine. The numbers also appeared to be random selections. She was desperate to know the meaning.

The colonel stopped in front of her and cast a glance at the lieutenant.

"Holt, Katryn. Doctor," the lieutenant said, with a glimpse at his tablet. "Failure analysis engineer. Zarcron."

"Hmm." The colonel sounded apathetic. "Group two." He stepped to the side, stopping in front of Kaz.

"Two?" Katryn blurted, before the lieutenant could give him Kaz's information. "What's group two?"

The colonel turned back to her, his eyes cold and surprised. Next to her, Kaz sucked in a sharp breath. She stood firm, hands clenched at her sides.

"Group two is kitchen duty," the colonel said slowly. "But you know, I think I've had a sudden change of heart about you. You're going to try your hand at mining, Doctor Holt." His gaze slid to Kaz, and he smiled for the first time since he'd entered. "So is your whispering friend here."

* * *

Katryn had never been so hot, even on Iythea, where the temperature often hovered within five percent of the allowable limit for the permanent shelters. The protective suit she wore made things worse, but it—and the single dose of corazamine everyone took each morning—was the only thing keeping her safe from the toxic atmosphere. And the hair? Well, she'd fought against having her head shaved when they'd been first lined up, but having her previously thick locks stuck to her neck would've been more miserable.

The bell rang as she picked up the sampler, and Katryn breathed a sigh of relief. It had been a longer fourteen hours than normal, but sometimes they suspected the Haederans adjusted the clocks backward. Whether that was for a brief increase in productivity or torment, no one knew. Most assumed the latter, but Katryn was certain it was the former. The Haederan guards had to deal with the same miserable conditions beneath the temporary shelters, after all. Their home world was more arid than Zarcron and most of them never broke a sweat on Iythea, but why increase their duty time?

She handed the sampler back to the sergeant manning the checkpoint in front of the lift, stripped off her disposable suit, and swallowed her disgust, as she always did, as he scanned the chip inserted under the skin of her upper arm. That demeaning process completed, he nodded, and Katryn stepped onto the lift with a dozen others. She smiled at the thought of seeing Kaz in thirty seconds—the Haederans weren't careless enough to place them on the same shift. It was too hard to hide their history as friends and occasional lovers, and though she'd earned him this mining detail as punishment, they'd been separated. Quick glances and smiles between shifts were all she'd seen of him for months now.

Sometimes she thought it was the only thing she had to live for anymore.

The lift moved faster the closer they got to the surface, and her smile grew, more at the thought of his face than of her bed . . . though that was appealing too. She dreamed of Zarcron most nights, of her parents, of cool rivers and snow-covered mountains, and occasionally of Xan rescuing her from this mess. It was a silly notion to have of a finance officer. But then, it was also a silly notion to have trained researchers and engineers mining for scraps of ore in an infernal wasteland. She and her fellow prisoners were well educated, respected, valuable. Why keep everyone here as slave labor?

Who knew what the Haederans were really up to? She'd never figure it out. So tonight . . . tonight she would make sure to dream of Kaz's arms around her instead of the home she'd never see again. It was hard to hide a smile at the thought.

But when the door opened and the night shift faces appeared in front of her, there was no Kaz.

Panic grabbed her. He'd always been waiting outside, every evening for over six months. There hadn't been an execution since the first week of the Haederans' occupation, but there was no other explanation for his absence. She glanced frantically around at the people who should have been familiar but now weren't.

"Kaz!"

Her voice cut through the silence, and the Haederan corporal standing guard at the top of the lift shaft frowned at her.

"Is there a problem?"

Katryn's eyes widened. "No problem." *A huge problem.*

"Then shut up and get moving."

She complied, following the other miners through the temporary inflated tunnel that led to the permanent station. Maybe Kaz was already below. Maybe he'd descended to the mine in another lift. Maybe the Haederans had pulled him off on some other detail. He'd been coughing more and more lately—perhaps he'd been removed from the mine completely. He couldn't be dead. What kind of deterrence was a secret execution?

Mulling over the possibilities, Katryn trudged into the smallest of the habitat's three greenhouses, now used as prisoner barracks. Another slap in the face—the private quarters she'd been entitled to by virtue of her position had been taken over by the Haederans, leaving her to bunk with the rest of the prisoners in the open dome. No privacy. No modesty. Not much comfort. The bleak scarlet landscape she'd once loved for its utter contrast to Zarcron was all too visible through the glass.

She flopped onto her bunk on the end of the second row and put her hands over her eyes. Any other day she would be asleep ten seconds after hitting the bed, but tonight her mind raced with thoughts of Kaz. Sleep was out of the question.

"Hey! Get out of here!" a voice called from across the dome.

It was the new technician shouting—or he had been the new technician in their past life—but Katryn couldn't remember his name. He was standing over his cot, hands on his hips, fury on his face.

"Get up, Kaz. Not your turn." The tech kicked at the cot.

Kaz was in bed? Katryn shot up and flew across the dome. Kaz lay in what was the tech's bunk during the night shift, a sickly gray color fading every part of him. She knelt beside him, ignoring the tech's glare. If she had to guess, most of his anger was fear, but at that moment she didn't care what the Haederans thought or did.

"Kaz? Kaz, what's wrong?" she asked.

Kaz only moaned and tried to roll toward her. He didn't make it and blinked up at her instead.

"Leave me here. I can't move."

"Kaz, you can't stay here. You know that. You need to get up." Katryn hesitated. "Can you?"

He closed his eyes and moaned again. Tentatively, she shook his shoulder.

"What's going on here?"

She sprang to her feet at the Haederan accent. Captain Minter, in charge of the barrack dome at night, stood behind her with a group of curious Iythean techs around him. It was a relief to see him instead of Corporal Royce, who would have dragged Kaz outside then and there, just to rid himself of the problem.

"He's sick, Captain. Please—I know it's his shift, but—"

Minter pushed past her and rolled Kaz to his side. His gray color had changed to an unhealthy yellow, incongruous with his normally tan skin.

"Fine. Take him to the infirmary and come right back."

"Thank you. Thank you." She put an arm under Kaz's shoulder and lifted him up, stifling a groan as she stood under his weight.

"And be quick about it!" Minter shouted after her, but she was already into the next tunnel.

CHAPTER TWO

It was strange how many people thought the desert was always hot. Windhaven, closer to the Haederan equator than even his thin blood would prefer, was cold in the winter, especially at night. Especially after . . . well, wasn't that why he was home? To forget what had happened? Forgetting apparently wasn't as easy as it used to be, since he'd been watching the sun rise above the faraway mountains for more than an hour now, unable to sleep. The only thing he'd forgotten over the past years was who he really was.

If the glass running from the floor all the way to the flat roof had been thinner, he might have heard the goldcrests perched in the cacti on the other side. Four more alighted on the arm of one giant cactus to peck at it as he leaned his forehead against the window to watch. They would kill the plant sooner or later, but they meant no harm. They just didn't know any better. How could they? Maybe if he reached a hand out, he could touch their feathers through the glass . . . take some of their innocence for himself.

"Hello there," he said to the fat one sitting closest to him. The gold-feathered wren chirped silently, accusingly, then flew off in its never-ending search for water. Like it knew what kind of man was speaking to it. Like it saw all the things he'd done. Things he couldn't think about now. His misplaced loyalties. The blood on his hands. He couldn't blame the bird for staying away, just like he couldn't blame the Holy One for deserting him.

Maybe he could touch the sun instead. Burn away the memories. It was hovering right there, just above the mountains, and it could end his pain. Everyone else's, too. But the glass was too damn thick . . .

He laid his forehead back against it, and asked once more for guidance he knew would never come. What was the point in continuing to pray? Because they said he had to?

"Gareth? It's warmer in bed."

Chase started at the unexpected voice behind him. At his name. It was always like that the first few nights home. Being on edge was fine out there—lifesaving, even—but embarrassing here in his sanctuary, and Isobel had managed to catch him off guard. He turned to see her propped up on an elbow, staring at him, her dark hair cascading over her shoulders. She'd kicked off the blanket, revealing the black silk gown she knew he loved. There was no question it was a welcome home surprise for him, one much appreciated after more than four months away.

"I didn't mean to wake you," he said. The tile was cold under his feet as he walked back to her, almost as cold as space. He couldn't fall into bed fast enough. "I'm sorry."

"You didn't wake me."

Chase smiled as he slipped between the sheets. "No?" he asked. "Then how long have you been watching me?"

She was right. The bed was warmer. Isobel herself was warmer. He wound his icy feet between her hot ones and she yelped in surprise. Was the fever back? She hadn't said anything in any of her messages, but that was just like her. Isobel never wanted him to worry about her when he was off-world.

"Only since you said good morning to the bird." Isobel laughed and reclaimed her feet.

"You had to have woken up to hear that." He shook his head. It was too hard not to smile at her too.

She laughed again and ran a finger across his cheek, at the dusting of offensive freckles there, her eyebrows raised in mock reproach.

"I know." It was almost as if he could see the dark flecks across his nose, the ones Isobel vocally abhorred. The ones he'd been lightening since their wedding, like most every other wealthy Haederan. Unless a mission became too precarious. "I was . . . busy."

"It was a bad one this time, then?" Her soft brown eyes turned anxious behind long lashes.

They're always bad these days. Have been for a while.

"No worse than usual," he lied.

If one considered forcing a fifteen-year-old to give up the location of his traitor father no worse than usual. There'd been no time for finesse with the boy, and this mission would haunt him for a long while. The child's father? Well, he deserved death as certainly as the beetles that infested the water condensers at Windhaven—anyone who provided the Commonwealth photos of the navy's orbital shipyards deserved to die. But his war wasn't with children. He'd told the boy that at the end, praying it gave him some measure of comfort.

Even knowing it was a lie.

For no matter what he'd promised the child, his superiors in the Haederan Imperial Security Command had their own ideas, and the son would soon meet the same fate as the father. Orders from on high this time—the emperor would never chance familial retaliation in such a sensitive case. Risk-averse the man was, oh yes. He thought of Sophie and Marc, both five years younger than the boy, and forced a smile. It wasn't hard to guess that this last assignment was a reminder that even his twins were required to respect imperial authority.

Isobel matched his expression with a mechanical smile of her own. After so long, she must know a lie when she heard one, but she would never ask. Especially not now, when the state-run mediavids showed another minor Commonwealth planet and deep-space station falling each week. He wasn't sure how much of her silence was respect for the secrecy of his job, and how much of it was a firm desire to remain oblivious to the more unpleasant facts of Haederan society. Not that she could live outside it altogether, but she pretended like an expert, and whatever the reason for her silence, he was grateful.

"I'm—I'm glad to hear it wasn't so bad," she said.

It was obvious she didn't believe him, and that was risky. Isobel of all people could never know his many doubts, his increasing doubts. The misgivings he was finding harder and harder to conceal from everyone in his life. Was it an early midlife crisis? Was the guilt finally becoming too much to bear? The only thing he was certain of was that Isobel must never find out.

Because sooner or later, everyone talked.

He closed his eyes against her touch and feigned sleep.

* * *

"My lord?"

He woke with a pounding head, minus one wife and plus one clear glass bottle of lightening fluid on his bare chest. Isobel hadn't been joking about the freckles.

"My lord?" The voice near his ear was low and insistent. "Are you awake?"

Zavis.

If he closed his eyes, maybe Zavis wouldn't notice he was awake. Maybe he'd leave. No—Zavis had been in the Windhaven household for far too long to fall for his master's charade. His most trusted servant would never leave him alone, especially his first day home.

"I'm sorry to wake you, my lord, but there's a visitor in the courtyard for you. A—a courier. One of yours."

At that, Chase forced one eye open. Zavis was hovering near

the bed, as sharply dressed and bright-eyed as ever. But he was anxious now, that much was obvious in the crease between his eyebrows. Something was wrong, something his normally unruffled valet couldn't hide.

"Where's Isobel?" he asked, parched. Why was his throat so dry? He'd been off-world too long, had become unacclimated to Haedera's weather. He reached for the side table, but the usual glass of water was missing. Yes, Zavis was truly anxious to forget that.

"Also in the courtyard, my lord. She wanted an early breakfast."

"Alone?"

"Yes—"

He swore, cutting Zavis off. "You should have known better!" Woe to the courier who'd disturbed Isobel's long hoped-for day alone with her husband.

The vial clattered to the floor as he sat up; he kicked it under the bed. With Zavis on his heels, he stalked to the courtyard, which was already warm in the midmorning sun. As he'd feared, Isobel was lounging in her usual spot between the fountain and the cactus that was as round as Haedera II's moon, a matching robe pulled around her sleep gown and a decidedly displeased expression on her face.

Her glare was directed at the courier, a young ISC lieutenant, who drew a deep breath of relief when Chase appeared. Somewhat belatedly, after one last nervous glance at Isobel, he saluted.

What had she said to him? Chase wanted to laugh that his slight wife had intimidated the young man, who was feared by every other Haederan simply by virtue of his job. But Isobel wasn't immune. *Especially Isobel.* He held out his hand.

"Hand it over."

"Yes, Colonel." The courier reached into his pocket and withdrew the cylinder.

Chase's heart skipped at the contents of the clear plastic. Paper orders, hand-delivered.

No.

"Zavis," he said, pressing his index finger to the seal. It turned red under his print. "Show the lieutenant out."

"But, sir," the lieutenant protested. "I need your answer."

He shot the lieutenant what he hoped was a dangerous look.

"Is there any acceptable answer but yes?"

"No, sir."

"Good. Then you can deliver that message. Now out." He held his breath as the courier and Zavis departed through the far gate, then turned worried eyes to Isobel. "I can't do this," he said. "I won't."

She managed a wan smile in return. "I'm sure whatever General Lient has in mind is important enough."

Isobel sounded skeptical but resolute. He loved her unquestioning acceptance of reality. *His reality.* The reality that included jumping whenever the head of the Imperial Security Command so much as suggested it. Especially with his future promotion in the works—head of ISC's Interstellar Counterintelligence Division. A desk job for the first time in a long while. Some dreaded it; he looked forward to it more and more each day.

"I hope you're right." It wouldn't just be important for them to call him back out now—it would be critical. *It's only been one day,* his mind screamed. *What are they thinking?* He skimmed the orders, and his skin prickled at the signature. "Isobel. These aren't from Lient."

Isobel frowned slightly, then her perfect mouth formed a silent expression of shock and understanding.

"It doesn't matter. I won't go." He tried to slip the courier capsule into his shirt pocket, only to realize he was half dressed. He let it dangle from his fingertips instead. Like a poison. "Not now," he said. "Not for this." Isobel knew better than to ask what *this* was, but *this* was not something he was going to waste his time on. Was it a joke?

"Don't cross him." She'd been pale before, but now her lips were white. "It's not worth it. Not even you—"

"I can't leave you. Do you think I can't see you're not well?" He hated the anguish in his voice, hated that he'd broken in front of her. "I'd never forgive myself if—"

She was up, her arms around him, before his mind finished the thought. "Then let's not waste the time we have left."

All his skill in reading people, all his years of experience, and her lack of denial was the only confession he would ever extract from her. Isobel's heated lips barely touched his, and his breath quickened as she pressed harder. He let her lead him back to the bedroom, let her make him forget the best she could. It never worked, but he would keep pretending it did, for her sake. For as long as they had left.

Hours later, he guessed he was halfway to the imperial palace in Rebet before she woke to find him gone.

CHAPTER THREE

KAZ HAD BEEN MISSING FROM THE MINING DETAIL FOR TWO WEEKS now. At least Katryn thought it was two weeks. Without his smile to look forward to, she'd become numb, distant to everyone and everything. The dreams of home had become more frequent, and the wish that Xan would save her was at the front of her mind every day. Silly, innocent, impossible wishes.

Maybe that was why she didn't care what might happen when she cornered Captain Minter inside the barrack dome that night. A supply ship was on the way, so the miners had been released early for the evening to be locked down in the dome when it arrived, and the Haederan officer looked to be in a good mood. Hopefully, the anticipation of a new stock of liquor had made him cheery enough to answer her questions.

"Where is he?" she asked without preamble. Haederans didn't deserve evening pleasantries.

Minter turned, eyebrows raised. "Excuse me?"

"Kaz Augus. The man I took to the infirmary two weeks ago. Why isn't he back yet?"

"Still sick, I suppose. Do I look like the medic?" Minter shrugged and turned away to watch the other prisoners filter in.

"Then you didn't—" Katryn vented a frustrated sigh at his dismissal.

"Didn't what?" Irritation crossed his face when he realized she was still standing next to him. "I didn't do anything to Augus. What's he to you, anyway?"

Oh no. Minter was, apparently, one of the very few who wasn't aware of their connection. It had to remain that way. Relationships were too easily used by the Haederans.

"He's a colleague. A colleague I'm worried about. You all don't have the best reputation here, in case you aren't aware."

Minter gave a short chuckle at that. "Well aware." His lip curled in annoyance. "You're not going to leave me alone unless I let you see him, will you?"

Katryn shook her head and held her breath, sensing an imminent change in heart.

"Fine," he said. "You've got twenty minutes. And no whining about being awake on time tomorrow either."

"I won't."

She had to force herself to walk steadily to the infirmary instead of running. Kaz was alive. For now. Resources meant everything when so few supply ships visited Iythea. A useless miner . . . a useless prisoner . . . it was surprising the Haederans hadn't decided he was a waste of resources already.

Kaz was alone in the infirmary, the sole Iythean medic gone on whatever other menial duty she'd been assigned to. He didn't lift his head when she walked in, and his skin had that horrid sallow tone, but he gave her a small smile. Her shoulders sank in relief as she knelt next to him.

"I've missed you." He reached out his hand.

She put her hand over his. "I've missed you, too," she whispered. "I've been so worried. What—what happened?"

He coughed. "Tumor in my liver. You'd have to ask the medic what kind, but it's some genetic fluke. It feeds off the gas." His eyes met hers, the sadness there broadcasting the rest of the prognosis.

No. It wasn't possible. "But you were tested," she said. "And the corazamine . . ."

"I guess not carefully enough." Kaz looked away. "And she said the corazamine doesn't work on me. I might as well have walked outside and been done with it for all the good it's been doing for me."

Someone had made a mistake. Everyone assigned to Iythea underwent extensive medical testing before arriving to prevent this very possibility. Even the permanent parts of the station couldn't protect certain people from the toxic Iythean gas that made the atmosphere uninhabitable, but for humans with normal genetics, ones for whom corazamine worked, it was safe. It didn't matter how he'd slipped through the screening, because with that broken gene, Kaz had no chance. There was only one thing to do.

"Then we have to get you off this planet. It might slow the tumor down enough, at least until you can get real medical care. It certainly wouldn't hurt. I'll beg them. I'll do anything. Minter let me come see you tonight, I'm sure he might—"

"Katryn." Kaz squeezed her hand. "You know we're not allowed to leave. I don't know what they're up to here, but they're not going to take the chance that someone will figure it out and talk off-world. This is it for me." *And for you,* she read in his expression.

"No." Her denial was fierce. "I won't accept that."

"I'm going to die. Soon. There's nothing you or anyone else can do about that now." Kaz closed his eyes. "I only wish . . ."

He was silent for so long that she shook his shoulder, terrified she'd heard his last words, that he was already gone. "What? What, Kaz? You only wish what?"

He opened his eyes and smiled at her. "That I wouldn't die here."

Katryn watched his shallow breathing as she held her own. What should have been a difficult decision came all too easily. "Then you're not going to die here."

"I always thought you were crazy," Kaz said, "but you normally show it in other ways. Ways I certainly do miss."

As did she. It had been so long . . .

Kaz knocking on her door.

His arms around her.

Kicking off the sheets the next morning.

She shook off the memories. "I'm not crazy. Listen to me, Kaz. They sent us back in early tonight because there's a supply ship coming in. When it leaves, we can get you out on it."

"Tell me you aren't serious." He coughed.

"Why not?" It wasn't as though they needed to get him to safety. Just off Iythea.

"Because for one thing, I don't think being executed when they find me stowing away is a better solution to this problem!"

"But it wouldn't be on Iythea. That's what you want most, right?" She hadn't realized how much she shared Kaz's wish until he'd spoken it out loud.

You have time. Kaz's time is running out.

"You're right. It wouldn't be on Iythea." He closed his eyes again, a grimace on his face. Would he be able to walk to the hangar dome? Would he even live long enough to get there? "A supply ship, you say? Then yes," he said after a long pause. She wondered what he was thinking, but Kaz would never tell. Never had. "If you have a plan to get me to it, let's do this."

"I—I think I can come up with something. If you can sit up."

With great effort, he did, and Katryn had second thoughts about his ability to make the short walk. There had to be another way. She scoured the small infirmary for something, anything that would help. A cane, perhaps. Ludrocin would be useful. The drug could make a stunned man run like he was fifteen years old, but it wasn't surprising the Haederans had taken all of that medication. Katryn sat on the edge of the cot and rubbed her eyes. There was no way to sneak him out. None. Not on short notice.

"Hold on," Kaz said.

Her eyes questioned him, but he had addressed a man

pushing the cargo cube down the hallway, an Iythean Research Association cook she'd seen in the past but had never met.

"Yeah, you," Kaz said as the cook paused at his order. "What's in the box?"

The cook glanced down and shrugged. "Plant experiments for the shuttle."

"That cube's shielded?" Katryn asked. *Good idea, Kaz.*

"Yeah. Gas would kill the plants if it wasn't."

She exchanged a nervous glance with Kaz.

"What if I wanted to deliver that cargo to the hangar dome instead of you? What would it take for you to want to switch jobs for the night?"

He grinned. "From you, Doctor?"

"From me." She pushed Kaz's concerned hand away from her shoulder and grimaced inside. "Whatever you want. When I get back," she hastily added. It was a flippant suggestion. Nothing like that was tolerated on Iythea anymore. Not between the prisoners, at least.

"Then you've bought yourself a box full of plants." The cook pushed the cube inside the room and walked off, hands in his pockets, whistling.

"You aren't really going to . . ." Kaz sounded dubious and jealous at the same time.

"With Minter watching everything that goes on in the barracks? Hardly. I may owe him in some other way, though. Now get in."

It was a tight squeeze between the cartons of arrowroot and bittercress—grown on Iythea in an attempt to dispel the effects of the gas—but Kaz fit. The green surrounding him made him look a little less ill. She pressed her lips to his, then backed away to close the cover.

"Wait." Kaz grabbed her arm. "How many Haederans do you think are on that ship?"

Did it really matter once he was discovered? One armed man was enough to shoot him.

"I don't know," she said. How would she know? "A dozen?"

Kaz mulled over that for a moment. "Second drawer from the left. There's a small box. Get it for me, will you?"

She rolled her eyes at the delay but did what he wanted. The white box was sealed and heavier than its size suggested.

"What is it?"

"Pills. Just in case. I wasn't ready before, but now . . . depending on what happens . . ." His voice cracked. "Katryn, I'm afraid of what they'll do to me."

This was for real, then, and there was nothing she could do to stop it. She handed him the case, and the tears started to fall as their fingers touched. A joke—she had to make a joke to cover up this nameless emotion.

"Poison pills aren't exactly an engineer's expertise, Kaz. Are you sure you're not a spy or something?"

A bad joke. Kaz loved her bad jokes.

He smiled and gestured for her to close the cube. Katryn pushed the button and engaged the levitation before guiding it out the door with a finger.

The marked cargo cube allowed her open access to the hangar dome. A Haederan corporal opened the last door for her and scanned the box. He moved aside to let her by when it came up clean, but the thirty seconds it had taken him to search the shielded container took thirty years off her life.

"We've been waiting on this one," he said. "Hurry up and get it out there." She looked toward the center of the dome at his instruction, and her forehead creased in confusion at what lay in front of her. The expected cargo ship was there, oh yes, but an unmarked courier ship sat next to it, venting exhaust.

Two ships?

The Haederans wouldn't be having such a rousing party with their newest delivery of alcohol, not with whoever had arrived on that courier ship. Lighter at the thought, she plodded toward the ship with the open cargo door, the cube floating beside her.

One tech at the end of the ship's ramp nodded at her while the other worked the box's controls to lower it onto the ramp. Removing her hand from the cube was the hardest thing she'd ever done, and she forced back tears as she watched the conveyer belt start, moving Kaz up the ramp and inside the ship.

Gone.

"You're done here. Back inside." The tech jerked his head back toward the door.

"Oh." She hadn't realized she was still standing there. "Sorry."

The ship's engines screeched, and the tears fell as she walked back across the ramp, unable to believe how much she felt Kaz's absence on Iythea already. The corporal opened the outer door for her—more out of expedience than courtesy—and when he pulled his mask down and turned back to watch the ships, she stopped in front of the viewing window behind him.

She would watch Kaz leave before she returned to the barracks. She would say one last goodbye. The dome roof opened, and the cargo ship lifted off silently, leaving the lone courier ship below.

The emptiness was physically painful.

"What are you doing?"

Ice rushed through her, an unfamiliar feeling on Iythea, and she spun around at Minter's voice.

"Watching the ship leave . . . wishing I was on it." Why not be honest?

Minter narrowed his eyes at her. She could tell the precise moment he realized he'd been had, because those narrowed eyes snapped open as round as the coins they used on Zarcron. He shoved her against the wall and swung the door to the hangar dome open, heedless of the fact he wore no mask.

"Corporal! Call that ship back!"

The corporal stared at him in bewilderment as the roof closed, sealing the dome.

"It's—it's too late, sir. They're already in the gas, and they'll be in comm blackout once they exit. It'll be weeks before we can get a message to them."

Minter swore as he stormed back inside. "Did you think this would accomplish anything, *Doctor*? That you saved him? All you've bought him is a little more time and a ghastly death when he's discovered."

"I bought him everything, you—"

She didn't hear the explosion through the heavy glass of the dome, but the flash caught everyone's eye, brilliant fireworks of yellow and orange that only died down when each fiery piece had fallen, mixing into the red of Iythea's surface. For a moment, Katryn wasn't the only one who stood there stunned. The corporal recovered first and ducked past her and Minter, shouting instructions into his handheld comm.

The case. It hadn't been full of suicide pills after all. Kaz wasn't an engineer—or, at least, not only an engineer. He had fooled everyone, even her. Katryn began to laugh, a feverish, high-pitched cry of understanding.

She only wished she'd seen Minter's stun pistol sooner.

* * *

"I thought my request was clear, sir. She was to be handed over to us unharmed. Was there anything vague about that desire in my transmission this morning?"

The words were a blur in the headache that seemed to have taken over Katryn's entire body, the voice an unfamiliar Haederan one.

"You didn't see the explosion, Captain Linden?" It was the horrid colonel in charge of the habitat on Iythea, and his voice made Katryn's stomach churn. "I'm not sure you could have missed it. Thirty of my men were on that ship. This woman was involved in the sabotage, and she'll be held responsible for it. I can't begin to imagine what interest the Imperial Security Command has in her, anyway."

No. No, the explosion was Kaz.

Kaz. Her head hurt more at the thought of him. Or was it her heart? Had he known what kind of trouble he was leaving her in?

"With all due respect, sir, I suggest you stop worrying about her and start worrying about your perimeter security. Our interest in this prisoner isn't your business." The new voice sounded smug—or perhaps bored.

There was a long pause. Why couldn't she lift her head?

"Then take her and get off my station."

"Gladly, sir."

Multiple hands lifted her from the hard ground and dragged her up a ramp into what she assumed was the courier ship. Katryn didn't fight them. She would go willingly with anyone who didn't seem like they intended to put a bullet in her head in the next ten seconds. The hands dropped her onto a seat, more comfortable than anything she'd sat on in months, and she opened her eyes. The muscle weakness slowly ebbed away—the headache didn't. She stared at the metal grate that made up the floor, unable to force her neck to move.

"Post-stun headaches are nasty. It'll go away faster if you don't move, though it seems you may have deserved this one. Colonel Ellicot certainly thought so, at least."

At that, she raised her head. The man who spoke from across the narrow cargo bay was no older than she, perhaps younger, with sandy brown hair and dark eyes that could have belonged to anyone from a half-dozen Commonwealth worlds. The uniform, she didn't recognize, but he was certainly no one friendly to her cause. Not with that accent. Katryn rubbed the side of her head and stared at him.

"Rhys Linden." He leaned toward her with an outstretched hand, and then pulled it back, as though he'd realized the absurdity of shaking hands with a woman he'd saved from probable execution. Or maybe he'd realized she couldn't move enough to meet him halfway.

"You're not Haederan Army." A ridiculous statement since this young captain had all but ordered the station colonel to release her to him. Of course he wasn't. "Haederan intelligence?" she guessed wildly.

How she wished Kaz was here. He would know. Or Xan. Xan could fix anything, even this. Whatever *this* was—besides engines spooling up and an enemy officer sitting across from her.

A chuckle crossed his lips. "You might say that."

His evasiveness was exasperating and telling at the same time. "What do you want with me?"

"I don't want you, not really." He tilted his head toward her. "When was the last time you talked to your brother?"

"My—my brother? Xan?"

"Cute nickname. He's Commonwealth Navy, is he not?"

Something was wrong. Terribly wrong. Why was he asking questions about Xan? Xan had the most boring job in existence, an accountant by any other name. She'd always made fun of him for it. He couldn't mean anything to this Haederan with his easy smile and sinister bearing and attire.

"He's—yes, but he's not on a ship." Her gut told her there was no point in remaining quiet, that he knew everything already. "He's only an accountant."

"Is that what he told you he does?" Linden smiled as the courier ship lifted off. "Interesting cover. An accountant . . . it fits him." He chuckled a bit to himself at that assessment.

"Cover?" Fear made one half mute, it seemed. She gathered her wits enough to ask the silly question. "Xan's a spy?"

Linden laughed out loud that time, and she hated the sound because it was charming and attractive and reminded her of Kaz.

"No one uses the word spy," he said. "Commonwealth Special Operations Forces, if you want to be exact. That's his first job, at least. His second is even more clandestine."

Even through her blinding headache, his meaning couldn't have been clearer.

"Xan's no traitor," she whispered. It wasn't possible. Xan loved Zarcron. He'd served the Commonwealth for years.

"That's a harsh word, don't you think? If it makes you feel any better, it wasn't his idea." He shrugged. "You might be right, though. Your brother has become less and less helpful since the attack on Iythea and finally disappeared altogether weeks ago. I hope a little encouragement will be enough to get him back on track."

"And I'm the encouragement."

Linden nodded once, cautiously, like he didn't want to offend her.

It was a terrifying implication. Katryn glanced out the window, but the view was blocked by pale scarlet gas as Iythea disappeared below the fog and was gone. She'd been wrong before, and being wrong had never been such a relief.

However this ended, Xan had already saved her.

CHAPTER FOUR

CHASE STARED DOWN THE LONG HALLWAY LEADING TO THE EMPEROR'S formal study. He knew what was waiting for him inside; he'd been here enough times. A large room with a vaulted and intricately engraved glass ceiling, longer than it was wide, with a low set of stairs cutting it in half and floor-to-ceiling windows on the left side. He could see himself in the polished marble floor of the front half before it turned to lush carpet, and the gold-and-diamond *alig* lizard statues that lined the niches on the right side were a millennium old.

A throne room by any other name. There wasn't even a desk in there. The courier capsule burned his skin through his pocket, and his identities—all three of them—weighed heavy on his shoulders as he walked as slowly as possible down the plush corridor.

If only he'd had the foresight to arrive at the palace in something other than the traveling clothes he'd picked off the floor at home. In his panic, he hadn't considered that His Majesty would be displeased by anything more casual than his dark green service uniform. No matter. However informally he was dressed, however out of uniform he was, security hadn't questioned him when he'd arrived—through an entrance on the east side reserved for the most trustworthy—and now only a wood door separated him from the emperor.

Well, a wood door and two imperial guardsmen in full navy-and-gold regalia, already eyeing him warily as he approached. Perhaps it was his unexpected appearance, perhaps it was the loose khaki pants and gauzy, untucked shirt. Frankly, they ought to be grateful he was wearing shoes.

"His Imperial Majesty is expecting you, my lord," the guardsman said with a brisk bow that managed to be defiant and courteous at the same time.

Expecting him? This was an unforeseen snag in his impromptu plan. Chase nodded at the guardsman's insipid smirk and pushed the door open. It wasn't the time to worry about what the emperor's ceremonial security thought of him. He knew who was really in charge of things, and that was all that mattered.

His Imperial Majesty, Devan Owin Arwel IV, First Prince of the House of Claerwen, the High Emperor of the Sacred Empire of Haedera—it was hard to not fill in his entire title whenever Chase saw him—was standing by the impressive window that overlooked the sheer cliffs of the northern edge of the imperial palace. Mist rose from outside, a product of the waterfall that plunged over the cliffs, the source of most of the water in this part of the world. A rainbow shimmered through the spray, casting its color through the window and against the emperor's embroidered shirt and the polished floor. There wasn't a more appropriate image for this situation—a rainbow, the harbinger of death and destruction.

The emperor turned at Chase's appearance and smiled. "Well. What a pleasant surprise."

"You think this is pleasant?" Chase jerked the cylinder from his pocket and held it at eye level. "Political officer? On *Defiant*? What kind of joke is this? You know I don't do space work anymore."

In truth, he hadn't ever wanted to do space work at all, but few ISC officers escaped it. His superiors had seen his required political officer assignment on *Gauntlet* years ago as somewhat of a joke—or, perhaps, punishment for his father's position. His father had always been loyal to the empire and his emperor, but ISC didn't trust anyone, even an honored and reliable Imperial Haederan Navy admiral. *You should have joined the navy, Lieutenant Chase,* they'd liked to say to him when he was fresh from the academy. *You won't find any favor here.*

He'd made sure to prove them wrong.

"It's no joke. Orders. Lient gave me the impression you don't question those." The emperor's lips thinned. "But since they say nothing about you reporting to me here in Rebet, it appears he was mistaken. If I'm not mistaken, you've missed your ride."

"I won't go. I already have orders."

Orders which dictated he stay on Haedera II for at least the next two years. It had been planned that way, as a kind of reward for his last assignment, and he didn't mind the planetary restriction. Leaving Isobel now was unthinkable, anyway. And for a full year?

Even more, he'd had career plans. ISC had plans for him. His promised position in Interstellar Counterintelligence would have kept him away from—well, from their secondary plans for him. The truth serum research, the work with the miracle drug lacrozenate, the program that would be the final death of his soul. But now, by the time he returned from Asria, they'd have filled that counterintel billet with someone else, and there would be nothing else left for him to do . . .

Something fearful stirred inside him, and before he could stop himself, before he could stay his treasonous hand, the cylinder hit the emperor's chest with a thud.

Chase's eyes widened in shock at what he'd done.

The emperor's eyes flickered downward to the tube, now lying innocently on the floor, then met his. Only for the briefest second, then, as if in invitation for Chase to follow, they flickered sideways toward the shadows.

Toward the crown prince, Owin, and a dark-haired stranger, both lounging under an unlit chandelier.

Crown prince and *stranger* was all Chase could discern through the sudden thudding of his heart. He hadn't been alone with the emperor in his throne room after all. This wasn't a grave mistake —it'd been a potentially fatal one.

You must salvage this . . .

"You will comply with those orders with no further argument," the emperor said, his gaze slowly moving back to Chase. "And you will remember whose study you have just barged into."

"I—" His breath became short. There was only one option left, however humiliating it would be. He fell to one knee, head bowed. "I am sorry for my offense, sire. And Your Highness as well. I was . . . I was out of line."

There was a snort from the stranger in the chair. The crown prince, Chase decided as he chanced a deferential nod to the side, merely looked bored.

"To say the least." The emperor's feet turned sideways. "Victor, let me introduce you to Colonel Gareth Chase. My . . ."

His voice drifted off into the mist outside, along with any hope Chase had of surviving his misstep. Chase suppressed a shiver as silence filled the room, as cold as the knife that would shortly be across his throat.

Holy One, protect me.

There was no answer, of course.

"My son-in-law," the emperor finally concluded.

He swallowed at the recognition but didn't dare move. Not yet.

The feet turned back toward him; the emperor's stare bored a hole in the back of his head.

Better than a knife at your throat.

"Get up, Gareth. You of all people look ridiculous on your knees."

Chase stood, swiping the courier container into his hand as he straightened.

"Sire, I—she's not well. And a political officer position—"

The emperor made a slight *not now* motion with his hand—

and his eyes—and turned to the stranger. The dark-haired, green-eyed stranger. He almost looked . . .

Asrian?

But that couldn't be.

The stranger stood and nodded toward Chase. "Victor Rendon." His mouth quirked up slightly. "It's a pleasure to meet you, Colonel."

He was the last to know something, and that was never a good thing. Victor Rendon, the King of Asria? A Commonwealth planet? He wasn't just the last to know, he was unsteady on his feet now. Caught off guard. It was a new feeling, one he didn't care for.

"Our guest," His Imperial Majesty said. "For the time being."

"And no longer," the Asrian added, "the King of Asria."

Was the man a mind reader?

"I see," Chase said.

The emperor laughed. "You can admit when you don't know something, you know. Not that you ever will." He glanced sideways at the Asrian, skipping over Owin with visible disregard. "*Defiant*, along with the rest of Alpha Fleet, will take Asria in eight weeks' time. I've agreed to hold the planet under a protectorate status for now. I need you there, in orbit. Ready."

One more planet would fall to the empire. Why was he so surprised?

"Ready for what?"

The hand-delivered orders made a bit more sense now, but something was off. A closed-door meeting with the emperor, the crown prince, and an Asrian? One he'd been allowed to walk right into?

The Asrian king—former king, or whatever he was now—spoke.

"Until recently, my niece was a Commonwealth Navy officer. She will not take the invasion of Asria well, to say the least. I expressed my concern about her acceptance of this occupation to

Devan, and he assured me you were the right person to handle any complications she might throw at us."

Chase narrowed his eyes at the familiarity. No one called the emperor by his first name, especially in his presence. He was His Imperial Majesty, even to Isobel and her siblings. He'd probably demanded the same of his late wife.

"Or so I had thought," the emperor said. "It seems my perception of your court decorum was erroneous. I hope my faith in your other skills isn't similarly misplaced."

He hated that his cheeks became red at that. "What complications do you expect from her?" he asked.

Victor Rendon merely made an indifferent gesture with his hand. Was he unacquainted with his niece, or was it something else? If only the emperor would give him five minutes alone with the man, but that didn't look like it was going to happen.

"That's for you to figure out. I'm sure you can handle one young woman, whatever she throws at you. Maybe you can use her. She might be a valuable asset to ISC."

"I don't run agents anymore, either." He hadn't run agents in years. Some of his officers did, naturally, but it wasn't something he had much desire to do anymore, and ISC played along. His Majesty had to know that, too.

"But you could," the emperor said with insincere patience. "In the meantime, I don't intend to give you a vacation. I know you feel the position of political officer is beneath you, but *Defiant* is in need of one." He shrugged, but the laugh in his eyes was anything but dismissive.

"What happened to the last one?" Chase asked. The status of ISC personnel with the fleet was of no interest to him. Avoiding the truth serum research and sticking to his regular interrogation schedule had been his only interest of late. That and spending as much time planetside as he possibly could.

"Died." The emperor raised his eyebrows at him. "Under suspicious circumstances, like the rest. I'm sure you can figure out what happened to Lieutenant Adler."

"The rest?"

A laugh. "You really have been out of touch. Four Imperial Haederan Navy political officers dead in the last six months. Lient has a real problem out there with the fleet, which means I have a real problem out there with the fleet."

Of course. Political officers weren't popular in the best of regimes, and His Majesty had made an art of threatening Haederan military with the Imperial Security Command. It was no wonder they were so hated. It didn't take an expert to figure out what was going on.

"Sire, is this a creative execution?" The sharp knife would have been easier.

The Asrian snorted in amusement again.

"And risk Isobel's wrath?" His father-in-law's face softened at last. "No. Simply a convenience. You need to get to Asria somehow, and Lient needs to fill a political officer slot. If it makes you feel any better, he didn't want to let you go."

That was no surprise. "I have to pack."

"The servants were able to scrounge enough of your belongings from your suite here. It's not as though you need much. Your trunk is waiting for you on the shuttle."

"I have other things to pack." Things the emperor had no idea about. If they wanted him to investigate Victor Rendon's niece, he needed his gear. She'd never trust a Haederan colonel, especially an ISC officer, but his alter ego?

Maybe.

"Captain Chase's belongings have been added to your trunk." Owin, who'd been silent the whole time, finally broke in, the same uninterested expression on his face. "I packed them myself."

So. He'd been wrong about that too. Did His Majesty know everything? Even his more secret work? He'd certainly known about his arrival at the palace—Isobel must have warned him. It was time for honesty.

"I need to say goodbye to my family. Your daughter. Your grandchildren." Not that family had ever changed the emperor's mind, but he had to try. More importantly, he needed to remind this Asrian who he was.

"You lost that opportunity when you decided to argue with me."

Try to stop me.

"You're too obvious. You won't be running back to Windhaven today." The emperor gestured at the guardsman at a side door.

The guardsman pulled the door open to admit two ISC officers, one a major Chase had never met, one a captain from his last mission. He frowned at both of them as they entered and bowed formally to the emperor.

The emperor smiled at him as if to say *See? Is a little deference to me really such a difficult thing?* "Major Reed and Captain Lewis are here to escort you to *Defiant.*"

"I don't need an escort." Not if he had a chance of escaping to Windhaven to say goodbye, he didn't.

"Until you can convince me that your loyalty hasn't slipped, you do. No one's safe from Imperial Security. Not even you." The emperor patted his cheek and grinned. "Enjoy your trip."

CHAPTER FIVE

THE CRIMSON GAS OF IYTHEA'S ATMOSPHERE TURNED DARK AS THE courier ship slipped above it, then darker as they entered hyperspace. With the stars gone, there was nothing to look at, and it was silly to pretend there was. Katryn turned her attention back inside the small cargo area, back to the young Haederan officer who was staring out the small porthole next to his jump seat, studiously avoiding her gaze. The throbbing headache from Captain Minter's stun pistol was fading away at last, and she chanced a question, though she didn't really want to know the answer.

"So now what?"

He started slightly at her voice, but she didn't care that she'd interrupted his thoughts. How exactly did—what had he said his name was? *Rhys Linden.* What a good Haederan name that was. How exactly did Rhys Linden intend this hostage thing to work? And more importantly—if not quite as urgently—how would she escape?

Linden caught himself, yawned, and turned toward her. The short hairs on the back of her neck stood as his eyes locked on hers.

"We're headed to Asria," he said. "Once we get there, I'll take you to a safe house where you'll wait and pray your brother comes to his senses. You'll be treated well as long as you accept this. Much better than you were on Iythea, I should point out. But don't get any ideas of escape—his life now depends on your cooperation, just as yours depends on his."

The chill of the cargo bay worked its way through her entire body. Her brother who'd betrayed everything he supposedly cared about. Her brother who'd been a Commonwealth Navy finance officer for all she knew—until less than an hour ago. Not —not a spy. Not a traitor to the Commonwealth and their own planet. How could she trust him to save her now? Her emotions were a churning ocean—anger over Xan's treason, fear for her future, hatred toward Linden, and selfish relief she'd been rescued from certain death on Iythea.

It was that last emotion which made her hate herself as well.

"I'd like your word that you won't try to escape," Linden went on, undaunted by her silence. "It would make things easier."

What a naïve expectation, especially for a Haederan. Did this man really believe she'd promise not to try? She wouldn't go willingly into whatever he had planned for her.

"And if I don't give it?" she asked.

He scratched his head and frowned, as if he hadn't expected a challenge so quickly. "Then I suppose you'll spend the trip drugged out of your mind in your cabin. I'd rather not have to do that—it would be a lot more work for me and quite unpleasant for you. This doesn't have to be a miserable voyage as long as you cooperate."

There was no real response to that kind of reasoning. Katryn leaned her head against the wall and considered her options.

"So how about it?" he asked. "In return, you'll have free run of the ship except the flight deck. And this ship, I probably don't need to point out, is also better than being on Iythea, despite being much smaller."

"You're Haederan," she finally said. "There's no way you're unaware of what's been going on in the habitats on Iythea. Of what you've already done to me. Why would I believe anything you say?"

"I saved your life." A hint of irritation crossed his face. "And I keep my promises."

For some reason, she believed him that time. Maybe it was the seriousness in his eyes. Maybe it was a desperate desire to believe someone. The months on Iythea had made her desperate for an ally, even a Haederan one. Slowly, she nodded.

"Good. I hope you're not claustrophobic. It's not a large ship, and cabins can feel small. And it's going to be a long trip. If you start having trouble, tell me, and maybe I can give you something to help."

He certainly had a lot of drugs on board. And his concern for her comfort was . . . not touching, exactly. Disturbing, if she had to pick a word. Why did this man—who'd basically kidnapped her—care if she was uncomfortable?

Katryn shook her head. "No claustrophobia."

"Good, then." Linden stood and ran his hands over his face. Katryn couldn't help but notice how smooth it was. How that one light-brown freckle near his left eye stood apart from the others. This man kept up with appearances, even alone on a courier ship.

"Your cabin is the first one through that door on the left," he went on, apparently oblivious to her inappropriate stare. "Mine is right next to it. The galley's down the corridor and doesn't have a door; you can't miss it. Help yourself to anything in there, and if you can't find it, feel free to ask. I requested provisions on Iythea, though what they decided to load for me is going to be a surprise for both of us. If you want to exercise, I usually work out here in the cargo bay—it's really the only place large enough. You can go anywhere except the flight deck, and you can't mistake that, either. Understand?"

Katryn nodded, too untrusting of the post-stun muscle weakness to stand with him. This netting jump seat would be her home for the next few hours. Even with a soft bunk awaiting her, she wouldn't chance having to crawl down the corridor to her cabin.

"Where are you going?" she asked. He couldn't leave. Not now. She wanted—no, she needed—more answers from him.

"I'm going to get some sleep. You should consider cleaning yourself up and then doing the same. No matter what I give you, that headache won't go away until you do."

With that, he darted out the door of the cargo bay, leaving her alone to watch the dark of space.

* * *

It turned out that watching space through the tiny window in her cabin was almost all she had to do for the next few weeks. It was either that or think of Kaz, and remembering him was something she couldn't yet do without falling apart. She'd explored every last part of the ship—staying away from the flight deck as ordered —but that took only half a day. Afterward, she'd hidden under a blanket in her bunk, too afraid to encounter Linden or the two pilots who she hadn't seen but knew were on board. Linden hadn't been exaggerating about how small the passenger cabins were, but living in a room the size of her bathroom back home was preferable to the open barracks on Iythea. She'd never take privacy for granted again.

She was doing push-ups on her bed one evening when there was a knock on the door. Annoyed by Linden's timing, Katryn stood to wipe the sweat from her face with a hand towel, then pushed the button to let him in. She hadn't seen him since the day he'd yanked her off Iythea and could have lasted the rest of the voyage without doing so, but there wasn't any point in pretending she wasn't inside. He'd probably checked the rest of the ship before bothering her in here.

He smiled at her from the corridor as the door slid open. Today that strange not-quite-Haederan Army uniform was gone, plain civilian clothes in its place. They appeared disposable like the thin gray jumpsuit she'd found in her wardrobe. Katryn looked away to check herself in the mirror, hating that the clothing made him look . . . normal. Haederans weren't supposed to look normal.

"You haven't been eating," he said.

"Most people say hello first." Katryn tossed the towel into the sink. He didn't get to act concerned. She'd decided that the night before as she'd lain awake thinking of Kaz. "Or good evening, or something." What was the usual nighttime greeting on Haedera, anyway?

Linden quirked his lip in a frustrated manner that she somehow found humorous. "Hello. Good evening. You haven't been eating."

"I swiped some ration bars from the galley a few days ago." The cherry and bacon bars were a strange combination, but it was better than starving.

He frowned and glanced toward the small cabinet over her sink.

Fear grabbed her, as vivid as anything she'd ever felt on Iythea. Should she not have taken them? Linden had said she had the run of the ship. He'd specifically included the galley. He hadn't said she had to eat there.

"Ration bars aren't real food," he said. "If you're trying to kill yourself, it's not going to work. There's a small med bay on board. If it comes down to it, I've got no qualms about strapping you down, shoving a tube down your nose, and force-feeding you."

Katryn stared at him in confusion, then burst into laughter as his meaning sank in. Linden was almost a copy of Captain Minter.

"Is something funny?"

"No." She choked the laughter down. "I mean, yes. You're as paranoid as the rest of them. I'm not trying to starve myself."

"Then why—"

"Look, I don't want to run into you or the pilots outside of this cabin. I don't feel like socializing with you, all right?" Her pulse sped up, though she was almost certain it was pride at her bravery this time.

Linden looked vaguely offended, and some of the pride turned to shame. "You don't have to socialize with me. You don't need to talk to me at all. You don't even," he said, wrinkling his nose at her and then at the towel in the sink, "have to shower first. Just eat something more substantial than a ration bar."

Had he just made a joke? Did Haederans make jokes? None of the Imperial Haederan Army soldiers on Iythea ever had, and Katryn was too surprised at the concept to keep arguing with him. She nodded and followed him to the galley instead. Linden searched through a few cabinets and drawers while she stood awkwardly by the viewing window.

"Do you drink tea?" he asked without turning around.

Katryn narrowed her eyes at his back. "Yes. I drink tea."

Her mouth watered. She hadn't tasted the stuff since the Haederans had taken over the research station on Iythea—though they flew it in for themselves, of course. Linden handed her a cup with a handful of whole leaves in the bottom, then poured boiling water on top.

"Haederan style." Linden cocked his head apologetically. "Sorry. You can pull them out when it's done steeping or drink around them." His angular features sharpened further as he glanced at the dark shadow that covered her scalp. "My grandmother claimed this kind was good for regrowing hair."

"It's all right."

His acknowledgment of her shorn hair wasn't, but the tea smelled like normalcy to her, so she'd forgive his notice. Katryn sat on the nearest chair and sniffed at the cup, willing her hand to stay away from the soft regrowth. It was one thing she'd learned on Iythea—never let the Haederans know your weaknesses.

Linden dug through another cabinet and pulled out a few full ration packs. "Is fake space meat all right with you?"

She shrugged. "Don't care."

He laughed out loud that time. "I'm kidding. It's lamb. The best frozen food Haedera II has to offer."

Maybe the ration bars had been a bad idea, because the scent of real food drifting from the convection oven in the wall made her stomach growl. Linden placed the lamb—along with steaming green vegetables and nuts of some sort—in front of her, and she blinked, afraid it would disappear once she made a move for it.

"Sorry it's not fresh." He'd mistaken her hunger for scorn. "It was a long way from Asria, and I figured we'd eat that older food before what they loaded the other day."

"It's better than what we've been eating on Iythea." She hoped it sounded enough like an accusation. She couldn't indict the soldiers there any longer—had never been able to, for that matter —but she could push Linden. He needed her alive.

"I bet it is."

Linden didn't meet her eyes but turned to grab his own meal instead. Was it her imagination, or did his shoulders sink a bit? *Good.*

"Hey, Rhys." The blue-uniformed Imperial Haederan Navy pilot who stepped inside nodded at Linden, not giving her a glance.

"Hey." Linden glanced up with a short wave and pulled out another frozen meal. "Dinner?"

"If you don't mind company."

"No." Linden pointed at Katryn, then shoved both packages in the oven. "Doctor Holt might, though."

"You let your prisoner make decisions like that?" The pilot flopped down across from her, gnawing on a ration bar. He focused on her face—at her lack of hair and the bruise on her cheek from hitting the ground back on Iythea.

"I don't mind," Katryn said hastily. Her cheeks flushed, and she turned away toward the viewing window. What else was she supposed to say? It certainly needed to seem like nothing bothered her, especially dinner with two Haederan officers.

"You're not looking so happy," Linden cut in.

"I'm not." The pilot wadded up his wrapper and tossed it against the closed door of the trash compactor. Linden picked it up and dropped it inside. "Some issues tonight. But . . . uh . . ." he trailed off, his gaze on Katryn.

"She knows where we're headed."

"Ah." The pilot glanced at her. "Well, then. The Commonwealth's set up a blockade near Thuen. Straight across the main route to Asria. We've just earned ourselves an extra four days going around it."

Linden sighed and practically tossed the first meal at him. "Don't you ever bring me good news?"

"Not when we're on the cusp of all-out war." The retort sounded flippant.

All-out war? Katryn's stomach settled down to her feet as the lamb sat in front of her, still steaming. Maybe she could buy herself more time before she forced the meal down her throat. She watched as Linden sat next to the pilot, and they both pressed fingertips to foreheads, muttering under their breath.

"Why do you do that?" she asked.

The pilot laughed, then, after a sharp glance out the door, focused on his dinner.

Linden's forehead creased like no one had ever asked him that question before. "All that time on Iythea, and you don't know much about Haedera, do you?" he asked. "I wish I could say I was surprised at how lax things are there. I suppose I can say I'm glad the things going on there aren't my problem." He took a bite of something that looked like fish, if the fish had whiled away the past five years in deep freeze.

"That's not an answer."

He sighed. "I thought you didn't want to socialize with Haederans."

She'd changed her mind—loneliness was a harsh thing—but she'd never admit that to Linden. Or to the arrogant pilot who'd stared at her hair and laughed at her innocent question about Haederan culture.

"No." Katryn picked up her fork. If only she could get away with stabbing that inappropriately charming freckle below his eye with it. "I suppose I don't." She jabbed at the lamb instead, ignoring the pilot's wide eyes.

CHAPTER SIX

CHASE KNELT ON THE FLOOR OF THE POLITICAL OFFICER'S CABIN, formerly Lieutenant Adler's, and unpacked his metal trunk piece by piece, solely to keep himself from commandeering a ride home. It was surprising how happy he was to be aboard *Defiant*—if only to be away from Captain Lewis's incessant apologies. It'd been a painfully awkward shuttle ride to the already en route cruiser, made more excruciating by the young officer's constant assurance that this escort duty had not been his idea, nor anyone else's in ISC.

As if it were really necessary to clarify who was responsible for this situation. No, when Lewis and Major Reed had dragged him out of the emperor's study, staying within striking distance the entire way to the shuttle site at Esrem, the fault had been clear. What must the two have thought of him when he'd exited the shuttle in *Defiant*'s secondary bay and they'd headed back to Haedera without him? He could practically see the speculations swirling about their minds: *What do you think the colonel did to deserve this one?* The rumors would fly at headquarters for weeks; formerly professional colleagues would cackle and whisper like a gaggle of insipid old women.

He pushed the gossip from his mind, more urgent issues

taking its place. It'd taken almost an hour to find his way to his new home on deck seven, and that meant, since he was required to report to the ship's commander within two hours of arriving, he was already behind schedule. Contrary to the courtesy given every other new hand shipped out with the cruiser, no one had stopped to help him through the maze of metal hallways and decks—worse, that wasn't a surprise. The anti-ISC animosity had begun already, spurred on by his uniform, unexpected and unwanted.

The ensign manning the entry hadn't even returned his salute when he'd requested formal permission to come aboard, and though he should have been long over what some young upstart thought of him and his position, the snub was still eating at him. Not because of any arrogance or wounded feelings, but because most ISC political officers didn't bother themselves with the barest military courtesies while in space and he did. Always had. Whether it was respect for his father or something deeper, he bothered, and the respect should have gone both ways. It was only right.

Of course, after the ensign's rebuff, there was also a grudging deference from most of the other troops he passed, even if it didn't extend to helping him find his way. Did it matter if the respect stemmed from fear? His father-in-law and Lient would say no. His conscience—that soft voice of the Holy One that he thought he heard some quiet nights—said otherwise. Sadly, the voice always flittered away into the ether before he could ask for clarification.

He hadn't gone through the unpacking procedure in years, but his hands worked as though they remembered the rolled-up socks, the crumpled uniforms, the leaking soap. The emperor hadn't been exaggerating when he'd said his personal things had been scrounged from the imperial palace. Chase couldn't remember leaving so many of his belongings in Isobel's rooms, but here they were: three bags of toiletries, one printed picture of Isobel and the children, two Imperial Haederan Army uniforms, four sets of his usual green Imperial Security fatigues, and one green ISC service uniform the color of the pine forests in the mountains outside Windhaven—as though he'd be wearing that aboard a warship headed for battle.

Those army utilities had captain rank, his preferred identity for any undercover work that might arise. Everyone trusted a middle-aged captain. Not that they would allow him to blend in on an Imperial Navy vessel, but they would be useful for trailing Avery Rendon on Haederan-occupied Asria. They also had to have been pilfered from Windhaven before he'd returned home from the last mission, which meant the emperor had planned this new assignment well.

Chase sat back on his heels and stared at the photo of his family. Was it a benevolent gesture from his father-in-law or a warning from his master? It had to be the latter, he decided as he ran a finger across Sophie's two-dimensional face. He'd have been more concerned about the subtleness had he ever said anything about his doubts, but this was pure Devan Owin Arwel IV.

Threaten those you know are loyal to you . . . the better to keep them that way.

Chase would never tell the emperor his backward way of preserving loyalty would catch up to him eventually. Even the most loyal Haederan subject didn't appreciate being threatened— no, especially the most loyal. Isobel herself chafed under the constant watch of ISC, the surveillance she would never have rid herself of even if she'd chosen a different husband. The imperial family must present a proper and loyal front at all costs, even if it meant terminating the more rebellious members. Never public, naturally, but accidents happened, and had happened to her youngest brother Glynn.

With a sigh and brief prayer, he tucked the photo below the mirror at his sink and picked up his shaving wand. Admiral Hellar wouldn't take kindly to him being late.

* * *

The commander of Alpha Fleet, and therefore *Defiant*'s de facto commander until after the invasion, poured himself more coffee, conspicuously not offering Chase a cup. He could have used one, too. He hadn't slept well his last night on Haedera—his first and last night with Isobel—and Hellar had an entire coffee bar next to his antique wood desk, including a polished silver salt shaker.

Salt. Stars. How long had it been since he'd put salt in his coffee? Fifteen years, at least, not since his last space tour. What would the admiral do if he simply stood up and grabbed his own cup? Smelling it from the other side of the desk was pure torture.

"I have to admit," Hellar said, shaking a bit too much salt into his cup, "I'm not entirely sure why the emperor thought it was necessary to assign another political officer to *Defiant*. I'm more unsure why it was necessary to hold us back to transfer you here. We're three days behind the rest of the fleet already, and I'm going to have to run *Defiant* hard to catch up. I don't need to remind you what kind of consequences a delay like this will mean."

He waved a hand in dismissal at his own prediction. "Surely His Majesty and ISC don't think we'll have any problems now. Not of the magnitude requiring a political officer's attention, at least. I'm afraid you won't have much to do for the next few months, Colonel."

Given a bit of luck, Hellar was probably right, but Chase wasn't going to let the admiral think he was in control of the ship. It was the empire's fleet, the empire's ship, and now, by extension, his. It didn't matter that this assignment was some sort of punishment on the emperor's part, or that Chase himself had no intention of exploiting that control. Hellar needed to understand exactly where he fit in the imperial hierarchy.

Even the admiral's success tamping down the small revolt on Haedera III fifteen years ago—as a senior executive officer on *Borealis*, he'd evacuated his entire company back to orbit with zero casualties after the commander had been killed—didn't mean he was untouchable. No one was. Hellar should realize that by now.

"With all due respect, Admiral," Chase said, "impending war

is exactly the situation where these problems come up. You obviously haven't heard the conversations in the corridors. I've not been here much longer than five minutes, and I can tell you that quite a few of your men are rather upset about this 'training exercise.' They know it's something else entirely and don't like being lied to. Their speculations are quite fascinating."

"Really." Hellar cocked his head to the side and eyed Chase with new interest. "You're starting out early, I see. And you did what about it, exactly?"

"Nothing. For now." Chase shrugged and tapped a finger on the arm of his chair. The complaints of a few low-ranking navy personnel might have bothered him eighteen years earlier, but these days? He had bigger problems to worry about. The empire had bigger problems to worry about. Minor rants about the lies of *Defiant*'s senior staff weren't a threat to anything except morale, and even that was debatable. Complaining kept men from focusing on their real problems. Unknown problems. With most of the crew too young to know actual war, they had no idea what they were headed for. "Right now, I'm a little more curious about Lieutenant Adler."

"Ah."

"You didn't think I wouldn't ask about him, did you?"

Hellar brought his coffee to his mouth, then hesitated before taking a sip. "This is beginning to feel uncomfortably like an interrogation, Colonel."

Wonderful—his reputation had preceded him. An exasperating, if possibly useful, circumstance. Best to let Hellar think . . . well, whatever he was thinking. Chase's expression didn't change.

"If it was, sir, you would know it."

A lie. A valuable one.

Hellar stood motionless against his viewscreen wall—dark now—and regarded Chase for a full minute before sitting like absolutely nothing unusual had transpired.

"We have the offender in custody." He leaned back in his chair and spread his hands. "It's a shame. Adler was an exceptional officer and deserves justice now. I certainly hope you'll make a decision as to Powell's fate quickly."

Specialist Second Class Ian Powell, Lieutenant Adler's alleged murderer. Yes, he'd read the file, but he wouldn't be making any decisions about Powell anytime soon. Or at all, if he decided he could get away with it. So much blood on his hands . . . he could stop that now by refusing to order Powell's execution. Powell didn't interest him right then, anyway. Adler's history with Hellar did.

"Adler was so exceptional that you reprimanded him three months ago for entering the engineering department without your chief's authorization?"

"He was getting nosy." Hellar rubbed his nose—it was cold in the office, like every other section aboard *Defiant*. Colder than usual for a starship, but then, ISC tended to keep their couriers warmer. They could afford it. "I hope it didn't cause him too much grief back home. I'm not in the business of destroying careers."

Even you are afraid of us. It was useful knowledge.

"Four reprimands from a Haederan Navy admiral earns you a medal with ISC. He only needed three more." Chase couldn't help laughing. It wasn't far from the truth, and nothing short of murdering an admiral would have ended Adler's career. Maybe not even that. "Nosy was his job. What are you hiding in there, sir?"

"A gambling ring." Chase didn't laugh at the intended joke, and Hellar sighed. "It's a safety issue, Colonel. I don't relish the idea of my political officers vaporizing if they touch the wrong piece of equipment."

"He was fully qualified for interstellar service." All ISC officers were. All the better to terrify the military.

"Yes, of course, but overprotectiveness isn't a bad thing. I also don't like safety inquiries mucking up our mission, and Adler was a kid. Too apt to step in something he shouldn't."

Young perhaps, but hardly an innocent child. Not after three years of imperial service. Adler would have had the same blood on his hands as he.

"He's also not the first political officer assigned to the Imperial Navy to end up dead under mysterious circumstances in the past six months," Chase said. "So you won't mind if I speak with Powell before I make any decisions as to his fate."

"I would expect nothing less. But I'm afraid Adler left quite a bit of unfinished business on his desk . . ." Hellar gave a little shake of his head, as if to say, *And now it's my problem, so I'm going to make it yours.*

Chase suppressed a sigh. "Understood, sir."

Bureaucratic work, a necessary evil. Adler had probably left weeks upon weeks of work undone, but it wasn't worth fighting the admiral on this, not yet. And it wasn't as though Chase was in a hurry to do the emperor's bidding regarding Powell, not this time. If he timed everything properly, he might manage to put off Powell's interrogation until after the invasion.

At that point, Avery Rendon would become his only problem. Powell wouldn't matter then. He could pawn the man off on someone else and avoid making a decision altogether. It was a tempting proposition.

"Once that's complete," Hellar went on, "I'll inform Captain Tanner you're to be given full access to the prisoner. But I don't know that you'll get much out of him."

You don't know anything.

"Maybe I won't. But as you said, Admiral . . ." Chase smoothed his sleeves as he stood to go. "I don't have much else to do for seven weeks."

CHAPTER SEVEN

She would escape.

No matter how Linden had threatened her and Xan, it was the only option—the only honorable option, at least. And honor was the only thing she had left.

Asria, Linden had said? Well, Asria was a Commonwealth planet, and a staunch Commonwealth supporter at that, one of the original treaty planets, like Zarcron. If that was where he was taking her, it wouldn't be hard to find someone sympathetic to her plight. It would be easy—it wasn't as though he could chase her around the planet without someone noticing. He couldn't even wear that horrible uniform on the surface while he was trying to reconnect with Xan. She would bide her time until they landed on Asria or some other planet for refueling and provisioning, and then she would escape.

What to do until then? Well. That was the question. As much as she didn't want to see Linden or that arrogant pilot, there wasn't much else to do but pace the main corridor or work out. She growled in frustration and punched the exit button to her cabin. Exercise helped brain function . . . so they said. Maybe Linden was on to something with his workouts in the cargo bay.

She was only two steps out her door when his opened.

Maybe it was a coincidence. Maybe he'd turn away from her and head to the flight deck, where he seemed to spend most of his time. No surprise there. Of course he'd rather spend the trip with his own people instead of a former Iythean prisoner who—

Linden jerked his chin at her, cutting off her silent and untimely question of what he thought of her.

"Good, you're awake. Med bay. Now."

Katryn backed against the wall. "Why?"

Hadn't she been eating enough? Spaceflight usually took her appetite away, like it did for most people, but she and Linden had shared another half-dozen awkward, silent meals since the first. Both pilots had joined them a few times—they and Linden seemed friendly. She was trying to eat, even if she couldn't manage much. He should know by now that she wasn't trying to kill herself. Not when there was a chance of escape once they reached Asria.

Instead of answering, he took her by the wrist and ran his fingers lightly over her upper arm.

"Did they stick you with a chip on Iythea?"

"Yes." Katryn jerked her arm away and massaged the lump under her skin. Linden didn't need to remind her of the humiliation of being injected in an assembly line, along with all the other prisoners on Iythea, and being tracked like livestock.

"Then I'm going to take it out. Come on." He headed down the hall without waiting for her to follow.

Her heart did something funny. "You can do that? I mean— they'll let you?" The prisoners had been threatened with all sorts of things if they'd interfered with the chips.

Linden turned briefly, a strange look on his face, then continued his walk to the small med bay without answering.

And it *was* small, half the size of her own room. Floor-to-ceiling cabinets lined one wall, and medical equipment she could mostly identify filled another. He pulled a sterile kit from one of the numbered cabinets, and she held her hand out.

"I'll do it."

Linden hesitated. His hand hovered between them, and for a second, it looked like he'd hand it over. He pulled the kit away from her instead and set it on the small counter.

"I think it's best I do it. I don't want a pilot walking in and thinking you did it on your own. That might not go over so well."

"You don't want to give me something sharp," she replied. He didn't answer, and she sighed. "You know how to do it?" she asked.

Not that it could be that difficult. It had been a twenty-something Haederan Army soldier wearing a military police patch—not a medic—who'd inserted it in the first place.

Linden nodded.

"Then fine. But I want to see what's in the injector first."

He smiled at her, the first real smile she'd seen from him, then pulled each piece from the kit and showed them to her one by one. Some off-brand Haederan disinfectant, a scalpel, two Brisian-made anesthetic injectors—she didn't trust those much more than the Haederan disinfectant—and dermtape. She rolled one of the injectors around in her hand, scanned the label, then handed it back.

"Does it meet with your approval, Doctor?"

Was he joking with her again? Or—sacred winds forbid—flirting with her? Resigned, she rolled up her sleeve, pulled the chair down from the wall, and sat.

"Ready?"

"I suppose." She bit her lip and looked away as he pressed the injector against her skin.

"There. Now we wait." For some reason she expected him to leave while the anesthetic took effect, but he only leaned against the wall and crossed his arms.

"Why are you doing this for me?" she asked. There had to be some sort of catch. Had he changed his mind? Was he going to drug her and lock her in her cabin now?

"Why not? I don't need to track you here. You're on a courier ship the size of a closet." He stretched his arms over his head and cracked his knuckles. "And you gave me your word."

He believed she'd keep it? Katryn looked at her arm.

"I think it's numb now." Anything to halt a conversation about promises. If he kept talking about that, kept assuming her honesty, there would be no way to hide her guilt. She'd spill everything she planned to do once they reached Asria. Not that she knew quite yet what that would be, but . . .

Linden pushed himself off the wall and squeezed her arm with two fingers, then shrugged.

"If you say so."

He flicked the scalpel against her skin before she could say another word. Immediate hot agony rushed through her arm like a thousand knife cuts in the same spot, and she squeezed her eyes shut, a curse on her lips.

Linden stared at the cut, then the chip on the floor where it had landed, his eyes narrowed.

"Did that hurt?"

"A little," she gasped through gritted teeth. Actually, it had hurt like he'd sliced her arm off, too much to touch it and stem the bleeding.

"I told you it wasn't numb enough," he said.

"You never said that." With difficulty, she met his gaze and held it. Accusing him. Well, he hadn't specifically said it, had he?

Linden scratched his forehead with the inside of his wrist and reached for the second anesthetic injector. With the other hand, he drew a finger around the small wound.

Katryn shivered.

"Feel that?"

"No," she lied. Anything to get him to stop touching her. She would take the pain as long as he looked away before he saw—

"Are you cold?" He frowned at the bumps on her arm, then shot her with the second injector.

"Yes," she managed to wheeze as she reached for the dermtape, her face hot. With her teeth, she ripped off a piece and stuck it over the cut with her palm. She'd bleed to death before spending another minute with him.

"It's bleeding." Linden's frown moved to the blood seeping underneath the clear tape. "Here. Let me check—it should be numb now." He placed a hand over the tape.

"I don't feel very well." Katryn stood, knocking the remnants of the kit onto the metal floor. "It's the blood. I don't like blood." She dashed around him and out the door before he could stop her.

"Are you going to pass out?" Linden shouted after her, his voice too close.

Her arm was tingling more from his touch than the wound he'd created. Cheeks blazing, she locked her door and collapsed on her bunk.

* * *

The sirens wailed, heralding the imminent arrival of the Haederan Army at the Iythea research station. The sound kept up as the supply ship lifted off the station with Kaz on board, only to explode into brilliant flames that trickled down to the red surface.

Something was wrong. There hadn't been a siren when the Haederan ship exploded, had there? No, the soldiers hadn't sounded an alarm, shocked as they had been at Kaz's home-made bomb. The siren must be a failure in the dome's environmental system, letting in the toxic Iythean atmosphere. Yes, that must be it, because she couldn't breathe. She needed a mask, needed—

Katryn woke, gasping for air.

A dream. It had been a dream, though she'd never had nightmares about Iythea before. Except . . . no, it hadn't been a nightmare, for the wailing of the siren hadn't ceased. Neither had her shortness of breath. The flashing red light above her door caught her eye, and she flung herself to the floor in an automatic movement, hands reaching for the emergency kit underneath her bunk. One of the pilots had shown her the second day en route, and she was thankful for that favor now. Mask, mask, there had to be a mask somewhere.

There.

She snapped the straps around her head with shaking hands and took a deep breath. It was a risk to check the rest of the courier ship, but staying in her cabin might mean death. And even though she'd implied the opposite to Kaz once, oh how she wanted to live now. *Live, live, live.* She repeated it to herself as she crept down the main corridor. *Asria, Asria, Asria.*

The flight deck door was open. Linden's warning to avoid the area didn't apply in an emergency, did it? Surely not, since she could see one of his pilot friends slumped over his console. Cautiously, not trusting either the artificial gravity or integrity of the hull, she made her way forward and put a cautious hand on his back.

He wasn't breathing and hadn't been for some time. What kind of accident wouldn't have allowed him to reach for the mask over his seat? Had it been catastrophic, or so subtle it'd taken him by surprise? Katryn took a step back. Her mask wouldn't protect her for long, not if the oxygen was leaking out from this section of the ship.

She checked the crew bunk on her way out, all too sure of what she'd find. As she'd expected, the secondary pilot lay there, face a dark blue. Checking his pulse was unnecessary. Quietly, with a reverence that felt odd, she folded his hands, covered his face, and moved aft. The atmosphere in her cabin must have held longer than on the open flight deck, protected by the sealed door.

But where was Linden?

She found him in his cabin ten seconds later, face down on the floor. Somehow it was a relief to have found him, though she'd be joining him in death shortly. How shortsighted she'd been to agree with Kaz that dying off Iythea was preferable to dying on the planet. At least there it might have been quick, a bullet to the back of her head. Now, once her own oxygen ran out, she'd suffocate slowly, surrounded by bodies.

Unless . . . Linden must have something in his cabin she could use to end this. Understandably, he never wore a weapon around her, but he had to have one secreted away somewhere. A pistol would make this fast and painless. Even a knife. Maybe drugs. Katryn knelt on the floor next to him and began to rummage through the emergency drawer under his bunk. There was nothing except his own mask and a small med kit. Why hadn't anyone put them on in time except her? She shoved the mask into her pocket and was about to stand to check the drawers on the side of the wall when a hand grabbed her by the ankle.

Her scream caught her by surprise.

Linden released her leg and looked up, his lips dark blue. "Escape. Pod. Aft."

She sat back on her knees and watched him struggle to breathe, watched his eyes close.

His people were responsible for the atrocities in Iythea. For Kaz's death. For the deaths of her colleagues, the ones she barely remembered. Linden had kidnapped her, threatened her, threatened Xan. That escape pod would be hers, not his. Even if there was enough oxygen there for two people, she would never give him that gift of life. Not the life he'd taken from her, and probably from Xan as well.

Yes. It was settled. She pushed herself back up. In the doorway, she turned for one last look. Linden moved his blue lips, eyes dark with fear, but no sound came out. Katryn paused, her chest tight.

It took less than two minutes to slap his mask across his face and drag his limp body to the escape pod on the side of the empty cargo bay.

CHAPTER EIGHT

SHE HAD BEEN WRONG ABOUT THE SIZE OF THE POD. IT WAS physically small, yes—enough to make her claustrophobic unless she took regular deep breaths—but there were supplies and oxygen enough for four people for two weeks. The morbid part of her brain desperately wanted to know what would have happened if the courier ship had had more passengers on board than her and Linden. There was another unoccupied cabin next to hers, after all. Would the pilots have had instructions to die aboard to protect whatever important passengers they might have been carrying? Duty was an odd thing—and fatal in some situations, it appeared. The very idea made her ill.

Unsure of the exact nature of the accident and whether the courier ship would hold together, she'd hadn't taken any chances on staying with it. After dragging Linden's limp body on board, she'd punched the jettison button above her head. They now floated through space together, her leaning lengthwise across the three seats on one side, him sprawled across the sole bunk across from her, unconscious. A small part of her wished he'd never wake up.

"Is that horrible of me to want?" she asked him after another few deep breaths.

He didn't reply. Just breathed, much too slowly for her comfort.

"Would you have dragged me in here if you'd found me lying unconscious on the floor?"

That was a ridiculous question. Of course Linden would have saved her. She was valuable to him, even if her value stemmed not from something intrinsic, but from something he could use against Xan. She was safe from the Haederans until she and Linden reached Asria . . . And then what? Torture? Imprisonment? No matter how kind he'd been, Linden was someone to fear, that much was certain. What would happen to her if he couldn't find Xan? Or if Xan refused to cooperate? Or if he caught her trying to escape?

The thought made her pull the knife from her pocket, a sharp dagger she'd found in the pod's supply kit. Rumor had it that Commonwealth worlds used poison pills for suicide in space, but that was a laughable thought when one could simply vent their ship into the icy, airless void. Would a knife be a more painless death than hypoxia?

She knelt beside Linden and placed the knife against his throat. Her cut wouldn't need to be accurate since he couldn't cry out. A few sharp, well-placed slashes, and any chance he had of waking would disappear like oxygen in the courier.

So much blood.

There would be no way to contain the slaughter, no way to hide the bloodbath from the recovery team when and if they were found. She couldn't subject anyone to that visual, especially if the Commonwealth found them first. Maybe not even if the Haederans did. The image of the escape pod, drenched in wine-colored stains, was more than she could stand. No, using the knife on him —or worse, both of them—was out of the question.

She drifted off to sleep on the floor, the knife clutched in her hand, and dreamed of Kaz.

* * *

After two days in the pod, she'd stopped trying to rouse Linden, who was alive but in deep unconsciousness. His shallow breathing bothered her, but his eyes moving under the lids—under that freckle—were even worse. She kept her gaze on the blackness of space instead, toward the stars that had always meant hope and adventure. What did they mean now? Death? Or was there some adventure left in the heavens?

She was sitting in her new favorite spot across the individual seats when the ship appeared outside. Stiff from her cramped position, Katryn uncurled herself and knelt on the floor for a better angle out the lower window. She wasn't an expert at starship recognition—they all looked the same to someone who used them as nothing more than transportation between research sites —but the Haederan flag and seal painted on the hull of the unidentifiable ship was unmistakable. A quick investigation of the pod and the flashing light under the bunk provided the reason for their sudden appearance.

They'd picked up a distress signal. *Of course.* Why hadn't she realized the pod had automatically activated one when it slipped out the back of the cargo bay? She could have found a way to disarm it—could have torn it out and left it on the courier ship for that matter—but there was no chance of the Commonwealth finding them first now. A thousand profanities rushed through her mind, but it was too late to do anything about it now. She shook Linden, but he only moaned in response.

"Hey. Captain. Seriously, now would be a great time to wake up."

He didn't reply at all that time, and Katryn wanted to scream at him. She wanted to scream at the ship outside. She wanted to scream at the pod for not having any supplemental oxygen to give him, and at herself for not grabbing all the extra masks she could find on the courier ship.

But before she could scream at anyone or anything, the tow beam latched on.

* * *

The brig on the Haederan whatever-it-was was cold, and the air was dry, with a sharp tang of oil underlying the chill. Katryn shivered—she never felt warm in space. Worse than the cold was how anxious she was, even after experiencing so many threats from the soldiers on Iythea. She should have been immune to them by now.

Even more surprising than the fear was the apprehension she felt over Linden's condition. Had she rescued him and drifted in space with him for two days only for him to die now? No one was answering her questions about him, so perhaps he was dead already. She tried to tell herself she was only worried about what the Haederans would do if they thought she was responsible for his death.

Because, unfortunately, that was what the Haederan Navy commander across from her was thinking.

"So," he said, rocking back in his chair, "you're saying you have nothing to do with Captain Linden's injuries." It was clear from his tone and expression what he thought of that story.

"He was like that when I found him in his cabin." It was a good thing this man couldn't read her mind, couldn't see how close she'd been to leaving Linden lying there on the floor of the courier—or slicing his throat in the escape pod. What would they have done to her then?

"And you didn't succumb to the scrubber failure on the courier ship like everyone else . . . why?"

So that's what had happened. Katryn suppressed another profanity. They could have stayed aboard after all. She might have been able to fix it—if her own oxygen had held out that long.

"I don't know. I assume the passenger cabins are sealed as a measure against that kind of emergency." Her suggestion didn't change the commander's stony expression, so she tried again. "Captain Linden must have tried to check on the flight crew and been overcome before he reached his cabin."

Or mine.

"There are half a dozen places on that ship where he could have found a mask, including the flight deck. Including his cabin. You already said you found the one under his bunk. Why didn't he put one on?"

What kind of question was that? How could she possibly know what was going on in Linden's head? For the love of all the sacred winds, she'd been asleep when everything happened.

"Do you want to go back to Iythea?" the commander asked as she stared uselessly at him.

Now that was a good, if slightly random, question. And *no, not really*, was the answer. But Iythea was preferable to whatever they planned to do with her on this ship. Wasn't it? She shook her head without knowing why.

"That's a good answer. If ISC has no further use of you, you're wanted for the murder of thirty Haederan soldiers who died when that supply ship exploded. I suppose we can add two or three to that tally on the courier ship. You're racking up quite the body count, Doctor Holt."

"I didn't kill Captain Linden! Or those pilots!" This conversation was not going how she'd planned it.

"Then how did you know they were dead?" The commander cocked his head at her. "You said you barely checked on them . . . the only way you would have known is if you'd killed them yourself."

"I didn't," she repeated. Was he being deliberately obtuse? Did he get a bonus if he discovered a murderer? "It was obvious they were dead. It wasn't hard to figure out what I was looking at. Neither were breathing, and without an emergency kit, there was nothing I could do for them."

"Well. I suppose we'll find out the truth when—if—Captain Linden wakes up to corroborate your story." It was almost a snarl.

"Which he did two hours ago."

Katryn turned at the new voice, afraid to hope.

Linden stood behind her with his hand on the doorframe to

the interrogation room, somewhat unsteady, true, but dressed, upright, and with lips that were pink. She tore her stare away from those pink lips. It wasn't the time or the place.

He gestured at her with a half smile that seemed out of place.

"Let's go."

She didn't need to be told twice. Katryn darted out the door beside him as the commander protested, ignoring the curious stares of the brig crew as they exited.

"What took you so long?" she asked. She'd meant it as a joke, but it came out accusingly.

He smiled, a real one, and she hated the expression a little less that time. Today it looked less like Kaz's smile and more like his own.

"Apparently, I was unconscious for quite a while, so first I had to argue with the doctor about releasing me. Then I needed to threaten a bunch of people into telling me where you were. Then they had to scrounge up a uniform for me, and that took more time than you'd expect. Then I needed to shower. And shave. Then I nearly passed out as I was getting dress—"

"Yeah. All right. I get it."

"They say you saved my life." He eyed her sideways as they passed through a crowded corridor, hung with bare lights that made the ISC courier look luxurious. "Thank you."

"That's funny, because they just spent six hours accusing me of murdering you. For some reason, they were pretty upset about that."

"Were they?" Linden asked idly. He didn't sound surprised at all. Or curious. "You almost did, you know."

Katryn ducked her head, avoiding his gaze. Did he remember her almost leaving him on the floor of his cabin? "Where are we going?"

"Guest quarters. You're on *Aeris*, by the way." His head twitched. "If you were curious."

Relief washed over her. For some reason, she'd feared he was taking her to another brig. Instead, she followed him up another two lifts, down one more, and through a large hangar filled with troops. How did he find his way around this maze of a ship? Clearly this man had spent much more time on interstellar ships than she. He finally gestured her inside a door just as her legs had begun to tire.

She could be across the room in four steps, but it was larger than the brig's interrogation room that Linden had rescued her from. No window out to space, but a shimmering viewscreen over the bunk provided much the same view, and a door on the left led to a private washroom. The rest of the place? Gray, steel, utilitarian, even the table bolted to the floor. Still, it was privacy, away from any Haederans. Finally. As soon as he left, she was going to take off all her clothes, shower until her skin threatened to peel off or the water shut down, and then sleep as long as he let her.

But Linden shut both of them inside.

"Hold on. You're staying here too?"

He perched on a chair at the small table against the far wall and pried off a boot.

"It's hard enough to get a cabin here as it is. *Aeris* is full up— you saw how crowded it is—and they certainly weren't going to give you one of your own. Believe me, I argued about the inappropriateness of this arrangement, but there simply isn't anywhere else to put us. I'm lucky I'm not sleeping on the floor of a hangar bay." The boot flew into a corner. "So unless you'd like to spend the next few days in the brig . . ." He raised his eyebrows in question and wrested the other boot off.

"No, but—"

Linden laughed and tossed the second boot into the corner next to its mate.

"You're going to be shy around someone you spent a week in an escape pod with? The cabin has a private head, and I've slept on the floor before. Doesn't bother me. I don't know why it bothers you. It's more privacy than you had on Iythea."

"Do not speak to me of Iythea." Her cheeks flushed at her boldness, then reddened even more at his grin. "And we were not in that pod for a week. It was two days, though it felt like six months. And no, as much as I appreciate the wonderful increase in privacy, I prefer not to live with someone who's using me as a hostage."

"That's not—" He crossed an ankle over his knee, leaned back, and frowned at her. "All right, that's . . . that's fair. But it's not for long, hardly long enough to be called living. They've located the courier, and it's fixable. We'll be on our way as soon as they can find new pilots for us—and replace all the scrubbers and test all the systems. It will be extensive testing, believe me."

He'd missed the point entirely. And for some reason, she found herself desperate to make him understand.

CHAPTER NINE

"Two days," Linden said later that evening over a meal of some sort of pale brown Haederan fish. Fresh, of course—*Aeris* had a stockpile of it. And fresh food, even this strange-colored and unusual kind, tasted like bliss. "They've found us a new flight crew, so a few final tests and a short wait for our departure release and the courier will be ready to go."

Katryn laid down the apple on her gold-rimmed plate. Her eyes had grown wide when fresh fruit and sparkling cinnamon water had been delivered with dinner, but Linden had ruined every bit of her appetite with his news. How had they fixed the ship that quickly? Not that she wanted to stay here on this warship with him, but continuing to Asria as a hostage? No, she didn't want to do that, either.

"Two days?" she asked. "Only two more days?"

"You're not happy to hear that? And here I thought you wanted to get away from me as quickly as possible. Maybe I was wrong." He shrugged and sipped his water, eyeing her over his glass.

Why had she eaten at all? The food, especially that beautiful apple, was a lump in her stomach now. Worse, his suggestion brought heat to her cheeks; his comments would sound flirtatious coming from any other man.

"That ship tried to kill me," she said. "I'm not exactly thrilled to step foot on it again."

"Is that all?"

"Of course that's not all," she snapped, jumping up from the table. The table that was conspicuously devoid of knives—not that she'd make it past whatever security was outside after she stabbed him.

Too bad.

"You were going to die out there on that rock." Linden took a calm bite of fish. "I did you a favor, and one day you'll realize that."

His frankness—and his clairvoyance—were more unnerving than his jokes. "So I'm supposed to thank you?"

She'd meant it to sound scathing, but it came out as a plea. For sympathy. For an explanation, maybe. For him to tell her what she was supposed to feel, because she certainly didn't know.

"I didn't say that."

Not in so many words. Katryn glanced from him to the door. It wouldn't be locked from the outside, would it? No—that would be a fire hazard, even on a ship this big. It didn't matter that there was nowhere to go once she was out. She'd take the chance.

She bolted.

Linden was faster. He was around the table and his arm was across the door before she could blink, blocking her intended path. Unable to stop her dash in time, she slammed into him, knocking her breath into the air. He pushed her gently away from the door—and himself—as she gasped for air. She stood there in the center of the cabin, foolishly silent.

"Sit down," he said, although it seemed more of a request than an order.

"Or what? You'll take me back to the brig?"

How could she have been so stupid? She'd gained enough of his trust to get near the door, but it hadn't been enough. He'd never take his eyes off her now; there would never be another opportunity.

"Or we won't be able to finish the first decent meal either of us have had in weeks." He bit his lip and stepped toward her. "Please? I was—I was enjoying this."

They were only a body's width apart now, and though he was back in that horrid green uniform, something was happening to her. She hated—*hated*—how her heart fluttered at his closeness. How he smelled fresh and clean and sort of like cloves, the exact opposite of everyone on Iythea.

You're being a silly woman.

She took another step away from the door and nodded. The distance from him cleared her head somewhat. Her traitorous, confused head. Kaz had only been dead—what? Days? Or had they already spent weeks on that courier ship? Well, days or weeks, it didn't matter. She had no right to find this man—this *Haederan*—attractive, no matter how clean he smelled.

Yes, that was it. He was cleaner than anyone she'd smelled in a long time, and her body was reacting. Nothing more. She wasn't attracted to him.

"Thank you." His shoulders relaxed as she took another few backward steps.

He certainly did a lot of thanking her, Katryn suddenly realized. Was she that agreeable of a prisoner? That would have to change once he let his guard down, but now . . . Linden was right about one thing. Decent food, and even his conversation, was more appealing than a futile escape attempt. Katryn forced her legs to walk back to the table, forced her hand to pick up the apple. The doorbell beeped as she sank her teeth into it.

Linden coughed once, grabbed his glass of cinnamon water, and opened the door. The commander who'd interrogated her earlier stood outside in a fresh uniform, hands on his hips. Katryn pushed her chair against the wall, wishing she could put another light-year between them.

"Good evening, sir. I thought you were done with her," Linden said.

"Well—I'd thought so too, but not quite. With your permission, I'd like to interview your prisoner again." His gaze swept around the cabin, landing conspicuously on the single bunk.

"About?"

He met Linden's eyes. "She was only questioned about harming the crew directly. I want to know if she had anything to do with the scrubber failure itself." He raised his chin, confident in his accusation.

"Ah." Linden shot her a quick glance. Katryn didn't think she looked down fast enough to hide the fear on her face. "Then no, sir."

"I—I'm sorry?"

"No." Linden took a sip of water. "As far as Imperial Security is concerned, sir, the matter is closed."

"I see."

By his tone, he clearly didn't. Katryn's breath became shallow. There was only one way this would end. How could Linden tell a commander no?

"Happy to hear it, sir," Linden said. "I hope you have a pleasant evening." He shut the door on the commander's shocked face.

* * *

She woke that night to the sound of Linden's soft snoring. True to his word, he'd pointed her toward the bunk after dinner that evening while he slept on the floor. Right in front of the door. Clearly, he wasn't trusting her after earlier. Escape from a Haederan warship had been a bad idea before, and now she was more likely than not to trip over him in the dark. What would Linden do then?

Katryn closed her eyes again. The entire situation—Iythea, the Haederans, Linden, being here on this ship—none of it was fair.

She missed Kaz. She even missed Nash, and before tonight she'd thought she'd been over his death for a good long while. Not that reflecting on the past would get her out of her situation. It certainly wouldn't save her from that Imperial Haederan Navy officer who seemed to want her dead. Because no matter how Linden had run him off earlier, there was no question that he'd be back. Probably in the morning, and with more security.

Tears stung her eyes. She squeezed them shut but began to sniffle anyway. Now, of all times? She was safe, warm, and fed—there was no reason for this sudden emotion. Embarrassed, she rolled over so her back was to Linden. Whether he was asleep or not, it was humiliating to let herself shed tears in front of him. Even in the dark.

"Are you crying?"

Oh no. Why hadn't she noticed that the snoring had stopped?

"No," she replied. "I'm not crying."

"Sure you are. I can hear it. What's wrong?"

Such a ridiculous question. Where did he want her to begin? Haederans invading Iythea, Kaz dying of a tumor, Kaz deciding to take his life into his own hands, her being shot with a stun pistol, Linden and his pilots kidnapping her, seeing those same pilots dead on the courier ship, floating in deep space for days, being dragged to the brig, being threatened . . . yes, it was truly a ridiculous question. Linden should know.

She propped herself up and wiped the tears away. He might know they were there, but he didn't need to see them.

"In general, or tonight?"

He smiled, and in the dim light of the cabin, it was somehow comforting. "You know, neither. I'm sorry for asking. You don't owe me any explanation."

Katryn drew in a shaky breath, her defenses shattered by his consideration. "That man. They're going to take me back tomorrow, aren't they? What will they do with me?"

She hadn't done anything, but there would be no convincing these Haederans. They would execute her for the deaths of the two pilots—who she would have saved had it been possible—all the while wishing they could do it twice as revenge for Kaz's destruction of the supply ship.

"Of course they're not going to take you back." Linden sounded genuinely surprised at the question. No, not just surprised. Surprise as well as confusion laced his voice. "What makes you think that?"

"Didn't you notice the look on his face? He doesn't agree that I had nothing to do with it, and he'll never believe you. He suspects I was involved, and—"

"He won't bother you. He can't, and I'm going to send him the paperwork tomorrow and make sure he knows it." Linden settled on the end of the bed next to her feet, but somehow, the closeness was calming instead of frightening. "You weren't kidding, were you? You really don't know who I am."

She shook her head. "You wouldn't tell me."

He'd implied he was Haederan intelligence of some sort when he'd first dragged her aboard the courier ship. The fact he'd ordered the station colonel to release her all but confirmed it. Did she need to know more?

Linden's eyes widened. "I thought you would have figured it out by now."

"How would I have done that?"

His confusion turned to amusement. "That's right. I suppose you're more into math than galactic politics—especially of Haedera. You're the type who barely leaves your lab, am I right?"

He was righter than she would ever admit. How dare he have her figured out when she didn't have any idea what he was like. "I don't have a lab. I spend my days collecting samples and developing more efficient testing procedures. And yes, it requires interaction with other humans."

"So you do like people."

Was he flirting? It sure sounded like it, and even worse, it felt like it, at least in her gut. Well, she'd shut down that nonsense right now before it began.

"I like people. I don't like Haederans."

Linden snorted at that. "You seemed to like me just fine while we were eating dinner." He frowned at her and half stood. "Do you want tea?"

"No. And don't stall."

He sat. "It's that obvious?"

Katryn jerked her head in a kind of affirmative movement.

Linden took a deep breath and settled back against the wall at the foot of her bunk.

"You guessed Haederan intelligence, which is close enough, I suppose. The Commonwealth has us identified as some sort of covert security service, which isn't quite as close. Technically, the Imperial Security Command surveils, investigates, and neutralizes internal and external threats against His Imperial Majesty and the Haederan Empire."

Neutralize.

Her stomach flipped at his unemotional words. He'd probably repeated them a hundred times over the course of his career, so frequently they scarcely carried any meaning for him anymore. Did he realize what he was saying?

"You mean you kill people," she said.

"If we need to. It's not something I take pride in."

Sure. "You take pride in your empire, though."

"Of course." His eyebrows pulled together. "Haedera has been good to me. Would I pledge my life and honor to an empire that wasn't?"

So many had. Was Linden truly this indoctrinated?

"And Xan . . . he's a threat to your empire?" That was impossible to believe. Xan was so mild mannered. He'd rescued spiders from the house as a child. He wasn't a threat to anyone.

"I did say intelligence was close enough. Your brother is useful. The Commonwealth is the threat. Massing near the Jonat System, building thousands of Comets to strike at our fleet, bringing planets into their organization as fast as they can—"

Katryn pulled the blanket tighter around her, suddenly chilled.

"They're protecting us from you. It's their sole purpose, what they were created for. If the Commonwealth is massing anything—" She slammed her mouth shut. *It's because you're attacking more systems. You're trying to expand your empire.*

Linden ignored her comment. That was for the best—but there was no doubt he had cataloged it away to use against her later. She'd have to learn to curb her tongue if she were to survive this.

"We don't answer to the Haederan military," he said. "Never have, never will. It's the other way around, in fact, though they're loathe to admit it." He rubbed his eyes and yawned. "It's the only way to restrain them, keep them from—"

"Deciding your emperor needs to go?"

He shot her a look. "All that to say . . . they won't take you. They may want to, but they can't. Not unless I need assistance from them, and I explicitly order it. Which I don't want to have to do," he added.

"Is that supposed to make me feel better?" She jerked her feet away from him. *Too close.*

He blinked at the sudden motion but didn't move. "Well . . . yes."

"It doesn't."

"Would tea?"

"Stop with the tea!" She looked around, anxious her outburst had been heard through the walls. "I don't want tea, and I don't want to talk to you anymore. I just—I want to go to sleep."

Or cry in peace. Please let me cry in peace.

"Fine." Linden held his hands up in some sort of polite appeal. "Then sleep."

He closed his eyes, and in thirty seconds was snoring, sitting there next to her feet. She watched him sleep for over two hours, thoughts and fears and wishes of what would happen to her on Asria filling her head.

CHAPTER TEN

It turned out the erstwhile political officer had had his own system of organization, one that took Chase a week to even begin to figure out. He worked through Adler's minor investigations first—and took his time with those. There were so many . . . it was no wonder *Defiant*'s crew had despised Adler. Powell was certainly not the only man who'd wanted him dead. Had they hated Chase so much during his stint as political officer on the *Gauntlet* eighteen years ago? He was still alive, so perhaps not.

There was the ordnance man who'd been caught with unsanctioned pornography, the Hawk mechanic who'd sent a message to his wife questioning the length of their last orbital deployment, and the two launch-control petty officers who'd come to blows one day over some innocuous name-calling. The rest of the investigations were so paltry he couldn't bring himself to look into them further.

In the end, after a few weeks of insincere and superficial investigating, he closed them all. No one would care that he wasn't fully doing the political officer's job, not with an invasion approaching. And if they did, well, didn't *Defiant* need all the personnel possible to fight in the invasion? He had a built-in defense for his idleness. Making sure the ship was fully manned was for the benefit of the emperor, of course. For the glory of the empire.

He'd dare them to say anything about it.

He began the communication censorship after that. Perhaps because of the impending invasion, the outgoing comm system had auto-selected triple the usual number of messages for human review. Chase took a four-day break to explore the ship before beginning that mess. It wasn't as though the messages were going anywhere.

An impromptu visit to the brig on the final day of his exploration ended with him being escorted out by a commander who apologetically told him to come back when Captain Tanner had approved it. It seemed Tanner wanted him to speak to Powell about as much as *he* wanted to speak to Powell. Chase wouldn't admit it was a relief. Delaying his more heinous work was turning out to be easier than he'd ever imagined.

Still, it didn't endear *Defiant*'s executive officer to him, and Chase sullenly returned to his quarters and his work. Temporarily, at least. After a day of reading more personal messages than he cared to see, he reported to Hellar in a fury, arguing that the comm blackout made the exercise moot. The communications would all be held until Asria was taken, if not longer, but the admiral was insistent. There would be no access to Powell until all of Adler's unfinished work was complete.

Delaying the inevitable on his own was one thing, but being denied something he pretended to want was another entirely. Chase took another day's break after that meeting to seethe over the further restriction. Reviewing each message by hand was tedious, mind-numbing work, and he cursed the emperor each time he flipped to a new communication that wouldn't reach its recipient for months. As if he needed any more proof of imperial bureaucracy . . . this had to be the reason political officers were drawn from the junior ISC team.

But if he needed a reminder that he was not one of those junior officers, the matter of Her Royal Highness Avery Rendon, formerly Cadet Rendon of the Commonwealth Navy, was a good one. The emperor's initial charge had never been far away in his mind, and as Chase brought up a channel of publicly released Commonwealth data, he wondered exactly what His Imperial Majesty meant for him to do with her. If the emperor was to hold Asria as a protectorate, under whatever agreement he'd made with her uncle, that meant any investigation on his part would need to be discreet. A rebellious princess had the potential to ruin any kind of tentative peace.

A few more taps and he had a listing of the latest Commonwealth Academy class. Another tap found Cadet Avery Rendon's biography. The young woman in the photo stared back at him, a hint of arrogance in the angle of her chin and her green eyes. Seafoam, Isobel would call them, as if seafoam was an everyday occurrence in their arid part of Haedera. Her dark hair matched the brushed metal of the wings on the chest of her Commonwealth uniform, which he suspected accounted for that wisp of conceit.

Yes, here it was—Cadet Rendon had been selected to fly Comets, space fighters designed specifically to intercept and push the Haederan fleet back toward its homeland. It was no surprise, then, that she'd been practically brainwashed by the Commonwealth. Maybe her uncle was paranoid. Maybe he wasn't. Still, she was only a young woman. How much of a threat could she be to whatever the emperor had planned?

He'd worry about her later.

This afternoon, he'd worry about the box. Locked and marked *Personal*, he'd found it in a drawer under a stack of Adler's spare uniforms while rearranging his own belongings for a third time. The fatigues appeared too small for the stocky man in Adler's personnel photos, but Chase supposed he would have gained some weight himself after six months in space. Many men did, so it wasn't unusual. Neither were the uniforms themselves— normally personal effects would have been sent home, but with *Defiant*'s upcoming mission, they'd apparently been left behind.

The box, on the other hand . . . after spending an hour trying to pick the lock with a clip, Chase sighed and tried another of Adler's code cards. Nothing worked, including bashing the metal with a hammer, and that was for the best. He didn't need to see pictures and mementos of loved ones, family that would never see Adler again.

He stuck the picture of *his* family on the ceiling above his bunk and slept for a long time.

* * *

He'd postponed his first interview with Powell long enough.

Defiant was only days from Asria now, and despite Chase's earlier plan of avoiding the whole mess entirely, the emperor would have his head if he didn't accomplish something during this forced tour. Still, he dressed as slowly as possible and shaved even slower. When he stepped outside his quarters, five minutes after their agreed-upon time, Captain Tanner stared at him like he was something he'd found on the bottom of his shoe. Something dangerous, but garbage nonetheless.

"I don't know why you're here at all," the executive officer finally said, seemingly resigned to Chase's presence on his ship. "I certainly don't know why you're interested in the Adler investigation. Powell already confessed, and we have more important things to deal with right now. He'd be dead already if His Majesty let us make our own personnel decisions. Really, Colonel, this is poor timing for an ISC inquiry."

It was a brash comment to make to an ISC officer, one that would usually lead to a formal rebuke, if not more, but Chase chose to ignore it.

"I read Hellar's report," he said. "From what I understand, Powell only confessed to having been in Adler's cabin the day before his death. That's hardly an admission of murder. He had no motive, and no other interactions with him. It doesn't make much sense—you've got to give me something better than that."

He leaned against his door and folded his arms, relishing the way Tanner stiffened at his casualness.

Uptight bastard.

"They were heard arguing," Tanner insisted.

"That doesn't mean anything." In truth, it meant quite a bit, but arguing with Tanner was too entertaining to concede the point immediately. "Aren't you the least bit concerned he's not guilty? Or that he might have an accomplice running around your ship?"

The answer was obvious, of course. *Defiant's* senior officers were simply glad Adler was gone—and displeased to see his replacement appear so soon. With the comm blackout and his own arrival requiring an imperial order, there was no doubt Hellar and Tanner had assumed the position would be left vacant indefinitely. More than assumed—they'd probably hoped. It didn't necessarily mean anything since dislike for ISC wasn't uncommon in the fleet, but Tanner was so obvious about it . . .

It was something to keep in mind.

Tanner looked at him without emotion. "Fine. This way."

He headed down the corridor, following a path that made Chase's head spin. Light grew bright, then dim. The floor clanged under his boots, and once he didn't duck fast enough, catching the very top of his head on . . . well, something hard. None of this was right. His feet and his heart belonged on the ground, preferably at Windhaven, not in some maze of metal and look-alike doors. Even the artificial gravity felt unnatural. He didn't belong here, trying to find a way to have another man killed quicker than necessary. He didn't want to have to order an execution at all.

What if I didn't? What if I refused? Made up a story? Cleared him? Would You protect me?

Instead of comfort, fear flashed through him. How much did the emperor suspect of his doubts? How much had Isobel suggested to him?

"Question for you," he called after Tanner as they rounded the corner past the enlisted mess. Talking kept his mind off the idea of Isobel unknowingly—or worse, intentionally—suggesting that her husband might not be as trustworthy as her father wished. "Is the food here always so terrible?"

"Budget cuts. But don't bother trying the wardroom." Tanner grunted. "Adler wasn't welcome there, and you're not either."

It was a conversation-stopper, obviously Tanner's intent—as if he had the power to deny the political officer access to anywhere on the ship. Still, who wanted to eat meal after meal in cold silence? Eating in his quarters was comfortable; eating in the enlisted mess gave him ample eavesdropping opportunities. Either worked. Chase didn't say another word until they reached the brig, where Tanner introduced him to the guards, then disappeared without another word. To the wardroom for a decent lunch, no doubt.

The pale officer on duty led him down an aisle of closed doors —did the man ever leave his post to use one of the dozen sunrooms on board? As a mid-grade officer, he could claim up to twenty minutes every day cycle if he was so inclined, more than enough to maintain some kind of healthy complexion. The disturbing idea that the lieutenant was as much a prisoner as whoever he guarded popped into Chase's head. Or maybe . . . maybe everyone on *Defiant* was a prisoner, including himself.

Stars, he was going soft.

The lieutenant punched in a code to open the door, revealing a room almost as small as the washroom in Chase's cabin. A man sat on a hard cot against the far wall, and he looked up at the sound. No sheets, no pillow, no blanket, no comfort at all—and now his day was about to get much worse.

Per Haederan Navy policy, Powell's head had been shaven. His pale skin matched the officer on duty's, which meant they'd both been on *Defiant* for weeks, if not months. But unlike the brig officer who had the usual intermingled Haederan background, the prisoner—older than he'd expected for a specialist—had an intriguing swath of freckles across his face. It was unusual for junior enlisted navy personnel to come from the higher Haederan social classes, but not unheard of. His personnel file hadn't said anything about a noble title, so either something had been missed or Powell's history was more interesting than he'd first assumed.

Likely there was a story there . . . something innocent he could start with to get Powell talking. If nothing else, their former shared status in the empire was common ground, and common ground would be useful.

Yes.

That was how he would approach this first meeting. He would be concerned at first. He would wonder out loud how such a man could have ended up in this position. He would give Powell time to make excuses, then suggest how his actions brought shame to his family. To the Haederan Empire. Guilt made people talk.

It would be simple. Interrogations weren't usually simple, but some were, and after the past weeks, he needed a break. Deserved one, in fact.

But all his plans were shattered when Powell's eyes locked on to his uniform. He jumped to attention, although he refrained from saluting. The look on his face—

Relief?

He'd never seen relief on the face of a prisoner. Ever. Fear, yes, terror, yes, even anger once when he'd allowed too much time for a prisoner to work up his courage before initial questioning. But never relief. Something was wrong, and Chase cursed fate for leading him into this situation unprepared. There was only one way to begin now. Silent, he waited for the prisoner to speak first.

Powell took a deep breath.

"Sir, I can't tell you how happy I am to see you."

Yes, something was very wrong.

CHAPTER ELEVEN

For a moment that seemed to stretch on for an hour, Chase stood in the doorway, staring somewhere between Powell's ear and the wall, his vision hazy. What had he ever done that fate was conspiring against him like this? First, he'd been yanked from Windhaven, then sent to this deep-space misery, and now he was standing in the brig, wordless like he hadn't been since he'd run his first interrogation so many years ago. He had to say something, and honesty was the only thing that came into his mind now. It was probably the wrong move, but rubbing his eyes and cursing under his breath was even worse.

"Most don't react like this to my appearance, Specialist," he said. A wave of heat slunk down his back. This wasn't good. This wasn't good at all.

"It's not—" Powell's eyes widened almost imperceptibly; a haunted expression replaced his relief.

Ah, there was the fear. Chase's heart began to slow. Fear he could handle. Fear made sense. Fear was familiar. The only problem was, it didn't look exactly like fear. It was almost . . .

Could it be shame?

Oh, blast it.

The answer was right there in front of him. It explained everything. Powell's visit—no, it had to have been *visits*—to Adler's quarters, his physical characteristics incongruous with his position, the spare uniforms of Adler's which couldn't have fit him in months. More than anything, it explained his relief at the appearance of a man who terrified everyone else who crossed his path. He was probably the answer to Powell's prayers.

Chase narrowed his eyes at the prisoner in front of him, who, haunted or not, stood with the same professionalism as before. One more piece of evidence, since it wasn't a courtesy he'd come to expect from navy personnel during his weeks on *Defiant*. Yes, Powell's denial had been a slip, likely from the weeks of isolation and surprise at seeing someone who might be able to save him. And now, it had embarrassed him. *Strange.* Powell was more afraid of being called out for his mistake than of his current situation.

Or maybe not so strange.

How had no one on *Defiant* made the connection? Was Powell that good of an actor? Had Adler implied the visits had been of a more personal nature? That kind of thing wasn't allowed on a military starship, of course, but who was going to argue with the political officer about what he did in his free time? Not even Hellar or Tanner would want to wander into that mess.

Powell's expression turned to something else—hope?—and then Chase was sure. The kid had ISC written all over him. Maybe Navy Special Intelligence Corps, but he'd take the chance Powell was the former. He'd been meeting with Adler, after all, not whoever NSIC had stationed aboard.

Chase took a silent, deep breath.

"What did Lient promise you if you took this assignment . . . Lieutenant?" he asked. Powell—though that couldn't be his real name—would have been persuaded into it. Like the despised political officer appointments, ISC undercover positions weren't a job most settled for. Too dangerous, too unglamorous. "A promotion? Or a transfer back to Haedera II?"

"Captain." Powell's knees buckled, and he sank heavily onto

the cot, hands over his face. "Brennin Kern. How did you know, sir? I thought I'd have a fight on my hands trying to prove who I was."

He still might, especially with Tanner, but there wasn't any point bringing that up yet. This Kern, or whoever he was, needed hope if he was going to talk.

"Years of experience. You want to tell me what's going on?"

"I didn't kill him, sir."

Why had he expected to hear something besides an immediate denial?

"Admiral Hellar's report says otherwise, Captain. His fairly detailed report, I might add. I didn't see anything in it that would point to anyone but you. Now, if something happened, something personal—we can work this out, keep it within ISC. I can't promise anything if that's the case, but—"

Kern snorted. "His report would say that." He ran a hand across his bare head, an automatic response. His fingers froze, like they'd only now realized he was bald. "But that's because . . ." He shot an anxious glance at the door.

"Microphone's off." Chase had made sure of that before entering. ISC's business was no one's business but ISC's.

Kern lowered his voice anyway. "He did it, sir."

He would have placed more money on Tanner, but somehow Kern's statement didn't strike him as strangely as it should.

. . . and Adler was a kid. Too apt to step in something he shouldn't, Hellar had said. Well, Adler had certainly stepped in something—something Hellar hadn't wanted him to find out. Then he'd taken care of an undercover ISC officer—who was doubtless getting just as nosy—by pinning Adler's murder on him.

Lient was going to have a stroke.

"That's quite an allegation," Chase said. "Hellar has almost thirty years of spotless service." The incident on Haedera III, though it was what he was best known for in the navy, was only the tip of his service to the empire. "And senior officers aren't known for fragging."

"I know, sir, but it's the truth." Kern leaned against the wall, any defensiveness he might have considered seemingly stolen from him. "Even Adler wasn't sure about it, not at first. He'd requested help from NSIC, and they'd denied him the personnel."

Sure about what? He'd skip that question for now, let Kern ramble.

"So he ended up with you. How long have you been on *Defiant*?"

Kern blinked in confusion. "I don't—I don't know anymore. Seven months before Adler was killed. He stuck me in the janitorial section, which let me wander the ship at will. It gave me access to every controlled area, including engineering. No one suspected we were running an investigation."

It was impossible to know if Kern was leaving parts of the story out on purpose or simply couldn't string words together in any kind of coherent fashion after so much time in isolation. That was the problem with these solitary cells—interrogations after so many weeks were almost useless. But that was a problem he'd created himself, wasn't it?

"Investigating what?" he prompted.

"Gambling, sir. You wouldn't believe the gambling that goes on here."

And here it was, right in front of him—the most naïve ISC officer ever to exist. Chase would have laughed, except that Kern's simplemindedness had resulted in Adler's death and his arrest, awaiting his own demise.

"Captain, there's gambling on every ship." He wanted to sigh but ran his palm across his face instead. How had these two been so careless with this investigation? Boredom? Did they have personal issues with Hellar? Perhaps this was some sort of vendetta. Things like this had happened before, but there was a procedure for it. "If that's what got Adler killed, it's a problem you two created on your own."

And it was a problem Kern would pay for, one way or the other.

"But Hellar's swiping a third of the onboard budget to pay off his own gambling debts. He's siphoning the mess funds. Haven't you noticed how bad the food is, sir?" Kern didn't sound naïve now, but confident. "He threatened the purser into it—told him he'd turn him in to ISC for some imagined offense if he didn't cooperate. And it was only a little at first. It would have taken Adler years to figure it out if Hellar had kept it that low. He didn't. Eventually, what he took wasn't enough to cover his losses, and he knew he was in big trouble. He was making plans to sell some armament to a cartel on Brisia. An entire cruiser load of Torchlight missiles and such."

In his mind, Chase whistled low and slow—then cringed. Treason was worse than murder.

"And you can prove this?" he asked.

Please be able to prove it. Because if Kern couldn't—

"Yes. All the proof's in an unmarked safe in Adler's cabin. I brought it by that morning and told him he needed to arrest Hellar immediately. He wanted to run everything by Lient first." Kern shook his head. "The man had no balls, no idea what it was really like to be the one making the decision. I told him if he didn't do it in the next five minutes, I'd break my cover and do it myself."

That must have been the argument Tanner had referred to. A slow ache was beginning somewhere deep in Chase's head, and it wasn't one pain meds would take care of. "Why didn't you?"

"He wouldn't give me my uniform or identification, and things were getting loud. I went back to my cabin and drafted an urgent message to Lient, hoping to have an answer in the next few days, but before I could send it, we went under some kind of comm blackout. When I went to confront Adler about it, to tell him that there was no choice but to arrest Hellar now, the admiral was coming out of his cabin and Adler was dead inside. I wasn't going to tell anyone who I really was, not after that."

"Why didn't he have you executed right then? Cover his tracks?"

Kern's voice turned bitter . . . or contemptuous, Chase couldn't tell which. "Hellar killed Adler out of panic. He's not bloodthirsty. And I was dead as soon as they arrested me. Why cast more suspicion on himself?"

"And the box?"

"You can find the code card behind the humidifying grate in Adler's cabin—your cabin now, I'd expect, sir. All my identification is in there, along with a chip to replace my falsified personnel data and biometrics in the ship's system with the correct information."

The slow ache turned to a pounding agony. Kern was telling the truth, there was no question of that. *Seven-week vacation, indeed.* There was no way the emperor could have predicted that the guilty party was *Defiant*'s commanding officer. And now it wasn't only Hellar's life at stake.

It was the entire invasion.

* * *

Chase had lain on his bunk for two hours, staring up at Isobel and asking for forgiveness, before making his decision. Kern knocked on his door at the end of the second hour, clean-shaven, dressed in a clean uniform from Adler's cabin, and looking healthier than anyone who'd spent months in solitary confinement had a right to.

The innocence—or cruelty—of youth.

There were looks, yes, as the two marched down the maze of corridors, but no comments. Not out loud, at least. Rumors must have spread around the ship already, although whether they were about Kern's identity or Hellar's guilt, Chase had no idea—and didn't want to. It didn't matter what the rest of the crew thought; it didn't even matter if the rumors made their way to Hellar before he did. This would, ultimately, end the same way.

Hellar's back was to them when they slipped inside his private office. The screen in front of him that'd been dark when Chase had first met him was now lit by white Haederan ships interspersed with potential Asrian interceptors. The strategy that Hellar knew better than anyone else in Alpha Fleet played out over and over as he checked for weak points. He turned at the interruption and smiled at Chase with the anticipation of a man who was realizing a dream.

"Colonel, now's not a good time." He flicked a finger at the screen. "We make Asria tomorrow, and—"

His gaze flashed to Kern, silently closing the door behind himself and Chase. In the span of thirty silent seconds, Hellar turned gray, except for the pulsating blue vein in his temple.

If not the easiest, it was certainly the fastest and least verbal confession Chase had ever compelled.

"I have a proposition for you," Chase said quietly, as Kern made his way next to the desk and switched off the viewscreen. "I've already talked to Captain Tanner, and since I've pronounced him *Defiant*'s commander once again, he was willing to approve it. He tells me you're the one with the best knowledge of tomorrow's strategy, and I'm inclined to believe him. As loathe as I am to let you have another day of freedom, I'm not going to be the one to sabotage this invasion by arresting you now. Captain Kern will take you into custody and is prepared to escort you back to Haedera after your mission here is complete. He'll be with you on the bridge during all military operations, and you are not to interfere with his presence in any way. Once you're home . . . I hope you'll do the right thing, Admiral."

Whatever Hellar's interpretation of the "right thing" was, be it suicide en route or confessing to the emperor. The fate of a Haederan Navy admiral, thankfully, would be decided at a level higher than himself. Not that Chase had to wonder about what that fate would be. The only question was—

"But I will warn you," he went on, "if you so much as imagine evading this final duty, only the Holy One will be able to save your family from His Majesty's vengeance."

Even the words made him sick. He ground his boots into the deck to keep himself from fleeing.

Forgive me.

"It was an accident." Hellar's words were strained, becoming high-pitched. "A mistake. You don't understand, Colonel. You have to listen to me. You have to hear what really happened!"

The claim of every man in Hellar's position, and it would do him no good now. Chase turned on his heel and ignored the protests following him down the corridor. His part in this mess was done.

It was time to figure out his plan for Avery Rendon.

CHAPTER TWELVE

KATRYN DROPPED THE SMALL BAG SHE'D ACCUMULATED ON *AERIS* ON the floor of her cabin of the courier ship. Amazing how one took personal items for granted before having them stolen away after an enemy invasion. Her current possessions weren't much—a few feminine-scented toiletries the men on the cruiser hadn't wanted, but they meant so much.

She took a deep breath. No headache, no dizziness. The ship seemed fine for now. She checked the mask under her bunk anyway, comforted by the flashing green lights on its side. Worrying about dying from an environmental system malfunction was preferable to worrying about what would happen to her once they reached Asria, and it was certainly preferable to worrying about what Xan had gotten himself into.

Linden hadn't said more than three words to her since the night she'd woken in tears, spending his days with his nose in a tablet instead. Every so often someone would appear at the door, and he'd stepped outside for a conversation. Though she couldn't understand the low voices outside, he wasn't leaving the cabin unguarded. Where would she have gone, anyway?

With a shiver, she stood to get a cup of water. No, not water. The courier was cold tonight, so it would have to be something hot, probably that awful Haederan tea that Linden seemed to prefer. It was better than nothing though, wasn't it? She managed to suppress a grumble as she headed for the galley. Reluctant gratitude was a funny thing.

So was the newly stocked galley. Linden must have had a talk with the cooks on *Aeris*, because the two small cabinets were stocked with not only the ubiquitous ration packages but a few bags of fresh fruit. And . . . Katryn squinted in confusion at the gold foil next to the apples. Freeze-dried coffee cubes? She picked one up and rolled it between her fingers. Commonwealth-made— on Ventana IV, if she had to guess.

"Do you like it?"

Katryn gasped and spun around, dropping the cubes onto the floor. Linden had snuck in while she'd been inspecting the supplies and was grinning at her from his usual chair. She nodded, wordless. He'd acquired coffee? For her—just for her?

"Here, let me get those." He pushed himself up and was across the galley in two strides.

She waved him off. "No, I've got it." They were right under her feet, after all. She bent down to gather the cubes up—and gasped in shock and pain as Linden's forehead slammed into hers. How had she not seen him lean down at the same time?

Linden jerked back and swore under his breath.

"I'm sorry!" She leapt to her feet and away from him. "I'm so sorry! I didn't see—"

"You didn't break me." He laughed, palm on his forehead. "Well . . . maybe a little."

"Let me take a look." Gingerly, she reached out a finger, accidentally brushing his hand as he lowered it. Her entire arm tingled at the touch. As for his head—there was already a lump, and it might turn into a bruise, but he deserved it. "I think you'll live."

My heart might not, though.

"Is that your expert opinion, Doctor?"

"I don't know. I'm not a medical doctor." She knelt down to

grab the cubes, mostly to hide the sudden flush on her cheeks. "Where did this dangerous coffee come from?"

"I negotiated for it. Had to trade some instant noodles for it and even that was a hard sell. It's not easy for us to get our hands on Commonwealth goods."

"I'm surprised you didn't take it." Shocked, actually, after what he'd told her about himself. Taking a bit of coffee from a Haederan Navy ship would be a small thing.

"I suspect you wouldn't have enjoyed it if you knew I'd appropriated it by another method."

She had no answer to that, nor to the sudden earnestness on his face. He'd been worried she wouldn't like his gift? That reaction was . . . well, it was confusing.

"Do you want some, too?" she asked. As loathe as she was to do anything for her captor, she had to thank him somehow.

Linden shook his head and held his hand out. Katryn dropped the cube into it. "No. Sit down. I'll make this and some tea and we can talk."

Talk? She ignored his order to sit and pulled a freezer pack of purple berries out of the deep freeze instead. "About what?"

"Whatever you want. It's what people do, after all." He unwrapped the cube, sniffed it, and tossed it into a cup.

But I don't want to talk to you, was on the tip of her tongue before it died out. It was a lie.

"Then let's talk about you. I barely know you, after all, even after weeks together." Her face turned red. Had she flirted with him this time?

He furrowed his brow at her over his shoulder and poured hot water into his cup. "If you'd like. So," he said, dropping into his chair across the table from her, his tea and her coffee in hand, "how much do you want to know?"

She passed him the freezer pack as he slid the coffee across to her. "Everything."

Without breaking eye contact, he placed the berries to his forehead and took a sip of tea.

"All right. I'm thirty-one, as far as Commonwealth time goes. I was born in and grew up in Saer. I hate science, and math even more. I have two older sisters, both of whom you'd probably like if you could get over them being Haederan. I joined the army right out of school and was recruited for this two years later."

"*This* being hostage-taking?"

Linden had sense enough to blush at that.

"That's secondary."

Right. Running double agents must be primary.

"Married?" It was her turn to blush.

"No. You?"

If he knew Xan, if Xan had been held prisoner by ISC, he must know she had been.

"He died. Shuttle accident." Though he must know that, too. "It was a long time ago, and Nash and I had only been married six months." She wiped the wetness from her eyes. That rationalization had never worked. "He was headed to Caige to do some research on the icecaps there. They picked up some cargo on the way—there were several undeclared oxygen canisters packaged inside one of the crates. The canisters overheated, and . . . They told me it was instantaneous."

She'd never believed that part. The smoke would have overcome the crew and passengers first. It must have been a horrible, terrifying, looming death.

Linden was silent for a long while. "I'm sorry," he finally said.

She shrugged. "You didn't load those containers."

"I can feel bad about it." Linden reached his hand across the table, and before she knew what she was doing, she'd taken hold of it. He squeezed, then pulled back, leaving her more alone than before.

"Happier topic," she said. Was there one? There was a gulf between them so big a starship couldn't cross it. What was she doing in this galley, making small talk with the enemy?

Linden opened his mouth, but static from the galley's comm on the far wall interrupted him.

"You in there, Captain?" The Haederan voice sounded on the verge of panic.

Katryn stiffened. Now what was wrong with the ship?

Linden jumped up and slammed his hand on the button to reply. "Yeah. What's going on?"

"Couple of Commonwealth interceptors off our port side."

"I'm on my way." He looked at Katryn, all compassion gone from his face. "You too. Time to do your job."

* * *

Linden hauled her down the corridor as the courier ship shook, ignoring her protests. Maybe—just maybe—she could step on his foot or slam his head against the wall. Because this wasn't good. Something was very wrong. He intended to use her to keep the Commonwealth ships from firing on them. Not that she wanted them to, but she didn't want a reminder of her status as a hostage, either.

He paused outside the locked door to the flight deck and pulled her close. "If you say a word, I will make you regret it. Understand?"

Katryn stared at him, mouth open.

Linden shook her by the shoulders, cutting through her fear. "Understand?"

Numb, she nodded, and he knocked on the door without letting go of her arm. The pilot who pushed it open was pale—which was preferable to blue and dead.

"They've fired four times now," he said. "Shields are holding, but won't if they keep pounding us like this."

"Can you raise them?" Linden frowned at the viewscreen.

"I can try." With a deep breath, the pilot waved his fingers at his control panel.

Linden hadn't let go of her. Katryn tried to take a step away, but he pulled her back against his side, hip to hip, as the small viewscreen lit up. The khaki-uniformed woman on it looked irritated by their intrusion.

"Feel like giving up yet?" she asked, focusing on Linden.

Katryn hated her immediately.

"Only if you want a dead Zarcronian citizen on your record." His voice had taken on a tone she'd only heard once. The bored, smug tone he'd used when addressing the colonel on Iythea.

"Then let her go." If the woman was surprised at her identity, she hid it well.

He chuckled quietly. "So you can turn us into a supernova? I don't think so." His free hand darted to the side, then brought up a pistol.

Against her head.

Katryn tried to shift away from him, but he pulled harder on her wrist and pushed harder with the gun. She wanted to look at him, to beg, but she could only hold her breath and stare at the woman on the screen. Judging by the officer's face, it wasn't a stun pistol Linden had pressed against her temple.

"There's no need for violence," the officer said in a false calm that suggested she would, in fact, welcome it.

"You started it by firing on an unarmed courier ship." Linden sounded cool, confident. "But I'll end it."

There was silence. Katryn thought she'd heard silence before, but this . . . this must be what people meant when they said silence was thick.

The woman made a motion with her hand, then looked from her to Linden.

"I've ordered them to stop firing for now. But if she's truly Zarcronian, I'm not allowing you to leave here with her. You've got an hour to hand her over."

The screen went black. The pistol fell to his side. Katryn didn't move. Could barely breathe.

"Go to your quarters." Linden spoke quietly and didn't look at her.

Katryn somehow managed to turn her head and stare at him. Her legs wouldn't let her move.

"Now!" His voiced echoed in the bare flight deck.

She backed into the empty navigator's chair, caught herself before she fell, and ran.

* * *

It was another hour—of no explosions—before her doorbell beeped. She ignored it, knowing it didn't matter. How long until Linden overrode the lock? Well, she wouldn't give him the chance. After the fourth beep, she opened the door. He stood in the corridor with a blank expression, looking serious and resigned.

"Leave me alone," she said. An ironic command since she'd let him in to begin with.

Instead of replying, he held out the pistol, handle first. She stared at it, then him. He raised it slightly in invitation.

With a shaking hand, she took it. "Am I supposed to shoot you with this?"

Linden rubbed the back of his neck and stepped around her to crumple on to her bunk.

"It's not charged."

Katryn blinked, her chest tight. With the pistol dangling from her hand, she glanced down, scarcely able to believe it . . . but it was as he said. With a light finger, she pressed the trigger, but the lights remained off. Dead, though she hadn't been able to see it from behind her—and neither had that Commonwealth officer.

Relief sparked inside her. Relief and something much hotter and unpleasant. Without thinking, she flung the pistol as hard as she could toward his head.

"Hey!" Linden ducked, his eyes wide. The pistol bounced off the wall behind him, then clattered to the floor in front of him. "You didn't need to throw it at me." He knelt on the floor to retrieve it from its final resting place and shoved it in his pocket.

"And you didn't need to put it to my head," she screamed at him.

"They would have destroyed this ship, Katryn." He climbed back on her bunk. Why wasn't he going away? "What did you want me to do? Let them?"

Linden had never actually called her by her name before.

"N—no. Are you going to let me go now?" He'd have to, right? That Commonwealth Navy woman had said so.

"Don't be silly. They're gone."

"Gone?"

They couldn't be gone. She'd envisioned herself walking off this Haederan ship onto a friendly one. Somewhere safe. She'd pictured herself collapsing on a bunk, knowing the Commonwealth would get her home eventually, and then this nightmare would be over. She'd see her family, except for Xan, probably. She'd been so certain . . .

"Gone. They're not reckless. A live hostage is better than a dead one, and she realized she didn't want to be the one to start an incident over you. Things are bad enough between the empire and the Commonwealth right now as it is."

"Oh." Katryn didn't know what else to say. "Oh." She needed to sit, but Linden was . . . It didn't matter. She sat down next to him on the bunk. "Oh," she said to her hands.

Linden took hold of her wrist. She looked up at him, confused by his gentle touch—and by the way her heart pounded at the feel of his fingers on her. He dropped it almost immediately, and she reached out without knowing why.

"You hurt me," she said, wishing she could dig her nails into his soft palm in retaliation.

"I didn't mean to," he said. "I'm sorry." He flipped her hand over, and his frown faded. At the lack of bruises, she assumed. He really hadn't grabbed her that hard. He had hurt her emotionally more than anything else. "I can get you some ice if you need it."

Katryn shook her head. "I'm all right."

"If you're sure." He looked at the door, then back at her. "I should go."

It was an automatic suggestion. He wanted to stay, that much was clear. And—and her heart and her mind wanted him to as well. Was it for comfort? Or something else? Whatever it was, she couldn't allow it.

"Yes." She jerked her hand away and headed for the sink before she did something she regretted. "You should."

CHAPTER THIRTEEN

Chase straightened the captain's pins on his collar one last time as he hurried down the street. His Imperial Haederan Army uniform still fit after several months of disuse, even if the shirt was looser than it should have been. Somehow, he'd managed to lose weight on the long voyage. Isobel would not approve—he would need to remedy that before heading home or he'd hear about both his new freckles and his decreasing waistline.

He'd followed Victor Rendon's niece out of the palace, had watched her lose her Haederan Army shadow in one of the dozens of shops that lined the curving road leading south into central Cadena—she was imaginative, he had to give her that. And if he'd calculated correctly, she would come out of the alleyway back onto the main street in less than two minutes.

Two minutes until his real mission began.

He'd spent four useless weeks pacing around his cabin on *Defiant* after the invasion. Kern and Hellar had departed for Haedera two days after the short battle, and with no assignment outside of the usual post-invasion deterrence, life on the cruiser had settled into an uneasy calm. He certainly hadn't had any political officer work to do. After the comm blackout was lifted, he'd sent a barrage of messages to Isobel, hoping to see her in person before her response arrived, and as each day passed with no word from the surface, he'd prayed the silence would continue.

It had not.

The Haederan Army occupation governor had sent an urgent message last week. Victor Rendon's niece was causing trouble, Taln Perrin had said. He was certain she was up to something. Chase had shaken his head as he'd packed up his things, just as certain that the governor had fallen prey to the deep-seated Haederan paranoia that made all their lives miserable. But even paranoia could be true sometimes.

He'd been watching Avery Rendon for a week now, and with no sign of anything untoward, it was time to deliver a warning. With any luck, the governor was wrong, and he'd be able to go home as soon as there was a ship headed for Haedera. Back to Windhaven, back to Isobel, back to his long-desired orders. If Perrin wasn't wrong . . . well, that's why he was here, wasn't it?

He pressed himself against the cool wall. The stone of the ancient building, wedged in between two modern skyscrapers, was chilled even in what passed for summer in Cadena. Would he ever feel warm again? Not until he made it back to Haedera and was in Isobel's arms, certainly. Quick footsteps, unquestionably feminine, sounded in the alley, and he waited, his breath short. *Patience.* As soon as they reached the corner, he stepped away from the wall.

His quarry slammed into him as she turned the corner to the main road. Chase grasped her arm, more to keep her from tripping over his feet than to restrain her. She gasped in shock at his touch, turning wide green eyes up to meet his. The expensive silk dress she wore blended in with everyone else, the dark brown waves that hung just past her shoulders made her look like almost every other young woman he'd seen in Cadena, but the family resemblance to Victor Rendon was remarkable. Up close, there was no doubt this was the suspect niece.

Her eyes ran across his uniform, taking in the Haederan green he knew she must detest, his rank and military police insignia, and his stun pistol. It was ISC issue—he'd deign to use an army uniform, not their weapons—but she had no way of knowing that. He stifled a laugh at her horrified expression, then smiled as he dropped her arm.

"I'm sorry. I really should pay more attention to where I'm going," Avery Rendon said, evidently deciding he was no threat to her. Things were starting out well. "Excuse me."

She tried to step around him, but he took a step in the same direction, trapping her against the wall. *Careful, now.* He couldn't use force . . . couldn't risk frightening her, not yet. If Perrin and Victor Rendon were correct that she was working for the Commonwealth, he needed to gain her trust. He needed to find out how much she'd told them. Per the emperor's suggestion, he might even be able to use her to feed the Commonwealth false intelligence. It would be slow, painstaking work this time, with no room for error.

"Your Highness, wait, please," he said, before she could move around him. "We've been looking for you."

Her face fell as the significance of his use of her title sank in; her shoulders deflated. She was so full of conflicting expressions —annoyance, hate, and fear—that it was difficult not to laugh. He bit his tongue, hard, but he wasn't sure it did any good.

"Keating said you were caught up in a protest. It must have been pretty bad for the two of you to be separated." He'd play dumb, at least for now. She couldn't know he'd been following her, couldn't know he knew she'd dumped hapless Sergeant Keating—tonight's guard—a few streets back.

"It was." Her voice shook a bit that time.

"Is that so." She'd barely denied what she'd done, and the way her voice had cracked said the rest. He had to respect her for trying, at least, even if her resistance was going to make his job more difficult. Well, he'd never shirked a challenge, had he? "You know you're not permitted outside the palace alone, no matter what demonstration you come across."

Some of her fear turned to the arrogance he'd seen in her academy photo, and he found himself vastly preferring that emotion.

"What I do is none of your concern, Captain—"

"Gareth Chase," he said, focusing on the two words. It was something to cling to, even if it was only a name—his real name, not the ridiculous title of His Imperial Highness that the emperor had stuck him with when he'd married Isobel.

"And that's where you're wrong," he continued. "As of today, General Perrin has me handling security for the royal family. That's just you, until we find your parents, so what you do is very much my concern. I'd hate for my sole responsibility to be injured in a protest."

He paused for a breath and to watch her shoulders sag at his reference to her parents, missing from their country home hours away in Sabino. But even he didn't know what'd happened to them. With the army in charge, they'd escaped, no doubt.

"And you know Asria's protectorate status is predicated on the behavior of certain individuals." Her parents, of course, plus the prime minster and herself, as well as a few targeted senior senators and ministers. "It would be unfortunate if that status were to be revoked because one of those individuals refused to follow policies agreed to in good faith by her own government."

If she were wise—and there was clear intelligence behind her socialite façade and affected Ventanan impression—she'd listen to him.

"They never should have agreed to those policies." Anger burned in those strange green eyes as she hissed at him.

He couldn't hide his smile that time, no matter how much more the expression would anger her. It was no wonder Perrin disliked her. What had the governor said? *The girl argued with me, Colonel. Even if she's not working for the Commonwealth, put a stop to her nonsense. I'm tired of dealing with her.*

Oddly, though, he found her stubbornness fascinating. Refreshing. Charming, even—much more so than her uncle. It was tedious to deal with people who caved at the first sight of his real uniform, and this one would be a challenge when the time came. Exhausting, most likely, but a challenge.

"Perhaps not," he said, trying to keep his grin in check, "but that's irrelevant right now. Neither one of us has control over what happened in the past, but I have my orders now." He glanced around at the dissipating crowds, praying he wouldn't have to drag her back to the palace. She looked like the type who'd try to scratch his eyes out. The exhaustion he'd predicted only seconds before washed over him. "Your Highness, I'd really like to not make a scene here."

Avery sighed and raised her hands in defeat, and he knew he'd won.

"Good. Where do you want to go now?" he asked.

"Go?" She frowned at him. "I don't understand."

"You must have wanted out badly to pull that stunt." Her eyes widened as she realized he knew what she'd done. "I can't let you wander around Cadena alone, but if you don't want to go home yet, I'll go with you anywhere you want to go. Almost anywhere." He laughed to conceal his unease. Letting her go anywhere she wanted was the first step in giving her the freedom to hang herself, and . . . was it already possible he was having reservations? "A ship off the planet isn't an option."

How he wished it was. *Iz, my love, I miss you so much.*

"I don't know," Avery said with more than a bit of wariness.

He steeled himself for what came next. It was war. What did she expect if she crossed the Haederan Empire? She had to know what she was up against, and nothing that was about to happen was his fault. It was hers and hers alone.

His internal argument didn't help his conscience.

"I've heard the temple by the senate building is spectacular," he said. "I just arrived on the surface a few days ago and haven't seen it yet." Tonight, though, standing with her now, he needed to be there more than he needed to be anywhere else. Maybe the

Holy One would speak to him on Asria. "Maybe you could show me?"

At his suggestion, those green eyes filled with confusion—and more than a little fear. His stomach sank, a reaction he didn't understand. He should have felt the thrill of anticipation, but he felt sick instead. Maybe Perrin was right about her, and he didn't want Perrin to be right. There was an innocence about her—not naïvety, exactly, for his people had invaded her planet, after all—but innocence.

And he was going to shatter it in the worst way possible.

* * *

The temple in the sprawling Asrian High Senate complex was the largest and most ornate place of worship he'd ever been in, which wasn't surprising. He'd had plenty of time on *Defiant* with which to study Asria over the past few months, and the fact that most Asrians were formal with their worship of the Holy One was mentioned in almost every briefing. There may not have been holy men wandering the place, just like there weren't on Haedera —though for different reasons—but they had all the formality and archaism. As he picked up the cup of consecrated water, Chase almost managed to convince himself that the old-fashioned ritual and the soaring ceiling were the real reasons for his unease.

Almost.

The water was ice as it cascaded over his palms. He was tempted to scrub them, to wash the blood of the last twenty years away, but the Asrian version of the ritual only dictated pouring, and he wouldn't humiliate himself like that—nor let Avery know of his guilt. Even so, he could feel her stare burning a hole into his back like the goldcrests at Windhaven always accused him of his many sins. She knew what he was without really knowing.

Hands physically clean, he reached for three candles and a match.

"I don't merit Your favor, but please keep them safe, even if I don't deserve to ask the same for myself," he whispered, hoping she couldn't hear the plea. What would she think of him if she did? And why did he care? Could it be pride? He'd never struggled with the emotion, even growing up in the imperial court, but it was possible. Or was it something else?

He struck the match against the side of the altar and golden light danced into being, the first warmth he'd felt on this cold planet, as he lit the candles one by one. He hesitated, then pulled a fourth toward the center and lit it too. The candles flickered in his side vision as he turned back to Avery, and he clung to the slight—imagined—feeling of holiness.

"You don't approve of me being here," he said.

"No." Her burning stare turned wary. "I don't approve at all."

She had no idea what living on an occupied planet was like, did she? Part of him wanted to drag her outside at gunpoint and tell her who he really was—how dare she disapprove of anything he chose to do? She had no say over where he went and what he did. Another part, the trained and patient ISC man, analyzed her reaction. And still another . . . well, he'd ignore that shameful part the best he could for now.

"We believe the same thing, in case you'd forgotten," he said instead of giving in to his fury. "I belong here as much as you do." He'd convince himself of that eventually.

Something strange crossed her face. Not quite anger, but he'd made a misstep somehow.

"I know what you believe." Avery took a deep breath, and he hardened himself for whatever admonishment was coming. "And I know you only believe it because your emperor forces you to. Why someone who's clearly only using faith for control would pretend to love Him is something I'll never understand. And you're too blind to see it. Or don't care. So yes, I know what you believe. And I think you should go believe it back where you came from. You don't belong in this building—or on Asria."

It was a punch to his gut. Asria—yes. He would give her that. The Haederan Empire didn't belong here. He knew it, could never argue it, and yet he had no control over what His Imperial Majesty had done. She was right, even if he could never admit it to anyone except himself.

But the temple? His faith—and hers!—was supposed to transcend such mortal things as empires and planets. Had the Holy One just confirmed his worst fears through her? Was he truly unwanted? His mind began to spin; he had to say something before she noticed his anguish.

"I could arrest you for saying that. All of it."

He swore to himself. *Another slip.* It was an ISC threat given in his ISC voice, and he glanced down at his uniform in panic before he realized he hadn't broken his cover. Army police had every right to detain her for speaking out. He hadn't made a mistake. And he hadn't really meant it—if he had, she'd already be halfway out the door, pleading for mercy.

Avery flopped on the bench behind her and began to pick at a nail.

"Then do it."

She was feigning confidence, but stars, as much as she'd just devastated him, he couldn't stop his laughter. The sound of it shocked him more than her reaction—how long had it been since he'd let himself go like that? Months, at least. Maybe it was the utter relief she hadn't found him out yet.

"Not this time," he said, struggling once more for a normal tone. "But if you talk to him like you talk to me, I'm beginning to see why Governor Perrin doesn't like you very much." He sat down next to her, and she paled a bit. "You hate us, don't you?"

Calm. Start assessing her. You know how to do this.

The familiar goal worked. Slowly, as he reminded himself of who he was and exactly what kind of power he held over her— even though she didn't know it yet—his pulse became normal.

Avery slid away and stared. Good. He'd already figured out how much proximity she could take. "You attacked us, unprovoked," she said. "You destroyed our world, our lives, our way of life. Wouldn't you if you were in my position?"

If he was in her position? The Commonwealth would never want to cross him like that. Not unless they wanted to see wrath like they'd never seen before. He shrugged and forced himself to remain seated. Acting casual around her was more difficult than he'd expected. "I probably would. I might even be angry enough to do something about it."

"That would be foolish." Her voice shook.

"It would. But desperate, angry people do foolish things sometimes, don't they?" He was pushing too hard now, but he couldn't stop himself. He could always back off later, pretend he'd been tormenting her for fun. It wasn't as though she was a hard read, and he could use that to his advantage.

"I wouldn't know."

"No?"

She took another deep breath at his question. Stars, but she was terrible at hiding her emotions. Maybe Perrin was wrong—no one would be desperate enough to ask her to hide anything for them.

"I hate every single one of you for what you've done to Asria." Her voice didn't shake that time—it became stronger, in fact. "Angry doesn't come close to how I feel about it, but I'm not reckless."

Time to drop it—for now.

"Good. Because I'd hate to see what would happen if you were."

She was lying. His gut tightened again as he stood, frantic to be away from her. It wasn't normal for a subject to get in his mind like this. It happened, of course—he wasn't a monster without any feelings—but it was happening more and more frequently lately, and he needed to figure out how to restrain his emotions. There was a job to do, and he couldn't let his fear of damnation get in the way, no matter what she said to him.

Whatever she was thinking right now was even more terrifying. She hadn't moved—he'd have heard the bench creak if she had—but she was certainly assessing him now, just as he'd been assessing her.

He decided in a fraction of a heartbeat that he didn't care. She could think whatever she wanted, and it wouldn't change her fate. The four candles flickered on the altar, casting an eerie shadow against the walls, and he focused on them instead of her.

One for Isobel.

One for Marc.

One for Sophie.

He drew a deep breath.

And one for Avery Rendon.

CHAPTER FOURTEEN

By the sacred winds, she hated push-ups.

And crunches.

And lunges.

And jogging the limited circuit in the empty cargo bay.

The constant turns were enough to make a person dizzy. But what else was there to do? There wasn't any freight through which to look for weights, and a search of her cabin and the galley for some kind of fitness equipment, makeshift or otherwise, had proved fruitless. She certainly wasn't going to knock on the flight deck door and ask what the pilots used.

Katryn's feet clanged on the metal grating below, echoing through the space, but she'd closed the door to the main corridor before beginning her workout. Linden wouldn't be able to hear, no matter how much noise she was making.

Linden.

He'd pretended to be thirty seconds from shooting her. He might as well have murdered Kaz himself. As she lowered herself to the deck for a second set of push-ups, the thought sent anger coursing down her spine—as well as several other feelings she tried to ignore.

The relief when he'd rescued her from the brig on *Aeris.*

His arms around her as the ship had come under fire.

His body against hers as he'd held a pistol to her temple.

What was wrong with her? Was she losing her mind?

But Linden hadn't shot her. He hadn't been able to, not with an uncharged weapon. He'd barely been on the planet when Kaz had stowed away in the supply ship. For how long? Perhaps an hour or two? Beyond being Haederan and therefore guilty by association, he had nothing to do with Kaz or what had happened to her and everyone else on Iythea.

So no, being attracted to him wasn't necessarily a problem—if she ignored the fact he'd kidnapped her, threatened her, then held a gun to her head, of all things. But it'd been unloaded. He wasn't going to kill her. He couldn't have killed her.

This was all just rationalization, wasn't it? Of course her feelings for him were a problem—it was described in all sorts of medical literature, and if there was one thing she was, it was well-read. Did psychologists have any idea what it was like to live the things they pontificated about, or did they simply sit in their safe offices on a planet that hadn't been destroyed by war and write about them?

Psychology. A bunch of mental sorcery and magic. Abstract justifications for behavior that would be completely appropriate in any other situation. Why couldn't she find a striking man of her own age attractive, no matter the circumstances? Being the enemy didn't stop him from being attractive, after all. It didn't stop him from having more confidence than she'd seen in years, and it didn't stop him from having that charming freckle and being sympathetic about Nash's death.

Katryn flopped to the deck, exhausted. The cargo bay was cooler than the rest of the ship, but she'd overdone her exercise. Worse, she'd used up her daily ration of water fifteen—no, sixteen hours earlier. There was no way she could clean up for another four hours, so she might as well sweat all over the steel floor instead of her bunk or her own floor.

Or maybe—this was an appealing idea—she'd head to the

galley and sweat on Linden's chair as she drank tea. That would be certain to anger him, and if she angered him, maybe some attraction would fade. She might be attracted to danger, but not anger. Never anger.

A soft hiss of the door jerked her from her thoughts.

One of the pilots. It has to be one of the pilots.

But as she lay there, gaping foolishly at the door, it was Linden who sauntered in, a towel around his neck, swinging his arms in front him. He'd traded the usual gray jumpsuit for a pair of knit shorts, and his shirt—

She sucked in a breath.

His shirt was missing.

For a long second, she couldn't break her stare. The green fatigues and shapeless jumpsuit had hidden some rather nice muscles—not that he was overly built. He wasn't even what her colleagues would have called chiseled, either. Just . . . defined. Her eyes widened at the indigo tattoos peeking over his solid shoulders, and she averted her gaze as quickly as she could.

To that freckle on his cheekbone.

Dammit.

"Oh." Linden looked down at her with a blank expression that was probably feigned, stretched a languid hand over his head, and pulled. "I didn't know you were here."

"You expect me to believe that?" Katryn blinked at the drawing of the lizard-like animal etched permanently on his tricep in gold ink as fresh heat washed through her. She sprang to her feet and tried to push by him, but he stepped in front of her. She would not look at his chest. She would not, even though it was right there, and the temptation to look down burned through her.

"I didn't. I swear." He dropped his arms to his sides and smiled. "But since you're here, I could use some help. And I think you could use some, too."

Why did he keep smiling at her? Did he think she'd fall for his charm?

Too late for that, Kat.

"No," she said. "I'm finished for the day. Excuse me. I'm going to get cleaned up."

"You're out of water, Kat." He shrugged. "For another four hours, if I'm not mistaken. You might as well help me."

Her name on his lips made her shake. *Control yourself.* "Help—help you?"

"Here." He tossed the towel at her and flopped down next to her to stretch. "You sit up there"—he pointed at the nearest bench—"and catch your breath."

"I am not out of breath." Not from exercising. She sat anyway. He was obviously baiting her into complying, but there was no way of escaping without admitting she couldn't handle his workout.

Linden grinned as he went through what had to be perfunctory stretches. He was showing off, that's what he was doing. It wasn't warm in the cargo bay—the sweat trickling down her back was enough to make her shiver—so what other reason did he have for showing up shirtless? Why was he all but preening in front of her like some Zarcronian red-tailed egret beginning a courtship dance? She was on the verge of saying something —*what?*—when he scooted toward her on the floor.

"All right. Toss me the ends."

Against her better judgment, she gripped the middle of the dark fabric and pulled it toward her, the resistance from his grip burning her forearms. Why hadn't she thought of this? It was certainly better than the push-ups she'd been doing for weeks.

Because it required being in the same room with Linden for more than ten minutes, that was why.

The cargo bay was silent as they alternated giving one another tension in the towel; only the gentle hiss of the pressurization system broke her churning thoughts of Xan, Asria, and, oh yes, those tattoos.

"I liked talking to you," she said out loud. Thinking was

driving her to distraction. She had to say something. "Before, you know, that happened."

Her face grew red at her impulsive confession, but Linden had leaned back—if she moved to cover her burning cheeks, he'd fall flat on his back, onto those gorgeous tattoos that she was dying to see the whole of, and she didn't hate him that much. Did she?

"Likewise." He curled forward and pulled down on the towel.

"And I wouldn't mind—I wouldn't mind having dinner with you again. Or even breakfast. Or whatever." *Loneliness.* It was only loneliness, no matter what those psychologists said. They didn't understand. "I hope you realize that's a little awkward and a lot scary for me for me to say, but—I really would enjoy it."

"Likewise." Linden curled toward her.

"You're awfully chatty tonight."

He arched an eyebrow at her. "I'm working out. Talking distracts me."

From what? Preening? She took a deep breath. "But what if—"

Before she could finish, the fabric slid from her sweaty grip. Linden had yanked on the towel harder than he had before, and before she could stop her forward momentum, she'd fallen forward off the bench.

Straight against Linden's bare chest.

His back did hit the deck that time, and he let out a muffled yelp.

"I'm sorry. I'm so sorry!" She tried to struggle upright, acutely aware of how she was straddling him. The grating dug into her knees through the thin fabric of her jumpsuit, and she fell flat against him.

Sacred winds, take me home now.

"You didn't hurt me." He gazed up at her, a sudden intensity in his eyes as he repeated her own words back to her.

Biological impossibility or not, she was fairly certain her heart had stopped. The intensity only meant one thing, and if she didn't move away from him right this second—

"Are you sure?" she asked, brushing his fingers with hers. "You hit so hard."

"Positive." He didn't move beneath her, though.

"I should make sure. Doctor and all, you know."

"I don't think a doctorate in engineering makes you a medical expert."

"Hmm, not in humans." Tentatively, her hand met the back of his head. "No blood," she said, running her fingers through his hair.

"No?" His voice grew rough.

"I think you'll live."

"I think you may need to take a closer look."

She lowered herself a bit more. Because this—this made sense. This was nothing more than biology, like Kaz had been at first.

And biology felt good.

"I could take a closer look, but—well, I don't do people so well, remember? Can you breathe?" she asked, running a finger across his lips.

Linden sucked in a breath and raised his head. "Not so very well."

She could feel his heart beating underneath her. Felt her own threatening to burst from her chest. "There's only one solution to that," she said, closing her eyes.

A rush of strange nothingness hit her as their lips met. She wasn't sure what was keeping her except her shaking legs. She'd collapsed on top of him, but she didn't care. It didn't matter that she smelled like sweat or that this was the worst idea in the world or that she'd regret it tomorrow. Because Linden responded immediately, his own lips warm and soft and tasting of tea and something more minty.

"We should take this somewhere else," he murmured. "Or I'll end up with permanent grid marks on my back, and we can't be having that."

Zarcronian red-tailed egret, indeed.

"It would certainly be a shame to destroy those tattoos you've clearly spent so much time and money on. What are they?"

"You'll have to find out for yourself." His eyes crinkled. "Preferably in a cabin with a locked door."

"But I'm sweaty." She didn't pull away or open her eyes, only spoke to that charming crease at the edge of his lips. Later, she'd have to remember to kiss that just-as-charming freckle on his upper cheek. Or maybe she'd do that first.

"So we'll shower first."

"I'm out of water."

"I'm not," he said against her open mouth. "Some of us plan our workouts better." A hand wound around her shoulder and pulled her closer. "But I'm not doing anything you don't want to do."

"No," she said, relaxing against him. "You're not. I want this. I mean—I want you. I want to see what's inked on your back."

Because this was her idea. Because this felt good. And that wasn't wrong.

"I was hoping that would be your answer."

With more strength than she'd realized he possessed, he sat up with an arm around her back, then pushed himself to his feet, still clinging to her. She wrapped her legs around his waist, pressed her lips back against his, and let him carry her out.

CHAPTER FIFTEEN

Taln Perrin had been right.

Victor Rendon had been right.

As much as Chase hated to admit it, Avery Rendon was up to something, and that something was much bigger than sneaking around to see that Royal Asrian Defense Forces lover of hers. No, her apparently rocky relationship with a certain Lieutenant Colonel Merritt Parker was the least of her worries—and his.

When he wasn't glued to her side as faux security personnel, which was most of the time, and he wasn't sleeping, which wasn't nearly as much as he'd like, he was trailing her around Cadena. He'd ordered the soldiers to back off, and like he'd hoped, Avery had made the most of her new freedom. Yes, she spent much of her days in her office at the senate building and in her rooms at the palace, but for a woman who claimed to be nominally faithful, she spent an inordinate amount of time in the senate temple.

And here was the reason.

Chase leaned forward and reached toward the bench in front of him. It was the one they said she always sat on, the one which was, perhaps not so coincidentally, nowhere near where she'd sat when she'd taken him here the night they'd met.

That loose leg—that was the key. It rattled on the tile floor, and he jerked his hand back as the sound echoed through the temple. Slowly, as he held his breath, he knelt and lifted up the entire bench, not daring to hope. It was always possible Perrin was wrong, and as much as he wanted Avery to be innocent, he'd feel like a fool if he'd been chasing wraiths.

But there it was—a small silver data chip lay in the divot under the leg.

He grabbed it with his free hand and set the bench back down as carefully as he could, only to stare at the chip in his palm. Such an innocent piece of metal and plastic that could mean everything —a threat to the empire, a risk to her life, and a lot of additional, painful work for him. He was further from seeing Isobel than he'd been in his entire life.

And what to do now? He couldn't copy it. As much as he wanted—no, needed—to know what was on the disk, he couldn't risk it not being here when whoever was waiting on the data came for it. Later, he could create a stack of disks with fake content . . . but that would have to come much later. He couldn't make a mistake now, not with the future queen of Asria in his sights.

Chase rolled the plastic between his fingers. Avery had only been on Asria for a few months, and it was unlikely she was working in some kind of complex agent network. No, whatever she was playing at had been hastily thrown together after the invasion—of that, he was almost certain. It wouldn't be surprising if the next agent in her network was her handler himself. Hastily developed networks were sloppy like that.

Yes, learning what intelligence she thought she was passing on would have to wait. He needed her and her handler, whoever that was. The Commonwealth was an obvious suspect, but it didn't appear she'd made any trips to their base in Rincon between arriving from Ventana and the invasion. The Defense Forces? It was always a possibility. Maybe those meetings with Colonel Parker weren't so innocent—or personal—as he'd been led to believe.

With a sigh, he knelt back down and replaced the chip. The flickering candles on the altar caught his eye as he stood, and he wandered over to light another four as he always did on his visits here. It worked on two fronts—first, as a brilliant cover for his frequent presence here, and second . . . no, scratch that. It was only a cover. Lighting candles and praying hadn't done anything to soothe the chill in his heart.

Another failure. Chase shoved his hand in his pocket and turned his comm back on as he headed outside. It lit up immediately. Perrin, of all the rotten luck. Six messages from the general, in fact.

He walked over to Perrin's office—slowly.

* * *

Perrin slammed his palm on the cheap army-issue desk, his face red. Maybe Chase's long walk had been a little too long.

"Why didn't you tell me about this?" he asked as Chase sat, full coffee cup in hand. Perrin's secretary must have suspected his true identity, because the man was always in a frenzy, coffee and all, whenever he saw Chase. "Why did I need to hear it from some sergeant on that security team you've got set up?"

"Tell you about what?" Chase stuck his nose in the cup and inhaled deeply. The coffee was hot, and it didn't taste terrible. Even so, it wasn't amazing, and that had never made much sense to him. So many worlds conquered, and his people still couldn't figure out how to make decent coffee.

"That you caught Merritt Parker and her picnicking in the mountains last week. After I forbade both of them from seeing each other. What do they think this is?"

This was worth six messages, four of them marked urgent? The general was enjoying the power that came with being away from Haedera a little too much.

"It didn't seem relevant at the time," Chase said, taking another sip. "I warned her once more to stay away from him. She was afraid I'd tell you about what happened, and I promised her I wouldn't say a word if she agreed not to see him again. It's no problem."

Sure, Avery and Parker had defied Perrin's wishes last week. Sure, he'd caught them up in the mountains and brought them right back to Cadena. So what? There was no harm done. Avery had promised not to do anything like that in the future, and he believed her—he'd let out part of his ISC personality and terrified her into agreeing to his demands that night. Didn't Perrin have anything better to do than track the two of them around town?

Doesn't he realize it's not his place to forbid a personal relationship? Or a possible professional one I might be able to exploit?

"You don't get to decide things like this," Perrin said. "Do you honestly believe I'm going to let her prance around Cadena, screwing whoever she chooses, flaunting everything I've told her to not do, rubbing her rebellion in my face? Arrest him. Now. And place those guards back on her, or I swear I'll—"

Chase held up a hand. "With all due respect, what's going on here is more important than making sure she doesn't rebel against whatever silly rules you've placed on her." It was definitely more important than preventing her from seeing Parker, especially if she was passing intelligence to him. He could shut down everything now, but that would be shortsighted. A free and unrestricted Avery Rendon was very useful to him. "I thank you for your information, but this is an ISC matter, one I must request you not interfere in further."

It seemed warning enough to him. The very wording was enough to frighten most Haederans into obedience, but Perrin was . . . Perrin. Chase drained the rest of his coffee, desperately wishing Perrin's secretary would barge in with more.

"Put the guards back on her or you're outed, Colonel. You won't get very far if she knows ISC is operating on Asria. She'll never say another word to you, and your investigation will be over. And arrest Parker. Today. This minute. I don't care what you do with him after that." The ubiquitous glass of liquor next to his tablet shook as Perrin slammed his fist on his desk once more.

Chase recrossed his legs and leaned back in his chair, letting the empty coffee cup dangle from his hand.

"Did you just threaten me? Sir?"

There was a long pause.

"No." A little of Perrin's rage faded into apprehension, though the red in his cheeks didn't change. "You know what, I don't care what you do with her. Let her run all over the damn planet and send whatever information she wants to the Commonwealth, for all I care. She's your mess, not mine. Although I hope ISC knows what they're doing with her. But do something about that Asrian snake or I will."

Stars. The man was insufferable. What would happen if he arrested Perrin instead of Parker?

Lots of paperwork, that's what would happen. Lots of paperwork and questions and . . . blast it. Perrin was nothing to the emperor. He was nothing as far as this investigation was concerned, and he certainly wasn't someone important enough to waste his time on. He couldn't make a mistake with Avery because he was afraid of the bluster of an army general nobody.

"You needn't worry about Colonel Parker," Chase said. Judging from Perrin's self-satisfied stare, it was the right thing to say. *Why so much hate?* "But I cannot have you interfering in my work here, Governor. I'll do as you request and put the guards back on her for a short time, but this is my operation to run. Do I make myself perfectly clear?"

"Do whatever you want." Perrin pulled a tablet toward him and tapped a stylus on his desk, head down.

"Good." Chase smiled as he stood, and the idea of escaping Perrin made it unforced. "If you need me, I'll be at the palace having tea." Pretending to guard Avery did have certain benefits, namely, access to quality tea and an excuse to socialize with her— to learn everything about her. She didn't even know she was being assessed. "Am I dismissed?"

Perrin looked up, glared, and waved a hand in dismissal.

* * *

He thought as he walked. About Isobel, about Sophie and Marc, about Asria, and about why he'd been so quick to agree to put increased security back on Avery. Cutting her off now would be myopic. It would protect her, but it would impede her from doing whatever she was up to, and that could be life-threatening for him.

It would protect her.

Chase repeated the words in time with his footsteps. He couldn't protect her. *He couldn't be caught protecting her.* She was Asrian, the enemy, the almost-leader of yet another conquered planet. And if that wasn't bad enough, she was blatantly disregarding the trouble she was already in and trying desperately to find even more for herself. Why?

He puzzled over her actions until he ended up on the front step of Parker's townhouse, not the palace as he'd told Perrin. Half of him—most of him—wanted to beat on the door, announce himself as Imperial Security, and get this taken care of easily and expeditiously. He knocked politely instead, all too conscious of the army captain rank on his collar and how Parker had condescended to him the week before when he'd caught him and Avery picnicking in the mountains. He'd promised Parker that evening that nothing would happen to Avery as long as he had anything to do with it, and—

The door swung open, and Parker stood in the dimly lit foyer, glaring at him.

"What do you want?"

Oh, good. Still pissed.

Of course he's still pissed. Last week you spent two hours calling him Mr. Parker just to get under his skin.

It had been entertaining at the time, but had he known he'd be groveling on Parker's doorstep just a few days later, he might have made a different decision. There was only one thing to do now, only one way to salvage this meeting. Chase swallowed every bit of his leftover pride.

"I'd like to speak with you if you have a moment, Colonel Parker."

Parker's eyes narrowed slightly at the unexpected politeness. "I don't think so."

He moved to swing the door shut, but Chase stuck his arm inside.

"Please, sir. I wouldn't have stopped by if it wasn't important."

Parker hesitated, then his shoulders deflated a bit as he moved back. "Then come in. I don't want the neighbors staring at you out there. And make it quick."

Chase stepped inside onto the marble floor and shut the door behind him. "Governor Perrin is angry about what happened last week. I didn't tell him," he interrupted as Parker opened his mouth, "but one of my men couldn't seem to keep his mouth shut. If you stay in Cadena, if you insist on seeing her, you're going to put yourself at risk."

"I don't care what that man does." Parker crossed his arms.

Well, this was going about as well as he'd expected.

"I didn't think you would, sir. But you'll be putting her at risk too, and I know you don't want to do that."

Parker stared at him, then ran his hands over his face and sighed.

"Do you have anywhere else you can go, sir? Just for a few weeks. Give the governor a bit of time to calm down, and then you can come home. If you promise to stay out of my way once you return, I might even let you know when it's safe to do so."

Like never. Even if the war ended, if the empire was run out of the system, Parker needed to run away from Avery and never return. Not that any man in love would ever take his advice, but if anyone knew about the hazards of marrying into a planetary royal family . . .

"Yeah. Yeah, fine." Parker looked around the small foyer, then down at his feet. "It's probably time for a holiday, anyway." He glanced back up. "Did you mean what you said last week?"

Maybe. Maybe not. Probably not.

"What did I say?"

"That I didn't need to worry about her safety when she was with you."

Oh. That.

Parker's statement didn't sound like a plea—his tone hadn't even changed—but it was. It had to be. The man was in love, his love was a target, and standing in front of him was the one person who'd offered to protect her.

Guilt seeped from his pores. *It depends on your definition of safety,* Chase wanted to say. It wasn't likely she'd be executed, at least not anytime soon, and as much as Perrin tried to reel her in, the general couldn't actually do anything about her. She was an ISC problem. His problem. He would break her, and she'd remain alive to regret his mercy.

So . . . yes. She'd be safe with him. Physically, at least.

That rationalization completed, he nodded at Parker. "I can't promise much, but I promise I'll do everything in my power to keep her safe from Perrin." He reached for the door, wanting to be anywhere else. If he was in Parker's position, he'd kill the man who'd just lied to him.

"Captain—" Parker's tone had changed to gratitude. "Thank you."

Chase nodded as he headed outside.

Don't thank me yet.

CHAPTER SIXTEEN

KATRYN RAISED HER HAND, ONLY TO LET IT FALL TO HER SIDE. WAS this her fourteenth attempt at knocking on Linden's door? Maybe the fifteenth? She couldn't remember how many times she'd lost her nerve since the afternoon she'd snuck out of his cabin, gathering clothing as she went. Linden had been asleep when she'd woken, their legs intertwined from earlier that morning. Or had it been evening? It was so hard to tell in deep space, even with the ubiquitous clocks—not that space travel was the only thing messing with her mind today.

The only solution to her predicament was to never leave her cabin. Not even once they arrived on Asria. It was that simple. Except now she was starving and thirsty and had exhausted the small supply of ration bars she'd hoarded in the cabinet over her sink. There was water in the sink, true, but she hadn't been able to bring herself to drink it—who knew what kind of microbes were living in the courier ship's piping? Some kind of strange Haederan bacteria she had no immunity to, for sure, and dying of thirst was preferable to vomiting for the next few weeks. Katryn took a tentative step toward the galley, making sure to silence her feet on the deck.

An electronic lock clicked somewhere inside the wall before

she'd taken three steps, and she froze, one foot in the air, as Linden's door slid open.

"Katryn."

Dammit.

There was no way to avoid him now. There was also, apparently, no way to avoid the flutter in her stomach at the sound of her name spoken in his lilting Haederan accent, and that was exactly the reaction she'd hoped to avoid. Maybe if she turned on her heel and dashed back toward her cabin—

"Lying Haederan bastard." Instead of running, the words flew out, and she clamped her hand over her mouth. The fluttering in her belly vanished in an instant. Attractive or not, he was dangerous, and she'd insulted him.

"Rhys."

"Excuse me?"

He leaned against the wall. "I'd prefer it if you'd call me Rhys instead of 'lying Haederan bastard.' I think we're on a first name basis now." Amusement, evident in the way his eyebrows lifted, replaced some of his irritation. "It would also be nice if you told me what I'm supposed to have lied about."

"I don't—" *What indeed?* "I don't know yet. I'll think of something."

"I know you must be angry."

"That's ridiculous. You don't know anything about me. I'm not angry." Ashamed, maybe. All right—ashamed and angry with herself. And hungry.

"Good. So we can talk, then." He tilted his head toward the galley.

"I don't want to talk to you." Her stomach growled.

"I heard that." Linden grinned. "Ran out of those ration bars you had stockpiled in your cabin, did you?"

"How did you—you've been in my cabin?" She'd have to stop leaving to work out in the cargo bay. Too bad. It had been a nice change from push-ups on her bunk, though she'd figured out how to rig a towel around a conduit and work her arms. She would never thank Linden for the idea.

"Of course." That vaguely confused look that was somehow charming crossed his face. "I have to make sure you're not making any weapons in there. So, food?"

"Yeah. Fine. Whatever."

At least if she followed him to the galley, she wouldn't have to look at his face for the next ten seconds. She couldn't do it without her cheeks turning bright red, and since he'd been keeping an eye on her location, there was no way he'd buy a claim of a recent workout. Linden grinned at her, without hiding it this time, and headed forward. Katryn stared at his back, then blinked. Admiring his physique, especially from behind, wasn't helpful, especially now. By the time she dragged her leaden legs after him into the galley, he was dropping one of her treasured coffee cubes into a cup.

"I'll do that," she interrupted.

"Katryn—" He held his palms out in front of him. "Please. Sit down and enjoy the coffee. I should have done this three days ago." His grin had disappeared, and he seemed . . . not angry, exactly. Tired? Maybe guilty? That had to be it.

He handed over the cup and she swirled it, focusing on the cube disintegrating in the hot water. Anything to keep her eyes off his back. Off his broad shoulders, off his close-cropped hair, off his single freckle—

Linden coughed into the back of his hand as he sat. "Look, I'm not that kind of person. This—I mean, what's happening here—that's not me. I want you to know that."

Katryn managed to raise her chin and make eye contact. "It seems you are that kind of person."

Wasn't he? As much as she wanted to see him as the man who'd kidnapped her from Iythea, the person who'd all but admitted to murdering his own people, he was different now. The man sitting before her wasn't that strange, frightening person she'd first met. He was . . . maybe he really was Rhys, like he'd said.

He sighed and examined her over his cup. "I've never done this. Any of it. I don't know what I can say to convince you of that."

"Are we talking about me"—the horrid thought sprang into her head before she could stop it—"or are we talking about my brother?"

"Both, I suppose." He set down his tea and folded his hands on the table. "I'll be honest with you. You may think everyone in the Commonwealth is loyal beyond reproach, but they're not, and if you think they are, you've been living in a fantasy world. My sources are willing. Usually. I mean, always. Until now. But Major Feye was a chance we couldn't pass up."

Oh. He was talking about Xan. Was it possible Rhys—*Linden!*—had already forgotten what they'd done the other day? She hadn't. The flush in her cheeks hadn't.

"You have to believe me," he said. "I need you to believe me, more than you know. As for what happened the other night . . ."

Oh, good. They were moving on from Xan.

"What happened that night isn't me either. But you . . . you saved my life. I know you didn't want to, I know you'd have been just as happy leaving me there for dead, but you gave me a chance. You saved me, and I suppose my feelings—I owe you everything for that decision. Then I woke up in sick bay and you were nowhere to be found, and . . . Katryn, I was scared. I was scared they'd done something to you, or that you hadn't survived whatever happened on the ship. And then when I saw you sitting there in the brig—I felt sick."

"You felt sick when you saw me?" The flush turned into an unpleasant heat.

"No! Not like that. It was relief. Relief that you were unharmed and that I'd gotten there in time. And disgust with myself."

"You were that worried about me?" Katryn swirled her coffee.

Had she been in imminent danger? She'd always been too afraid to ask. The Haederan Navy commander's appearance in their cabin suggested she may have been.

The corner of his lip lifted up. "I suppose I knew they wouldn't harm you, not if they'd positively identified you and saw you'd already been detained by Imperial Security—they wouldn't risk angering us like that. You should be grateful for that. But they'd have pushed me a bit, and I didn't want you to be upset, especially with me. I'd pulled you off Iythea and that left me responsible for your safety. You can think what you want, but that's not a situation I take lightly."

Her heart began to race. "Upset is a bit of an understatement for how I felt on that ship."

"I'm sure."

"But not with you exactly." She lifted the cup to her lips to hide the admission.

"I'm glad to hear that." The upturned lip turned into an unaffected smile. "And I have a confession to make."

"What's that?"

"Part of the reason I've been hiding in my cabin the past few days was to give you space. Don't think I don't know you've been out there in the corridor trying to work up the courage to knock on my door. I wasn't going to confront you about what happened if you weren't ready to talk about it." He laughed. "Though I was becoming a little concerned you'd starve to death in there. I decided this morning that I was going to sneak some more ration bars inside once you left for the cargo bay this evening."

Katryn put her head into her hands. "How long did you think you could get away with that before I started wondering where they came from?"

"I was hoping a few weeks, if not longer." His eyes sparkled when she glanced up under her eyelashes. "I'm guessing I probably underestimated you in that regard."

"I'd say so. I'm sure you know I can count better than that."

She couldn't move her head in case he saw her smiling like a fool. "But you said that was only part of the reason."

"Yeah. The other part was because I'm exhausted. I hardly slept on *Aeris*, and I've needed to catch up on my sleep."

Katryn licked her lips. "Hypoxia and a brush with death will do that to you."

"Yes, I suppose it will. So will . . . other things."

They were way past pretending there was nothing between them now. "Was my presence that distracting for you?"

Obviously.

"Oh yes." He began to chuckle and reached a hand out across the table. "Distracting is a brilliant way to phrase it. You see, you smell really good. I spent those nights lying in front of that door wondering if I'd ever get close enough to decide of what."

Her hand met his. "It's soap. Whatever inexpensive, caustic Haederan soap they stocked for you." The laugh she intended didn't quite materialize. The scent of that cheap soap was yet another reminder of Iythea. "You, on the other hand, smell like cloves, and I'd love to hear the explanation for that."

"Cloves?" His forehead crinkled. "What are cloves?"

"They're a spice, and they kind of smell like—" How to explain foreign spices to a Haederan? "It doesn't matter. They smell like you." She wound her fingers through his. They felt good. They felt *alive*.

"We can't do this." His voice grew husky, but he didn't pull his hand away. "You—you're an Imperial Security Command prisoner."

"And you didn't force me to do anything I didn't want to. In fact, if I'm remembering correctly, it was my idea."

"That's not the point."

Katryn yanked her hand away and crossed her arms. "Then what is?"

"Maybe the fact that it's illegal, immoral, and unethical?"

"You certainly weren't thinking that the other night!"

Her own reaction surprised her more than his rejection. She

didn't love him. Good in bed didn't mean a good man—she knew that. *Loneliness. Remember the loneliness?*

"Katryn." He reached out for her, stopped, and ran his hands over his face. "I wasn't thinking at all that night. Only about how much I wanted you. And it doesn't matter how much that is. If things were different, then maybe yes, but they're not, and we can't—"

Her stomach dropped all the way to the floor. What an odd reaction—it'd just been sex, hadn't it? Katryn slipped out of her chair and around the table. "But we can do this." She pushed his coffee away and pulled him up, then, meeting no resistance, led him to the sofa facing the window.

"What exactly is *this*?" he asked with a curious mix of eagerness and fear.

"Not what you think. Not right now, anyway." Katryn fell onto the soft cushion and held her hand out. He flopped next to her and put his arm around her shoulder. It shouldn't make her feel safe—*he* shouldn't make her feel safe—but against the strength of his body, her racing heart began to calm. "For now, we're going to sit here, stare out into space, and pretend we're the only two people in the galaxy."

No Xan, no Commonwealth, no Haederan Empire, no Imperial Security Command.

Just two people.

Rhys grinned and pulled her closer. "That sounds perfect to me."

CHAPTER SEVENTEEN

There wasn't enough coffee on Asria for what he was about to face. Chase downed another cup of weak green tea as he pulled his boots on. It was dark outside the window of the barracks at Alcaris, the former Defense Forces headquarters, and the four hours of sleep he'd managed to get after leaving Parker's house the evening before was about a third of what he needed right now.

But duty called, and delivering bad news to the palace this early in the morning had its own kind of visceral charm. Avery would be furious when he informed her that her Asrian body-guards were to be relieved of their duties, and if he made the notification this early, maybe he could avoid her. If he couldn't avoid her . . . well, seeing the enraged look on her face might not be so bad either.

He took a flyer to the palace—it was becoming too cold in the mornings to walk anywhere he didn't need to—and dashed down the stairs from the roof instead of waiting on the lift tube. The Haederan Army guards outside the doors to the private residence section looked as tired as he did, and he gestured them inside with him. An entourage was always good, and these Asrians needed to be kept on their toes.

"Find Langley," he ordered them, shaking off the morning chill. One disappeared down a long hallway, returning less than a minute later with Drexel Langley, Avery's head bodyguard. Langley blinked back his fatigue and glared at Chase.

"Good morning." Chase gave him his best attempt at a brilliant smile.

Langley made a snorting noise. "Little early, don't you think?"

"Early? No, I don't think it's too early." He almost choked on the lie. "Mr. Langley, I'm here to inform you that your services, and those of Wynne Ferran, will no longer be needed in the palace. The Haederan Army has assumed all responsibility for Her Highness's security as of this morning."

That woke Langley up faster than any coffee could.

"You what?" It was almost a roar.

"The Haederan Army has assumed all responsibility for Her Highness's security as of this morning," Chase repeated calmly.

"I heard you the first time. And if you think—"

"I'm not thinking anything. I'm ordering you out of here, now." On second thought, catching them off guard was good, but it was still too early for this nonsense. "Don't make me have you dragged out of here."

"I'm not leaving her alone with you." Langley took a step toward him, only stopping when the two guards moved closer to him. "Do you think I'm an idiot? Do you think I don't know something else is going on? Is this the first step in moving her to Sabino where she'll disappear as well?"

They hadn't found her parents yet? Odd. Perhaps they hadn't escaped after all.

"I realize you're worried about her," Chase replied. *As you should be.* "But this is protection, nothing more. With what's happened to the king and queen, this is what's best for everyone involved right now."

Langley sighed, then huffed, then swallowed.

"It's not even sunrise. I'm sure there's a reason for this commotion."

The feminine voice cut in, and all four of them turned toward Avery, standing in the dark hallway behind Langley, looking rumpled and half asleep.

Langley tried to smile. "They're just delivering word that Wynne and I are relieved of our duties here. Permanently."

"What? Why?" Her green eyes grew wide as she focused on Chase. "You're not . . . You're not arresting them!"

Why had she jumped to that conclusion? It was a strange assumption, even though he'd shown up in what might as well have been the middle of the night. Blast it. He'd fallen into ISC procedure without realizing it. Did she know who he really was? His heart began to pound.

"Is there any reason we should?" Chase asked. His heart settled a bit as he spoke. "No. It's because Governor Perrin wants it this way. He's displeased at the lax security here, especially after the situation with your father. They're permitted to visit, but they're not to be alone with you."

Avery, stricken mute for once, glanced from him to Langley to the two soldiers. He hadn't known it was possible for her to be at a loss for words.

"Fine," she finally said. "But in the future, I'd prefer if you wait until later in the day for anything like this. I'm going back to sleep for another hour. Then I'm going to my office."

"You'll go to your office when and if I say you can," he said. "You're free to do what you want in the residence only, and I'm leaving two guards here to make sure you stay." They needed something else to do besides watching a locked door, anyway.

"You do what you need to do." She stalked back to her rooms for that extra hour of sleep he envied, and reluctantly, he let her go.

* * *

He slept in the next morning, too exhausted to have bothered removing his boots the night before. Things were fine at the palace. Langley and Ferran had been taken off Avery's security, he'd managed to convince Langley to explain the remaining security systems and procedures to him, and then he'd escorted Avery to her office—for a short workday, thank the stars. She'd dashed out of her office after only six hours, pale and muttering about wanting to go home immediately. Having not found any coffee in the entire senate building all day, he hadn't argued. Yes, he deserved a bit more sleep—the army would notify him if anything happened with Avery. It wasn't as though she'd be dropping data chips anywhere for a few days; he'd scared her enough to ensure that.

It was well past midday when he dragged himself from his cot, brewed some strong black Haederan tea, and checked his overnight messages. Nothing important, and that was a relief. No one needed to know he'd slept for fourteen hours straight.

It took another few hours of messages and reports—along with three more cups of tea—before he made his way to the palace to check on things. The army guards shouldn't have made any mistakes with Avery's security on the first day, but one never knew. He'd told them he wouldn't be back for a few days, after all, and it would be just like them to make the most of his absence, especially in the evening.

A panicked sergeant met him in the main gallery outside the ballroom.

"Sir, we've got a problem. There's a big mess at Alcaris. Some sort of attack, they're saying. And she's gone missing. She hasn't set off any of the sensors, so she hasn't left the palace grounds, but—"

"Why didn't you call?" It was a fight to tone down his ISC voice, but frightening the man would do more harm than good.

"We were looking for her on our own—"

We were trying to hide our screwup from you.

"—and I think we're getting close."

Chase pushed him aside and darted through the foyer. The ballroom—well, yes, there were some Haederan soldiers in there, but there were always soldiers in places they didn't belong. He didn't bother examining them further. A quick search of each room he passed on the way up the marble staircase was fruitless. Avery's rooms were dark, empty, and cold.

Dammit.

He stood in the center of her parlor, eyes closed. *One day.* No, they'd been responsible for her less than one day, and they'd already lost her. An unreal level of incompetence, though one he should have expected. ISC always forgot what it was like to deal with people who were not ISC, and he was just as guilty of that forgetfulness, it appeared. With a deep breath, he clenched his fists and opened his eyes. Standing in Avery's empty quarters was nothing but a waste of time. He'd send teams through the gardens, and after that, they'd need to widen the search through central Cadena—

A distant light flickered through the trees, drawing his attention. Chase squinted out the parlor window, then motioned the nearest soldier over. "What's out that way?"

"Don't know, sir." The corporal wrinkled his forehead. "Some old chapel, I think. We don't even patrol there unless the sensors are tripped."

The sudden release of stress made his legs weak.

Found you.

* * *

Like the corporal had claimed, the source of the flickering light was a chapel, or at least had been. Time hadn't been kind to the gray stone building, but then, maybe the vines that covered the near side were some kind of Asrian architectural feature. Who really knew what they liked in this part of the quadrant. Water dripped from the bronze faucet outside the door, and dim light glimmered through one of the windows, though it was darker than he'd seen from Avery's rooms. Chase took a breath and pushed the door open.

Avery was sitting cross-legged in the center of the floor with one candle lit on the stone altar in front her. And what an odd altar it was—circular, like the one in the main temple, but with even more carved into the wooden sides. Asrians were certainly preoccupied with circles in their version of the faith.

"What are you doing?" he blurted out, too relieved he'd found her to be angry about where. The soldiers behind him tried to move closer, but he waved them away with a rapid flick of his wrist behind his back. What, did they intend to grab her and carry her back to the palace?

"What do you think I'm doing?" she asked. "It's a chapel. I'm praying."

"You? In the dark?" Who sat around and prayed in a dark chapel in the middle of pitch-black gardens? Not Avery Rendon, that was for sure. What was she really doing here? "Whatever you're doing, it's time to go. There's been an attack on Alcaris. There's concern they may strike the palace next."

And if they did, he and Avery weren't going to be anywhere near it.

She scrambled to her feet and brushed the dust from her hands, but it wasn't fear or concern on her face. "Do you really expect me to be worried about that? I don't think I'm the one in danger from anyone attacking your base."

Stars, she was right. Rebels wouldn't risk attacking the palace, either, not with her living there. Maybe the soldiers had the right idea. He was going to have to drag her out of here kicking and screaming. "I don't care if you're worried about it or not. You're leaving now."

At that, she frowned at him, her eyes dark in the candlelight. "Where are we going?"

Yes, that had worried her.

"Back to the palace." He glanced at the rest of the candles on the altar. Some were smoking, like she'd blown them out right before he'd arrived. "Somewhere with a bit more light and a whole lot more security. Only until we figure out what's going on," he added hastily. "It could be a false alarm."

Or it could be Perrin ruining everything I've been trying to set up.

She took a step away from him, toward that odd altar, and wiped her hands on her pants again. "I don't want to leave."

"Come on." He extended his hand, though he didn't expect her to take it. "I just want to make sure you're safe."

Her eyes wavered from him to the soldiers behind him, but she didn't move.

"Do you want five minutes to finish praying?" he asked. "That's all I can give you."

"Yes," she whispered. She didn't say another word to him, just lit a few more candles on the altar and stood there with her back to him, her lips moving silently. Maybe he'd been wrong about her. Maybe she wasn't as afraid of death as he'd believed. Or maybe she was so afraid of it—or something else—that prayer was the only thing she could think to do.

Chase waited patiently until she turned back toward him, then he motioned to the rest of the soldiers to follow behind as they walked outside. Avery stuck close beside him as they made their way through the dark gardens and into a service entrance in the back of the palace. *Good.* She was finally starting to see him as an ally. That would come in handy later, and he'd play up that bond.

He escorted her to the main library, sat her on one of the couches, the one farthest from the soldiers milling about, then sank down next to her. She didn't move away like he'd assumed she would, and that was a relief as well. Building rapport was a precarious thing, and breathing the wrong way could stall it.

"What's going on?" she asked, weaving her fingers in and out between each other. "I know this isn't a false alarm."

"I don't know." It wasn't a complete lie. "Let's sit tight for a while, and we'll figure this out. I won't leave you, all right? Not until we find out what's happening."

Let's. We'll. We. I won't leave you. Some might call it manipulative, but he called it preparation.

Avery nodded and dropped her head into her hands.

"Captain?" The lieutenant who appeared at his side looked more annoyed than intimidated.

Chase sighed to himself as he looked up.

"Governor Perrin needs a word with you, sir. He said it's urgent."

Of course it was urgent. Was it ever not urgent with the man?

"I'm sorry, but I can't leave her here alone." He chanced a glance at Avery. She'd wrapped her arms around her chest and was staring into the distance, though he doubted she was seeing anything outside her own mind.

The lieutenant glanced around the library, filled with Haederan soldiers. "It'll be quick, sir. She's safe here."

It was never quick with Perrin, but fighting him right now was pointless. Not when there was something larger going on. Chase sighed audibly and stood. "I'll be back as soon as I can," he said to Avery, and followed the lieutenant out.

Instead of leading him up to the roof to catch an aeroflyer to Perrin's Alcaris office, the lieutenant led him across the main hallway and pushed a large set of wooden doors open. "In the ballroom, sir."

Perrin was at the palace? That was a strange turn of events. Maybe Alcaris really had been attacked. Chase glanced back through the library doors. Avery was watching him and the lieutenant from the sofa, arms around herself, but a little of the blank look was gone. He nodded reassuringly at her and walked inside.

Perrin turned from a group of soldiers as he did.

"You're done here, Colonel," he announced.

Chase tilted his head, but Perrin continued on like he hadn't even realized what he'd said.

"We've quashed that attack on Alcaris. An officially sanctioned one, approved by Prime Minister Baylen himself, it seems. I'm done with the Defense Forces, I'm done with the senate, and I'm done with Her Highness. I have one small piece of business to handle with her and the prime minister tonight, then when you're ready, she'll be in our detention facility on Slouhn Road down-town. I trust when Imperial Security is through with her, she won't be a threat to Haedera or my power any longer."

Chase fought the rage, but he could feel his ears turning red as the remaining soldiers cast their curious—and then anxious, as his identity sank in—stares on him.

"Ruining this operation was the biggest mistake of your life, General," he said evenly. "If I were you, I'd start praying it wasn't a terminal one."

He turned and walked away before Perrin could reply.

CHAPTER EIGHTEEN

FREEDOM WAS GETTING CLOSER AND CLOSER. KATRYN COULD ALMOST taste it as the shuttle which had brought them from the courier ship settled onto Asrian soil. A Commonwealth planet. She could feel it in the tension Rhys carried throughout his entire body, even though they were a seat's width apart in the empty cargo bay. He knew she'd try to escape once they landed. It was the only explanation for his anxiety. And if he was prepared for her to run, things would be more difficult than she'd anticipated.

"You're not going to try anything, are you?" Rhys asked as one of the pilots worked to open the door. "It won't be worth the consequences, I promise you that."

Katryn didn't answer. Her emotions would be obvious if she spoke or even moved to shake her head. She stared out the opposite window, watching the trees in the distance sway in a strong breeze. How long had it been since she'd felt that kind of wind on her face? Her fingers flexed as the shuttle made the same familiar post-landing noises she'd heard her entire life, creaking and popping and relaxing.

"Good," he said, apparently mistaking her silence for compliance. He stood as unfamiliar, tangy surface air flooded the bay from the opened door, and she followed him down the ramp like an obedient little prisoner with no rebellious thoughts of her own.

So close. So close. So close.

Would she be able to run? Would she need to sneak off? Or—this was a dreadful idea—must she bide her time until more people were around? No, that was silly. They were at a shuttleport in the capital city of Cadena. There were people here. Lots of people. She'd disappear very soon. An ally would be harder to find, but even that wasn't an insurmountable challenge. She'd only need to ask around, would only need to figure out the right questions to ask and the right kinds of people to approach.

Her mind wouldn't settle as she and Rhys walked the short distance inside the terminal. Neither would her stomach. This was it. In an hour at most, she'd be free. Or hiding in a public building somewhere, but that was preferable to her current situation. Rhys pushed the button to slide the door open and placed an intimate hand on her back to guide her inside. Like he cared about her. Like the things they'd done on the courier ship mattered to him. Her skin prickled, and she took a step inside before she could second-guess her decision to flee.

She froze at the sight.

There were dozens of people in the terminal, yes.

Dozens of men in green Imperial Haederan Army uniforms.

She couldn't move. She couldn't breathe, either. Her head turned from side to side, and she blinked, trying to clear the horrific vision from her mind. Because that's all it was—a vision. She was imagining things. She'd dreamed about Iythea before, hadn't she? This was the same thing, and at any moment, she'd wake up.

Or—fear washed over her—maybe they weren't on Asria. Maybe Rhys had lied. Maybe she'd given him too much credit, and he'd taken her to an imperial-controlled planet. Because this —this was not how Asria was supposed to be. Asria was her last hope, a place where she would be safe.

Rhys gave her another gentle shove.

"Oh," he said when she didn't move. His lip curled up in a reluctant smile as she fought to get her breathing under control, but there was no malice underlying it. Perhaps a sliver of pity and regret. "I suppose I forgot to tell you. Asria's ours now."

* * *

So this was to be her prison.

All things considered, it could be much worse than the large bedroom, bathroom, and sitting area on the tenth floor of the luxury hotel in central Cadena. A light blue coverlet lay over the large mattress; the cozy chair by the window matched it. The crystal lighting was expensive—she knew the style from a short vacation on Ventana IV several years ago—and the soft flooring under her feet wasn't far behind.

And clean. It was so clean that she could smell the nothingness of it as she paced off the size. Twenty-seven steps from wall to wall, over three times the size of her room back on Iythea.

If it wasn't for the Imperial Security Command troops who occupied the rest of the building, it would have been like being on holiday. Her quarters were certainly better than living in a habitat on Iythea. They were certainly better than sharing a cot with another prisoner. Weren't they? There were even drapes that blocked all the light from outside if she chose, though there was no doubt there were some kind of cameras in the room. It couldn't be more different from the barracks on that red planet.

What would her colleagues on Iythea think of this hotel? Would they be jealous of her privacy, her fresh clothes? Would they begrudge her the good food and clean water that was certainly on its way to her? None of them had felt anything like the silk coverlet on the bed in months—not even since before the Haederan invasion of the complex. Iythea had always been about little luxuries, not large ones. Scarcity had always prevailed.

Or would they hate her for her change in fortune? Kaz would, especially if he'd truly been a Commonwealth spy. Would he have expected her to kill herself to prevent the Haederans from taking her off-world? Would he have wanted her to try to kill Rhys? She could have easily done so in the pod. Why hadn't she? It hadn't been the idea of the blood; she knew that now.

Rhys, for his part, had disappeared as soon as he'd shown her inside—for meetings and updates with his horrid colleagues about her, no doubt. Katryn had napped, taken a shower, found fresh clothing in the closet, and made herself tea. There wasn't anything else to do now besides stare out the window at the Asrians on the streets below. She'd spent hours trying to catch someone's attention, but no one had glanced in her direction.

So now what? Escape, of course. Clearly, Xan was somewhere on Asria, maybe even in Cadena itself. Rhys wouldn't harm either of them, would he? It was hard to imagine that he would—not the man she'd spent weeks in space with. Not the man she'd shared meals with and laughed with and . . . done other things with. On the other hand, even his own people were afraid of him. She needed an ally, and she needed one fast.

She was fiddling with the empty cup of tea, contemplating her next move, when the door across the room opened. Rhys stood there, back in the green Imperial Security uniform she hadn't missed at all, with two other men dressed the same beside him.

"Roll up your sleeve," he said without preamble, setting a small case on the table next to her by the window. It was the most he'd said to her since they'd arrived.

"Why?"

He gave her a soulless smile, then unsnapped the case. "Tracking chip."

Her face became hot as she surveyed the room for an escape route. "You took one out already."

"That was an army chip. This one is not." His words were cool and clipped.

Katryn wrapped her arms around her chest. "No."

"Roll it up." He glanced back at the two other Imperial Security men behind him. "Or this will only be worse."

The shorter man shifted at his suggestion, and something in her snapped.

"What's the matter, *Rhys*? Afraid you can't handle one prisoner on your own? Need help holding her down so you can violate her?" Her eyes met his for a fraction of a second, but he looked away, taking her hope with him.

"Just do it, Doctor Holt." It wasn't quite anger in his voice. More—more like exasperation. "Now."

She could fight them, but what would be the point? There was no way she could take on all three of them—probably not even Rhys by himself. Katryn sighed and jerked her sleeve down from her shoulder, not up as he'd demanded. A tiny bit of rebellion, true, but it helped to mend the crack that had started in her heart.

Rhys exhaled. "Thank you."

The disinfectant stung her skin, dry from too many weeks in space. She'd have to dig through the bathroom later and find something to help with that. Katryn looked away as he placed the injector against her arm, but didn't flinch as the chip broke her skin. She didn't touch the small lump or look at him as he packed his things up and disappeared back out the door with his friends. Because this—trusting the wrong person—it shouldn't have been a surprise.

Except for Kaz, she'd always been a terrible judge of character.

The city visibly slowed as the sun set. Hundreds of people turned to dozens, dozens turned to a handful, until finally the only people left on the street below wore green. The lights flickered out too, slowly at first, then the entire city went dark in sections. Katryn glanced at the small light by her bed. It was lit, though the buildings across the street had gone black. The door opened behind her, and she looked back out the window to avoid the last person she wanted to see.

"Have you moved out of that chair since the last time I was here?"

She shook her head at Rhys's question.

"I didn't think so." A pocket opened, plastic crinkled. "Here," he said. "Eat something. Please."

Katryn stared at the ration bar he held out, but didn't move. "Why is it so dark out there?"

He sighed and set the bar on the bed, then sat next to it. "We shut down the power grid every night. It helps keep problems at a minimum. Except in certain buildings, of course—there's a generator in the basement here. I wouldn't leave yours on too long, though." He nodded at the small light by the bed table. "Light usually means Haederans, or Haederan sympathizers. I don't want you to become a target."

"You're going to start worrying about me now?"

"I didn't have a choice, Katryn."

Something moved inside of her at his use of her name, too intimate for someone who'd done what he'd just done.

"Of course you had a choice. Were you going to let them beat me up if I'd fought you earlier?"

"I brought them with me because I was hoping they'd frighten you into doing what I needed to you to do, and that further measures wouldn't be necessary." He held up his hands. "They wouldn't have harmed you. Just held you still for me."

"That's supposed to be better?"

He didn't answer.

"Go away, Captain."

"Katryn." He stood and waved off the light, leaving nothing but the moons illuminating the room. "Come here."

"No."

He blew out a deep breath. "I'm sorry. I'm sorry for what I did earlier, I'm sorry you're here at all, and I'm sorry—look, I'm just sorry. I know those words can't make up for anything I've done, and I wish I knew what could."

"You could let me go."

"That's not going to happen. You know I have orders. If I violate them . . ."

"Then no, there's nothing that can make up for what you've done."

To me, to Xan, to Asria, to the people on Iythea.

"How about you dance with me?"

"Dance with you?" Had he been drinking before he'd come up here? She'd just said—

Rhys held out a hand. "I know you'll never let me sit there and hold you, and I can't have you released—so that's the best I can offer right now. Please?"

The moons lit his face enough that she could see the earnestness there. The honesty. He might be using her, but he cared for her in some twisted way—that much was obvious. She could use that. She could gain his trust, and then maybe . . . well, she could use it for something. Convince him to let her go, eventually. To let Xan go. They wouldn't even need to go home, only to a planet the war hadn't yet touched. Yes, that would have to be the new strategy.

Katryn pushed herself up on legs stiff from sitting all day and took his hand.

"That's better than sitting in that chair all night, right?" He pulled her closer, and she leaned her head against his chest. Enemy or not, it felt good. His free hand reached out and brushed the lump on her arm. "Does this hurt?"

Katryn shook her head, willing tears away. "Not much. Not anymore." Not physically, at least. The defilement, the knowledge that someone, somewhere, could tell exactly where she was and probably whether she was awake or asleep or hungry—that would never go away. But Rhys couldn't know how tarnished she really felt.

"Good," he said, swaying back and forth. "Good."

They moved like that, unspeaking, for several minutes. She should pull away, force him to leave. But the loneliness and fear won out, and she clung to him, her eyes closed.

"I'm leaving tomorrow," Rhys said suddenly. "There are some things I need to do. You'll be safe here, and I'll be back as soon as I can."

Already? "You're seeing Xan, aren't you?"

His drawn-out silence answered for him.

"Can I see him?"

"I don't—I don't know yet. I don't know exactly where he is. So maybe. Let's talk about that tomorrow before I go. Right now . . . let's dance."

"This isn't dancing, Rhys."

"No?" A low chuckle. Good. Amusement meant that he had no idea what she was thinking. "I suppose not. But there are worse ways to spend an evening, I suspect."

She gripped the back of his shirt harder, ignoring the warming —and the warning—in her gut. *Just biology.* "Yes. There are."

CHAPTER NINETEEN

The plain silver band and two silver stars he'd swiped from Perrin's evidence locker sat on his desk in his new office in downtown Cadena, mocking him. Chase gave the ring a spin and watched it swirl until it collapsed in a clattering heap. Merritt Parker had wanted to marry her, had given her this ring scarcely a day prior, and now he was dead, killed trying to take Alcaris back from the Haederan Army. He couldn't bring himself to feel glad about that.

He shoved the ring in his chest pocket and picked up the stars that had come from Parker's uniform, giving them only a cursory glance before they joined the ring. It didn't matter what Avery had done, what kind of treason against the Haederan Empire she'd committed—she deserved to have them back.

And if he was the one to give them to her . . .

He took his time going downstairs. Took the stairs instead of a lift tube, in fact. Anything to delay seeing the devastation in her eyes. But why did he care? He shouldn't. By the time he reached the basement, more out of breath than he should have been, he'd almost convinced himself he didn't.

The control center for the temporary prison at the bottom of the fifty-story building—an upscale office building before the occupation—was right inside the security door. Chase stopped inside the small room, filled with live video feeds from each cell and a selection of stun rifles, and the scene was familiar enough to ease a little of his anxiety. Despite having Perrin in charge, maybe not all of the army was as incompetent as he'd feared.

"What's she been up to, Lieutenant . . . ?" he asked the officer in charge.

"Noall, sir. And crying, mostly," he replied, pointing at one of the screens. Avery was standing on her tiptoes on the hard bench, eyeing the ceiling. Even through the feed, her eyes were visibly swollen and red. "Trying to find a way out when she takes a break from that."

"Mm." Sounded about right. What else was there to say? "I'm going to pay her a visit. No one is to interrupt." He headed toward the door and stopped. "Got a bottle of water and some pain meds I could have?"

"Yeah, probably, sir." Noall dug through a drawer filled with medical supplies and came out with a sealed kit.

Chase shoved it under his arm and headed down the hall to Avery's cell. The guards pulled the door open for him, and though he'd expected her to make a run for it, she didn't do much of anything but look curiously at him as he entered.

"What do you want?" she asked.

It wasn't a rude question, exactly. At least, it didn't sound nearly as rude as when Parker had asked him the same thing a few nights ago. She was angry with him—he was Haederan, after all—but less so than with her jailers. He'd spent a long time making sure of that.

"Just to give you this." Chase pushed the water more securely under his arm and brought the ring and stars from his pocket. Her eyes began to water when she recognized them, and he made a motion to lay them on the bench. "I'll just leave them here, then." He hadn't meant to upset her more, hadn't known she'd cry over them.

"No. Please. I'll take them." He handed them over and she put the ring straight on. "I—I appreciate it."

"It's no problem." He unwrapped the package and examined the contents before handing them over. "Sennyl. And water. You're still going to have one hell of a headache." If she'd been crying as long as Noall had said she'd been—and Chase had no reason to doubt him—she was going to be in pain for a while no matter what meds she took.

Avery popped the medicine in her mouth and swallowed, looking warily at him.

"Where's Prime Minister Baylen?" she asked. "Is he all right?"

"He's thinking things over, just like you," Chase said. The prime minster was the last person she needed to worry about. Didn't she realize that? "But if you're ready, I can take you back to Governor Perrin now. I can't promise how much more time he's willing to give the two of you."

A lie. Perrin didn't want anything to do with her anymore, no matter how much support she agreed to. And he was only delaying the inevitable, like he had with Powell.

She sat the water on the floor and rubbed her head. "No. It's not going to happen, so if he sent you here to talk me into it, you can tell him that."

That response wasn't surprising.

"Believe me, you don't want to know what he'll do if I tell him you said that, so I'll forget I heard it." He couldn't contain a small laugh at the idea of Perrin's reaction. The general's head might explode.

A sudden thought struck him—maybe Perrin hadn't permanently ruined things after all. He'd give her one last chance to confess, one last chance to admit what she'd been doing before things got serious. He'd lucked out before, hadn't he?

"I'm curious though," he said. "Why not just do what we want? Things would be a lot easier for you if you'd stop fighting this. You had to have seen his request coming a long time ago."

If she was smart, she'd have a good answer. And if she was

like everyone else, she'd already be tired of this prison cell. She'd say anything, would promise anything, would sell out her own father, all for a chance at her release. He'd obtained a few of his agents this way. People jumped at the chance.

Avery chewed on her lip before answering. "Because I'm Asrian."

Blast it. The statement was quiet, hesitant, like she'd always been around him, but also—confident. She was stronger than he'd ever given her credit for.

"You're that certain?" he asked.

Please don't be that certain.

Avery didn't reply, just traced her fingers over the silver stars in her hands, and he knew what he had to do.

"I wish you felt differently." His shoulders sank as he spoke, as she turned away from him. He blew out a deep breath and knocked on the door to be freed, putting together his long-unused ISC uniform in his mind.

* * *

Chase gave her three days to think over her situation. Three days to worry, three days to miss him and the protection she thought he provided, three days to agonize about Perrin. He needed her defenses down—and if he was the least bit honest with himself, he needed the break.

He dressed slowly, already unaccustomed to the subtle differences in the buttons of his ISC shirt. He'd assembled everything yesterday, then hung the uniform from a hook on the wall, all too visible, as a way to ease himself back into his real life. Looking at it brought heat to his face instead, made his hands shake as he worked the buttons on the dark green shirt. It was only a shade darker than the army uniform he'd been wearing so long, but the crossed swords on the left side of his collar and the single platinum starburst on the right allowed no doubt of his true identity. He was no harmless army captain.

No, he was something he wished he wasn't. Maybe, just maybe, if he wished the swords away, they'd disappear. Maybe he'd be transported instantaneously back to Haedera, back to Windhaven, back to Isobel. He'd blink once more, then wake in the desert with her brilliant smile welcoming him home. But when the door opened, he wasn't standing in the desert outside the estate, but opposite the control room in the basement prison.

Too bad.

"Colonel." Noall jumped to his feet when he saw him, his eyes wide.

"Relax, Lieutenant. I'm not here for you."

"Y—yes, sir. I mean, no, sir. I—what can I do for you?"

"I need to borrow four of your men. Quickly."

He'd need them. Avery would panic when she saw him— unless, as that nagging feeling kept trying to convince him, she already knew who he was. Though that might not matter. Knowing it and seeing it confirmed right in front of her were two different things.

"Yes, sir." Noall leaned toward the comm board and pushed a few buttons. "Glace, Sergeant Faughn, I need you in here immediately." He turned to Chase. "Two is all I have right now, sir. If you had . . . perhaps . . ." He trailed off, his eyes wide, though now he kept looking past Chase, out the door.

Ah, Noall had wanted some sort of notice of his appearance. Of his identity. Didn't the Imperial Haederan Army remember what Haedera was like? ISC never gave notice unless it suited their purpose, and that was a rare situation indeed.

"Perhaps what?" Chase asked, raising his eyebrows. Noall had unintentionally turned himself into one last entertaining distraction before his real work began.

"Warned us . . ." His forehead crinkled. "Never mind, sir."

"Noted, Lieutenant. But that would defeat the purpose of things, wouldn't it?"

The poor kid turned pale at that, and Chase grimaced.

Cowards, the lot of them. How had they taken an entire planet? On the other hand, it made ISC's job easier.

"Lieutenant?" The sergeant who stuck his head into the control center froze when he saw Chase, then stiffened to attention. "Colonel."

Why was everyone so surprised? If it wasn't him, it would be another ISC officer sooner or later. They had no idea how lucky they were that it was him and not . . . well, Lient would terrify them into capitulation in less time than he had, even if the head of Imperial Security wasn't exactly given to dropping in anywhere but a library.

"Go wake up the prisoner in sixteen," Chase told them. "I'll be along shortly." Avery needed to be wide awake when she saw him for the first time. "And don't harm her," he added. "I don't care what she does, you're not to harm her."

Faughn bobbed his head and dashed off, and Chase leaned against one of the consoles to watch the proceedings on the live feed—much to Noall's dismay, he noticed with no small amount of delight.

The cell grew a bit brighter as the door opened, and Avery blinked a few times, then sat up and looked toward the opening. Before Chase could wonder how she'd react, she darted for it, apparently indifferent to the soldiers blocking her path. Faughn knocked her to the ground, hard, and Chase swore under his breath as he dashed down the hallway. He made it there in time to see a young private land a solid kick to her side.

"That's enough," Chase ordered, the cold voice he hadn't used in so long firmly back in place. Couldn't they follow a simple order? On the other hand, he couldn't be too angry—they'd just inadvertently reinforced his position as her savior. "Get her up."

They jerked her to her feet, and she kicked backward at them like an awkward young colt. Would she not stop struggling? They were going to hurt her even more, and though he'd warned them not to use force like this, there wasn't much he could do about it if she kept fighting like she was. They'd react out of self-defense.

She managed one strong kick against the sergeant's shin, and he brought his stun pistol up against her skull.

Chase wanted to sigh. This wasn't what he'd planned, and if he had to delay their first talk because of some overzealous soldier . . . it might throw everything off.

"I'd stop now, if I were you," he warned her. "You won't like what they do next." Not with that stun pistol against her head, she wouldn't.

She blinked at his voice, like she'd noticed him standing there for the first time. Blinked and froze, so motionless it didn't look like she was even breathing. For almost a minute she stood there, that blasted stun pistol against her neck, staring at him. Staring at his uniform. Her eyes began to flicker about the cell, occasionally landing on the open door behind him, but it didn't seem she could help herself from gaping at those swords on his collar. No, before this second, she'd had absolutely no idea who he really was.

It was difficult not to grin.

"Please." Her voice was raspy with fear.

He took a step toward her. "I'd rather they not do that again" —*I'll kill them if they do*—"but that depends on your cooperation." Another step. "And that cooperation starts with you not attacking my men."

On second thought, though, he wouldn't mind all that much if she tried—these soldiers could use someone to keep them on their toes. She'd almost gotten out the door thanks to their incompetence, and then where would he be? No, the additional ISC personnel he'd requested from Lient over and over couldn't arrive on Asria soon enough. If His Majesty had had the appropriate foresight, they'd have arrived with the fleet.

But he still needed her to trust him, and that wasn't going to happen if these soldiers beat the life out of her. He sighed internally. There was no winning here for either of them.

She shook her head, and the sergeant pushed his gun harder against her neck.

"No?" Maybe he'd underestimated her. But likely not. He chanced taking his eyes off the soldier with the gun to wave the door shut. She wasn't going to try anything right now. Not until the shock wore off, and that would take five minutes, if not more. "I think it's an easy request. But maybe you're right. You don't know what else I want."

Avery closed her eyes.

"Or maybe you do." The small chuckle that escaped was unprofessional perhaps, but he couldn't hold in his laughter any longer. He waved at the soldiers to release her. It was too risky to have them holding her like they were. Someone was going to get shot. "Sit down."

She didn't flinch, didn't argue, didn't blink, only padded back to the bench and put her head in her hands. Like he couldn't see her if she couldn't see him.

If only that were so.

He stood there for what seemed like an hour, watching her, waiting for her breathing to slow—by the way she was moving, they'd broken at least one rib when they'd kicked her—and waiting to get his own emotions under control. Laughing at her more would do more harm than good at this point.

"Aren't you even a little curious?" he asked, as her gasps for air became less frequent.

She jumped. Perhaps she'd hoped he'd disappeared. "A—about —" Her voice wasn't raspy now, but shaking. "About w—what?"

"Who I really am."

She didn't do anything but shake her head.

"Then you already know."

Of course she knew. It was plainly obvious. They'd had a cordial enough relationship before. He'd made certain of that, and giving her that ring back had been the last step—there was only one reason she'd be this terrified of him.

Avery glanced up quickly, then back down at his boots.

"Look at me." He grasped her chin and pulled her face up

toward him. She fought that too, so he squeezed harder until she stilled, those seafoam eyes that met his full of pain, fear, and betrayal. "Why are you so worried?"

There was no answer. Not an immediate one, at least, and that was what he wanted. He dug his fingers in harder, and she gasped.

"Because I know what you are, Colonel." The words were barely a whisper, delivered as she focused on his collar. She twisted her head, and he let her go that time.

"Oh?" Brilliant news. That brainwashing academy she'd attended had done his job for him. "Yes, I suppose anyone educated on Ventana would. And that frightens you this much?"

It was a question with intent. No matter the look on her face, no matter that he could almost feel the terror radiating from her, she could always use another reminder that he was someone to be feared.

"I asked you a question."

"Yes," she whispered. "It does."

"Good."

She began to cry at that. From a single word. Perhaps he'd pushed her too far, too early. *Give her a little hope, quickly.*

"Although I can't imagine why it would," he went on. "You certainly weren't afraid of me the night we met; the night you couldn't wait to tell me how much you hated me."

The night she'd accused him of being a hypocrite and implied he couldn't serve an empire that cheapened life while also worshipping the Holy One. He still heard her words at night, still argued to himself about the things she'd said. He would never admit she was right.

He shook off the guilt. "I've shown you quite a bit of leniency and consideration since then, given the circumstances. Much more than you deserve. Yet you're sitting here acting like I'm about to torture you."

Yes. Watching her eyes widen and her hands shake at his

implication kept his mind off the shame which had suddenly flooded him.

"You will."

"I would prefer it doesn't come to that." She didn't know how lucky she was that it wouldn't. "But I'm glad we have an understanding now."

She pressed her back against the wall, and he stifled another laugh. Yes, she was well and truly convinced that her situation was dire. He'd decide her ultimate fate another day, but fear always . . . usually . . . most of the time . . . worked to his advantage.

"We'll talk more later," he said. "I only wanted to introduce myself again, but it looks like you did my job for me. Thank you for that." He smiled at her as he backed toward the door. Smiles kept them off their guard. Smiles gave them hope, hope that he could rip out from under them at the right time. And smiling at her, with her overly responsive emotions, was just too easy. She had no training, no clue. "Tomorrow, then."

Noall was hovering in the hall when he made his way outside, followed by the two soldiers.

"Sir," he said, quite a bit more composed than earlier, "I need to apologize for my men's actions. I assure you it won't happen again. We'll make sure of that."

"It's fine." Chase strode toward the control center—and freedom—with Noall darting along after him. "I'll send a medic by in a few hours to see her. After that, keep her fed and stay away from her." He hoped he'd emphasized that last bit enough. "Your men can wait outside while the medic fixes her up. I don't want anyone besides him in there, understand?"

Not yet, anyway.

Noall bobbed his head. "Perfectly, sir."

"Also, I want the rest of your prisoners transferred out. I don't care where. As for you—call another few guards in. And welcome to your new home for the next few weeks. I don't want your men talking while she's here."

Noall didn't look quite as thrilled at his restriction to the dungeon, but nodded again.

"Good," Chase said. "I'll be back in a few days for her."

For now . . . for now it was time to spend those few days at the temple.

CHAPTER TWENTY

IT NEVER MATTERED HOW PREPARED HE WAS OR HOW MANY TIMES IT'D happened in the past, the first official interrogation session was always stressful—for the prisoner too, Chase supposed. But then, Avery probably hadn't had the dreams he'd had last night. Nightmares, really.

Or maybe she had.

On the other hand, though every subject was different, there was something vaguely comforting about the familiar anxiety. Unlike direct surveillance, especially in an unfamiliar city, interrogation was something he was skilled at. Something he could do in his sleep. Avery had already confessed, after all, much faster than he'd ever imagined. Actually getting the information out of her would take longer, but they'd made a good start. The key, of course, was getting it out of her before it became useless.

He was flicking through his tablet notes with a finger when the army guards pounded on the door outside, but before he could say a word, the door slid open. Chase took a breath to reprimand them for their lack of protocol—their lack of security—but they tossed Avery on the floor in front of him before he could speak, a broken heap of clothing and dark hair.

What in the quadrant . . .

"What happened?" he asked.

"Sorry, sir," one of them muttered.

They dashed back into the corridor before he could say another word. Avery pushed herself up to a sitting position as the door closed, pulled her hair from her face, and clasped a hand over her eye. Was that relief he detected? Yes, under the terror, there was some of that too, and that tiny bit of her emotion washed over him. If she was relieved to see him, then maybe things weren't as bad as he feared. He ordered her to stand and tamped the relief back down. It wasn't the time or the place to bask in it.

She shook her head, furiously, and his gaze landed on her left eye, swollen and red beneath her palm. Had they—had they hit her? By the fear she was projecting, fear that filled the entire room, it hadn't been an accident. He'd given the guards such simple orders, yet they were so difficult for some to follow.

"Let me see."

Avery pushed herself back from him instead. She shook her head again, sending her hair flying about. Her breath came in short, panting gasps. "Hurts," she managed to say. He could barely hear the word.

"I'm sure it does. Let me see it."

They'd hit her with a pistol, he was sure of that now, and he didn't need her blinded. He also didn't need to be calling the medic in already—didn't Noall's men understand there was a procedure for this kind of thing?

Apparently not.

Instead of removing her hand for him to check, Avery scooted another few paces away from him. Chase crossed the room in three steps and crouched in front of her, startling her enough to freeze her in place. With more caution than she deserved, he pried her hand away . . . too gently, perhaps, but he didn't want her blood on his hands.

It was tough not to whistle at the damage they'd done. A long slash—not deep, but lengthy—cut across her upper cheekbone.

That entire side of her face had started to swell, and the tears in her eyes weren't from fear this time. No, she hurt—they'd certainly done a number on her in the span of five short minutes. The only question was—

"Why did they do this?"

He'd read the army's report later, but Avery's version of events, immediate and raw, would be more truthful. She wasn't in any condition to make up a story now.

She blinked at his question—or at least tried. The motion turned to a long shudder as she tried to pull away.

"Answer me." His impatience was beginning to show, but he couldn't stop it.

Avery twitched, then swallowed. "Because I didn't hit them hard enough first."

He wanted to sigh. Naturally, she was defiant. She was scarcely a week into her imprisonment—all but the frailest could hold out for a week. And Avery Rendon? She'd be more resilient than most. It was unlikely she had any training in this kind of thing, but one never knew . . .

Well, if she had, it would be a challenge—and he'd never backed away from a challenge. But it was also a definite problem as far as expediency was concerned. Instead of letting her see his frustration, he stood. Allowing her defiance to go unchecked set a precedent he didn't want to deal with later.

But now what?

"I suppose it's time to have a discussion about your lack of cooperation," he said, reaching for the handcuffs on the table behind him. "I've been tolerant of this for far too long. Get up. If I have to tell you again, you'll be begging me to send you back to the guards."

Vague threats. Always useful, especially to someone with her imagination.

Avery looked up at him for the briefest moment, and then darted for the door on her hands and knees. His throat closed up at the sheer fact she'd attempted something, but he grabbed her by the foot before she made it three paces. Before his heart could follow his throat, he pressed her cheek against the floor and his knee against the small of her back. She twisted toward the door once more and let out a sound he'd never heard, so he pulled her wrist behind her and yanked her fingers back. That time, she stopped.

"No you don't," he said, giving enough pressure to be uncomfortable, but not nearly enough to cause pain. "Aren't you tired of this?"

Silent now, she lifted a tearstained cheek off the floor and tried to spiral from his grip. Stars, he didn't want to hurt her, but . . .

"Keeping fighting, then." He let a little more of his weight press against the small of her back. "But it's going to hurt, and you're still going to lose."

Slowly, so slowly he didn't feel it at first, she eased into the concrete, a sure sign of surrender. Another interrogator might have wanted a verbal agreement of defeat, but what would be the point? Requiring that would be nothing more than unnecessary humiliation, and the look on her face—yes, they were well past the physical struggle now. It would be a mental challenge from here forward. And not a moment too soon. He didn't want to have to hurt her further. Not yet.

"Now get up," he said, jumping to his feet. "And don't try that again."

It took her a while, but she stood, hand pressed on her eye, shaking uncontrollably. The tremors only made it easier to twist her arm behind her back.

"What are—what are you doing?" she whispered back at him, trying to pull her wrist free. "I did what you asked."

He snapped the metal on before she could escape his hold.

"No, you didn't. You're still fighting, and I've grown rather tired of it. I want to treat you with respect, but I can only do that if I get the same in return. Now relax. We're only going to talk for now."

The order sounded harsh, but right now, harsh was better for her than soothing—though she'd never believe that if he told her. For whatever reason, most prisoners had an inexplicable tendency to believe words spoken in anything other than anger were a prelude to brainwashing, and that, understandably, tended to shut down conversation.

Brainwashing. A laughable idea, though sometimes an appealing one. It would have made the Elex Feye situation easier. The truth serum certainly hadn't.

Avery flinched a bit at his tone as she reached for her battered cheekbone with her free hand.

"Don't . . ."

Chase seized that hand, too. It was hard not to smile at where her mind had just gone. Did she think he was going to beat her like the guards had? Beatings rarely earned one any useful intelligence, and more importantly, were a waste of his energy. Best to let someone else expend that energy if needed. He managed to contain his chuckle, barely, as he secured her other wrist behind her.

"But I need to fill out a report before we begin, because I'm not going to take the blame for whatever you did to anger them. You can wait right here while I do that and consider how you got yourself into this situation and how you might best avoid it in the future. Do you need to see the medic first?"

She blinked at him a few times. He could almost see the neurons firing as she argued with herself.

"No." She didn't sound certain.

"Your decision. Remember that." Chase pushed her in front of the table where he could grab her if she tried to escape again—or collapsed. "Don't move from this spot."

He sat, only to stare blankly at his tablet before making a few idle comments. When had this job become so exhausting?

"Colonel."

The whisper was soft, hesitant. Ah, she was going to admit her pain was more than she could tolerate. That hadn't taken long. He kept scratching at the tablet. Over the years, he'd cultivated a reputation for meticulously detailed interrogation notes, and he wasn't about to change the drill now. She could wait a few minutes.

Metal clinked in front of him, and he battled the impulse to raise his head. Avery was trying to pull her wrists free—to what end? Even if she managed to pick the handcuffs—unlikely, since they searched her every time she was moved from her cell—did she think she'd make it out of this room before he or the guards grabbed her?

The clinking turned to sniffling, and he was able to focus on his transcript again. Ten minutes later, he pushed the button on the tablet to transmit the rather abbreviated report to Haedera, rubbed his eyes, and wondered if anyone but Lient's cadre of low-level clerks would ever read the information he'd just typed up. Perhaps someone would—this was Avery Rendon, of all people. She wouldn't just disappear.

"I'm curious about something," he said to her, making his way around the table. Avery's shoulders tensed as he came closer, even though he'd stopped a respectful distance away. "All the records we have say you were never commissioned. Yet you suggested the other day that that might not be the case."

No, she'd corrected him when he'd called her Your Highness. *It's actually Lieutenant Rendon,* she'd told him, no doubt hoping for some kind of leniency. Prisoner of war status, perhaps. Too bad ISC didn't care anything about that.

And why should they? She had no documentation proving she was a member of the Commonwealth Navy. He'd never seen her wearing a uniform. If he was honest with himself, it wouldn't have mattered if he had, but he hadn't, and that was that. Avery Rendon was an enemy intelligence agent, illegally working on a Haederan protectorate planet, and he had every right to treat her as he would any other traitorous civilian. His conscience—in that regard, at least—was clear.

"So which is it?" he asked. "When did this start?"

She inhaled sharply, then glanced up at him and gasped.

Chase took a few steps forward, close enough to make her uncomfortable.

"Does your eye hurt?" It had to be agonizing by this point, but she had to be the one to ask.

Silent, Avery began to shift her hands up and down behind her, preparing for yet another struggle against the restraints.

"Stop that." He accompanied the order with a jab of his thumb to the pressure point near her elbow. She had to be hurting herself doing that, but the medic, when and if he called him in, wouldn't be allowed to treat those bruises. If she couldn't stand there for ten minutes without fighting while he wrote an unenthusiastic report, she deserved whatever minor injuries she inflicted on herself.

"Does your eye hurt?" he repeated.

Without looking up, she nodded.

"I offered the medic before." He crossed his arms and regarded her with his best attempt at confusion. "You said no."

No surprise there. She'd only said no because she didn't want to be indebted to him further. It was a common enough response. Didn't she know she couldn't hold out like that forever? He controlled her food, her sleep, her medical care, and her pain. She was already indebted to him more than she could imagine.

"I changed my mind." Her voice was hoarse.

"Hmm. I thought you might."

He walked off to crack open the door, ignoring how her shoulders sagged in surrender. The army guards who were supposed to be waiting outside were absent, and he rapped on the wall until one came running down the hallway.

"Medic," he said. "Now."

The pale-faced sergeant nodded and ran the way he'd come. Chase refrained from rolling his eyes as he ducked back inside.

"He'll be along shortly, though it's anyone's guess as to when the summons will be delivered to him. In the future, you'll do well to remember that while I have no inclination or desire to withhold medical care from prisoners, the Haederan Army's unresponsiveness when it comes to assisting you is not something I can do much about."

She opened her mouth to argue against his lie but was saved from another stupid remark by the medic, who entered the room out of breath from his run down the hallway. He wore an ISC uniform with the rank of senior corpsman, which was both surprising and relieving. Maybe the medic could give him some answers. But first things first.

Chase waved at Avery. "Check her eye."

She flinched but didn't otherwise move as the medic ran his finger across her cheekbone and followed it with the scanner. Maybe she was learning. Maybe she was in that much pain.

"Orbital fracture." The medic shrugged after his examination and backed toward Chase. "You can let it heal on its own. Let me know if it still looks bad in a week, and I can try dermtape, but it just takes time."

"Ice?"

"It'll help with the swelling. And the pain, if that's acceptable." He reached in his pocket and handed over a few flat cold packs. "Anything else, sir?"

"My office. An hour. They'll give you directions."

The man would end up waiting, of course—he hadn't planned to be done with Avery for another three or four—but she couldn't know of his timeframe. He'd just twisted her perception of time with scarcely any effort at all. And he did need to speak to someone, anyone, as long as they were Haederan. An ISC someone was even better.

The medic nodded on his way out. Chase pulled Avery toward an empty chair and shoved her into it, then held the cold pack up to her face.

"I'm going to release your hands so you can hold this. Don't even think of attacking me."

Avery shifted. "Ice is all he can do?" Her voice broke.

He resisted the urge to rub his own cheek. "He has better

things to do than waste his time on your bad decisions. Do you want the ice or not?"

She nodded. He didn't believe she wouldn't try something eventually, but she was too focused on the pain right now to overwhelm him. He reached behind her and undid the handcuffs, then flung the pack at her from a few paces away, just in case. With shaking hands, she tried to open it, but her fingers slipped off the plastic again and again. It was surprising she could move them at all.

She glanced up at him with no small amount of fear, like he was going to punish her for the failure.

"I can't open it."

Neither could he, most of the time. They were always sealed a little too well, and there was nothing sharp in the room, naturally.

"Then I guess you'll have to wait until you can." His head ached a bit from watching her, but he stomped down that sympathy as he pulled a chair across from hers. "Let's talk about that apparent discrepancy in your work history while you keep at it."

Avery's hands stilled, and she began to shake. She swallowed hard, though how there was anything left in her mouth to swallow, he didn't know.

"I can help you, Lieutenant. I want to." Somehow, he hid the cringe that worked its way through his body. It was the first time he'd called her by her name or rank or anything else belonging to her since this had begun. A failure on his part—de-individualizing a prisoner wasn't usually this difficult, but he'd had to give her something back to ease her fear. He kept his voice soft, calm, to hide his mistake. "You just need to talk to me."

A few tears splashed on the package in her lap.

"That's right. I know you didn't lie about your rank. I know you lied to Perrin about your relationship with the Commonwealth, and you know what? I probably would have done the same thing." Hell, he'd probably lied to Perrin more in the last week than this woman had ever considered doing. "I don't blame you one bit for whatever story you told him. But why the discrepancy? Why are our records wrong?"

Avery looked up at him and wiped her face with her sleeve, smearing blood on the already-dirty fabric.

"Everything happened afterward."

She didn't say anything else, just focused on the plastic, then on her feet.

"After? After what? Your return? The invasion? Were you recruited on Ventana or Asria?"

Avery fumbled with the package.

Chase exhaled deeply. "You can stay silent as long as you want, but know this: they are going to nail you for treason unless I can give them a good reason not to. I'm your best hope of salvation right now."

She froze, stiffened, and narrowed her good eye at him. "You cannot accuse me of treason, Colonel. I am not Haederan."

Such a charming emphasis on the word *not*.

"Of course you are." He began to laugh, partly to anger her, partly because . . . well, how else was he supposed to react? She'd transformed from terrified prisoner to haughty Asrian aristocrat in the span of one second. Treasonous, yes, but also—dare he even think it?

Oh, why not? Half his thoughts were treasonous these days.

Yes. She was amusing. She'd been amusing since the day they'd met. He'd knock her back to terrified prisoner when the time was right, but for now, he'd relish her ironic arrogance—it was certainly more comfortable than her fear.

"Maybe not ethnically Haederan," he went on, letting his gaze linger on the green eyes she'd once mentioned she hated. He didn't blame her for that. At least he could lighten his freckles when Isobel so desired, remove the mark of his family's nobility that was paradoxically undesirable at home. It was useful for missions, yes, but there was also something freeing about ignoring his responsibilities, if only with a small part of his body.

Something that you, Your Highness, can't escape.

"But you became subject to imperial law the second that surrender was signed," he continued. "Not that timing matters when we're also talking espionage and sedition and who knows what else."

Avery raised the pack to her mouth and tore into it with her teeth. Her wrists were as bruised as her face. "I don't know what you're talking about."

"I think you do."

She stared at him, as stubborn as the day they'd met, slapped the ice against her eye, and pressed her lips shut.

* * *

The medic was leaning against the door to his office, tapping a foot, arms crossed. He straightened and stopped tapping when Chase appeared, but didn't uncross his arms—typical home world ISC. No respect for anyone, even a senior officer.

It felt good.

"Sorry about that." Chase unkeyed the lock on the door and motioned the medic inside. "Took longer than I thought. You know how it goes."

"I know." The medic grinned. "That's why I've only been here five minutes."

Chase laughed and tossed him a pouch of water from his supply, then collapsed in a chair by the floor-to-ceiling window. It was raining so hard he couldn't even see the building across the street. Did it ever stop?

"I was surprised to see you," Chase said. "Where did you come from ... uh ..."

That sounded ruder than he'd intended. But switching from interrogation mode to social politeness had always been difficult, even for him. The medic was ISC. He'd understand.

"Draven Mercer, sir. Sounds like you haven't been clued in about the garrison uptown yet."

Chase shook his head. "Little isolated here."

Had ISC finally arrived on Asria in force? Too little, too late for him.

Mercer took the chair next to him. "Temporary headquarters in some hotel a few klicks away. And we took possession last week of a building at Alcaris for a detention center." He glanced around, out the window at the torrent of water. "You might move your prisoner there?"

"I can't move her now." Chase rubbed his eyes. "Wish I could."

Blast Perrin, throwing off his schedule like he had and bringing Avery to this temporary army prison. If what Mercer said was true, she could have been at an ISC facility at Alcaris right now, more secure, more terrified, more pliable. He might be bending her this very moment, turning her into the most perfectly placed Haederan agent he'd ever made, instead of simply trying to extract information by brute force. And he could be spending his nights in a hotel instead of this sparse office with a cot, eating field rations and bathing in a bathroom sink.

"Of course, sir. I'm at your disposal here—whatever you need."

"I hope I won't need your assistance again for a while." As long as the army guards followed his orders. Make her uncomfortable so she'd look forward to the protection he provided during their sessions, yes. Beat her within a hair of her life, no. Why was that kind of delicate work so hard for some people to understand? "I'll tell you what I do need—some decent food. Any ideas?"

Mercer chuckled and made an expression completely out of place on the face of a grown man. At least, it would have been out of place if Chase didn't know exactly what was going through his head.

"Not out in town," he said. "Not unless you like fresh eel for breakfast, which I personally do not care for. Right now, we're stuck with local food or field rations they're shipping down from orbit, and rumor says they're going to stop that soon."

Of course they were.

"Eel it is, then." What a horrific thought. Chase made a mental note to stretch out the field rations he'd hoarded in his desk. "Anyone interesting land after the invasion?"

"Not Lient or any of the command staff, if that's what you're wondering. But a few intel types you might know." Mercer rattled off a few names. "I'm not sure who else. I don't spend much time there," he apologized. "Too much work to be done at Alcaris—and now here."

"That's all right," Chase said. "I think I'll pay one of those names a visit."

CHAPTER TWENTY-ONE

THE SENATE TEMPLE WAS ALL BUT EMPTY—LIKE IT WAS DURING MOST of his visits—and quiet except for the soft murmurings of the man at the main altar. Chase couldn't quite make out the words, but it didn't sound like a prayer. No, the tone—and the pacing that accompanied it—sounded more like raging frustration than any kind of supplication, but he didn't mind interrupting. Not this time, and not this man.

Rhys Linden.

How long had it been since he'd seen Linden? It must have been months—not since turning over Elex Feye to Linden to run. And the last he'd known, Linden—and Feye—weren't supposed to be anywhere near Asria.

He wasn't paying as much attention to his surroundings as he was supposed to be, either. Chase padded silently down the center aisle, hand on his stun pistol, softening his footsteps on the marble. It had been hard enough to find Linden tonight, and dropping him right where he stood had a certain appeal, if only to teach him a lesson about self-awareness and personal security. But he wouldn't tarnish the sanctity of the place by using a weapon here. Instead, with a grin on his face, he whispered Linden's name from a pace away.

Linden started, dropped a match, then spun toward him, hand on his own pistol. His shoulders relaxed almost immediately.

"Hell, sir. You could have said you were back there."

"And miss that look on your face? I don't think so." He clasped Linden's hand in his. "Stars, Rhys, you don't know how good it is to see a familiar face. I was beginning to think I was alone on this planet. What are you doing here?"

Linden seemed to deflate. It was hard to tell for sure in the candlelight, but he looked pale, much paler than normal. Recent long-haul spaceflight, or was it something else?

"In the temple or on Asria, sir?"

One didn't need to have much experience in reading people to know something was wrong. Linden was a lot of things, but unlike most of ISC, he wasn't usually this cagey.

"Well, both, I suppose."

"In the temple . . . about what you'd expect. It's been a rough few weeks, and sometimes . . . well, sometimes you need a little beauty around while you think. Or yell at someone or something. On Asria?" Linden glanced around, even though they were alone. "Not here."

"ISC building?"

Linden clearly wanted to talk to him, and Chase didn't mind. Over five years of working together made for the kind of camaraderie he missed sometimes.

Linden looked at his feet. "Not there, either. I—I'm staying at a flat nearby for the time being. Waiting on a source. We can go there."

Strange. This had to be something good—he owed Mercer for the tip.

"Then lead on, Captain," Chase said.

* * *

Linden turned on the portable jammer and kicked back in his chair with some sort of local Asrian brewed beverage in his hand

—ISC had never been all that formal among themselves. Then again, it would be hard to be formal in this one-room flat with a concrete floor and toilet in the corner, sitting out in the open. A few uniforms were slung over a stool by a pull-down table—that explained why Linden had looked a little wrinkled earlier. The one thing the flat did have going for it was a respectable view of the glittering Cadena lights and street below.

"Elex Feye," Linden began with a sigh. "What a mess."

Chase couldn't help how his eyebrows shot up as he sat, his own drink in hand. "On Asria?"

Something tightened in his gut. There were coincidences, but very few good ones, and this could be a very good one indeed. Feye might be Special Operations Forces, but the commando-type work the Commonwealth Navy group was ostensibly known for across the quadrant wasn't his specialty—agent-handling was.

Was it possible . . . ?

"Yeah." Linden took a long swallow. "As far as I know. I mean, he was. I followed him and that partner of his all the way here from Sairik, got stuck on *Adrul* during the invasion, and by the time I made my way to the surface, they'd both disappeared. Vanished. Like wraiths."

Chase frowned. "That shouldn't have happened."

His partner Zenos Hadley was good at disappearing, Feye had always insisted, but if any of their Commonwealth agents were reliable, it was him. Chase had made certain of that himself. The lacrozenate—the truth serum ISC had been working to perfect since a Commonwealth source had delivered the formula a few years ago—had worked its magic, and after watching the videos of his interrogations, after seeing himself give up hours upon hours of classified information, Feye had known he'd had no choice.

Work for me, and I won't let the Commonwealth know of the things you've told me here, he'd told Feye—and Feye hadn't been able to agree to his demands fast enough. He'd skimmed enough of Linden's reports to know that Feye was reporting back as regularly as ISC could expect from a planet-hopping source hiding his second job. So what was the problem?

Linden stared at his beer. "Well, it happened. He's on the surface, I'm sure of it—even Zenos Hadley can't get them off-world right now. But trying to find someone who doesn't want to be found on a war-torn planet has made my life miserable. I spend half my time sitting in this hovel waiting for him to answer my messages, and the other half wandering around Cadena hoping I'll run into him on the street. I've got some people watching potential hideouts, but you know how it goes—not enough people yet. And if he's not in Cadena anymore . . . it's up to my backup plan, and I'd rather it not come to that."

Oh, perfect. Another headache was building. They hadn't been able to inject Feye with a tracking chip, not without the Commonwealth finding it, so if he'd disappeared, it was possible he was well and truly gone.

But at least he wasn't the only one needing more ISC on Asria. If he'd requested, and Linden had requested, and the general in charge of headquarters had requested . . . maybe things would start happening. Lient had the men, but getting them this far from Haedera on whatever the navy had available for transport was another matter.

Avery might be his first priority, but he couldn't shake the idea that Feye's disappearance was partly his fault. Maybe Feye wasn't as reliable an agent as they'd all assumed. Maybe he'd made a mistake during his interrogation and indoctrination. They could have held him longer, could have done all sorts of things to ensure his compliance. But he'd thought extreme measures hadn't been necessary.

"Anything I can do to help?" Chase asked. "What's this backup plan of yours?"

Linden grinned and recrossed his legs. "The backup plan? Get this. He's got this sister, right? You remember—widow, engineer, he told us all about her." He flushed a bit. "I found her on Iythea, working as a prisoner in some army mine."

Chase laughed out loud for the first time in what felt like years —though the beer had helped his mood. Linden was capable of more manipulation and plotting than he'd ever given him credit for. He had a brilliant career in the making as long as he didn't screw this one up.

"I take it she's not on Iythea anymore?" he asked.

"Hell no, sir." Linden laughed in return. "She's stashed away at headquarters downtown, in a room much nicer than this one" —he waved his hand toward the toilet—"terrified I'll kill her if her brother doesn't reappear soon."

More death. The beer sloshed in his stomach. "What do you plan on doing with her if he doesn't?" He didn't really want to know, but he had to ask.

"I don't quite know yet." Something strange, almost like melancholy, crossed Linden's face. "But it's academic, because he'll show," he said. "Soon. I sent him a message three days ago letting him know that Katryn Holt is on the surface. He loves his sister, you know that." Linden stood, drained his bottle, and reached for one more. "It's not a problem, sir—you'll be the first to know if it becomes one. Another drink?"

* * *

Chase couldn't tell which one of them was more exhausted. Even with her swollen eye and dirty hair, Avery looked more tired than afraid, and he stifled his own yawn as he checked for new bruises. It didn't look like the guards had done much damage to her overnight, though the bruise on her side where they'd kicked her early on wasn't healing as it should. He bit back a sigh. Mercer would have to pay her another visit soon, and that would put him behind schedule once more.

But he didn't have a choice. The emperor had made it clear—

No.

The emperor hadn't made a damn thing clear. He and Victor Rendon didn't care how abused Avery was as long as she survived to face them, and as much pain as she must be in from the bruises, cuts, and burns, she wasn't anywhere close to being fatally injured. He and Mercer had made sure of that. Yes, this compassion was all on him, and he needed to put a stop to it.

"So," he said, settling in his usual chair, pushing the unwanted concern and his own questions away, "what should we talk about today?"

Avery's forehead creased at his unexpected question, and she flinched as the movement pulled at her injured eye.

"What about your family?" he blurted out before he could stop himself. Well, it was as good a subject as any. Who knew what other conversation it might lead to? Maybe the king and queen had been involved in some kind of resistance group. Stranger things had happened, and even if they were dead, perhaps he could lead ISC to an entire cell.

"They're dead." Avery's voice was dull, scratchy.

"You don't know that."

She stared at her hands, cuffed in her lap.

"Perrin could have lied," he said. "Until you have proof, there's always hope."

She still didn't answer, wouldn't look at him, and that wasn't good for either of them. Perrin probably hadn't lied about her parents, but she needed to cling to the hope that they were alive. With Merritt Parker gone, she couldn't possibly believe she had anything else to live for, and a prisoner with nothing to live for was a prisoner who wasn't going to start talking any time soon. What would be the point? He could put a gun to her head right now and she wouldn't fight it.

If only he had some kind of proof her father was alive . . . something he could show her to give her that shred of hope to hold on to. But he didn't, and asking Perrin about her parents' fate was out of the question. Maybe angering her was the next best thing. Anger kept people alive, too, if only out of sheer stubbornness.

He swallowed hard. Angering her and watching her eyes flash

with rage could be entertaining, but this time, it wouldn't be anything other than painful.

"Anyway, I suppose it doesn't matter if they're alive or not." He kept his voice light, though the effort made him sick. "Rumors in the palace say the king didn't love you. He certainly doesn't miss you, wherever he is, or he'd be doing something to get you out of here."

Come on. Get angry. Challenge me.

As he'd hoped, her good eye flashed as she looked up at him.

"He did!" Then, quieter, to her hands, she said, "He just wasn't good at showing it."

"Especially after your brother disappeared, I'd imagine."

"Yes." Avery blinked, then gave him a confused look. "Why are you asking about this?"

Well, you're talking to me, aren't you? "Because I'm tired," he admitted. That was true, even if it wasn't his only reason. "I don't want to talk about anything else right now. And I'm curious about what went so wrong. Tell me about him."

"About Quen?" She sounded mistrustful, but . . . also hopeful, like someone who'd kept a secret for too long.

He nodded.

"Quen." Avery licked at her cracked and bleeding lips and shifted. "Quen . . . he was always the golden child. Always happy, always joking. Everyone was happier when he was in the room, even the ki—our uncle. He was such a prankster. To me, our parents, the servants, the king. Everyone. It wasn't malicious—he made everyone around him laugh. That's what I remember, at least. But when he turned thirteen, things changed."

"They usually do." He couldn't remember what thirteen was in Haederan years, but Avery's point was clear. How he dreaded those upcoming times with Marc and Sophie.

"This wasn't regular rebellion. I think he realized Uncle Victor wouldn't be having children and everything would fall to him. There were whispers about it everywhere in Cadena. So he rebelled. He'd disappear for days at a time, usually with some girl from school, and security would have to haul him back to Cadena. My father would scream at him. The ki—our uncle was never a screamer, but he had this look of disappointment that could control everyone except Quen. But they kept it quiet within the palace, so the senate still—"

Her voice cracked. "There wasn't anyone else. Some distant cousins and ambitious politicians, but not enough senators seriously entertained the thought of one of them as sovereign, and for some reason, I was a very distant second choice. When the senate started talking about Quen succeeding my uncle and eventually our father, if it came to that, things got worse. One day . . ."

She licked her lips again. Chase reached behind him for a small pouch of juice and handed it over. Her mouth tilted up on the left side, just enough, as it always did when he deigned to show her the least bit of kindness. It wasn't enough to be called a smile, and it certainly didn't reach her eyes, but she trusted him. After all this. She wasn't the first by far, and she wouldn't be the last, but it never stopped amazing him how prisoners reacted to his techniques.

Avery took a long sip, then sat the pouch in her lap and brushed her dirty curls behind her ears. They fell right back across her face and she tried again, then gave up and finished the juice, the hair hanging over her eyes.

He should have sheared it off when she'd first been transferred to ISC custody, and it was only that familiar, traitorous sympathy that had stayed his hand—and the fact it would've been done for him in an ISC detention facility. Perhaps that would be tomorrow's undertaking . . . though if he did so, the guards might take it as permission to harden her treatment in ways he might not approve. Why had she needed to remind him, however unintentionally, of his failure to follow policy? Forgetting was one thing— he was doing the work of two or three ISC officers right now, after all—but forgetting, being reminded, and then declining to follow regulations was another matter. Of course, she was still wearing Merritt Parker's ring, as well . . . something else he hadn't been able to bring himself to take from her. Lient would have a fit if he saw her now.

"One day he started a fire in an older wing of the palace," she went on, oblivious to his discomfort and her upcoming humiliation. "He'd disabled the fire detection and suppression systems first, and most of the wing was a total loss. Almost twenty rooms. I was only eleven, but he blamed me, even though they'd seen me on the security cameras in a garden on the other side of the grounds at the same time, and they knew I had nothing to do with it. I—I of course denied it. When security confronted him, Quen flew into a rage, struck one of the guards, accused me of lying. That night I found a dead bird on my pillow with a note saying I was next. I told Drex—"

Her voice broke. It was surprising that someone who'd been through what she'd already been through was this upset about a bird. Or was it something else? He filed away her emotional reaction for later.

She took a deep breath. "I told Drex, and the next day Father sent Quen to Sabino for a year. He and Mother thought some time away from the palace would help—it would hide his problems from the senate, too—but it only made things worse. Sometimes I think Drex is the only reason Quen didn't actually hurt me."

Something odd moved in his chest—that protective reaction toward her that he'd first sensed around Perrin.

"He really didn't want the job, did he?"

"Of course not. No one did. Would you rather run a winery or a planet?"

He wasn't going to answer that, though the answer was obvious to anyone who knew him. Probably even to Avery. He'd mentioned Windhaven to her, naturally, and he could never keep the fondness from his voice when he talked about the estate.

"I would do my duty, naturally," he replied without enthusiasm. Duty was exactly why he was sitting here in an interrogation room instead of in a courtyard at Windhaven, enjoying the sun and mountains in the distance. "As should anyone with these kinds of responsibilities."

For the first time, he felt untethered. Confused. Who was running this interrogation? He wasn't sure it was him anymore.

"And what if your duty is not what you thought? Not what you're told? Duty to one's planet is not one's sole responsibility." A bit of that familiar arrogance from her academy photo flashed across her bruised face. "Sometimes not even a minor one. We may have callings that are different from what society has dictated for us."

She sounded like she was standing in front of her father, arguing about some minor restriction or another, instead of sitting here with him, beaten and terrified. Yes, prisoner or not, this bitter version of Avery Rendon was a frightening thing. She'd be one to watch in the senate chambers one day.

Where had that thought come from? He blinked away the vision that would never come true.

"So your brother didn't want it and your father didn't want it. Did you?"

"No." Her voice was steel. "I didn't. I had dreams, and they never involved Asria."

"What about now?"

"They still don't." Somehow, if it was possible, her tone became sharper. "But I am Asrian. I am a Rendon. I will do what they demand of me."

No matter what you and your empire have to say about it, was left unsaid.

"Did they demand you risk your life for the Commonwealth?"

Avery's cheeks flushed. Her chest moved in and out as she stared at him, silent. "That was my decision," she finally said, her gaze falling to her lap.

"And the Commonwealth's." She'd claimed it before, but she was verifying it now. It was a minor detail, but useful nonetheless. They'd circle back to it another ten times before they were finished. "Did they give you a choice?"

"I wanted to do it. I would have hunted them down if they hadn't found me first."

"I'd be cautious saying that so loudly. Least of all in front of me." He tilted his head in feigned concern. "The senate would be disappointed in you if they knew you pushed aside your responsibilities to an entire star system for some foolhardy exercise in espionage, don't you think? What do you think they'd have to say about it?"

Guilt was a powerful thing. He of all people knew that. And guilt always kept Avery talking.

"Perhaps." Her answer was quiet, unsure. "I don't know what they'd do."

And suddenly, with that tentative claim of hers, he was exhausted. What a horrific waste of time this was. She didn't know anything. She hadn't told the Commonwealth anything important, if she'd told them anything at all. No, Avery Rendon was nothing more than a bitter member of a planetary royal family, tied to her ancestors' history against her will, playing a game that she hadn't quite understood the stakes of. Well, she'd learn soon. Chase pushed himself to his feet and stuck his head outside to call for the guards.

CHAPTER TWENTY-TWO

Being a prisoner was, first and foremost, boring.

No, that wasn't quite right. Iythea hadn't been boring, after all. It had been hostile, it had been stressful, it had been exhausting, it had been anxiety-inducing—but not boring. Boring was definitely preferable to laboring in a mine for hours, days on end. At least here, she had more food than she wanted, clothes that were laundered every other day, and a deep bathtub. And this tub . . . oh, how she never wanted to leave it. On Iythea she'd wiped herself down with damp rags, but here there was all the hot water she could stand, plus a selection of aromatic bath oils whose scent clung to her skin long after she'd exited the water. They smelled better while she was in the water though, and along with her sore muscles, weak even now from the long voyage, the smell of the mine faded gradually away.

Still, one's body could only take so much, and she'd become more and more concerned over the past few days that she'd fall asleep in the soothing bath. Katryn stepped out, not caring how much water she was dripping all over the floor. There wasn't anything else to do but clean it up later, was there? She picked her way across the damp floor toward her full closet to make her only decision of the evening.

Whatever else she thought about the Haederans, they were doing a decent job of caring for her, like Rhys had promised. Overcompensating for her prior treatment, perhaps? Her clothes were always clean—and fashionable on Asria, or so it appeared from her survey of the people in the street below. She chuckled at the idea of one of her hardened ISC guards out shopping for her as she pulled a pale blue tunic over her head. The sun was setting, but she wasn't ready for sleep, so there was no point in dressing like she was.

As thoughtful as they'd been with the clothing, they hadn't seen fit to give her a chronometer—but with a window and their strict food-delivery schedule, it wasn't difficult to determine the time of day. And they were late with dinner this evening. At least a half hour late, if she had to guess by the angle of the sun and the growling of her stomach.

Katryn flopped in the chair by the window to watch the Asrians dissipate from the street below and considered her options. There hadn't been any opportunity to steal ration bars like on the courier ship, and a quiet, fearful place in her mind screamed that the Haederans had forgotten about her—that she'd starve to death up here before she was brave enough to leave and forage for food. But that was ridiculous. Likely they'd forgotten about dinner tonight and they'd show up in the morning. Or they were simply running behind schedule. Or something. She wanted to swing the door open and ask whatever Imperial Security officer was manning the chair outside, but they'd warned her about that, hadn't they?

Well, even before the Haederans had arrived on Iythea, she'd never been known for listening to instructions. Before she could think better of it, she dashed across the room and cracked open the door. It took a second for her to realize she'd pressed her eyes closed. With a prayer to the winds, she opened them.

No one. The chair was empty; the corridor was silent.

Katryn leaned her forehead against the doorframe. If she could get to the emergency stairs—if there wasn't any kind of security system—if no one noticed her leaving through the door downstairs—

Her bare feet moved onto the soft carpet. Along with neglecting to provide her a clock, they hadn't given her shoes either, but that oversight wasn't a problem. Now her footsteps needed to be silent for this to work. Even if security was around the corner, they'd never hear her. Katryn took another step. And then another. Freedom. She could feel it, just through that door and down the stairs and—

"What are you doing?"

Katryn froze, then spun around, wordless.

He'd come up behind her. It was the younger major with dark hair and a scar over his left eyebrow, the one who liked to whistle as he walked down the hallway. She'd only seen him twice before, and both times, she'd heard him coming through her closed door.

Why hadn't he been whistling tonight?

He blinked at her, then narrowed his eyes. "You're not supposed to be out here."

"Dinner," she gasped. "It wasn't—and I didn't—"

The major held up a bag in his right hand. "It's here. There was some mix-up in the kitchen, and they forgot about you. Had to get them to reopen, so it's cold tonight."

"Right." Security hadn't forgotten about her. Katryn backed toward her room, foolishly aware of her bare feet. "I'm sorry."

"Don't be sorry," he said as he followed her inside and tossed the bag on the table by the window. "Just don't do it again."

"No." Katryn shook her head as she backed against the window, hand on the bag. "I won't."

His expression relaxed as he considered her. "You look like you could use some fresh air though, Doctor Holt."

"Fresh air?" She scarcely remembered what that was. There hadn't been any such thing on Iythea, or on the ship to Asria, and her window here didn't open. "Are you offering to let me out?"

"Well"—he seemed to hedge a bit as he headed back toward

the door—"Not out. But there's a courtyard downstairs. Maybe you'd like to eat dinner there?"

"Really?"

"Why not?" He shrugged. "Find a sweater. It's cold."

* * *

The major hadn't lied. Katryn wrapped her arms around herself as he slid open the door and motioned her to come out. Dried leaves spun in little cyclones in the corners of the courtyard and crunched under her feet, though the trees were green. It was early autumn in Cadena, then? The chill was unmistakable, a deep sensation she couldn't shake, the feeling that brought the promise of winter.

It felt like home.

Trying not to stumble in the too-large men's shoes he'd provided, she followed him to a small table under an overhang with an electric heater and dug through the bag. The presentation might be lacking, but there was no doubt something good was inside. Linden's men didn't seem to be lacking the small luxuries she'd taken for granted until Iythea, especially in the culinary area.

"Captain Linden asked me to"—the major raised his eyebrows as he sat across from her—"be 'nice' to you when and if I saw you. Most of the senior officers are in a meeting, so I figured being nice included sneaking you out here for a bite." He shot her a quick grin. "Don't tell."

"Nice?" Katryn's hand froze halfway inside the bag. That didn't sound like Rhys. Or maybe it did. She shook her head and pulled out a pouch of sparkling cinnamon water. "I don't need anyone to be nice to me." Even as she spoke, she gulped in a lungful of fresh air.

His laugh warmed the courtyard. "We can go back inside if you'd like."

Not without a fight.

"No. I think I needed this." She shivered. "Where is he?"

"Captain Linden?" He shrugged. "Can't say."

"Is he in Cadena?"

"Maybe. I can't say because I don't know. He doesn't tell me about his jobs, and I don't tell him about mine."

That was a nonanswer if she'd ever heard one. Katryn turned her attention to the food. Dinner was a sandwich, though one much better than the sludge they'd been fed in the habitats after the invasion. It was a Haederan cook tonight—or an Asrian who was finally learning—for the chicken was slathered in something that looked spicy. She wiped away half and replaced the bread.

"What is your job?" she asked. "What's your name, for that matter?"

"This and that. And none of your business. You ask too many questions—are you like this with Linden?"

Well, that was blunt. Even Rhys had told her what he did. The major had accompanied the statement with a smile, though.

"Worse," she replied. "You're a terrible conversationalist."

He chuckled. "My wife tells me that all the time."

Well, so much for seducing her way out of the building. *Probably*. Wife didn't mean he couldn't be manipulated—he was a long way from home, after all. Time to poke around and find out.

"How does she feel about you being so far away from Haedera?" she asked.

His face fell. No, definitely no chance.

"She's not thrilled, of course. Tells me so in every comm she sends. But"—he glanced conspiratorially around—"they say eventually we'll be able to bring our families out here. She claims Asria's not safe, and it's going to take some convincing to assure her that the revolts and insurgencies won't last forever, but eventually Cadena will be as secure as it ever was. More so, in fact."

"Because you're here now."

The Imperial Security Command surveils, investigates, and neutralizes internal and external threats against His Imperial Majesty and the Haederan Empire.

An odd feeling slunk down her spine, and it didn't have anything to do with the rapidly chilling evening air. This man was the enemy. It wasn't a coincidence that he'd used the word *secure* when his wife had used the word *safe*. Cadena must have a local police force—maybe even a regional one, as the capital city and the seat of the system's government—so ISC was here for one reason only.

To smash the opposition, Rhys had implied with his pretty words and verbal evasion.

The major nodded in that same half-ashamed way Rhys had when she'd first met him on Iythea, then sighed. "You're right," he said, like he'd read her mind. "I'm a terrible conversationalist. You don't want to hear about the problems on Asria right now."

Katryn stared at the sandwich, her appetite gone. Why had they made it so spicy? She wasn't Haederan. She could have eaten bland Asrian fish and been happy with it, just to prove to this man that she could.

"What's Cadena like?" she asked.

Since I'll never get to experience it for myself.

"I wish we could show you. Maybe, eventually . . ." He frowned, then shrugged. "Like any other cosmopolitan planetary capital, I would imagine. Certainly similar enough to Rebet to not seem exotic to anyone who's traveled the empire. Too many people and too much traffic for me."

She knew that from watching the street below her room. Cars and lower-level aeroflyers made for quite the scene, one which only died out when the curfew began. It might be a silent panorama through the glass, but Cadena was hardly asleep.

"So you're not a city person," she said.

"Not in the least. You?"

She shook her head and crunched a few leaves with her thick-soled boots. The sound was surprisingly satisfying. "I completed my dissertation research in the swamps on the southern rim of Owakla on the failure modes of pilings exposed to constant ionizing radiation. My group didn't see another soul the entire time we were there." Nash had been with her, and they'd fallen in love, so it hadn't mattered.

Nash. She was always saying goodbye to the people she cared about, and in the worst ways. Nash and Rhys and . . . oh, she couldn't forget Kaz. What would Kaz—who'd likely been some sort of Commonwealth operative—say about her having dinner with this Haederan tonight?

Forget this guy. What would Kaz say about what Rhys and I did?

The major's face had lit up at the mention of swamps. "I grew up in Maaft, on the edge of the Zrab Slough. Klicks and klicks of some of the most beautiful land on Haedera II, though those cocky bastards in Rebet would argue otherwise, of course. They don't know a good thing when they see it."

Katryn raised her eyebrows at his enthusiasm as she tossed the remains of dinner back into the bag.

"Sorry." He shrugged again. "I miss home."

"Me too." The words spilled out.

His gaze fell to his boots. Good. She'd shamed him.

"I think—I think it's time to get back inside, Doctor. You look like you're about to start shivering."

He wasn't wrong. "I'm getting close. Will you—will you be around tomorrow night?"

Even if he didn't bring her back outside, a quick conversation as he dropped off her dinner would be enough. Even if he was Haederan. It was either that or sleep her afternoons away, and that wasn't something she was prepared to do quite yet, even if her recent fatigue was all-consuming. The rain in Cadena needed to stop before it put her in a permanent state of hibernation.

"I'm headed off-planet for a few months." He kicked back in his chair and brushed a fallen leaf from his shoulder. "Leave tomorrow afternoon. Sorry. Maybe if—"

He broke off, probably realizing neither of them knew what would've happened to her by the time he returned.

"Oh."

Yet another person was leaving her, even if he was only dinner conversation—after suggesting she may not live to see the next year. Katryn swooped up a handful of leaves to take upstairs as décor for the bland side table and stood. No more Haederan company. From now on, evenings would be for planning her escape.

CHAPTER TWENTY-THREE

How many weeks had it been? Chase couldn't bring himself to check his notes. Three? Maybe four? It didn't help that he'd been attempting to adjust himself to Asrian time since he'd arrived on-planet, but so far, he'd only succeeded in confusing himself more with the afternoon coffee, late nights, and early mornings. The insistent darkness in the army prison, except in the small room he'd commandeered for interrogations, didn't help matters. Still, it was unusual for him, like it was unusual for anyone with almost twenty years of interplanetary travel experience.

Stars. Twenty years. He was getting old. Most in ISC—not to mention the navy—didn't last much past fifteen.

He wet his mouth with a pouch of water as the guards dropped Avery in the chair across from him. She didn't look at him, which was normal for her, but this evening something was different.

Chase lifted her chin with a finger. She didn't pull away, just gazed past his shoulder at the opposite wall and closed her eyes. They were sunken, yes, with huge dark circles beneath them, but that could have been from crying. She'd been crying a lot the past few days, they'd told him, and the more they tried to force her to stop, the worse she became. He couldn't see any new marks on her skin, but it must have been a bad night for her to look like this —he dreaded reading the army's write-up.

But even with the abuse they'd surely dealt out for her conduct, something was wrong. They'd been together for weeks now, and the rapport went both ways: Avery trusted him in the warped and complete fashion he'd engineered, and he bore her terror as a regrettable side effect of that bond. Some days it was stronger than others, and tonight, he felt it in his soul.

Did that mean he still had one?

He pushed away the inane thought and scooted toward her.

"You didn't behave last night, did you?" A sigh, full of the false patience he'd spent a career perfecting. "Where are you hurt?"

"Everywhere." Avery shot him a glance, full of fear, then focused on the wall.

Right. His suspicion grew stronger. "When's the last time you ate?"

The guards were only allowed to provide one meal a day, but it was enough food that she shouldn't look like this. When she didn't answer, he grabbed her by the hand. She tried to jerk from his grip, but he held firm, fingers pressed against her inner wrist—thankful she hadn't discovered he was close enough to kick.

"Don't touch me. Please." She began to sob, tried to pry his fingers off. "I'm fine. I lied to you. I'm sorry I lied to you. I won't do it again, I swear. But they didn't do anything. They didn't hurt me—"

"Hold still." The patience, insincere as it was, began to slip. He checked her injuries at the start of every session—and she never fought him, knowing he'd allow her whatever medical care she needed—so this kind of overreaction was exasperating at best and alarming at worst. He wanted to slam his free hand over her mouth to shut her up but pushed harder on her wrist instead. It was difficult to count her pulse with her fighting his hold and protesting her innocence, but he didn't need to make an accurate count to feel her heart racing—and it wasn't from fear this time, of that he was all but certain.

"When's the last time you drank something?"

Avery's tears slowed; her jaw tightened. For the briefest instant, her eyes met his, and he knew. Those expressive eyes had done her in again.

"Wrong move," he told her, then released her hand and headed outside. The guard on duty took a step back when Chase reappeared in the hall—if he knew what was good for him, he'd have been in another building.

"Why didn't you tell me she hasn't been eating?" Chase asked without preamble. This man standing in front of him was probably the wrong person to ask, but his fury was growing second by second, and he wasn't going to waste time searching for someone better to lay into.

"Sir, your orders were one ration pack every day and a half. That's what she's been getting. It's plenty for someone who's just lying around in a cell."

Chase jabbed his finger toward the closed door. Avery was probably slumped on the floor behind it at this point. "And if you had any sense at all, you'd have realized she's not eating that one ration pack. Would you care to give me an explanation for that?"

"Colonel." Lieutenant Noall appeared, fastening the last two buttons of his shirt, sounding breathless as usual. "Is there a problem, sir?"

"When I told you to limit her rations"—Chase tried not to grind his teeth—"I thought it was understood that she was to eat what you provided. And that if she, for whatever reason, decided to stop eating and drinking, that you would tell me. Immediately. Not three days later when she's on the verge of passing out from dehydration."

"Sir, she's been eating. Until a few days ago, at least—but I only thought—and she's drinking water. Not much, but it seemed . . ."

The incompetence. After all this, was he going to have to pause things to move her to Alcaris? It was the last thing he wanted to do. Moving her would make her ask questions. It would make her think she had some say over her future. No, that couldn't happen.

He held up his hand. "Don't think. Do as you're ordered, no more, no less. From now on you're going to stand in there and watch her until she's eaten a sufficient amount if that's what it takes. Understood?"

"Understood, sir." Noall looked at his feet. "Shall I call the medic in?"

"No. Take her back to her cell and offer her some food and a bit of juice. After you do that, then find Senior Corpsman Mercer and get him over here. Don't touch her otherwise—don't even breathe in her direction—until he or I return and tell you what to do. You've put me behind schedule. Don't let it happen again."

He stormed up from the basement prison, fury building deep in his chest—though he couldn't decide whether it was directed at Avery, the guards, Noall, or himself.

* * *

It took several tries to light the first candle, especially with his hands shaking like they were. Why was Cadena so damp in autumn? Did the residents notice how horrific the weather was, or had they become immune to the gray storm clouds that had swept through the city in the past week? He certainly wasn't immune— he could feel the chill in his bones. Not for the first time, he closed his eyes and visualized Windhaven—the arid hills, warm valleys, and green mountains. And Isobel's smile . . . she'd never understood how much it warmed his soul.

How would he live without her?

Chase pushed the thoughts of her silken skin from his mind. It wasn't the time or the place for that kind of distraction. Mercer would be arriving at the prison soon, and he'd be expecting orders when he did. What to tell him? Simply that he didn't want

Avery to die? That he wasn't going to let her starve herself to death?

Mercer wouldn't question that—Avery was a high-level prisoner, and there was no hiding who she was—but there was so much more to it. He couldn't let anyone, especially anyone in ISC, know of his misgivings of her treatment. The only thing to do—the only thing he could think to do—was to slow down, push on, finish the mission, and hope she came out of the other side unscathed. Not that she had a chance of that. He'd known from the moment they'd met that he'd eventually break her, hadn't he?

"Holy One, tell me what to do with her."

No answer to his whispered plea, as usual. He lit the first three candles like he always did, except this time he paused and scanned the empty temple before lighting Avery's. How would he explain four candles if someone else happened by? One for an invented, illegitimate child? For the empire? For himself? Well, a secret child or selfishness were both better explanations than constantly worrying about and praying for a prisoner he was supposed to feel nothing but animosity for.

But there wasn't anyone here to see his inappropriate plea to the Holy One, not even Linden this time. Chase arranged the candles in a straight line and made his way to the first row of benches. They wouldn't miss him in that dungeon for an hour or so. And for that hour, he'd pretend nothing was wrong.

That Isobel wasn't dying.

That he hadn't built a career on fear and violence.

That his empire hadn't conquered yet another world with sheer brutality.

And that he didn't have a prisoner trying to kill herself.

Not that he blamed her, much. Avery didn't know what was going to happen to her once he was through, and though he hated to admit it, neither did he. What if he couldn't turn her? She seemed past that stage by this point, so it was purely an information-gathering mission now. And what if he couldn't even do that? What if she made sure he couldn't? What if whatever intelligence she possessed was already out of date? She wouldn't succeed in killing herself today, not with Noall's men keeping a close watch and Mercer on his way, but what if she managed it tomorrow? Or next week? What if the emperor changed his mind about letting her live?

Could he live with himself if she died?

A goldcrest chirped in his left ear, reproachfully, like usual, and he jerked upright toward the source of the sound. No, it wasn't a goldcrest—he wasn't on Haedera like he'd imagined for a fraction of a second—but a small red bird that had made its way inside the temple and was squawking at him from one of the high arches above, puffing out its feathers in the cool air. Thin silver lines edged its wings; a gray tuft stood up from its brow. It cocked its head at him and screeched.

Chase glared at it despite its beauty. Didn't this animal understand? Guilting him would do no good, because he couldn't fix any of this. He couldn't change Haedera, he couldn't change the situation, and he couldn't change himself. He certainly couldn't do anything about the fact that he was sitting in yet another holy building, just short of begging and pleading and crying, and yet the Holy One had slammed a door in his face as surely as He'd created the universe. All the miracles in the quadrant, yet he was alone.

"So what do I do now?" he asked the bird. "You decided to come in here and interrupt me, so maybe you have an idea."

Its hidden eyelid flashed up. It wasn't exactly a reply, but at least it wasn't avoiding him like the Windhaven birds. That was something, wasn't it? Was someone finally listening to him?

"I've tried to pray. I'm sure you heard me doing it earlier—I know it sounded like pleading, but it was prayer, truly. And He ignores me, no matter how much I beg, so don't tell me to keep doing that."

Was this what his life had been reduced to? Chatting with a tiny feathered creature that sat there cocking its head back and forth and screeching at him? Official dinners at the imperial palace made for more stimulating conversation. So did listening to Avery ramble about her espionage adventures—stories that had to be made up. At first they'd irritated him, and then they'd made him angry, but now they were all he wanted to hear from her.

Even the one about her running an entire agent chain from Cadena all the way to Molino, one with over a hundred Asrians reporting directly to the Commonwealth. He'd had to listen to her, naturally—there was usually a grain of truth in every story a subject told—but he could tell there was scarcely any in that one. Even so, he'd made his usual meticulous notes and typed them up that night, shaking his head the whole while. He'd wanted to strangle her himself. And now? She could make up whatever tales she wanted as long as she talked again.

Chase looked back at the bird.

"You probably don't want to hear about her, do you? That's fine, because I don't want to talk about her. She's nothing but a job, and a rather messy one at that." He shoved his hands in his pockets and leaned back. "She challenged me, you know. Right to my face. Called me a hypocrite the very night we met. Can you believe that?"

The bird screeched again.

"But suppose, by chance, she's right. So what if I am? Can you blame me? He's hidden His face, abandoned me, and I've still been doing everything I can. He claims His faithfulness is eternal and His love never-ending, but it's all a lie. That kind of betrayal isn't something you can understand, I'm sure."

The bird—a western crested sparrow, from the Asrian ornithology records he'd flipped through on *Defiant*—chirped once more at this accusation and flew off through the open door.

He sighed. "Thanks for that. You're worse than the ones at home." Wrapping his arms around his chest did nothing to protect him from the chill of the temple as he leaned forward and took a deep breath, letting the scent of incense replace the cold. If he couldn't feel the Holy One's presence, at least he could go through the motions of faith and prayer.

Holy One, protect her.

From the soldiers, from His Majesty, from her uncle, from herself.

From—

He stood and stared at the candles, almost burned down to the wick now. Dare he say it? Saying it would be admitting his wrongdoing, and thinking the words, saying them—it would mean Avery was right. That he was a hypocrite, a sinner, lost for all time.

Protect her from me.

After today, Avery was going to hate him more than she already did. Nothing would be pleasant from now on, especially after what Mercer was about to do to her. But whatever happened, no matter how alone in his desires he was, he wouldn't—*couldn't* —let her die.

He put out the fire with his fingers, candle by candle, and headed out the door.

CHAPTER TWENTY-FOUR

It was dark downstairs when he returned, still cold. Chase cornered Mercer in the hallway outside the control room.

"Nothing?" he asked.

Mercer shook his head. "They gave her two meals while you were gone, but she didn't touch either of them."

"Right then." Chase let his chin fall to his chest. What good had prayer done? "I'll meet you in there."

Mercer tossed him a ration bar—ISC policy—and headed in the opposite direction toward the infirmary, whistling.

Chase shook his head. Avery wouldn't be whistling in about five minutes. In fact, the effect of the jubilant tune in this dungeon was downright ghastly. Didn't Mercer realize that?

Did he care?

"Hey, Doc?" he called down the hall.

Mercer turned. "Mmm?"

"Go easy on her this time, all right?"

Mercer nodded politely and resumed his whistling. Chase grabbed a few guards on his way to Avery's cell. She wasn't quite sleeping, but she wasn't quite awake, either. Weak, that's what she was.

He held out the ration bar. "Last chance. Are you going to eat it?"

"I'm not hungry." She wrinkled her nose, then put her head back down and closed her eyes.

Sure. Chase motioned to the guards, then stood back as they attached the leg shackles, then the chain around her waist and through the handcuffs. Avery fought them this time, yes, but barely. It seemed to be nothing more than a ritual at this point. *See? I haven't given up yet.* Or maybe it was his presence, quiet and unmoving by the door, holding the rejected bar. Maybe she was too weak to struggle. She didn't even flinch when he brought the hated blindfold from his pocket, and that was more unsettling than anything else.

Like he'd expected, she made a tired pretense at cooperation until they entered the small medical room, though her stilted walk wasn't only from the restraints. But she had to have known things were different when they'd first removed her from her cell—she was never shackled like this, and he wasn't given to delivering her to the interrogation room himself.

Luck was on his side, though. It wasn't until he removed the blindfold, and her wide eyes landed on Mercer, sitting next to the gurney and his table of equipment, that she realized what they intended to do. There was fear there then, fear like he'd only seen once before—the day he'd first appeared in her cell wearing his ISC uniform.

And when her body caught up, she tried to bolt.

He should have left the blindfold on until she'd been secured—that was a mistake he wouldn't make again. Chase seized her arm even tighter, and Avery whimpered as he and the soldier on her right pushed her toward the bed. He'd never have called her frail before, but now?

Starvation does have its benefits.

The straps went across her chest, waist, and shins easier than he'd anticipated, though she begged and pleaded and screamed and tried to twist her way free. Chase put his palm over her eyebrows and kept her from moving as they placed a strap across her forehead.

"You brought this on yourself. Fighting is a waste of time." The ration bar was heavy in his pocket. "Now, we can do this one of two ways—either you hold still and let the medic do his job, or you keep fighting. One way will be uncomfortable, and the other will hurt like you won't believe. Your choice."

That sounded too cruel, even for him, and Avery had never responded well to cruel. But he had no doubt which choice she'd pick. *Hurt like you won't believe* was a bit of an exaggeration perhaps, but he'd threaten all sorts of things if it kept her from doing something stupid. She'd never win—and couldn't be allowed to come close.

She stared at him for a few seconds, motionless, and he began to exhale. Of course she'd seen reason. She wasn't struggling anymore, just running her tongue over those cracked lips, and that meant—

He was the one to flinch that time.

That meant she'd been working up enough saliva to spit at him. Or at least she'd been trying—she was much too dehydrated for him to feel anything. Still, it was a measure of defiance he hadn't anticipated.

"Do that again and I'll tape your mouth closed myself," he said.

She pressed her lips together, so he released her forehead and turned to the medic. Mercer held up the equipment and raised his eyebrows. Chase nodded, then motioned for two of the soldiers with his fingers. Not for the first time, he cursed the fact that this hastily arranged clinic room didn't have the normal restraint fields that would have been universal in an ISC detention facility. Avery was going to panic when they held her head down, and for some reason, he didn't want to be the one doing it.

And struggle she did, as soon as the first soldier touched her shoulder. Maybe her hunger strike hadn't taken as much of her energy as he'd assumed, because she fought with such stamina that Chase was terrified they'd hurt her. When she twisted her neck awkwardly to the side for the third time in twenty seconds, he took a step back.

"Hold up a second."

Mercer froze at his order as Avery gagged, but didn't let go of the tube. "They need to hold her still," he said, almost a growl. "Or I'm going to knock her out."

Chase motioned the guards away and leaned in toward Avery. "If you don't stop resisting, he's going to sedate you, and I know you'd rather be awake. Your decision."

Just enough of a choice that she believed she had some control over the situation . . .

"I don't want this." The words were a soft whisper. She didn't move her gaze from the ceiling. "It hurts."

"I don't care what you want. It only hurts because you won't stop fighting," he replied. And fine, also because Mercer was shoving a tube down her nose, but this wasn't the time for sympathy.

Not a lot of it, at least. He pulled out the ration bar and held it over her head so she could see. She could have one last chance if she wanted it—he could be reasonable when talked into it. And somehow, without a word, she'd done just that.

Avery shook her head as furiously as the restraints allowed.

How else did she expect this to end? He steeled himself against the scratching sensation in the back of his own mouth, and, against his better judgment, pushed a stray curl from her eyes. Avery recoiled at his touch, distracted from the tube halfway down her throat, and Mercer pounced. She flailed when she realized he'd moved again, then her limited movements came to a sudden stop—when Mercer exhaled, she knew she'd lost.

Chase sighed and grabbed the nearest chair as Mercer taped the tube to her cheek.

"There," he said. "The worst part's over. And it's not so bad now, is it?" Avery didn't answer, only closed her swollen and damp eyes and tipped her head back toward the ceiling. He pointed at one of the soldiers. "You, outside, at the door. The rest of you—back to whatever you were doing."

They complied without any argument, and for that, he was grateful. There wasn't any point in humiliating her more than necessary. This was medical treatment, not punishment. Wasn't it? If he kept insisting this to himself, it might become the truth.

"Water now?" he asked.

Without looking at him, Avery twitched, which he took for a yes. Mercer put a small cup to her mouth, and she took a few sips, only to choke it right back out.

"That happens sometimes. The gagging." Chase tilted the gurney upright a bit more, then wiped the liquid from her chin with some gauze. She was going to hate what came next, more than being held down, but they should have started with it to begin with. He nodded at Mercer. "Get some fluids in her before you start?"

Avery's gaze flickered to the IV kit Mercer picked up, so Chase gently angled her face toward him.

"No—no drugs." She squeezed her eyes shut, but it was obvious she was crying.

"Who said anything about drugs?" Chase asked. There went any ideas of giving her pain relief. The last thing he needed was for her to tell someone, even one of those soldiers, that he'd drugged her. There couldn't be any rumors about him giving her lacrozenate. "He's only going to rehydrate you." He pulled the strap from her forehead and brushed the hair out of her face—it wasn't much freedom, but it was all she was getting. She'd already learned to be grateful for small kindnesses, and she'd be grateful for this, too. "Don't look at him. I know it's uncomfortable, but he's not going to hurt you if he can help it. You'll feel better after this, right? Relax."

A laughable suggestion. Avery didn't want to feel better, and she couldn't relax, not here. She hated and feared him, especially now. They were doing the exact opposite of what she wanted, in the most inhumane and humiliating way possible.

Mercer must have thought it was an asinine comment, for he glanced over with an inscrutable look on his face.

"It's under control, sir."

Right. *Under control.* What Mercer meant was, *Why the hell are you in here, sir? You should have left with the guards. This isn't procedure.*

And it wasn't. Avery wasn't going anywhere, so it wasn't as though he was needed to hold her down any longer, and this wasn't an interrogation session—though he always had the option of making it one. It was the right choice, too, the one he should make. She was too distracted by the pain to focus on resistance now.

He brushed Mercer off with a wave, along with his own misgivings.

"Here's an idea," he said to Avery. "Until he's finished, it's your turn to ask the questions. You ask me anything, and I'll answer as best I can."

She cringed as the needle entered the inside of her elbow, then opened those seafoam eyes and fixed them on his—not Mercer's ministrations this time, thank the stars. Not surprising. Likely she'd rather pretend the medic didn't exist.

"Anything?" she asked, her voice raspy.

"Anything."

Her forehead creased, like she suspected it might be a trick, and her mouth opened and shut a few times before she spoke.

"You seemed kind when we first met. Even though you're Haederan. What kind of man—why do you do these things?"

She pressed her lips closed and looked away, like she was terrified she'd offended him.

"It's a job," he lied. "It's nothing personal."

Or maybe it wasn't so much of a lie. It'd been a job when he started, but now? He couldn't disentangle Gareth the man from Colonel Chase the ISC officer from His Imperial Highness, the emperor's least favored son-in-law. All of it was his life now, and he hated himself for it. He grabbed a clean piece of gauze and wiped the blood from her nose. Mercer was going to kill him for interfering, but the blood was making him sick.

"Then everything you said, everything you did in front of me in the temple. Was it a lie?"

At least she'd stopped stuttering, though he suspected that was temporary. And him? It was hard to speak for a moment, for fear he might begin. Instead, he watched Mercer open the IV and start the feeding process.

"No lie," he told her, after a long breath. *Holy One, why is this so difficult?* Why did this Asrian woman make him feel so ashamed about something he'd been doing for the past however-many years with barely a speck of guilt? "My mother—she made sure I learned. She taught me since before I could walk."

At least she'd tried, before sending him off to the imperial court to be raised by her distant relatives. Her decision had never made much sense. His mother had called the current Haederan religious practices a perversion—so why had she sent him to that *alig*'s lair in Rebet? On one of his last days at home, in a fit of passion, she'd even thrown the same words at him that Avery had spoken so harshly the night they'd met—*His Majesty uses our faith for control, and everyone's too afraid of him to do a thing about it. Don't forget that. Control isn't what this is about.*

Whether she'd ever spoken of her misgivings to his father or not, Chase had never been able to decide. Probably not. She'd died before he'd risen in the ISC ranks, and for that, he would always be grateful. The fear of her own son's eventual betrayal would have killed her in a more painful way than the accident ever could have.

Avery eyed him with more wariness than he thought possible. Or maybe it was disbelief. He couldn't blame her for that.

"But that doesn't mean you—" She gagged again.

"Sorry." Mercer shrugged, unrepentance personified.

Chase shot him a sharp look as he wiped her chin. *Slow and easy there, Doc.*

"That doesn't mean you believe it," she said quietly, slowly.

He sat back, clutching the damp gauze. "What can I say to prove I do?"

"Nothing. There's nothing. You can't prove it. Nothing you can ever say will make me believe you're telling the truth." She closed her eyes, then opened them. "Do you hate Asria?"

Did he—what a strange question. But then, she was likely the undeclared queen of Asria, whether he and the emperor wanted to admit it or not. Naturally she'd be curious about his thoughts, no matter how miserable she was right now.

It was just that hating an occupied planet, or conquered person, or even a prisoner . . . it wasn't something he'd ever considered. Asria was a job. A war. One more planet in the empire's unceasing quest for power.

And it wasn't as though they were treating their newest conquest poorly—Asria was a protectorate of all things, thanks to Avery's uncle. The Imperial Haederan Navy remained in orbit, partially to quash any Asrian rebellions, partially to keep the Commonwealth away, but also to defend the system against outside threats. There hadn't been any threats from outside the quadrant in three hundred years, of course, but there was always the chance. And if it happened, Haedera would defend Asria.

Because Asria was part of the Second Haederan Empire now.

"I don't hate Asria," he said. "This is a job, nothing more, nothing less. And there's nothing to hate about it." Her forehead creased, and he added, "It's cooler in Cadena than I'm used to. And it rains a lot. And I'm homesick. There are lots of things I miss about Haedera. But I don't hate Asria, no."

"This is . . ." Her breath became rapid, like the very act of swallowing hurt. "This is a dry year."

The claim was quiet, hesitant. He gave her a wisp of a smile. "Then I don't think I'm looking forward to a normal one."

"You—" Her lips twitched. "You're going to freeze when winter comes. All of you are."

At first, he thought she was making an ill-timed joke, but no, every Haederan freezing to death in the first snow was probably her most fervent wish. Chase stifled a laugh. He'd survived worse than some snow.

No, Lieutenant, I'm going to be alive and on-planet for much longer than I care to stay.

"We might." Against his will, a bit of respect flooded him. Maybe she wasn't as weak as he'd assumed. Broken and terrified, she wanted him dead and wasn't afraid to let him know. He glanced over at Mercer to check his progress. "Almost done. Time for one more."

Her lips moved silently a few times.

"If you don't hate Asria . . . Do you hate me?" The question was barely a whisper.

He drew back a bit. "Why would I hate you?"

She looked frantically at Mercer, then back. "I'm Asrian. And I—"

I spied for the Commonwealth. I passed them classified information about this and that. I committed treason, I lied to you, I fought you, I defied you, I resisted you . . .

If only confessions were that straightforward.

"I don't hate you for that," he said, shaking his head. "I don't hate you for anything."

Hating you would make this easy.

"All done." Mercer sat back, uninterested in their entire conversation. What kind of things did ISC medics hear during interrogations over the course of a career? Nothing they wanted to remember, that was certain, and forgetting the chats they heard was safer for everyone involved.

"Can I—" Avery seemed to be dragging up what was left of her courage from deep inside. "Can I go back now?"

"No." After what had been an almost amicable conversation, the word fell flat, heavy.

"Two hours," Mercer added, reinforcing it with his index and middle fingers.

"You heard him. I'm not letting you have privacy so you can throw it all back up." Merciless, yes, but he needed to stop himself from caring. "And you need more fluids before I allow you back in your cell. Consider it a chance for a few straight hours of good rest. Really, you ought to be more appreciative."

Her cheeks grew red at his admonishment, but she didn't cry as Mercer removed the tube—just pressed herself into the bed and feigned sleep. Chase turned away and flipped on his comm. Another six messages from Perrin. Nothing new there. One more from Rhys, marked urgent. He resisted the urge to read it—if Rhys said it was urgent, there was no doubt it was, and he couldn't be running to the ISC building now. Self-control was a dreary thing. Rhys could wait.

* * *

Mercer shook him awake two hours later, and Chase raised his head from the spare med table. Three army guards stood in the doorway; Avery lay unblinking on the bed, her gaze focused on them. She didn't look happy, but she didn't look half dead anymore, either. Her face was swollen, her nose was bloody, and her dark hair was knotted, but there was color in her cheeks, and her eyes weren't sunken like they'd been at the start of their last session. No, now they were defiant. Through his fatigue, a little relief seeped in. Behind schedule or not, he couldn't allow permanent harm to come to her, and her condition was a definite improvement over twelve hours ago.

He yawned and stumbled to his feet. He must have been more tired than he'd realized, for he helped the guards escort Avery back to her cell only somewhat aware of what his legs were doing. Even with his hold on her arm, she didn't stop trembling until the guards removed the shackles, then she collapsed in a heap right there on the ground in front of him. Those long, dark eyelashes fluttered closed, but there was no way she was sleeping. Probably just hoping they'd all go away.

Instead of doing what she hoped, he crouched in front of her and seized her by the chin, eliciting a cry of pain as he pulled her head from the cold concrete.

"I don't care if you hate the food," he said quietly, wide awake at last. "I don't care if you're doing this to anger the guards. I don't care if you're doing this because eating is the one thing you can control. And I certainly don't care if you're trying to escape by starving yourself to death."

Her entire body, slack and exhausted before, tensed at that.

Strange.

He'd meant it as an offhand remark, an almost-meaningless threat, but . . .

He tossed the exhaustion away. Avery had just told him something without saying a word. She didn't even know she'd said anything, but this woman, who was more afraid of death than anyone he'd ever met, was willing to kill herself by the only means available—an unpleasant and protracted means. There was something important he was missing here, something critical, and if he didn't figure it out—

Realization struck like a starship entering hyperspace, and it almost made him shake.

He'd been wrong about her. He'd been wrong about this being a waste of time, wrong about her being nothing more than a bitter aristocrat, wrong about her not giving the Commonwealth any valuable information, and wrong about her not knowing anything.

She has a secret so important she's willing to die to keep it.

He gave her the slightest hint of a smile, enough to cover his surprise.

"I don't care why you did it. But you understand that I can't let it happen. Starting now, if you skip any meal they provide, I'll take you back to that room, and next time I won't order the medic to keep you comfortable. In fact, I'll have him do everything he can to make it as excruciating as possible." He tightened his fingers enough to leave bruises. "Understand?"

Avery didn't answer out loud, but the fear in her eyes did it for her.

"Good." He released her chin and tossed a Defense Forces ration bar he'd found in the infirmary to the floor beside her. The familiar food was a kindness she didn't deserve. "Six hours. It better be gone in six hours."

She wasn't going to eat it. He knew that. By the looks the guards gave him as he left, they knew that, too. He and Mercer were going to have to repeat the entire horrific process the next day, and he wouldn't be able to stand it that time. Perhaps Mercer could handle things on his own tomorrow.

But when he checked the live feed in Avery's cell two hours later—after his own dinner and a quick nap—she was sleeping, the empty wrapper folded neatly next to her head. A sliver of capitulation at last.

CHAPTER TWENTY-FIVE

DAYS HAD BECOME DULL—TOO MONOTONOUS, ESPECIALLY FOR someone who'd never thrived on routine. Tea upon waking, breakfast, a light lunch, dinner, a shower or a long bath, all broken up by Katryn's watch out the window. Asrians filled the streets until they didn't, then green uniforms slowly faded away until it was silent and tranquil below her.

Maybe this was worse than a prison. She could see free people going about their lives—a little altered, perhaps, but most on this occupied planet seemed to be making their livings undisturbed by their conquerors. Was anyone as miserable as she was? Was anyone else as trapped? She was surrounded by luxury, yes, but she hadn't seen Rhys and she hadn't seen the friendly major . . . come to think of it, she hadn't seen the same guard more than twice for the past week. Did they think she'd try to become too friendly with them? Coerce them into sending a message or helping her escape?

With a sigh, she stood from the chair where she'd spent too many evenings and stretched. The room was wearing on her, the same view, the same lamp, the same sheets. If she dared open the door, it would be the same carpet and the same chair sitting across the hall. She wanted to scream, but that would invite her guard in, and she didn't want that. Besides, after sitting in one position for so long, sleep sounded more appealing than screaming. It had for days now.

If only Rhys would appear, even for a brief talk—though she'd never turn down more. It was hard to admit she missed conversation with him just as much as she missed his body. Which made her more of a traitor? Wanting his body or wanting his mind?

Raised voices from outside her door diverted her attention from the philosophical question. *Something new?* Something interesting, at least. She'd take whatever came.

"You're needed downstairs," an unfamiliar man was saying.

"Not now." The guard who'd brought her dinner sounded bored. Annoyed, maybe. "Shift change in an hour—I'll do it then."

"He wanted to see you in the next five minutes. Don't make me tell him you said no." Concern tinged the new voice.

Something clanked, like the chair had just hit the wall. Katryn pushed her ear against the door, cursing the Haederans for disconnecting the viewscreen that would have given her a view down the corridors. Had he left? Really and truly left? Yes, there were heavy booted footsteps on the carpet, but she couldn't decide if it was one or two sets.

This could be her chance.

She cracked open the door a hair, surprised it moved from the inside—though it was a hotel, after all. Maybe they hadn't been able to reprogram the lock. Should she call out to them? Pretend to be needing something? Or simply slip toward the emergency stairs while her guard was away? If only she had shoes—it'd been chilly enough when the major had taken her to the courtyard, and walking barefoot around what was allegedly a cosmopolitan city would draw attention she didn't need.

On the other hand, barefoot out there was better than barefoot in here.

The emergency stairs it was. She made it to the door, her heart pounding so hard they must have been able to hear it downstairs.

Her hand hovered over the keypad. Open it—or would an alarm sound? Would it be silent, or would she hear it?

Katryn fought the sudden desire to dash back to her room and hide under the covers. Such a silly, childish thought. Wasn't she beyond those kinds of fears? After Iythea, she should be. Linden and his men needed her alive, after all. What else could they possibly do to her until they found Xan?

Buoyed by that strange hope, she jabbed at the open button. The door slid open, so silently she might have imagined it, and before she knew it, she was two floors down, though her stomach was still up in the hall outside her door.

Eight to go.

Did she hear footsteps? Or was it just her heart? Her brain heard them, but her brain also liked to lie when it was under stress, and escaping from an ISC stronghold was anxiety like she'd never felt—even after being forced to work in the mines, even after watching Kaz disappear on that supply ship. Because this was a bad idea. If they caught her, she could say goodbye to the comfortable hotel room and that deep tub and luxurious bath oils. Was it worth it? She didn't have a plan besides trying to find Xan, and she couldn't even be certain he was in Cadena. But yes— she had to warn him. Or at the very least make sure the Haederans couldn't use her as leverage against him.

Six to go.

She didn't know where to start looking for him. He had to be hiding out somewhere, but where? If he was truly Special Operations Forces like Rhys had said, he'd know how not to be found— unlike her. She could stumble unknowingly into the very people who'd be looking for them both. Or worse, perhaps—the army. Did they still want her for the supply ship incident? Would they bother notifying ISC if she was arrested? Or would they simply shoot her on sight? Colonel Ellicot had seemed angry enough at Rhys to ignore anything he said, regardless of who Rhys claimed answered to who.

Two to go.

An even more horrifying thought struck her as she reached the ground floor. What if the exit opened to another courtyard? What if she'd made it this far only to trap herself? No, it was an emergency exit. It would open onto a street, or an alley at the very least, and if it was open and unguarded—she'd be free.

Please be open.

Her legs were on fire. Strange for a mad dash down the stairs. Was the feeling fear more than exertion? It had to be, but at the same time, her breath was coming in painful spurts. Katryn leaned against the door, trying to force oxygen back into her lungs, but it was no use. How long before her guard came back and discovered she was missing? It shouldn't be for a while—he'd already delivered dinner, after all—but could she risk it? Her whole being wanted to climb the stairs back to her prison. The desired compliance felt odd and unfamiliar, but then again, so did the fear.

Going back wasn't an option, though. She was almost free, and almost free wasn't something she'd ever take for granted. With one more deep breath, she pushed open the door and took a step outside. No alarm sounded, so she closed the door as softly as she could.

The alley was silent, the stone cold and damp. Curfew hadn't yet descended on the city, though the crowds were thinner than twenty minutes ago, even on the main street. Katryn picked her way south, thankful no one had cast a second glance at her bare feet and lack of overcoat. But where to find Xan? More importantly, where would she hide?

Cadena wasn't the biggest city on Asria, that much she knew. Still, it wasn't a small town—it wasn't even a small city. And if Xan didn't want to be found, she wouldn't be able to find him. Especially barefoot, already half frozen, with no credit, and, soon, with dozens of ISC officers looking for her.

Yes, this had been a bad idea.

Katryn sank to a bench around the corner from the hotel and considered her options. Shoes would have to come first, if only so she wouldn't be miserable until Rhys and his people found her. A restaurant, perhaps. Asrians dined shoeless in the public restaurants in major cities, that much she knew. She could duck inside and steal a pair from the pile by the door, then be on her way before anyone noticed.

And then what?

Find Xan.

He was no doubt working on Asria under an assumed name, so it wasn't as though she could visit every flat in town and ask the neighbors about him, even if she could find every residential area. Would he be desperate enough for a taste of his old life that he'd break whatever new routine he'd set up? He'd need to buy food, and Xan never could go without his cup of Zarcronian coffee.

Could the Haederans possibly know about his predilection for the kind of spiced coffee that was likely scarce on Asria? There couldn't be that many Zarcronian coffee bistros in Cadena, so it would be easy enough to search every one—of course, the Haederans would have the same idea, but it was worth the risk of them seeing her. Desperation and stupidity were not the same thing, and if someone considered them such, they'd never been in a hopeless situation like hers.

Yes. Her plan might be a colossal failure, but at least it was a plan. She'd find a warm place to spend the night, then start looking for Xan right after the curfew ended tomorrow morning.

But first, it was time to find some shoes.

* * *

The morning dawned cool and bright. Katryn shook off the chill as she rounded the corner toward the first Zarcronian restaurant she'd seen the night before. There were Haederan soldiers on the street, yes, but they didn't give her a second glance. Maybe she wasn't as wanted by the Imperial Haederan Army as she'd feared. They certainly hadn't hassled her in the park where she'd spent the night huddled under a bush, her head resting on her used suede shoes. She'd been more exhausted than she'd expected, and sleep had come easily. Too easily—perhaps it was the shock of escaping.

And ISC? None of those uniforms had crossed her path—though they could very well be in civilian clothes. Rhys had always been in uniform while acting officially, and so had everyone else in the hotel, but from what he'd told her about his organization, it was a possibility. The uniforms instilled fear, yes, but so did never knowing if you were being watched. But there was no point in worrying about something she couldn't change or see. She'd know when and if they grabbed her.

It won't be worth the consequences, I promise you that.

Hot fear flashed through her at the idea. Rhys's words wouldn't leave her mind—wouldn't leave her heart. Had he meant it? Or had it been an idle threat? What would they do if she was caught?

She kept walking anyway, focused on the café. *Like home.* She hadn't realized how much she missed it—she'd dreamed of it on Iythea, of course, but now it was obvious those dreams had been a way to escape her horrific situation. They hadn't meant she'd missed home, yet here she was on this strange Cadena street, her eyes tearing up at the smallest reminder. Maybe leaving her home planet permanently had been a bad idea, but space had called to her. Strange planets and more interesting research than Zarcron could offer awaited her. Xan had understood even if Mimi and Aba hadn't.

No matter how much her mouth watered over the spiced coffee inside—a drink she wasn't nearly as tied to as Xan—there was no way she could go inside without any credit. She passed by the large window three times instead, searching the customers inside in what she hoped was an unobtrusive manner. Xan—and Kaz!—would no doubt sneer at her technique, but it was the best she could do.

But each time she wandered by, her stomach protesting at the temptation of food more loudly than before, there was no Xan. Had he changed his appearance? Quite possibly . . . but more than likely, he just wasn't there. She'd have to keep looking, keep walking, keep hiding. It was an exhausting thought—and now she'd need to find something to eat and drink as well.

What if the snow came early? Was it too early for snow in Cadena? Maybe not, and she'd been lucky enough to avoid it so far. The park wouldn't be nearly as comfortable if she was wet and shivering.

Katryn turned south and paused in the sun that illuminated the side street. A bit of warmth, finally. It wasn't going to burn her face at this morning angle, but somehow, she wouldn't have minded if it did. Strange how something so simple could bring about such a change in mind-set—for now she knew she'd find Xan, no matter how long it took, and they'd escape this planet and get him out of all the trouble he'd gotten them both into—

A hand slammed against her mouth; strong arms pinned her against the wall. Her stomach threatened to leap into her throat. For the briefest of moments, she considered struggling, but what would be the point?

It won't be worth the consequences.

If running would get her punished, yes, fighting would only make things worse. She'd go back with them wherever they wanted her, placidly and without resisting. That would earn her some favor, at least, and she could explain the rest to Rhys. Rhys wouldn't harm her.

"Katryn," a familiar voice growled.

Not Asrian.

Not Haederan.

Not one of the myriad accents of the scientists she'd known on Iythea.

It was Zarcronian.

CHAPTER TWENTY-SIX

"Xan?" She blinked as her attacker released her, but his familiar face, mild yet anxious, didn't shift into something sinister like her gut insisted it would. "Xan! What the—"

"Shut up." Xan pushed her down the alley at a far faster pace than was comfortable. "Do you want everyone within six blocks to hear you?"

That was the last thing she wanted. But he owed her so many answers. Even if the Haederans were looking for her—which they doubtless were by now—he owed her answers, and quickly. She stumbled along next to him, shivering in the rapidly chilling air as the early morning sun disappeared behind another building.

"Where are we going?"

He huffed, a sound she knew all too well. Being a traitor didn't change everything, it appeared—this was her fourteen-year-old brother all over again.

"I don't know, Kat. You've kind of put me in a bad position. What are you doing here?"

"I've put *you* in a bad position? What am *I* doing here? Are you kidding me?" He was delusional. Xan was silent in return, so she added, "Don't you have—aren't you staying somewhere?"

Hiding somewhere, she thought, while he pretended to be loyal to the Commonwealth?

He appeared beside her and held up his hand to stop her, his eyes strangely feverish and bright. "How much do you know?"

It was all she could do to not slap him. Katryn shivered, then the tears started. She took a step back to put him out of striking distance.

"I know all of it! I know you're not a Commonwealth Navy finance officer, and I know you've never been out with the fleet, and I know—" Sacred winds, she wanted nothing more than to punch him straight in the nose until he fell backward onto the rough stone. But if he was a—well, she was going to call him a spy, even if Linden said the word was inappropriate—he could deflect any move she made, couldn't he? "And I know you betrayed us. I know you betrayed the Commonwealth. He told me everything."

Xan swore under his breath.

"Then it's true? You did all those things?" Her heart sank. She hadn't realized how much she'd hoped Rhys had been lying.

"Rhys Linden told you that?"

As muddled as her brain was, it may as well have been a confession. If Xan was truly a Commonwealth Navy finance officer, he wouldn't know Rhys. He wouldn't be acquainted with any Haederan, much less an ISC officer. He'd know a bunch of . . . accountants.

"Yes," she said, trying to forget the memory of Rhys's body beneath hers. "Rhys Linden told me that. Right after he kidnapped me from Iythea where I'd been slaving away in a mine for months, all for your new friends! Right after someone I cared about—who was loyal—died for us. Right after the Haederans threatened to execute me. How could you?"

Planetsider or not, he loosed a string of curses that would have been appropriate for a navy officer.

"Don't stand there and curse at me!" Her scream echoed against the alley walls.

"I don't know what to say to you right now." Xan's face went blank. "Sacred winds above, Kat. Let's find somewhere to talk."

* * *

Xan certainly knew the shadier neighborhoods of Cadena. But shady in Cadena meant plenty of the single-cell box hotels like the one they were standing in front of now, so maybe that wasn't such a bad thing. He pressed a credit chip against the machine by the sliding door—was it Asrian or Haederan currency?

Whatever it was, it was valid, for the door slid immediately open, and against her better judgment, Katryn stepped inside. It was warm at least, paneled in light wood that couldn't have been local—more likely manufactured in a cheap workshop somewhere. Two stacked bunks took up most of the space, only allowing for a small tea kettle and coffee maker against the far end two or three paces away. He slid the door shut behind them and latched it as she perched on the lower bunk.

"Do you want some coffee first?" he asked, jabbing his finger at the auto-brewer. "Or tea?"

"I want answers."

He glanced toward the coffee, almost disappointed. "I'm afraid I don't have the answers you want."

Katryn clenched her fists. What a waste of time this had been. What a waste of dreams. He was supposed to have fixed all this. Immediately. Steal a ship and get them off-world or something.

"Then tell me what you can."

Xan glanced around, probably looking for something stronger than coffee before he admitted to whatever heinous things he'd done, then stuck two cups under the brewer anyway.

"Fine. Kat, I was never a Commonwealth Navy finance officer. Ever. Not from the beginning, not even when I first graduated from the academy. But you have to understand, I couldn't—"

She snorted. "I figured as much. And that's not the lie I'm

upset about." Hadn't Kaz lived the same lie, after all? She couldn't blame either of them for that.

"Yeah. But—" He handed over her steaming cup and collapsed on the narrow bed next to her, head in his hands. "We had a mission go wrong a few years ago. I can't say when or where, but it went really wrong, and I ended up on—on Haedera. They did things to me. Things I don't remember and things I would rather forget. And I didn't fall for any of it. I never broke. But then one morning—

His voice broke.

"One morning they dragged me back to the interrogation room and showed me this video. The things they'd recorded me saying—important details, things no one should have heard. About our capabilities, our agents, their locations . . . Kat, I don't understand, even now. I would never—"

"But you did."

He looked up, honest confusion sprawled across his face. "I told you I don't remember. I can't recall saying any of it. But it was too late. They told me those recordings were already on their way to Ventana, that I'd betrayed the Commonwealth, that I'd be imprisoned for the rest of my life . . . if they let me live at all. Unless—they said they'd call the ship back if I agreed to work for them."

"And you agreed?" There it was, that same strange desire to punch him in the face. Or maybe toss her coffee all over him. "Prison would have been more honorable!"

"Easy for you to say." He looked up and snapped at her—easygoing Xan, who'd always been the mellow one. "Once I got here, and no, I can't tell you why, I thought I could disappear. Then the invasion . . . Kat, I had disappeared, but then Linden started sending me messages saying he was on Asria too, and that you were with him, and that he'd kill you unless I surfaced."

Rhys wouldn't have—would he?

"And did you? Surface?" Likely not, since she hadn't seen a glimpse of Rhys since the night he'd said goodbye.

Xan shook his head. "He doesn't know I've received his messages, and he won't act on anything less than certainty. I don't like flattering him, but I'll give him that. As long as I pretend I don't know ISC is operating in Cadena, as long as I keep doing the other thing they expect me to do, you're safe."

"What's the other thing?"

"I really can't say." He shrugged. "A mission. A classified one. For the Commonwealth."

Oh, so he'd be closemouthed now. Katryn still wanted to throttle him, but the broken look on his face . . . she reached her free hand out instead. Xan refused to take it.

"I'm sorry," she said. "This was three years ago, wasn't it? When your messages stopped coming for a few months?"

It hadn't been that much of a question at the time—she'd thought he was in deep space, after all. Even so, the navy realized how much messages from home meant to people, and communication delays were generally caused by the long interstellar distances, not any kind of navy policy on family separation.

Except three years ago. When Xan had finally reappeared after months of no communication, he'd blamed a comm blackout on his ship. The Commonwealth had even sent an official communiqué apologizing for the length of the blackout. It'd all made sense, and she hadn't questioned the explanation—until now.

He nodded. "The Commonwealth—in case of detention, they're supposed to keep sending them, to make it seem like nothing's wrong. We write a series of them when we swear in, enough to last a year, and update them every so often. Someone screwed up there." He took a long, shuddering breath, and scooted next to her. "I didn't want anyone to worry. I'm sorry you did."

The change in proximity felt like manipulation, but when she searched through her memories, this was Xan. She'd held him one night for hours when was eight and he five, all because he'd cried over moving once more as Aba chased his dream as a diving instructor to another Zarcronian port. How could someone so sensitive, so intelligent, be a traitor? Or was that life? Bad luck, bad decisions, bad outcomes? Was it bad luck they'd loaded those cylinders on Nash's ship? Or that she'd chosen Iythea over a half-dozen other planets that were still free?

And she had missed Xan, especially knowing now how close he'd come to death. Especially with Iythea. Mimi and Aba—well, it'd been years since she'd seen them during her final year of school, but Xan—he was different. He'd always been there, even when he was halfway across the quadrant. Even though he'd lied about the direction his life had taken after the academy.

And the Haederan thing—yes, forgiveness would have to come so much later, probably after she convinced him to turn himself in to the Commonwealth, but . . . right now, she would enjoy his presence. Because he'd said everything would work out, hadn't he? He could do everything and anything to make the situation right.

She stuck her nose in the cup of coffee he'd brewed and faked a smile over the rim. It was a start, at least.

"I guess neither one of us have had a great few years."

Xan hesitated, then grabbed his own cup and wound his hands around it. "How bad was it on Iythea?"

Her smile, however forced, faded. Why did he have to ask about Iythea? He should know the answer to that.

"It was—it was bad." Her eyes flickered to the coffee, then back to him. She needed to see the pain and guilt in his eyes— emotions that would mean he regretted what he'd done. "I could handle the hard work, but not the other things. The Haederan Army executed people. People I knew. Right in front of us as a warning. Sometimes they shot them. Sometimes they just shoved them outside and . . ." Well, Xan would know what happened if someone left the habitats on Iythea. It was a slow, painful death.

And he's working for them.

Whether he'd been coerced or not, the thought made her heart ache again.

"And then—I got involved in something. Something I shouldn't have, and the Haederans—I think they would have killed me in the next few hours if—" She'd almost called him Rhys. "If Captain Linden hadn't shown up. And he threatened and blustered and said the same thing would happen if I didn't cooperate. If you didn't cooperate."

"Has he hurt you?" Xan's face had turned blank. She hated the expression, no doubt trained into him by the Commonwealth.

"No—no." He'd frightened her a few times, but did that matter now? Especially after she'd slept with him? What would Xan say to that? Rhys wouldn't mention it to Xan, would he? "He just threatened a lot. It wasn't so bad on the way here."

In fact, several weeks of it were sheer bliss.

Xan blew out a breath. "Good. That's good."

"And now?" She was afraid to ask the question. "Can you help me? Is Zarcron safe? Can I get back there?" It hadn't occurred to her before that the long-range interstellar routes might be controlled by Haedera as well.

"Maybe. I don't know. I mean, yes, I'll help you. But I need time, and I need to hide you somewhere while I figure this out." He took a sip of what had to be lukewarm coffee by now, then tilted his head. "How did you manage to get away, anyway? I never marked my big sister for a sneak."

"They left the room unguarded." Katryn shrugged. "And the emergency stairs weren't alarmed, so—"

His coffee hit the fake wood floor with a splash. Xan flung himself toward her, and she wasn't fast enough to avoid his grip. Her cup went flying, matching the stain his coffee had left on the floor. His hands were all over her, searching, prying.

"Xan! What—"

"Where is it?" Voice raised, he ran a hand under her shirt.

"Where is what?" She managed to free herself, managed to jump off the bed and against the door. With shaking hands, she tried to right her shirt, pulled at an awkward angle across her shoulders.

"The tracking chip. They let you go, Kat, just like they let me go."

CHAPTER TWENTY-SEVEN

Her fingertips brushed the small lump on her upper arm before she leaned forward and vomited the coffee all over the floor. Some idle thought told her she should drag the sheet off the bunk and clean it before she did anything else, but she could only stare at the mess.

"Xan." She retched one more time before he jerked her upright. "I forgot—I—"

"You forgot you had an ISC chip in you?"

His fingers dug into her skin, prying around the chip, surveying and clawing. For the first time, the mild stare she'd become so used to became incredulous.

"I—I wanted out of that hotel. And I've been so tired—I can't think clearly. I can barely move. I think they must be drugging my food or something." The accusation flew out before she realized what she was saying. That had to be it. Why else would she be beyond exhausted? "I never thought—"

Xan let go of her to pull a smooth-edged knife from his pocket, and her stomach revolted. How could she have been so foolish? Because she'd wanted to escape, that was how. She hadn't even remembered Rhys injecting the chip that awful night they'd arrived on-planet. The tracking chips on Iythea had become such a part of her life that they were simply another fragment of her body, like a navel piercing or tattoo or dental implant. And focusing on what the Haederans had done to her only made the situation worse. Forgetting was easier.

And now . . .

She'd led ISC right to Xan.

But she could fix this, couldn't she? Everything was fixable. Every mistake could be corrected, couldn't it? Even one as shattering as this one.

"Am I that much of a liability to you?" she asked. She could see the answer in his eyes, and the questions flew out in a rush. "What if I let them catch me? Is it too late? Can you get away? Go back into hiding? You are hiding somewhere, aren't you? I won't make you take me there. I don't know where it is, so I can't tell them, anyway."

"Katta—" he began.

Xan hadn't called her that in years, had become too grown-up for the diminutive nickname, he'd said. He ran the hand holding the knife across the back of his neck; his eyes darted toward the tinted window.

"I could lie," she interrupted. "I could say I didn't find you. That I wandered around for hours, and—look, I shouldn't have run into you earlier. It's statistically impossible, even if I knew where to start searching. Finding you was dumb luck, and if they let me go like you think they did, they'll never be expecting me to turn myself back in. I'll say I was tired and cold and saw some soldiers and got scared, and—"

"Do you know who you're crossing?" His shoulders drooped, but he let the knife fall to his side, then sheathed it. "You can't lie to them. Not ISC. Do you know what they'll do if they suspect you're lying? Do I need to spell it out for you?"

They did things to me—things I don't remember and things I would rather forget.

Her imagination didn't stretch that far, and for once, she was glad.

"Y—yes. I know who I'm crossing. I've been doing it for weeks now, and I'm not afraid to keep doing it if it'll help you. Until they have you back, they need me. I'm the only bait that they have, and they know it. Please. Will it work?"

"I can't let you go back to them. Kat . . ."

"You don't have another choice, do you?" Her stomach churned at the thought of turning herself in, the memories of being trapped in that room, but she backed toward the door anyway. "It's too late. I love you, Xan." She wanted more than anything to put her arms around him one last time, to kiss him and squeeze him and tell him everything would be fine, but he would grab her and keep her here if she did. "Be safe, all right? And—" Hot tears began to fall. "And try to fix this. For Mimi and Aba."

She thought she heard his voice as she dashed out of the box and toward the main street, but whether it was on purpose or not, he never caught up with her.

* * *

Katryn had thought the interrogation room on the Haederan cruiser was cold, but she hadn't known the meaning of the word. No, this cell was the very definition of cold. The air sliced into her lungs and the metal bench underneath her might as well have been a block of ice. She shifted, but with her hands cuffed behind her, there wasn't any way to get comfortable. Was she still in Cadena? The drive had been long, but the windows in the transport had been blacked out, so there was no way to know. Perhaps executions didn't take place in the capital. Perhaps this prison was far into some Asrian desert, leaving her with no hope of escape.

The major who'd sat with her while she'd dined, yet refused to tell her his name, had found her on the street in front of the Zarcronian restaurant. His appearance was more proof that Xan was right about her escape being a trap—clearly he hadn't left Asria the morning after he'd taken her to the courtyard. He hadn't mistreated her either, exactly, but he'd left her in this freezing cell after cinching the cuffs as tight as he could. Well, if that was the only punishment she was going to face, life wasn't so bad. Unless death by hypothermia was a new method of Haederan execution. She wouldn't put that past them.

Katryn shifted her legs underneath her. Was it better than being outside in the snowflakes that had begun to fly as they'd dragged her inside the transport? Her feet weren't damp any longer, so that was an improvement of sorts. Silver linings and all, and she'd take what she could get. Better, she'd been exhausted enough to fall asleep against the cold wall earlier. It was impossible to tell for how long, but she'd woken with a bit more stamina than she'd had earlier, even if her fingers had gone numb.

That optimism allowed her thoughts to slip to Xan. She'd let him go, yes, and for what? He had to realize what a gift she'd given him. Would he right his wrongs? Or was it more likely he'd continue with whatever he'd been up to—whatever that was?

Doors slammed somewhere down the hallway, and the major appeared in front of the bars holding her in. He looked exhausted—and annoyed.

"Rhys sent you?" she asked.

He shrugged.

"So where is he?"

"Busy." He leaned against the wall outside, arms crossed. "You get to talk to me."

Busy looking for Xan, probably. It was hard not to roll her eyes, but the hope that sprang into her heart kept her from doing anything rash. They hadn't found him yet.

"I don't think so," she said. "You're a poor conversationalist, remember?"

He chuckled without any humor. "That's fine. I'll see if you've changed your mind in a few hours." He turned to go, and she shivered so loudly that he twisted back toward her. "Unless you've changed it now. You seem rather uncomfortable."

Drawing this out wasn't helping anyone. Hadn't she promised

Xan she'd lie to protect him? Delaying her story wasn't making her eventual surrender look believable, either, and she truly was freezing—beyond cold. No, she could talk now, though she'd have vastly preferred whatever wrath Rhys would have subjected her to. Rhys she could handle. This man was unfamiliar, and that meant he was unpredictable.

"I wanted to find him," she said. "So when I heard an argument outside my door and realized the guard had left his post, I decided to try."

"And did you? Find him?"

"If I had, do you think I'd be here right now?"

I'd be halfway to Zarcron.

He raised his eyebrows.

"Fine. No. I wandered around all last night freezing, wondering where I'd start looking for him. And I saw Gem—that eel restaurant on Draus Road—and decided I'd wait there, see if he showed. He told me once how he loves grilled Asrian eel, and that if he ever made it out this far, it was the first place he'd go."

She suppressed a disgusted face. Eel was the last thing Xan would be caught eating. It was the last thing she'd be caught eating, for that matter, if they hadn't served it to her for breakfast almost every morning. A lifetime in sea ports had guaranteed neither of them would ever touch the stuff off-world.

"Someone said they saw you with a man. In Honten."

The chill in the cell settled into her core at his mention of the neighborhood in which she'd spent the morning searching for Xan. Honten Hospitality owned the box hotel they'd stayed in. It'd been stamped right across the inside of the door. *Someone had seen them, someone had talked.* Had it been voluntarily, or had ISC threatened someone into doing it? This man looked like he was capable of it.

"I was cold last night. I found a man who was . . ." She swallowed. "Who was willing to keep me warm. I didn't get his name. But he didn't know who I was, or that I'd—" Katryn threw a high-pitched panic into her voice. "You're not going to harm him, are you? He doesn't know anything! He wanted some company, and I wanted some warmth. It wasn't Xan, I swear!"

It was working. She wouldn't risk holding her breath, but she could see the disappointment etched in his face. He'd screwed up apprehending her so early, and he knew it.

"Where did he take you to . . . uh . . ." Disappointment turned to disgust. "Keep warm?"

And now the fact-checking questions had started.

"A hotel. On Nattan Street." She didn't know if the street existed, but if it didn't, she would plead ignorance of Cadena. They'd had her locked up for all but one day, after all. She could play dumb if desperately needed. "Or maybe it was Nappet. I'm not sure."

"And you don't remember the name of the hotel, of course." It wasn't a question.

She shook her head, and he uncrossed his arms and stepped toward the bars.

"Can you show me where it is? Or point it out on a map? Describe it? Tall, short, old, skyscraper, color of the building?"

"I don't have a very good sense of direction. And I'm not sure what it looked like. It was dark and the road wasn't very well lit."

"Wasn't it now." He pressed his lips together and stared at her. "You're full of it, Doctor Holt."

Well, he'd figured it out sooner than she'd expected. Nothing to lose now.

"And you screwed up, Major." She pushed her back against the wall to stop the shaking, but it wasn't like he couldn't already tell she was freezing. Admitting it wouldn't make things worse, not now. "Twice now. Or do you think I'm too stupid to realize you wanted me to escape the same way the night you were late bringing me dinner? Don't blame me. I don't know where Xan went, so you can't manipulate or threaten me into telling you. And you can tell Rhys Linden that he can't manipulate me anymore either. He can find Xan on his own, because I'm not going to help ISC any longer."

His fingers flexed in frustration, then he keyed in a long code on the door and stepped inside.

"Wrong decision. I can't believe you've forgotten what Captain Linden told you would happen if you or your brother decided not to cooperate. Did you mention that to Major Feye during your little family reunion? Did you tell him that your days are numbered?"

Katryn didn't flinch. Rhys wouldn't. He wanted her alive. ISC did too, didn't they? Or maybe they didn't, because the major was stalking toward her now, his jaw tight. Maybe she'd pushed too far, caused too many problems. It wouldn't be the first time. Had she learned nothing since Iythea?

He yanked her up by the wrist, and that time she did recoil.

"What are you doing?" She pulled her arm away, but his grip tightened.

"Taking you back to headquarters." The handcuffs fell away with a painful click, and he pushed her toward the door. "I hope you enjoyed your last night of freedom, because you won't be having another. Captain Linden may be running this operation, but if Major Feye doesn't show soon, I'll cut your throat myself."

CHAPTER TWENTY-EIGHT

CHASE'S COMM DINGED ONCE MORE AS HE KEYED IN HIS CODE TO THE prison door. Some people never learned not to bother him. With a sigh, he pulled out the comm. Probably Rhys. Or Mercer. Or Perrin. Who else knew or cared he was here?

Or—he swallowed a smile at the thought—maybe it was Isobel. It could be a forwarded message or two from Haedera, though she'd never been the best at sending messages. His hand moved of its own accord, hopeful for the best.

My lord,
I'm in orbit now. I want an update on her tomorrow. In person. They
will have instructions for you at the ISC building if you decide to finally
show your face there. Don't be late.
-L

Chase swore under his breath.
Not Isobel.
Lient had found him. And not only had his boss found him, he was here. In the Asrian system, in orbit, mocking him with his title as he was wont to do. Mocking him and waiting on an update.

An update on nothing, because Chase had thought, not for the first time, that he had all the time in the world to work a prisoner. He swallowed his panic and pushed open the door to the interrogation room. Avery was already in there, and . . . well, Lient's visit was going to require a slight change in tactics today.

Because *she lies to me, then refuses to speak for an hour, then makes up even more insane stories* was never going to work with Lient. Whether his new strategy worked or not . . . he'd have to see.

Avery stiffened at the sound of his footsteps, then tried to pull away when he touched her to remove the blindfold.

"They tell me you didn't fight much this time," he said to her, trying to calm his racing heart. If she wasn't fighting the guards or him, that meant they'd turned a corner. Her resistance was finally wearing her out—and not an hour too soon. "I'm glad to hear it. I hope that means you're finally starting to realize this pointless struggle is a waste of time. A waste of . . . well, a waste of every-thing, no?"

She didn't say anything in reply, so he began his routine check of her injuries. She stared blankly at the wall as he lifted her shirt enough to check her side. Her ribs were healing nicely, as was that large scrape on her upper arm—he'd never asked the guards how she'd gotten that one.

But her face was another story. They must have hit her with a pistol again, and recently, for most of her cheek from her jaw all the way to her eye was a mixture of purplish-blue. Chase sighed inside. Ice wouldn't fix this one, and the army refused to stock dermtape in their prisons. He'd have to remind Mercer to bring some next time he stopped by.

As gently as he could, he ran his finger across the bruise. She flinched and whimpered once, then closed her eyes—only this time it wasn't from fear. Had she fallen asleep right in front of him? It was hard to believe, but her sudden slow breathing didn't lie.

I don't have time for this.

He drew his right hand back far enough to hurt, then flung it forward, striking her directly on her undamaged cheek.

Her eyes flew open in shock, but surprisingly, he didn't see much additional pain there. Fury, yes. Disbelief, yes. Fear, yes. Even a bit of humiliation. Good. The fear was all he'd been aiming for, but he'd take its accompanying emotions.

Did you honestly believe I'd never harm you myself?

Judging by the look on her face, she had.

"Am I boring you already?" he asked as she brushed her hands against the mark he'd left. "Or have you not been getting enough sleep?"

At least the guards were doing one thing right. No more than three hours of sleep at a time. More than that, and her defiance increased exponentially. Less than that, and she might as well be babbling incoherently at him in some ancient colonial language. But three hours of deep sleep, interspersed with the Imperial Haederan Army's particular brand of beatings—yes, that seemed to work. And when she was particularly cooperative and gave him a steady feed of information during a session, he gave her more sleep. It was a system that worked well for both of them.

"You know I haven't," she all but spat at him.

He let her have a small, innocent smile.

"This is a Haederan Army prison, not Imperial Security." How lucky she was that it wasn't. "I don't have any say in what goes on down here." He picked up his comm, skimmed Lient's message, cursed to himself, and set it back down. "Only whether or not you stay. And so far, you haven't given me any reason to have you moved to better quarters."

Better quarters. A place where they didn't starve her, didn't wake her up every two hours, didn't chain her to the wall if she made the mistake of closing her eyes when she was supposed to be awake, didn't beat her for not obeying their orders without hesitation. Would she ever experience her fearless, luxurious life again? It was hard to say. Solitary confinement in an ISC prison on Haedera for the rest of her short life seemed more likely at this point—but he had to make it seem as though she had a chance for something better.

"In fact," he went on, "just before you came in, I replied to another request for your transfer to Haedera, asking for more time. I can safely say that won't be the better treatment you want."

That part wasn't a lie. The unexpected message might as well have been a request for her transfer—there was no doubt that was what Lient's sudden appearance on Asria meant. What else was so important to make the head of ISC travel weeks on a military transport to a backwater planet like Asria? Eight or nine weeks back to Haedera with Lient and Avery and a group of ISC guards —there wasn't a more unpleasant idea in the quadrant.

Her hand froze on her cheek. "What?"

Chase let his shoulders sink, then pulled his chair right across from her. If there was one thing Avery hated, one thing that made her pliable, it was physical proximity to him.

"You didn't think they'd give me forever to do this, did you?" he asked. "I can't put them off much longer. You have to give me something I can use. No more stories. No more lies."

"When?" She began to shake, though she made a valiant effort to hide it.

"They've called me up tomorrow to discuss this." He jabbed his finger toward the stars, up where Lient waited, no doubt disappointed and angry and impatient. "I need to have something to tell them before that. If they don't like what I have to say, I suppose you would leave the next day, on the first courier ship out. That's not up to me."

Was his claim an exaggeration? Was that the real reason Lient was here? Did he intend to take Avery back to Haedera? She was Victor Rendon's niece, after all, and if there was anything he'd learned from his humiliating encounter with the man, it was that he had the ear of the emperor.

For some reason, the idea of subjecting her to the emperor's and Rendon's plans made his stomach twist. But if he could keep her on Asria, perhaps she'd come out of this unscathed. But how long could that last?

"I can't go there," she whispered.

"I would tend to agree with that. I don't want to send you there either"—that was truer than he wanted to admit—"but the decision will be out of my hands soon."

Her gaze darted to her feet, his eyes, the metal around her wrists, the door, the floor, his desk, and then her hands.

Then, finally, back at him.

"I'll show you where the second location is." The words seemed to fly out of her mouth.

Her second drop location? She couldn't be serious. As much as he wanted to find Feye—if that's who she was indeed working for—she wasn't getting out of here that easily, not yet. Naïve, indeed.

"Show me?" he asked. "That won't be necessary. You'll tell me. Now."

Her breathing grew rapid; her stare flickered around the room. "I don't remember until I'm walking there. It's in the Old City, and the streets are confusing—"

More games. She was lying—he should have known.

He stood, kicking his chair away from her as he did. When he flung the door open, there were three soldiers hovering outside like they were supposed to.

"Take her back," he told Noall. "I'll comm further instructions tomorrow evening."

"But, sir—" Noall looked panicked, like he'd been the one responsible for this short session.

"Twelve hours, then she can sleep and eat. Do whatever you need to do to make sure she doesn't until then."

He steeled himself against the image of Avery kneeling in front of a cot, hands and feet chained, with a guard behind to strike her whenever her head fell to the bed. That particular torment, more mental than physical, was an ISC technique, though. However Noall's men planned on keeping her awake this afternoon, he wouldn't ask. It was an unfair punishment, perhaps, but he had to do something about the panic roiling through his blood.

What do you care what Lient decides to do with her if she doesn't talk?

The guards moved past them into the interview room. Avery screamed something unintelligible as they approached her. Chase pushed himself against the wall inside the door, placing himself out of the way as they yanked her from the chair.

"It's a warehouse in the Old City," she sobbed at him, oblivious to the soldiers. Tears fell as they pulled her toward the door.

"Shut up." Noall struck her on the back of the head as they dragged her by them.

Chase held his breath. She wasn't lying this time. Could this be the break he needed? The one she needed? He lifted his chin at Noall.

"Let her say what she wants to say."

"On Ameto Road." Avery drew in a long, shuddering breath and tried to pull away from Noall. "There's a loose brick on one side of the building, and—"

He mouthed a silent prayer that the guards wouldn't do something to ruin the situation. "The signal?"

"I was supposed to leave the window in my office at the senate building tinted open that night."

He regarded her for a long time as she trembled, partially to frighten her—make her wonder if she'd said enough—and partially to determine his next course of action. It wasn't enough, but it was a start.

"Don't ever lie to me again." He nodded at Noall, and the guards dropped her back in the chair, then disappeared back into the corridor. He leaned against the table, arms folded, and watched her until the tears subsided. It took a while, but if she were to survive this, she needed to be calm.

"You know you've been here too long for that information to be of any use to me," he finally told her. "They won't trust a single piece of intelligence you leave there now. If you'd been up front with me from the beginning, told me the truth, things might have been different. But now . . . You're going to have to do better than that. I'll call them back in otherwise. Last chance."

Fresh tears tracked down her cheeks. One small push and she'd fall right over the edge. *Calm . . . slow . . .*

He shrugged, like he didn't care if she spoke or not.

"You've already told me enough that the Commonwealth won't want anything to do with you ever again. If that's what you're worried about, you might as well tell me everything. It doesn't matter what you do any longer as far as they're concerned."

Accusing her of treason was a risk, probably the greatest he'd taken so far. If she didn't go for it, she'd shut down completely, and then what? Lient had forced him into an endgame.

More excuses. Lient wasn't to blame here. He'd done this to himself.

"I—I don't know what you want anymore." Her stare grew distant. "I don't know anything."

Neither did he. There was so much . . . What was on the chip, how many she'd left at the temple, where that backup site really was, who—

He swallowed. Yes, that was it. An easy bit of information. And if her contact happened to be Elex Feye, so much the better. Rhys would be thrilled.

"I'm sure you know where your contact is," he said, keeping his voice level.

She wiped most of the tears away and stared at her feet.

"Yes," she said after a few deep breaths, though he could barely understand the word. "I know where he is. I'll tell you where to find him."

That last—that meant something. She was desperate for him to believe her.

"That'll do. For now." He switched on the tablet behind him and laid it in her lap. She looked at it dully. "Write it down. I want details. When I get back, we'll pay him a visit."

With her hands cuffed and shaking like they were, it took her almost a half hour to find the herb shop where her contact was allegedly hiding out. An herb shop somewhere in the Old City. If that didn't have Zenos Hadley's name on it, Chase wasn't sure what did. And where Hadley was, Elex Feye wasn't far away.

"And his name?"

She looked up and began to cry. "Please. I—"

A mysterious pity washed over him, though it didn't quite feel like pity. Perhaps it was shame, an emotion he couldn't pinpoint because he couldn't remember ever feeling it like this. And suddenly—Chase blinked at her as she shook—suddenly she wasn't Avery Rendon, princess-elect of Asria, but Kai, the young dark-haired boy from Haedera whose only crime was being born to the wrong father. And Kai was lying there on the floor in front of him, eyes closed, every finger broken, begging for mercy, and—

Avery's words in the temple that first night crashed back into him.

I know what you believe. And I know you only believe it because your emperor forces you to. Why someone who's clearly only using faith for control would pretend to love Him is something I'll never understand. And you're too blind to see it.

"You know what?" he said to her. "It doesn't matter right now."

He'd find out on his own, and there wasn't any sense in pushing her too far today. She would be easy now. She'd broken. She'd betrayed the Commonwealth, and now things would be straightforward. He would give her a break. She didn't deserve it, but he couldn't harm her further. Not now.

"It—it doesn't matter?" she asked. The question was cautious, like she couldn't believe her good fortune.

Chase shook his head and gently pried the tablet from her hands. Tomorrow he'd visit Lient, and then, if all went well, he'd soon be back on Asria, visiting the herb shop with Rhys and a dozen other officers. It was obvious Zenos Hadley and Elex Feye were hiding out there, and once they had Feye back, things would be easy—for everyone.

He smiled at her, though he was certain it made him look more exhausted than pleased. "You've been cooperative today. I appreciate that. I'll make sure they let you get some sleep."

* * *

The orbital shuttle docked hard with the Imperial Haederan Navy cruiser *Renown,* floating on the other side of the planet from Cadena like a jewel in the dark. There wasn't much time to admire the view. Chase sucked in one last lungful of surface air before the hatch opened and a familiar man ducked inside before he had the chance to orient himself to the new gravity.

Familiar, perhaps, but so excessively ordinary that Chase might have laughed on any other day. With his average height, average build, bland, emotionless face, and the typically muddled ethnic background of the Haederan lower classes, Callum Lient didn't stand out anywhere. Today his ISC uniform was missing, replaced by faded Imperial Haederan Navy fatigues that looked like they hadn't seen a steamer in five years. Blending in until it was too late had always been Lient's technique.

"It's about time you surfaced," he said to Chase with something that might be called a smile.

"Sir." Chase gave a half salute as he stood.

Lient merely sighed as they exited the shuttle—he'd never believe the half salute was for his benefit.

"I trust you had a pleasant flight?" he asked.

"If by pleasant you mean short, yes."

Lient chuckled as they headed toward the door. "Still not used to it, are you? At least we know it's not in the genes."

"Hardly." Chase slammed his hand against the door opener. Being on a cruiser was bad enough—standing around in a hangar bay chatting about his father wasn't going to happen. Who needed to play the comparison game anymore? His pulse slowed as they entered the corridor outside. The solid corridor with emergency kits every so often and no windows. "But I know you're not here to talk about my dislike of spaceflight."

"It does make a good welcome, you must admit."

"Sir." Lient was screwing with him now. "Perhaps you should tell His Majesty that I'd be more effective if I was down there and not up here."

"Don't test him. Or me." Lient's bland face grew grim as they turned one more corner, and he pushed open the door to a small observation deck. "Victor Rendon would like to know how his niece is."

"You came all this way to ask that?" Chase flopped on the nearest couch. After weeks of sleeping on a cot, maybe spending the night in orbit wouldn't be so bad if he could sleep here. It was hard not to sink back against the dark cushions, but he wouldn't do that in front of Lient. There were limits to his insubordination —not many, but some. "You have my reports, and I'm not certain Mr. Rendon really wants to know the answer to that question. What have you told him?"

Lient spread his hands as he paced before the viewing window. "Only that we were able to determine that she was working for the Commonwealth as he suspected, and that naturally we had an obligation to find out just how much classified military information had been compromised."

Chase blew out a deep breath. *Dangerous game.* "What was his reaction?" Hell, he knew what his reaction would be if Avery was one of his family members.

"He turned pale." Lient shrugged, like he didn't really care if Victor Rendon had vomited all over the emperor's marble floor at the news. "And left the room."

I bet he did.

"So?" Lient went on, oblivious to his silence. "How is she?"

"How is—" What, did the man want details? Now? He had the interrogation notes and ample time to read them on the way from Haedera. Verbally recounting Avery's experience, especially in front of Lient, was the last thing he wanted to do. "You know how she is, sir. Uncomfortable. Unhappy. Finally talking a bit."

"You're taking your time with her. I'm surprised."

"It's a slow process." Lient knew that. He hadn't come up in the interrogation corps, but he'd witnessed dozens, if not hundreds, of them.

"There's always lacrozenate. Even if you have to wait until she's on Haedera."

"Sir—" Lient couldn't be serious. He'd never dose Avery with it. Not even if it was safe. "It's not reliable yet. Are you going to be the one to tell that man we're experimenting on his niece? Because I'm not." His invented fear of Victor Rendon was a hazy excuse. He had to think of another one, and quickly. "And His Majesty didn't want her harmed. That rules out lacrozenate, and it also slows down a traditional interrogation, naturally."

"He didn't say anything of the sort to me." Lient's nose crinkled.

It was a warning, but Chase pressed on. "To me, sir. In private."

Lient wouldn't dare confirm that fabrication with the emperor. And if he pushed the issue, if he found out the truth, it would be much too late for any kind of real reprimand. Tempers tended to calm during a weeks-long interstellar voyage, and Lient would eventually come to his senses.

"Hmm." Lient tapped a finger on his thigh. Once. It was a movement that would probably terrify most people, but he'd become immune to Lient's subtle and not-so-subtle threats over the years.

"What exactly are you here to tell me, sir?" he asked. Move on, and Lient would forget about him taking his time with Avery.

Lient stared at him for a long time. Chase tried to ignore the horizon of Asria behind him, tried to forget his blatant lie. "Be careful," he said slowly, after the planet had precessed an entire degree by Chase's estimation. "Victor Rendon is not Haederan, and he most certainly does not run ISC. Just—be cautious, all right?"

"I always am." What did Lient know that he didn't?

"Indeed." Lient leaned back against the viewscreen while Chase tried not to cringe at his proximity to the void. "But this one—it's a delicate situation."

"I already knew that, sir." He'd known that as soon as the emperor had first mentioned Avery's name so long ago. And Lient knew he wasn't careless. Lient also didn't show concern—ever, about anything.

What was this really about?

"Yes, but he has plans for her once you're through," Lient replied. "A few years imprisonment. With us, of course. From your reports, it seems it'll be necessary to soften her up a bit. Then a few more years of close indoctrination. After that, Mr. Rendon gets his niece back, and His Majesty gets a perfect propaganda tool. Politically, we cannot mess this up."

As if ISC ever worried about that. ISC transcended such trivial things as politics.

"She hasn't shown much suggestibility," Chase said. "Indoctrination will be a challenge."

He forced a smile. Had he shown too much doubt? Lient would jump on it if he had, like *okaucros* fighting for carcasses outside Windhaven. His claim was true, though. Contrary to the emperor's initial wish, Avery Rendon was the last person he'd want to turn, the last agent he'd ever want to run. It was probably his fault, too. She hated him enough to resist almost every suggestion he'd tried to plant in her mind. And why wouldn't she? He'd spent weeks trying to get her on his side, and it'd all been for nothing.

But, upon further reflection, none of this was his fault. It was Perrin's fault for throwing off his timing, Perrin's fault for having Parker murdered. Unfortunately, that excuse would never be accepted.

"If she decides to keep fighting us after all that, she dies."

Lient shrugged. "Preferably after a few doses of lacrozenate. But that's a long way off, and I'm certain you can make her see reason before such measures are necessary. I'm sure I don't need to make the stakes much clearer here."

He barely heard Lient's last words, only able to focus on the first.

She dies.

Suddenly, as his knees went weak, though he was already sitting, he was even more grateful for the sofa. Avery had done something to him, what with all her accusations and rebelliousness and initial lack of fear and indictment of his faith. She'd taken away his nerve. Because no. Just no. He couldn't let that happen. What he was doing to her was bad enough. What His Majesty had planned for her . . . turning her was the only option now.

"Given time, I'm certain I can convince her." It seemed like the only thing to say. "Things are moving—I need a little while longer."

The door hissed open behind him, and Lient's face grew annoyed.

"Yes?" he called out.

Chase spun to see one of Lient's aides standing in the doorway.

"I'm sorry, sir," he said. "Urgent planetside comm for Colonel Chase."

Lient waved a hand. "Transfer it in here." His glare at Chase said, *This had better be good.*

Chase stepped toward the comm panel with the aide, who typed in a series of numbers before handing him the receiver. "This is Colonel Chase."

The voice on the other end sounded like Lieutenant Noall, but with the short delay from the surface and the man's rapid speech, it was hard to tell. It was even harder to make out the rushed words. Because it had sounded like Noall had said . . .

But that wasn't possible. It couldn't be possible.

"Say that again?" Chase asked, his mouth dry.

Don't say that again. Say anything but what I think you just said.

Nausea washed over him. He was going to vomit on this polished, stainless floor, standing here in the middle of space with Lient not twenty paces away. Because what he thought he'd heard . . . it was the second worst news of his life. Perhaps the last bad news he'd ever receive.

"What do you mean, she's gone?"

CHAPTER TWENTY-NINE

How many times could he watch the surveillance tapes? It had only taken twice to positively identify Zenos Hadley in a Haederan Army uniform escorting Avery up from the basement prison to the aeroflyer pad on the twentieth floor. Numb, Chase swiped his finger across the screen for the sixth time.

Hadley walked down the hall, Noall next to him. The Commonwealth officer handed a chip to Noall—forged transfer documents, no doubt—before the lieutenant opened the cell door. The camera switched inside. Avery jerked in recognition. Hadley backhanded her across the face, then Noall's men secured her and Hadley and an army guard dragged her out.

He watched it another four times, as if it would change the past.

"Sir?"

He jumped at Mercer's voice behind him and hit pause just as Hadley pushed Avery up the ramp into an army aeroflyer.

"I have her medical files for you, Colonel."

"Ah." He took the chip Mercer held out. "Yes."

"They'll be hiding in Cadena for a while. There's no way she's in any shape to do anything but disappear for the next few days, and that's only if they've got a damn good field kit. A week is more likely. Maybe two."

"Yes." Why couldn't he manage more than one word? "Thank you."

"You're headed to Alcaris then, sir? I've called a flyer—they're about twenty minutes out."

"For me? You should have waited. I'm not done here." Reaming out Noall hadn't done much for his panic, not with an official report and probably discipline to follow, but chiding Mercer—innocent, in this case—made him feel a little better, at least.

"For me, but there's room. I'm sorry—they sent an urgent request, so I thought I'd let you know."

Panic or not, he had to laugh inside. "It's always urgent with them, isn't it?"

Mercer cracked a smile. "Always. Especially since the army stopped letting us borrow their medical personnel for routine treatment. No rest the past two weeks."

"They did?" More panic subsided. Maybe everyone else was as screwed up as he felt. "They ought to know better than that."

"It's punitive. Or juvenile retaliation, depending on your point of view. They're pissed at us."

The Imperial Haederan Army was always pissed at ISC. Pissed, but powerless to do anything about it except play childish games. "Why now?"

Mercer hesitated, then sighed. "Well, there were rumors about what's going on over there, but that's all they were—rumors. Then two weeks ago, one of the docs was called over to the army side to do emergency surgery on one of those Defense Forces guys in the brig there. Appendicitis or something. Nothing serious, but their medical people were tied up with other things. He said the guards wouldn't let him out of their sight, which he thought was pretty strange."

Chase didn't reply. It wasn't unlike the army to treat ISC officers with as much disrespect as they thought they could get away with. And a doctor? He couldn't do much about it except put up with the treatment and report back to ops later.

"Anyway, on his way off base, he took a wrong turn and ended up in front of what he thought was the transport building. Those army police about removed his arm trying to get him away from the door. When they called the transport for him, one of them apologized for the overreaction—said they had a few secret high-level Asrian prisoners in there. Ones they'd captured the night the Defense Forces tried to retake the base."

"Secret?"

"Doc said he called them secret. I guess he didn't understand the meaning of the word."

Sounded like the army. "But a few—that's not possible."

As isolated as he'd been, even he knew the story. A small group of Defense Forces officers, Merritt Parker included, had attacked the army's headquarters at Alcaris the night Perrin had ordered Avery's arrest. Perrin and his men had murdered over half of them, then rubbed the Commonwealth's nose in it. The Commonwealth had threatened who knew what, and Perrin, ever the coward, had caved. The surviving prisoners were still being held at Alcaris, yes, but transparently now. They were to be transferred to the Imperial Haederan Navy's new prison camp on Emot once barracks were complete. The army had promised.

An unsettled feeling rose in his chest. *Nosiness is a good look on you, my lord,* Lient always said. *Though it'll catch up with you one day.*

"The army made an agreement with the Commonwealth," he said to Mercer. "Perrin had better watch his step if they're playing games over there with any of them."

"Right." Mercer took a step back. "I don't know what's going on, sir. Like I said—it was a rumor, several people removed now. I've told you everything."

Chase waved his hand. "It's all right. Probably nothing." *Or everything.* He closed his eyes and took a breath. "You know what, Draven? I think I'll catch that flyer with you."

* * *

Perrin's office at Alcaris was the last place he wanted to be, but the first place he needed to be. Chase knocked on the interior door, ignoring the curious and not-quite-surreptitious glances of Perrin's secretary. It was another minute—a long one—before Perrin called him inside. The nerve of the man. He'd never have acted like this on Haedera.

"Shouldn't you be out looking for your prisoner, Colonel?" Perrin asked in bold greeting. "Scuttlebutt says you lost her."

"Does it?" Chase brushed a piece of lint from his sleeve as he sat, not waiting to be invited. "Rumors certainly do fly, don't they?"

Perrin gazed at him over his glass of evening liquor. "They certainly do."

"And it's funny you mention it, because I heard a strange one earlier today. Something about some mystery Defense Forces prisoners you're holding at Alcaris."

A laugh. "Mystery prisoners? The only Defense Forces prisoners I have are leaving for Emot in another week. They'll be the navy's problem then, and good riddance to the bastards. You know they're here and where they're going. The whole planet knows. Even the Commonwealth does. Screw them and their transparency." He took a sip. "Though what's the Commonwealth going to do if some have health issues that prevent that kind of travel? Or are too high-risk for a low-security camp? They can't blame me for holding some back."

Chase took a silent breath. Perrin's implied threat wasn't worth mentioning yet. "You're saying the Commonwealth isn't aware of your secret prison? The one an ISC medical officer mistook for a transportation building? Sir?"

Perrin slapped his hands on the table as he stood, his face as red as the sun setting behind him.

"Get out. Now. And don't come back. I don't want to see you anywhere near this building again."

Chase stood but didn't move toward the door. Perrin wasn't this bad at hiding something important. Was he?

"In one moment. I'm not quite done with you. Sir." The chill in his voice worked on everyone else—it would certainly work on Taln Perrin, the spineless bastard. "It's my duty to make certain you aren't placing the empire and His Imperial Majesty at risk by violating any signed agreements."

"You think I'm violating that agreement?" Perrin smiled. "You may want to look a little closer to home, Colonel. Hiding undisclosed prisoners sounds exactly like something ISC would have its hands in. I know you people love to throw the word treason around, but it seems you might want to work on restraining your own men before you come barging in here accusing me of it."

Dammit. Chase swallowed the curse just in time. Maybe Perrin was right. Who knew what the newer ISC officers were up to on Asria? Still, it was unlikely they'd be doing it at Alcaris—too many watchful eyes and loose mouths. It wasn't impossible, though. For the first time in weeks, he wanted a drink.

"If you're up to something here, Governor," he said, more out of fatigue than any kind of real threat, "I'll personally make sure you regret it."

Perrin's smile turned cold. "Out."

* * *

He should be out in Cadena now, helping Linden and his men search for Avery, but the nagging feeling, the sense he'd missed something important—well, it meant something. Chase tapped his fingers on the desk he'd commandeered at the ISC detention facility. It was easy enough to bring up the list of Defense Forces prisoners from that night. Whatever else he thought of Perrin, the man did require meticulous records. Anyone could appreciate that.

Seven killed during the attack.

Fifty-three captured.

Twenty-seven executed by Perrin's men the same night.

Seventeen held at Alcaris, scheduled for transfer to Emot next week.

And two—two had already been shipped off-planet?

What was Perrin up to now? Was he trying to get a bullet through his head?

Chase rubbed his temples. On second thought, maybe it made a bit of sense. The barracks at the Emot camp had to be going up quickly, so maybe Perrin had transferred a few low-risk prisoners there first as a deceptive show of good faith to the Commonwealth. He'd all but said he wasn't planning on following through, after all.

He downed a pouch of water as he brought up the transfer records. It probably didn't mean anything, but then again, coincidences were very rarely actual coincidences. And if it was a coincidence, the names Perrin had chosen would be a fascinating insight into how the man's mind worked. That was knowledge he couldn't turn down. He tossed the pouch into the trash and glanced back at the screen.

The chilled water, already heavy in his stomach, threatened to come right back up as he blinked at the words.

This couldn't be right.

Perrin had made a mistake. Listed the wrong prisoner. The second of the two names—this man wasn't on Emot. Couldn't be on Emot.

Because he was dead.

Lieutenant Colonel Merritt Parker.

* * *

Blast the comm lag between Asria and Emot. Seventeen minutes was too long to wait for Admiral Treton's answer. The line clicked two more times, and the admiral's voice came back in a rush. At least someone knew how to make the most of the delay.

"I'm sorry Colonel, but the men you're looking for aren't here.

They were scheduled to arrive in early Verert, Emot time, but never showed. Their transfers were ordered by the governor's office directly, but when I checked with them, they informed me both prisoners were shot while trying to escape during transfer to the shuttle site in Cadena. I'm sending you the transfer order and official incident report now. Give it an hour and let me know if they don't arrive. Sorry I couldn't be of more help."

The heavily doctored official incident report, no doubt. Perrin hadn't honestly believed he'd get away with this, had he? Probably he did—he'd have no way of knowing ISC would eventually come asking questions. Or maybe he'd known and didn't care.

And this was an ISC matter, wasn't it?

Yes. Perrin's lie about Parker's death had contributed to Avery's resistance and the length of her imprisonment. He could have used Parker—he probably wouldn't have, but he could have. No, this wasn't personal at all.

That rationalization worked for now. Chase shook his head and pressed the transmit button to send his response on its journey.

"Thank you, Admiral. I'll be looking forward to reading it. Have a nice evening."

He grabbed another pouch of water, then kicked back in his chair. There was no real reason outside of revenge to transfer Parker to ISC custody. The Commonwealth would be furious if they found out Perrin was abusing him, but did it really matter in the end? They wouldn't act over one or two men.

Do something about that Asrian snake or I will.

Perrin's words flew back at him. This was all because Merritt Parker had loved her, and Perrin couldn't stand them flaunting it in the middle of an occupation. Ridiculous.

He needed a drink. Because Parker didn't deserve whatever Perrin was doing to him. He was rash to challenge the Haederan Empire, yes, of course, but hadn't Chase been rash himself when he'd first met Isobel so many years ago? He'd been beyond foolish for her, a young, dark-haired girl with eyes that saw into his soul and a smile that welcomed him to the imperial court even as he cried for his parents on those lonely nights. He'd cowered in front of her father five years later, a young man with nothing but some family history and a promising ISC career, and begged the emperor for permission to marry her.

He was lucky to have kept his head. No, foolish didn't begin to describe him back then—reckless and irresponsible and thoughtless, maybe—but it certainly described him now.

Because Perrin was about to find out what it felt like to lose his own prisoner.

* * *

For the fourth time in an hour, Chase checked his pocket for Parker's hurriedly written transfer order. Going back to his office to write up another would take almost an hour and, more importantly, would raise too many questions. Because ISC officers didn't sound unsure, didn't make mistakes, and certainly didn't forget paperwork.

Unless they were anxious about stealing a general's prisoner.

He took a deep breath and used his authorization card to override the security lock and camera on the side door. Even on Asria, Haederan Army buildings weren't as private as they wished—from ISC, at least. As he'd expected, an army sergeant came running down the corridor, hand on his stun pistol.

"Sir, this is a secure—" He skidded to a halt when he recognized the uniform in front of him.

"You think I don't know that?" Chase growled at him, bringing the chip containing the transfer order out. "Stop wasting my time and take me to see Lieutenant Colonel Parker. Immediately."

"I'm sorry, sir, but—"

Chase raised his eyebrows. "Yes. You know who he is, and you know where he is."

The sergeant rolled the chip between his fingers. "What is this?"

"Transfer order. ISC wants him."

"Colonel, I don't—"

Perrin really had them under his thumb, didn't he? "Now, sergeant."

The sergeant sighed and headed in the direction he'd come. "I'm sorry, sir. No one was supposed to know . . ." He trailed off as he led Chase through another secured door, this one almost as heavy as the exterior door he'd entered through.

"No one? I assume that doesn't include ISC. Or are you hiding something from us?" An unnecessary question, but watching the man turn pale was entertaining. For a brief second, it took his mind off Avery.

"No! Of course not, sir. I'm certain the commandant isn't including His Imperial Majesty in that 'no one.'"

Chase gave him a friendly smile as they entered a small row of cells. "I'm happy to hear you say that. The emperor will be pleased as well."

"Thank you." The sergeant put his hand on the third door from the end. "He's not in good shape, Colonel. If you planned on walking back to ISC, that's not going to happen. You're going to have to borrow security to cart him out to your transport."

"Ah." What did that mean? "That bad?"

"Governor Perrin's orders, sir. He was to be, and I'm quoting here, 'not treated with any kind of care.'"

Do you honestly believe I'm going to let her prance around Cadena, screwing whoever she chooses, flaunting everything I've told her to not do, rubbing her rebellion in my face? Arrest him. Now.

This was his fault.

Chase hoped the dim light in the corridor hid the sudden flush on his cheeks. He'd stopped lightening his freckles once Avery had been arrested, so perhaps they helped hide his sudden emotion as well. He could have arrested Parker weeks ago, as soon as Perrin had commanded it, and if he'd been in ISC custody the entire time . . . he'd have been relatively safe. How bad was he now?

His mouth went dry. "All right. You've suitably warned me, and it's much appreciated. Open it up."

The sergeant nodded, keyed in the code, and slid open the heavy door. The cell was dark—no surprise there—and it took forever for his eyes to adjust. Steel walls. Not even a cot. It was freezing inside, almost as cold as the autumn air outside. And there in the corner lay a motionless body wearing nothing but a torn, dirty pair of tactical pants. Was he—

The body moaned.

Hell.

After more than twenty years in ISC, no amount or nature of physical brutality should shock him. He didn't partake in it, of course, but it wasn't as though he'd never seen the results of less restrained interrogators. But this . . .

Parker's hair was gone, which only made him look paler in the dim light. His face was covered in bruises, his shirtless chest laced with shallow yet bloody cuts. The last time Chase had seen him, Parker had been standing in his foyer in Cadena, eyes defiant, but those same eyes were dark with pain now, staring distantly past Chase at the open door. There was no way he could make it—his left ankle was twisted backward at an unnatural angle.

"What happened to his leg?" Chase asked, trying to sound disgusted instead of horrified.

"Broke them, sir. More than once. He kept trying to escape."

And some claimed shackles were inhumane. That was, of course, debatable, but inhumane or not, they weren't as painful as a broken leg, and the army had access to them. Why not use them on a prisoner prone to escape attempts?

Because breaking Parker's legs wasn't to keep him from running.

"Made it easier for other things, too," the sergeant added. "Not me"—he flushed—"but a few here are a bit too into their own power."

Chase swallowed bile. "I—I see."

It surprised a few of his colleagues, but there were some lines he just didn't cross, some cruelties he didn't permit to be inflicted on his prisoners, no matter how reticent they were. He'd warned Noall more than once what would happen if his men tried that sort of thing with Avery, and they'd obeyed, of course. They'd be dead if they hadn't.

He stuck his hand in his pocket, searching in vain for the ring he'd given back to her weeks ago. It wasn't there, of course. She'd been wearing it when he'd left to visit Lient, and she was probably wearing it now, wherever she was. Something odd and unwelcome twisted in his gut, and it took a moment to realize it was relief. Relief she wasn't seeing Parker in this condition. Not the broken ankle, not the purple bruise that cut all the way across his abdomen, not what looked like a rope burn around his neck.

Holy One, how is he alive?

"Sir?" The sergeant's voice sounded far away. "Shall I call a few men for escort?"

Last chance. He could—no, should—walk away. Leave Parker here. Pretend he never saw him.

Because Parker was the enemy. He'd fought against the Haederan Navy during the invasion, and he was probably working alongside Avery for the Commonwealth. By all rights, he deserved to die here in this cell, alone and in pain.

And because Parker wasn't his problem. Avery Rendon was his problem, and right now she was—well, who knew where she was. Probably hiding with Elex Feye, the rat. He should be looking for both of them instead of wasting his time here.

He blinked, back in the present.

"You should have mentioned straightaway he was this bad off," he told the sergeant. Vague threats. Always vague threats. "The infirmary is full for the next few hours, and there's nothing I can do with him now."

That much was true. He had Mercer on standby, but Parker needed surgery, and Mercer had said anything more than basic aid would have to wait until the morning. It worked with his cover anyway—a hard-ass ISC colonel was a much more believable story than a sympathetic one, spiriting away an abused detainee for medical care.

The sergeant stuttered a useless apology.

"And if you and your colleagues are responsible for this," Chase went on, "I'll not have you escort Colonel Parker to the ISC building. I'll send people tomorrow morning for him. Touch him before then and you'll be in the adjacent interrogation room."

He turned to go before he decided to carry out Parker on his own, then remembered.

"Oh. I almost forgot. Lieutenant Colonel Kanmar? The other one you're holding here? I want him, too. I'll send that order over later tonight. I'd suggest you stay late to process it as soon as it arrives."

For whatever this Stev Kanmar of the RADF Space Operations Directorate had done, he didn't deserve to be here either. It would be his good deed for the month. Maybe the year. Both Kanmar and Parker would be safe at the navy's prison camp on Emot. Unhappy and angry, perhaps, but safe, and pissing off Perrin with the officers' disappearance would be a happier side effect.

Even better? The soldiers wouldn't dare touch Parker now. Chase was certain of that as he walked out the door and drank in the early evening sun. They wouldn't breathe a word of his visit to Perrin, not while knowing their prisoner was bound for an ISC interrogation. Not a single one would want to be responsible for fouling that up before it began. It was a risk, yes, but one he'd have to take.

And now? Now he had another name, another candle to light.

CHAPTER THIRTY

Linden stuck the chip into the comm desk in the garrison building at Alcaris and glanced at Chase.

"Latest message," he said. "Elex says he and Lieutenant Rendon are safe underground at Villiers and says he'll hand her over as soon as possible. That bodyguard of hers? He had some chip with him. Some kind of data she was desperate to get out."

Drexel Langley? No surprise there. "Where's he now?" Chase asked.

Linden glanced away for the briefest moment. "Dead, he says. But get this—actually, you should probably read it yourself."

Chase leaned forward, read, and whistled. Yes, he'd been hopeful Feye's appearance on Asria had something to do with Avery, but he'd never dared believe he was right. If they'd been able to raid the traditional herbal shop as planned, perhaps, but those men had been diverted to Cadena and the surrounding mountains to search for Avery instead. But they were related. He'd been right. And now this on top of that bit of luck?

"Verium."

Even as he said the word, he didn't believe it. Good thing the conference room they'd requisitioned was shielded. He'd wondered about the choice when Linden had shown him in here, but this was big—big enough that the rest of ISC didn't need to hear.

"Did you know we were using it?" Linden asked.

Chase shook his head. "I didn't know we could."

Verium was a hypothetical, as far as he knew, way to hide a starship's signature in hyperspace. Unstable and hard to mine, the method only worked on a small scale in laboratories. Only it appeared it wasn't hypothetical anymore—and worse, Avery Rendon knew it.

All this time, all the questioning, and he hadn't come close to finding out what she was desperately trying to hide. All her stories, her fear, her willingness to die for her secrets . . . it made sense now. And to think he'd once thought she had nothing to do with the Commonwealth—it was enough to make one commit ritual suicide in front of the emperor with their family watching. He massaged his temples instead. They'd get her back—but blast it, it needed to be before she got her information to the Commonwealth.

"Apparently the navy has their own secrets," he said, choking down the anxiety.

"They shouldn't. And here's why." Linden waved through the diagrams, a disgusted expression on his face. "Look at this. Pages and pages of sketches and formulas. Everything the Common- wealth would need to start up their own program—minus access to the actual verium, of course."

It didn't matter that the Commonwealth didn't have any. They'd find their own verium sooner rather than later. Almost thirty planets in the quadrant were still under Commonwealth control, and if even a dozen of them had adequate verium deposits, it would only be a matter of months until their enemy leveled the playing field. The Haederan Empire couldn't allow that to happen.

No. ISC couldn't allow that to happen.

Chase squinted at one of the sketches. Too technical for him. "And we have access to it, I assume?"

"Sure. Why do you think we took Thaopra, Hanides, and the rest?" His expression grew grim. "Iythea, too."

Linden knew more about this disaster than he did. *Strange.* "It's not something the Commonwealth needs to get their hands on, though. At least he got the data away from her. Lieutenant Rendon didn't make a copy, did she?"

"No way to know," Linden replied. "But even if she did, handing the data to the Asrian Defense Forces won't do any good. They might have verium here, but they can't do anything with it without us noticing. She's going to need to get off the planet."

"Then that's probably what she'll try next." Chase pulled out the chip and stuck it in his pocket. It wasn't something to leave lying around, even in this comm room deep in the ISC building. "Major Feye is aware?"

"I'm fairly certain he's going to use that desire to get her to us. Sounds like in the next few days, as soon as he can talk her out of leaving—says he has a plan for that, but he's keeping it quiet for now."

It made him nervous when sources began hiding things, but Chase clapped Linden on the shoulder. "Nice work. Get them both back, and I may have to forgive Noall for losing her in the first place. You can go apologize to him for me. What do you need me to do?"

"Not scare her away?" Linden grinned. "Everything's already set up, sir. He's planning to get a little lost and run into a checkpoint in the mountains. They're ready for her there. If, for some reason, they don't go through that way, I've got a team ready at Alcaris for them."

"You think he'll try something?"

"No. But you never know. I'm not going to ignore a few easy contingency plans out of complacency."

The anxiety had been clawing at Chase's throat, but Linden sounded so sure. Maybe this was almost over.

"It'll be fine, sir," Linden said, giving Chase a sideways look.

"There's too much security for them to get off the planet, and if they do, they'll never make it past the blockade. We'll get them."

He raised his eyebrows. "Oh, and to think I almost forgot the best part. There's one tiny little complication to this entire situation—or maybe you'd consider it a bonus. Major Feye also says that she was sworn in yesterday at the Defense Forces base at Villiers. Lieutenant Rendon is officially Avery Carina Victoria Rendon, Her Majesty the Queen of Asria."

The anxiety fell away like rocks skipping down canyon walls.

Brilliant.

* * *

Chase checked the time once more. The navy was getting too full of themselves lately, giving him this twenty-minute departure window. Linden had asked for two hours to give them plenty of time—Feye was supposed to have handed Avery over at a specific checkpoint outside Cadena, but at the last minute had sent word. Avery was suspicious, he'd told Linden. They'd be coming to Alcaris together in an attempt to hijack one of the navy orbital shuttles that sat next to his ISC one. A worrying change in plans, to be sure, but it was for the best—shoving Avery into a shuttle just paces away from where she showed up was easier than dragging her through the mountains.

Every fiber of his being wanted to race upstairs to the security gallery to back up Rhys, but he couldn't risk Avery seeing him first. Linden had made that clear. *Don't scare her off, sir. Please?* She and Feye would be gone if that happened. So he sat in the shuttle that would take him, Rhys, Feye, and Avery to *Aurora*, waiting with the door open and his ears perked for anything that might be happening in the gallery.

He hadn't failed.

He hadn't failed.

Feye had sent word fifteen minutes ago through a comm Linden had handed him in Cadena during their last visit, and now he and Avery were on the verge of arriving upstairs in the hangar where he sat. He should have known Feye hadn't betrayed ISC—how could he have? Even the best agents had second thoughts, and it wasn't as though Feye's had lasted that long . . . though, to be fair, those reservations were rapidly taken care of when family members became involved. He didn't especially approve of Rhys's decision to involve the sister, but that was over and done with now—or would be, once he made sure ISC's plans for her were acceptable. Linden should have made sure of that, but he'd check just in case.

And tomorrow—tomorrow he and Rhys and Feye and Avery would leave *Aurora* for Haedera.

Home.

Home to Windhaven, home to Isobel, home to Sophie and Marc. His heart began to race. He couldn't let himself get excited about seeing them yet. It was nine weeks at the very least to Haedera, and there was so much work to be done on the courier. Feye would need to be debriefed, and Avery . . . well, he'd see about Avery. There would be more questioning, certainly, and depending on how she cooperated, it could go easily or it could be exhausting.

Please let it go well.

Loud voices from outside drew him from his thoughts. Chase whispered a prayer as he ducked outside—yes. There they were, exiting the far lift tube.

Rhys.

Avery.

A group of Haederan Army soldiers.

But where was Elex Feye?

He pushed aside the question as he darted down the ramp to meet them. Feye needed to be here now. If he wasn't, if someone had to go looking for him, they'd miss the window. They'd be stuck on Asria one more day, and that one day would seem an eternity. For a moment, he thought he felt the breeze at Windhaven on his face, but it was only the wind blowing out of the open lift door.

Linden quickened his stride to widen the gap between himself and the soldiers.

"He's dead," he said under his breath, eyes wide in shock. "He tried to take my gun, and . . ."

Dead?

Chase held up his hand. "Not now." His head began to spin. "They're loading the body?"

Dead?

Linden nodded as the soldiers approached behind him, dragging Avery along. Her eyes were red and wet, and half the curls behind her neck had escaped. She hadn't come willingly, then.

Not that he'd expected it. Hoped, perhaps, that Feye had made her see reason, but he hadn't expected it. She tried to double over when she saw him, likely to slip away, but the soldiers pulled her back up. Linden twisted her around, one hand on the army cuffs they'd used upstairs, the other on the ISC ones on his tactical vest. Policy, of course—like his own, Linden's cuffs had an additional layer of fingerprint security that could be activated if needed.

Chase checked his chronometer again.

Thirty seconds.

They didn't have time for this. "Not now," he said. "Launch window closes soon. You can swap them once we get up there. You"—he pointed at the nearest soldier—"with us."

Linden pursed his lips at the unorthodox order, but shoved his cuffs back in his vest without a word.

Let him disagree. Avery wasn't going anywhere this time. Even if she had the skill, she was too afraid to do anything. Her wide eyes, dark with fear, never left his as they pulled her aboard the shuttle and secured her harness. Chase flopped down across from her and fastened his own as the engines spooled to takeoff power.

Just in time.

At the sound of the engines roaring to life, Avery looked out the window and closed her eyes. The sun was rising—the last Asrian sunrise she'd ever see. But there were Haederan sunrises that were just as beautiful, and in a few years, she'd be allowed to see one. He would make sure she survived her time in whatever grim ISC prison she was headed for, and then he would hand her over to Victor Rendon, compliant at last, the perfect propaganda tool, and then he would retire. No more worrying about her safety, no more truth serum, no more ISC.

He might even spend the first few months of his retirement finding Merritt Parker. If Parker was on Emot—which he would likely be for a few years, at least—it would be easy. And if he could convince Parker to come to Haedera for a visit . . . well, that would make Avery happy.

Suggestible.

It would make her suggestible. Because this was about indoctrination. Nothing more. He couldn't care what happened to her. He couldn't care about her happiness or joy.

Didn't care.

He blinked back the idea of a reunion between Avery and Parker as the sunrise faded to the dark of space. Linden's anxiety was tangible beside him as the stars popped out. Chase ignored his constant shifting and focused his attention on Avery. It was never too early for the questioning to begin, and the more off guard she was, the better.

"I'm curious," he said to her. "Who else knows how to duplicate the verium technology?"

Who else does ISC need to track down and neutralize?

She jerked upright and stared at him for the first time since they'd left the planet. Even with her hands behind her back, he could see her shake.

"Ah." He chuckled at the look on her face, terror like he'd never seen, then shot Linden one of his own. *Stop fidgeting, Rhys.* "You're so easy to read." How long had he wanted to say those words to her? "It's almost too easy, really. You didn't tell anyone else what you learned, did you?"

The tears fell at that, but they fell silently.

"I didn't think so." He'd been afraid she had, of course, but her reaction left no room for doubt. She was too paranoid to spread the information around, and finally, that had worked in his favor. "And since I don't need to worry about you anymore, that leaves only your source. A physicist, am I right? I'm sure he won't be difficult to find and silence. You'll help with that, of course. We can talk about how to find him on the way to Haedera."

Nine weeks. Even if he would have had to debrief Feye, he and Avery would have almost nine weeks to talk. How to play it? He could go harsh—threaten her with the things that would happen to her on Haedera if she didn't open up to him. It'd never worked well before, but on a small courier ship with only one thing on the other end . . . maybe. Or he could give her one last bit of freedom to explore the ship and see the stars, make her grateful enough that she'd tell him what he wanted to know. They'd been friendly once, after all.

It didn't matter yet. He'd figure it out once they were on board.

"And once we arrive . . ." he said. "Well, you do make quite the valuable hostage, Your Majesty. I'm sure we can think of some other use for you. Who knows? You might even grow to enjoy Haedera. Your uncle certainly has."

If she had any sense at all, she would learn to love her new home. Asria was her past, and Haedera was just as beautiful, if not more. And no matter what she thought this very second, living in exile was better than death—even if the shadow of execution would hang over her for the rest of her life.

Her breath quickened; the tears fell harder. He wanted to do something, anything to stop them, but that wouldn't be his problem soon. She'd learn. They wouldn't tolerate that where she was headed. They wouldn't put up with half the deceitfulness and manipulation she'd shown over the past few months.

Why did his stomach tighten at the idea? He didn't care what happened to her. Everyone needed to believe that.

"Colonel?" The pilot broke in over the intercom.

What now? Chase shook off his own anxiety and steeled his tone. "Go ahead."

"You have a priority comm from *Stargazer* waiting, sir."

He suppressed a sigh. "Right."

Of course he did. *Stargazer* was in the middle of troop turnover, and there was always someone who wanted to go home or didn't want to go home—and they usually insisted on making a nuisance of themselves. Like he had, and that's how dispatch knew there was a nearby and much-needed ISC presence.

You really screwed this one up.

He could rush Linden, could rush the soldiers, but now . . . he couldn't say no to this kind of request, no matter how much of a hurry he was in. Well, he'd handle it quickly, and whoever was responsible would regret the day they'd yanked him from his primary mission and delayed their departure to Haedera.

He reached for his harness clasps. Avery's eyes were wide, filled with tears, but her breathing had slowed. Was she relieved to see him leave, if only for five minutes? How dare she not realize his presence was the only reason she was as unbroken as she was?

A little of his anger at *Stargazer*'s senior officers narrowed in on her and her lack of gratitude. It was an unsettling feeling, one he didn't want, so he grinned at her and patted her knee as he stood. Watching her struggle to control her emotions always put him in a better mood.

Her whimper resonated through the flight deck hatch behind him.

* * *

Stars, he was exhausted. It'd been ten hours of meetings and interviews on *Stargazer*, another five hours of writing up his findings and pissing off a whole bunch of people. Chase had stolen less than an hour of sleep on the floor of the docking bay while waiting for his second ride to *Aurora*, though how they'd expected him to sleep in front of the void, protected by only a thin metal door, he didn't know.

Now, as he refrained from leaning his head against the side of the lift tube that took him to the small holding area outside *Aurora*'s largest flight bay, sleep was all he could think about. He jerked upright as the door slid open, revealing three navy security guards behind a reception desk. Luckily for them, they only straightened, gave him a cell number, and pointed down the row of doors.

Somber bastards, aren't they? Maybe Avery had given them trouble, although she hadn't looked like she was capable of that when he'd left her in Linden's competent hands. Maybe they didn't know how to handle a female prisoner. Maybe brig duty on *Aurora* was simply as unpleasant as it was on *Defiant*. Who knew? The only thing he knew was that he had no idea what he was going to say to Avery, and he needed to figure something out quickly.

The numbers started at twenty and went backward from the main door, and Chase counted as he walked down the cell bank. The doors were shut, the cells empty except for Avery's. Linden would have made certain the area was cleared for such a high-security detainee. Let the navy deal with moving their own prisoners for a day or so, if they'd had any to begin with. The army had done more work in the prison in downtown Cadena, so they had no right to complain.

Light caught his eye—one of the doors was open. *Strange.* He quickened his pace.

Not six.

Not six.

Not six.

His quick stride became a run, and he had to stick out his arm to stop himself at the open door, his heart pounding.

And inside—it wasn't Avery. A man in a green ISC uniform sat on the floor, knees pulled against his chest, head down on his knees.

"Rhys?"

Linden looked up, his face pale. Vomit stained his collar, though it looked like he'd tried to scrub it away. He stared at Chase with bloodshot eyes but didn't say a word.

Not that he needed to.

Avery was gone.

RHYS KNOCKED ON THE DOOR ONE MORNING AS SHE WAS FINISHING breakfast, weeks after the ISC major had dumped her back at the hotel with one last admonishment and threat. Without Rhys, it had been weeks of boredom, weeks of plotting more escape attempts that never happened, weeks of the same bland local Asrian food and Haederan tea, weeks of worrying about Xan, and weeks of nonanswers from the Imperial Security people who refused to tell her anything about Rhys's new whereabouts or of their plans for her.

And weeks of keeping her own secret. It'd taken Katryn that long to figure out the reason for her constant fatigue and nausea.

Rhys looked bad. Tired. The shadows under his eyes and wrinkles in the sleeve of his uniform pants, usually ironed to whatever exacting standards he followed, gave him away. *Let's talk downstairs* was all he said.

They went silently, except for her thumping heart. Could Rhys hear it? Surely he must be able to. He led her into a small conference room on the first floor, but it wasn't empty like she'd expected. An Imperial Security colonel she'd never met, never even seen, stood by the window, his hands clasped behind his back and a blank look on his face. Rhys shut the door behind them.

"I need to tell you something," he said slowly. "Though I think you should sit down first."

He didn't need to say anything more.

Xan was dead.

It was obvious from Rhys's quiet hello and the way he spoke and the way he'd brought a witness so she couldn't attack him.

Katryn shook her heard. "I need to tell you something first." If she delayed the delivery of his news, then maybe it hadn't really happened. Xan wasn't really dead until Rhys and this emotionless man told her he was.

Rhys glanced at the colonel, askance in his eyes. The colonel unclasped his hands and waved them in a *do whatever you need to do* motion.

"Did something happen?" Rhys asked. "They told me—they told me you've been treated well. That you cooperated, and—"

"No. I mean, yes. I've been bored and frightened but they haven't mistreated me." Besides not letting her leave her room after her one night of freedom and feeding her Asrian eel for breakfast, but those seemed like such minor problems now. "But I'm—" She glanced at the colonel, but he didn't make a move to leave. He narrowed his eyes at her, in fact. "I'm pregnant," she whispered.

Rhys's jaw tightened.

Before he could say anything, the colonel grabbed her by the arm. Katryn protested, but he marched her outside the conference room and down the hallway past at least ten other officers into a small courtyard she'd only been allowed to visit once. She hated the man already. Rhys tried to follow them out, but the colonel slammed the door in his face. Katryn stood in the center of the paving stones, arms wrapped around herself, as he turned to her.

"Did he force himself on you?" he asked.

"What?" It was the last thing she'd expected to hear. He'd brought her out here—to freeze—just to ask that?

"It's a simple question, one I'd like an immediate answer to." His cool voice turned angry. "Did Captain Linden rape you?" Each word might as well have been pulled separately from his lips.

"No!" Then, more quietly. "No. I care about him. I thought he cared about me. We—"

The colonel snorted at that. Actually snorted at her. Unbelievable. No, hate wasn't a strong enough word for her feelings toward this man.

"You won't care much about him when you hear what he came back to tell you," he said. "And after that? You and I are going to have a long discussion about this. Alone."

She narrowed her eyes at him. This man was the last person she wanted to talk to about anything. Maybe Rhys could get rid of him somehow. She'd told the truth, and what business was it of his? "What does he have to say to me?"

He jerked his head back toward the door. "He'll tell you himself. I'm tired of doing everyone else's dirty work. Let's go."

Katryn followed him back inside, back to Rhys, who was still standing by the door, watching them. Watching her. They both trailed the colonel back to the conference room he'd so abruptly yanked her out of, and she faced Rhys.

"So? What do you need to tell me?"

Rhys licked his lips, silent.

"Is Xan dead?"

He nodded.

"What happened?"

"I can't tell you."

How many times could her heart snap in two? Katryn lunged at him, a scream erupting from somewhere deep in her chest. She managed to land one good scratch across Rhys's cheek before the colonel pried her away and pulled her arms behind her. Lack of hands didn't stop her from kicking though, so she lashed out at Rhys with her feet, over and over.

"Stop," the colonel said as she began to cry. He sounded as

tired as Rhys. "If we're going to clean up this mess, crying and beating on him won't help."

"She needed to do it, sir. And I deserve it." Rhys stepped closer and tried to wipe her tears away with his hand. Katryn turned her face toward the window instead. "He—he killed himself. I can't give you more details than that. Katryn, I'm so sorry." He glanced at the colonel, and his voice became rushed. "I wish I could tell you more and that I had better news for you, but I can't, and I don't."

"You have to."

"I can't. Please believe me. The only thing I can tell you is that I've been recalled to Haedera over this."

"Good. I never want to see you again."

The colonel's grip loosened. Katryn pulled her arms away from him and shook her sleeves back down while he began to pace by the door. The movement made her more irritable. All she wanted him to do was stand still. Or better, leave. Rhys didn't reply, and she finally managed to look at him. He didn't look angry—or happy—about her news. He didn't look sad about his. He looked . . . afraid?

"Katryn . . . I won't be returning to Asria."

"Good," she repeated, though she couldn't muster as much malice that time. Rhys was involved in Xan's death somehow, so why did the idea of never seeing him break her heart?

"I won't see you again. Ever." Rhys sighed and rubbed his face. "Some things happened, and I . . . ." He drew in a deep breath. "I'm in a lot of trouble."

Something strange and light touched her soul.

"How much trouble?" she asked with more force than she probably had a right to.

Rhys blinked at her. His mouth seemed to be glued shut.

"Are they going to kill you?"

His continued silence answered for him.

"Then why go back there?" Katryn threw her hands into the air, her vehement defense of the man involved in Xan's death too surprising for her to do anything else. Rhys was probably as surprised—the colonel just looked shocked. "If things went that badly, then stay on Asria! Go somewhere else. Anywhere else! Anywhere but Haedera. There's an entire quadrant out there, Rhys!"

The colonel's eyebrows lifted at the familiarity.

I told you he didn't rape me, you idiot.

"I have honor." Rhys shrugged. "This is what's expected of me."

Honor? Did he know the meaning of the word?

"This is not honor." Her voice shook. "It's a waste of life. Xan's already gone, and now . . . They've brainwashed you, can't you see that?" Why was that so difficult for him to understand?

"It's what's expected of me," he repeated slowly, like he was figuring it out himself for the first time. "If I fight this, if I disappear and don't arrive on Haedera as scheduled, he will wonder why. And then he will find out about you. If I do my duty, this all ends right here, right now. I can't save myself, but I can save you. I can save my family. Do you understand what I'm saying, Katryn?"

No. She didn't. Every time he spoke, her mind became more muddled. Now it was a gray haze that wrapped around her. "Who? Who's he?"

"The emperor," the colonel broke in. "Or were you not listening when he said he was in a lot of trouble?"

Hateful man. Panic built in her chest as she turned toward him. "Can't you do anything to help him? Or are you punishing him, too?"

"He's taking me to Haedera," Rhys cut in. "Tomorrow. There's nothing he can do. There's nothing I can do. And if you want to stay safe, you'll listen to me."

"There has to be something I can—"

"You could marry me."

Rhys made the suggestion as casually as if he'd said they could go for a walk after dinner. Yet there was something in his tone that suggested that, no, it wasn't a spur-of-the-moment suggestion.

"Marry you?" She'd meant that she'd lie for him or hide him somewhere. Not marry him. She didn't love him. Cared for him, yes, of course, but love? Love was such a nebulous thing, especially now. And Rhys didn't love her. Was this the kind of thing they did on Haedera? It wasn't something they did on her own planet. "I can't—I can't marry you. You have no right to ask that of me."

"You're right." Rhys's left shoulder lifted, like he wanted to shrug but couldn't muster the effort. "I may as well have destroyed your life. I've certainly destroyed mine. I have no right to ask anything of you." His eyes grew glassy; his voice choked with emotion. "But Haederan law doesn't allow for the child to be called Linden unless we're married. I can handle my fate, but knowing I'll never meet my child—"

"Captain Linden." The colonel stepped toward him. "Out. Now."

"Sir, I—"

"Out."

Oh, what now? Katryn flopped into the nearest chair and crossed her arms as Rhys headed—however reluctantly—out the door. She hoped he was listening from the hallway, doing whatever he could to protect her from this man.

The colonel slammed the door shut and turned toward her. "You will not marry Captain Linden."

She hadn't had any plans to—had thought Rhys had lost his mind, in fact—until this man had ordered her to do the opposite. Who did he think he was? Just like everyone else who'd ever told her to do something she didn't want to do, his very presence grated on her like a dull itch on her back she couldn't reach to scratch.

"And you," she replied, tightening her arms around her, "will not tell me what I can and can't do."

His eyebrows flew up. "You are challenging the wrong person, Doctor Holt. I would think twice before you do so again."

A hot flash of fear ran through her. Maybe she'd just made a grave mistake, even though something told her he was all bluster. No real threat to her. Violent men were violent, and he didn't look like he was capable of hurting her.

Still, he was ISC . . .

"Give me one good reason I shouldn't do what he's asked of me. If he's going to die—if he's never going to meet this child—if I never have to live with him as his wife—if I won't see him after tomorrow—then why not?"

"Because it's—" The colonel made a few strange sputtering sounds. "It's absolutely inappropriate, and you know it."

Oh, please. When had she ever cared about propriety?

"What do I need to do to file the paperwork?"

"He needs permission from his commanding officer. That's me, and I won't give it."

"That's not what I asked."

He crossed his arms again, and she choked back a laugh. He'd mirrored her stance and wasn't even aware of it.

"Tell me why you want to do this," he said, calmer this time.

Katryn opened her mouth, then closed it.

"Because he was—" Her laugh faded away. *Stupid tears.* "Because he was kind to me. Even though I'm the enemy and he didn't have to be and—"

The colonel shoved his hands in his pockets and began to pace. Past her chair, past the door behind which Rhys was probably doing his own pacing, past the window where the rain had started once more. His unease was making her stomach turn circles, but he finally stopped and sat down next to her.

"Do you really want to do this?" The question was soft, gentle. "There could be complications in the future."

"That major Rhys sent after me when I escaped, you mean." She shivered when she thought of him. "He threatened to cut my throat."

"The—" His eyes grew cold. "Did he now?"

She nodded.

"That was . . . an unsanctioned threat." He stared at her, thoughtful, like a hunter after an *octeleon*, and she wanted to bolt. "Well, no matter. He was working with Captain Linden, and now that the operation's over, you won't see him again. But no, he's not the complication." He continued to stare at her, assessing, not answering her question.

Katryn shifted uncomfortably at the silence. What kind of complications was he implying, then? "Your emperor."

"You don't need to worry about that, either." He jerked his head to the side. "I'll make sure that doesn't happen. But it's always possible things may happen that none of us can predict. You would not be marrying someone with no history, no ties to Haedera. He has family—he has—"

She suddenly felt a burning desire to save him from his stilted explanation.

"I'm fine with that uncertainty. Whatever it is, I'm fine with it."

For hadn't her life been uncertain since the Haederan Empire had taken Iythea? This wasn't going to change her life nearly as much as an enemy invasion had. It wouldn't change things as much as marrying Nash, or agreeing to the Iythea position, or saying goodbye to Xan on Zarcron, or finishing her doctorate. And uncertainty wasn't even the right word, though this strange Haederan would never understand. This was simply one more adventure.

The colonel ran his hands over his face. "You just need to sign the paperwork. Beside him. That's all, since I assume you don't want some sort of blessing."

Katryn shook her head. "Just legalities."

"Then I'll have everything set up by this evening." He stood and rapped on the door for Rhys, who came back in with no small amount of trepidation on his face.

"Rhys." Katryn held her arms out for him, not caring about

their audience. He fell against her, so warm. So alive. And yet so desperate for the tiniest splinter of happiness that she now controlled. How could she destroy what little hope—what little joy—he had left? "I'll do it."

"You don't have to," he said against her cheek. "I was wrong to ask."

"Maybe. But I want to do it anyway." She took a deep breath and looked sideways at the colonel. "You leave tomorrow, you said?"

He sighed and scratched at his forehead. "I can probably buy Captain Linden another few days on Asria. No one will think anything of it if the journey to Haedera takes a little longer than usual. His Majesty will certainly be none the wiser. Space travel can be unpredictably slow, after all, especially during a war."

"Is that so?" she asked, an odd fluttering feeling beginning to settle in her stomach. Finally, another ally, in the most unexpected place.

He nodded, a strange glint in his eyes.

Rhys grinned and pulled her closer.

* * *

It was cold for this time of year—maybe this was something she needed to get used to if she was to make Asria her new home. Katryn tugged at her coat to block the fierce mountain wind that signaled certain snow. The crew was almost done loading the shuttle that would take Rhys and the colonel to the courier ship in orbit—the ship that was waiting, fueled and provisioned, to take them to Haedera. Part of her wanted to run across the ramp and scatter their belongings in every direction to delay the inevitable, but . . .

That was what it was. The inevitable. The unavoidable. Rhys was leaving, and he was never coming back.

She shivered, and Rhys stepped closer, his eyes on the workers. "You'll stay in the hotel for the next few weeks. After that,

Colonel Chase has set everything up for you." His hand shook a bit as he reached for hers. "I don't know details. It's—it's best if I don't know anything."

"That man has a name?" She laughed to cover the sick feeling in her stomach. "I was starting to believe he didn't."

Rhys laughed back, though it was hollow.

"He has a name." He paused. "Katryn—"

"Don't apologize. Please don't apologize." He'd spent most of the past four days doing just that. "I'm not bitter about this. Not about what's happened to me. But you . . . I wish more than anything that I could murder your emperor with my bare hands. I wish I could change your mind about returning."

I wish Xan was here.

He made a choking sound. "That's probably not the best thing to say right here," he said, with a quick glance at the two Imperial Security men behind them.

"Let them get flustered. If they honestly believe he's in any danger from me, then they deserve all the stress they get."

"They're going to get it from you, I think. I almost feel sorry for them."

On the other side of the ramp, Chase nodded at one of the crewmen and headed toward them.

"Time to go." Rhys sighed, though the brave expression she'd become so used to was firmly in place. "Are you going to be all right?"

"If I said no, would you stay? Try to fix this in some other way?"

"I told you I keep my promises." His entire body sagged, and she knew the answer before he said anything. "I'm doing this for you, Katryn. Remember that."

He kissed her cheek and was gone.

CHAPTER THIRTY-TWO

THE LUSH CARPETING IN THE HALLWAY OUTSIDE THE EMPEROR'S private study was a mockery under Chase's leather dress boots.

So were the wall hangings and the carvings on the ceiling and his green pants, gaudy above the crimson rug. And the cool air, artificial of course.

He'd grown up here, had run down these very corridors chasing after Isobel and her brothers and sisters, and yet—and yet, right now, it was the least familiar place on Haedera. In the quadrant, actually, since Cadena, the last place he'd ever wanted to go, had seemed more recognizable. More like home. The paintings that moved with the rhythm of his breath seemed unholy somehow, especially since the breath of the man next to him would shortly be ended.

Chase glanced beside him. Linden sat frozen on the low bench, hadn't moved for the past half hour, though it'd seemed Chase himself had shifted back and forth every second. Even stood and paced a few times. Because this—this waiting, this uncertainty that wasn't—this was what real torture was. People could withstand starvation and pain, but anticipation of the same? No, that broke them. A useful technique, until it happened to you.

He ran through his arguments in his head, ignoring the

wraithlike echoes of children's laughter in his mind. His Imperial Majesty had pages and pages of reasons and excuses and pleas, sent while they were en route from Asria. He'd spent over eight weeks writing and pleading and praying, then sleeping a few hours on a stiff bunk only to wake up and do it all over. The emperor also had Lient's arguments, and if there was one person he always listened to, it was Lient. Still, he knew, and Lient knew, and most importantly, Linden knew . . .

There was only one way this would end.

Linden cleared his throat and brought a small piece of folded paper from his pocket.

"Give this to her?" he asked.

"Rhys . . ."

But what was there to say? *Don't worry about a note because you'll see her as soon as we make it back to Asria?* That was a lie, and they both knew it.

"Please, sir." Linden's voice was steady.

"All right. Of course." Chase shoved the note in the pocket of his formal jacket. "But Rhys—"

The door in front of them opened. The guardsman who exited the emperor's study gave them a brief, emotionless look and motioned them inside, no sign of the sneer that usually accompanied Chase's appearance. Linden stood first and smoothed out his green jacket, conspicuously and intentionally decorated with every award he'd ever been honored with, down to the most inconsequential. If nothing else, he was putting on a brave face, and if he could do it, then so could Chase.

His Imperial Majesty was standing right by the same window where Chase had seen him before leaving for Asria so many months ago—though there was no underlying humor in his eyes today. Chase fell to one knee after a quick glance to make sure Linden had done the same. Bowing to the man was the last thing he wanted to do, but if there was any chance for Linden at all, they needed to play the game.

"So," the emperor said to the back of his head. "She got away.

With a verium-enhanced Shrike fighter, no less. That's quite the blunder."

By his side, Linden shifted. Chase didn't risk a glance. If only his heart would stop pounding, he could think, could form words. "It was a mistake, sire. One I take full responsibility for."

"So your dozens of communications stated. You certainly were busy on the way home—and you managed to get Lient on your side, as well. I'm impressed." There was a long pause. "Stand up, Colonel."

Colonel. Not his name, not his imperial title. Not even the earlship he'd inherited from his father—the lower-ranking title the palace staff used when they wanted to remind him of his place. This was official, this was formal, and—damn the hot tears that were forming. Chase blinked them away as he stood, his knees objecting; he couldn't show weakness. Linden's head was still down, his eyes closed.

"I understand your reluctance to allow Captain Linden to take the blame for this outrageous breach of trust," the emperor said, "though I'm shocked that you allowed it to happen in the first place. I really did think better of you, and I thought better of Callum. But we'll talk about your fate later—a fate which you may yet earn some influence over."

What did that mean?

The emperor reached for the table beside the window, for the pistol lying innocently next to his morning tea. A testament to how much control he had over ISC—over Haedera itself. Not one subject would dare reach for it, even the very few who were allowed inside the palace armed.

"You screwed up," he said. "You fix it."

Chase stared at the weapon in his outstretched hand. His Majesty couldn't expect—but the look on the emperor's face was anything but joking.

Never.

He'd never shoot Linden; he'd never kill anyone else. He

shoved his hands in his pockets, a reckless act of insubordination he'd never even been bold enough to do in front of Lient.

"No."

Linden's head flew up at his refusal.

The emperor chuckled. "No? Are you honestly going to stand there and disobey a direct order from me? Your sovereign? The person who has the power of life and death over you?" His tone was light, but there was something . . .

"Captain Linden did nothing wrong." That wasn't quite true, but no matter what Avery had been allowed to do, Rhys hadn't made any mistake worth dying for. He'd argue that until his last breath. Desperation was overtaking him now; that Holt woman's face was right there in the front of his mind. "If you need to take someone's life, take mine."

"You always did like taking the easy way out. But you're not getting away from your obligations that easily."

Death was easy? Said who?

"He's entitled to last rites." The words rushed out. "You cannot in good conscience deny him that." He'd already done it himself on the courier, but at least he could buy Linden a few more hours with that minor lie. "I'll do them myself, and—"

"Traitors are not."

No matter that Linden was anything but a traitor. This was an excuse. Chase clenched his fists in his pockets. "I won't do it."

"Then you will answer for that disobedience as well." The emperor raised the pistol. "Anything to say, Mister Linden?"

Linden shook his head. Eyes closed. Teeth gritted.

Chase didn't close his eyes as the shot echoed through the study. He would never forget—no, would never let himself forget— Linden falling forward onto that gleaming marble floor. After a few long, slowing breaths, he pulled his hands from his pockets and knelt back down. It was only to close Linden's eyes, and this time, he made sure to face away from the emperor. There couldn't be any indication that he was kneeling to the man. He couldn't formulate a prayer, not even the words he'd been trained to say since child-hood. Because this was his fault. He'd pleaded the entire way to Haedera, but the Holy One had stopped listening to his prayers.

"Isobel is here," the emperor said, like nothing had happened. He set the pistol on the table next to him and waved his guardsmen toward Linden's body. "You may as well say goodbye before you head back to Asria."

Chase's throat closed up. *How generous of you, Your Majesty.*

"Thank you. Sire." He rose, nodded, and retreated before he could put his hands around the man's neck. Seeing Isobel would fix . . . well, almost anything.

* * *

Her suite was quiet.

Chase walked down the long hallway that led to the private bedroom and sitting room, fighting tears. Isobel's rooms in the imperial palace were never quiet. There were always servants or friends or children visiting whenever she was in Rebet. Wherever Isobel was, there was happiness and loud joy. There was never silence. Perhaps her father had lied. Perhaps she was out. Perhaps—

"My lord. No one said—"

Yes, yes, he surprised everyone simply by existing. This time it was Meira, Isobel's favorite lady's maid, who jumped at his appearance. She seemed to gather her composure as she nodded at him, though she'd cringed a bit as she came out of the sitting room, like she'd heard the shot from the emperor's study. But that was impossible. It had to be impossible, didn't it? They were on the other side of the palace.

"I'm so glad you're here," Meira said instead. "But—"

"He said Isobel was here." Chase looked around her into the sitting room. It was dark, with only one small table lamp lit. The heavy velvet drapes were closed too, and that didn't make sense—Isobel liked the sun, even inside. Why was Meira standing there like she was blocking his way? "But it's so quiet . . ."

"Who is it?" a new voice called. Male. Clinical. "Tell them she doesn't need to be bothered. I've already told them to stay away; they can clean the place later."

Holy One, no.

He pushed past Meira and darted into the bedroom. Isobel was asleep on her side, her delicate hands under her chin and her dark hair loose and strewn across the pillow. Flushed—though maybe that was how she'd always looked. How long had it been since he'd last seen her? From his very first off-world mission, they'd made it a rule never to count the days. Counting the days did nothing but lengthen them.

The emperor's personal doctor, the voice he'd recognized, was rising from a chair at the side of the bed. His shoulders sagged when he noticed Chase.

"My lord." A quick nod. "Apologies. I didn't know you were back on Haedera, and—"

"Never mind that." Chase stood in the doorway, not wanting to ask. If he didn't ask, it wouldn't be true. "How bad is she?"

"We've tried everything, my lord. But you know how the virus progresses. She hid it for so long, and it was so advanced when she admitted—"

"How. Bad. Is. She?"

He rarely used his ISC tone on servants, and he'd never used it on someone on the emperor's personal staff. He'd hear about it later, no doubt, though he was beyond caring about his lengthening list of sins toward his father-in-law.

But Isobel—his stomach began to churn. Why had he bothered asking? He could tell how bad she was.

The doctor flinched. "A few days. No more than a week. I'm glad—I'm glad you made it back, my lord. She'll want to see you when she wakes up."

If she wakes up.

This was one more punishment, in a roundabout way, but it

would never succeed. His Majesty didn't understand love, didn't understand that being on Haedera when Isobel died was his most fervent wish. No, he'd been sent here because the emperor thought it would tear his heart out even more.

As if they'd already disturbed her too much, Isobel made a soft noise and shifted. Chase pushed by the doctor and yanked a chair toward the bed. Isobel's hand was as soft as always when he grabbed it, but the skin was paper-thin, and dark veins showed through.

Her eyes flickered open. "Gareth."

"Iz." He tried to smile at her. "Hey."

She rubbed her eyes with her free hand. "I'm seeing things."

How many times could his heart crack in one hour? "No, you're not. I came back to Rebet to—" *To witness the execution of one of my best men.* "To see you."

"You've been gone so long. Has it been a year? I didn't think . . ."

"I know. It's been a long while, hasn't it?" He adjusted the covers around her shoulder. "But I'm back now."

"For how long?"

Even though she'd asked, she didn't want to know the answer, either. Years of marriage meant he could read her soul easier than he'd ever thought possible.

"I'm not sure." He needed to head back to Asria, yes, but he could stay here a while, couldn't he? Lient would be merciful, and Isobel's father . . . well, he'd worry about that problem later. The emperor wasn't going to boot him from the palace until she was gone—maybe not even after. "Long enough."

Tears filled her dark eyes. "I'm sorry."

Chase squeezed her hand in between his and kissed it. "For what?"

"For going out there in the first place. For not telling anyone I thought I was sick."

"Oh, Isobel. You don't need to apologize for that."

And that was true. It wasn't her fault she'd visited Carew in the middle of an epidemic. The local governor hadn't informed the Imperial Security Command of the crisis in his region, and he'd died for that oversight. It wasn't her fault a vaccine hadn't been available until a year later. It wasn't even her fault for lying about it. The Carew fever wasn't contagious, but fear had spread across Haedera that year only a few short weeks after the outbreak had begun. Sufferers had been attacked, shunned, murdered. Isobel would have never shamed her father—or husband—like that. Traditionalist Haederan, she was.

Like he had been.

Where had that thought come from?

Isobel closed her eyes. "Then you'll stay with me until . . ."

He pressed her hand to his cheek and closed his, too.

"Until the very end, I swear it. I promise I won't leave you."

Until your father summons me again.

CHAPTER THIRTY-THREE

"My lord? You need to wake up. Quickly. Please, my lord."

"Go away," Chase mumbled. "One more hour."

No matter how much he lectured, Zavis would never learn to not wake him up after nights like these. He dragged his eyes open to admonish Zavis again, then blinked in confusion. It was too dark, much darker than it ever was at Windhaven, and it was cold. Windhaven was never this cool because he couldn't stand the cold and Isobel was amenable enough to allow him the warmth he desired. It was a dream, then. He was on Asria in that sterile office building downtown, dozens of floors up from the provisional prison, and Lieutenant Noall was calling his name.

No.

It wasn't Noall, and it wasn't any of his men, and it wasn't Zavis. It was a feminine voice, light and airy and without a hint of fear—some anxiety, perhaps—which meant it wasn't anyone in the Imperial Haederan Army prison in Cadena. It was Meira calling his name, and he was in Isobel's rooms in the imperial palace in Rebet, back on Haedera. Rhys was dead and Isobel was almost dead.

A nightmare would have been better.

Chase blinked, sat up, and looked around. Expensive

draperies covered the windows, and dim light glittered from the opulent chandeliers over the bed, scattering radiance across Isobel's translucent skin. She was asleep, a hand tucked under her chin, and a slight young woman was hovering over his left shoulder, adjusting the blankets over Isobel while simultaneously pulling them off him.

"My lord, they're here for you." Meira glanced toward the sitting room and brushed a nervous hand across her cheek like she was aiming for a loose curl, though her hair was braided at the back of her neck. "He—he wants to see you immediately."

The streams of light through the draperies suggested it was late in the morning, the day after Linden's death. His Majesty hadn't waited long—probably long enough for breakfast and a few cups of tea. Not even punishment could get in the way of the emperor's morning tea habit.

Meira shoved a cup of tea in his face and he drained it in one gulp. Who? Who was here for him? Who wanted him immediately? Even Meira—no, especially Meira—should know better than to pull him away from Isobel now. His eyes finally adjusted to the light outside the open door. There were four imperial guardsmen milling about in Isobel's sitting room, his summons from the emperor. Well, he'd expected that, hadn't he? The tongue lashings he'd received from Lient in the past couldn't compare to what was on the horizon for him. He could only pray it would be fast and easy and he could be back here within the hour.

He squeezed Isobel's hand and kissed her icy cheek, then let Meira help him smooth out the wrinkles in his jacket. She wasn't nearly as good at it as Zavis, but what he did he care? Did it matter how he looked now? His Majesty ought to be grateful he was wearing a uniform of any sort.

With one last glance at Isobel, sleeping comfortably, he wandered into the sitting room and nodded at the guardsmen, his heart racing. They escorted him back to the emperor's study without a word. Were they unnerved about guarding the wayward son-in-law? He'd always been uncomfortable with their presence when he played the part of a prince of the Haederan Empire—he of all people didn't need their protection, and it was silly to pretend he did. They were only ceremonial anyway, since ISC, uniformed and not, handled real palace security. And now . . . would these frauds listen in on the upbraiding he was sure to receive?

Well, he didn't care. They could listen all they wanted. His Majesty could scream and reprimand all he wanted, and then he would go back to Isobel, and then when she was ready for the next life, he'd return to Asria. He wouldn't be able to find Avery, but he'd find her source—or sources—and he'd make them talk. No mistakes next time. He'd make everything right. This was but one tiny breakdown in an otherwise illustrious career, and he only needed to survive the next few days. Everything would be better afterward.

The guardsmen pushed the door open—no waiting in the hallway of his past this time. Good. Waiting was the worst part, which, come to think of it, made it strange that he wasn't being subjected to it.

He didn't have much time to puzzle over that omission though, since the emperor wasn't near his favorite window this morning—instead, he was standing on the bottom tread of the stairs that led to the back portion of the study. That formality, unknown to the inner circle of the imperial family, didn't bode well for him. Chase bowed anyway; when he stood, the guardsmen were gone, and he and the emperor were alone in his study. There wasn't to be an audience, but that was small consolation.

"How is she?"

Chase started at the question. He hadn't expected concern —if that's what this was, and he wasn't yet convinced of that.

"The same as yesterday, sire. Mostly unconscious. It won't be long now. I—I do appreciate you bringing her here." As much as Isobel had loved Windhaven, she'd always wanted to die in

Rebet. He brushed his failure to the back of his mind. He should have been the one to bring her here.

"Hmm." The emperor began to pace on the low stair, hands behind his back. "About yesterday . . ."

He trailed off in such a strange manner—his father-in-law wasn't given to delaying a reprimand like this. Was he meant to apologize, to head this off before it began? The emperor had stopped pacing and was looking at him expectantly, but apologizing was the last thing Chase was going to do. His behavior yesterday had been the action of a zealous and caring commander, nothing more, nothing less. He pressed his lips together and took a slow, deep breath, remaining motionless.

"Your behavior was shocking, offensive, and borderline treasonous," the emperor finished.

Yes, yes, yes. Get on with it.

"I realize that, for whatever reason, you think you have Callum under your thumb, but you will not act like that around me." The last words grew in ferocity and volume until he was almost screaming, but Chase didn't flinch. "Have you forgotten who I am? What I've done for you? What I can do to you?"

Crossing his arms at this point was oh so tempting, but it'd be counterproductive. The admonishment would end. Eventually. Whether it was about his refusal to move his family to the imperial palace or the fact that the Chase family portraits his own mother had painted hung in a place of honor over the Claerwen ones at Windhaven, they always ended. Chase stood and waited.

"You will find a way to get that Shrike back, and then you will go back to Asria and find that woman. You'll bring her here to stand before me and answer for her crimes."

The man didn't have a clue, did he? Avery was long gone. Probably on Ventana IV by now. Did he expect Chase to kidnap her from the Commonwealth's capital planet?

Perhaps a small strike team—

But no. He wouldn't bring Avery to Haedera even if he could. On Ventana she was almost out of the reach of ISC, and he couldn't be more relieved about that. If only she was cooperative enough to stay there and out of a war zone. She had to stay safe. She had to let the Commonwealth protect her.

And you know her better than that . . .

The Shrike was another matter. He had no issues with the Haederan Empire retrieving their own property. A verium-enhanced ship, no less—how had Avery been so lucky and the crew of *Aurora* been so unlucky for her to choose one for her escape? Yes, they had to get that back. But if that small strike team was sent to Ventana to recover it, there was always the chance they'd create a side mission of their own and decide to bring back Avery along with it. She'd be easy to find.

He suppressed a cringe.

"Sire, the fighter is likely in Commonwealth hands by now, and—"

The emperor's face turned scarlet. "Did I ask you to speak? To make more excuses for your failure?"

Chase slammed his mouth shut. "No, sir."

"Then shut up. Lient has your new orders. You can stop by and pick them up once I'm done with you."

They weren't done already?

"Because I don't care if you succeed the second time around. You're going to drag her in here yourself, and even that feat won't absolve you of these mistakes. It won't change a thing except for her manner of death, which I'll personally ensure is protracted and painful. You've gone too far, and I won't stand for it." The emperor twisted sideways toward the door that led out through the desert gardens and raised his voice. "Captain. You can bring him in now."

What—

Something was wrong. Something was terribly wrong. Linden was dead. Lient was apparently in his office at ISC headquarters over ten kilometers away, awaiting Chase's visit to pick up new orders. He was probably writing a reprimand of his own, too. No one else knew he was back on Haedera, not even anyone at Windhaven. Not even Zavis. So who was *him*?

The door clicked open. A wave of green blew in on the hot midmorning breeze, as uncomfortable as the exhaust of a courier ship. Five ISC men—Captain Brennin Kern among them—with a small child in their midst.

His knees buckled; his mouth went dry.

Marc.

His son beamed in recognition, then darted for him with a happy screech.

"Father!"

Run.

Run away and don't look back.

He thought he'd screamed the order, but Marc didn't stop his sprint until he slammed into his legs. Small arms wrapped around his waist, and he curled his fingers through Marc's hair, coffee brown like Isobel's. It was all he could do to avoid picking up the boy and running straight out the door. They wouldn't make it five paces. Instead, he tightened his grip on the hair until Marc flinched.

"Aren't you forgetting something, Marc?" His father-in-law's voice softened.

"Yes, sir. I'm sorry." Marc released his legs and knelt before his grandfather, head lowered, like Chase had taught him so long ago. "Good morning, Your Majesty."

"And that, Gareth, is the proper way to treat your sovereign." The emperor's chin jerked toward the men surrounding Chase. "Hold him."

Before he could react, firm hands twisted his arms behind his back and yanked him away from the stairs. Chase was trembling too hard to fight them; his stomach heaved. He tried to bend forward so he didn't vomit all over himself, but they hauled him right back up, forcing the morning's tea into his mouth.

Marc spun toward him at the noise, his excitement gone. Still down on one knee—his sovereign hadn't invited him to stand yet. He and Isobel had trained the boy well.

"Father?"

It was a sob. Even a ten-year-old knew something was wrong. A ten-year-old knew his father wasn't immune from ISC. But it wasn't him in danger, it wasn't—

Sunlight splashed across his eyes, the reflection blinding him.

A knife.

Finally, too late, he found his voice. "Don't touch him! Take me instead!" He pulled one arm free and elbowed the nearest officer in the ribs, only to have his wrist jerked back once more. Metal cut into his skin, and he swore. The bastards were going to handcuff him?

Like hell they were.

He jerked away and stumbled toward the stairs, hands grabbing at him. The emperor ignored the scene and took a step down, closer to Marc.

His son turned back toward the emperor, eyes wide and filled with tears.

"Me?" He was nearly incoherent, tears spilling down his cheeks. "Grandpapa, why—"

The knife flashed across his throat.

The pressure on his arms eased as Marc stilled on the cold marble floor, and Chase fell forward with a cry. He didn't look at his baby. Couldn't focus on the blood. Just pulled Marc's limp body against his chest and buried his face in his hair. In the corner of his vision he thought the emperor's shoes had moved up a few stairs, but he didn't care if the man was standing over him or not. What else could his father-in-law do to him? He'd offered his own death twice in two days now, and the offer had been refused both times. No, in some sick twist of fate, he'd been ordered to live.

But living would have to come later. Much later. Because all he could do now was sob.

Until the thought came.

Sophie.

CHAPTER THIRTY-FOUR

SSHE WAS THE ONLY THING HE COULD THINK OF AS HE DARTED BACK TO Isobel's rooms, past the guards outside and past the doctor, who was asleep on a chair in the corner of the sitting room. No one stopped him, not even the ISC officers who'd released him once Marc's body had fallen to the floor. Strange. He must look like hell.

Meira was perched on a chair by the side window, reading a paper book with what daylight shone around the edges of the drapes. Her mouth opened and closed a few times when she saw him, then she covered it like she was about to be sick.

"How is she?" he asked, the words sand through his lips. He couldn't stop them, though he didn't want to know.

Meira didn't reply, only jerked to her feet and edged toward the bed, putting herself between him and Isobel.

He took a step toward her. Straighten, he had to straighten. Wave on some lights, let her see his uniform. Intimidate her out of the way. Remind her who he was. It'd always worked before—on everyone who crossed him. His body wouldn't obey his commands, though.

"Get out of my way," he said instead. "This second. I—I need her."

"No." She didn't move her hand from her mouth. "Don't you dare come near her with those clothes on."

Too numb to say anything about her insubordination, too dazed to explain the blood wasn't his fault, Chase stripped off the jacket of his dress uniform and let it fall to the floor. Meira's horrified look didn't change. *Was there blood on his shirt, too?* With shaking fingers, he began to work the buttons, but it was a lost cause. He yanked the edges apart, scattering silver buttons across the floor.

"Go home," he told her. "Now. Find Zavis, and the two of you take Sophie somewhere safe. I don't care where, but don't return to Windhaven or Rebet until I find you. Only me. Don't come out of hiding for anyone else. Don't tell anyone you're leaving the palace and don't tell anyone where you're taking her. Especially ISC."

"But Lady Isobel—"

"Is dying." There wasn't time for anything but painful candor. "She doesn't need you anymore, but Sophie does. Say goodbye and go."

Meira stared at him. At his stricken face, at his bare chest, at the pile of bloody clothes at his feet. Outside, an unearthly wind began to howl. A storm? If she didn't leave immediately, she'd be stuck here until it ended.

"Now!"

He hollered at her like he'd never screamed at a servant before, then turned toward Isobel. The door closed behind him, but he couldn't force his head to swivel to check, not even the least little bit. No, he could only stare at Isobel. Her eyes were closed, her breathing shallow, but she was as beautiful as the first day he'd seen her so long ago. They'd come so far, had been through so much triumph and pain. And now? Without thinking, he crawled into bed next to her. Her hands and feet were like ice. Isobel's feet hadn't been cold in years.

"I love you," he murmured against her ear. "I'm going to miss you so much. But we're going to be fine. You know that, don't you? Please don't hang on for us if you're tired of fighting. We're all right."

His voice cracked, and he buried his face in her shoulder, gasping for air. It was too hard to say. But maybe—maybe if he said it, it would become true. That was a lie, he knew it was a lie, but he had to—

No. He didn't need to lie to himself.

He had to reassure her that she could go.

"We're going to be just fine," he repeated. "Me and Sophie and —and Marc. All of us."

He hadn't known grief could hurt, hadn't known his chest could close in on itself. The sheets felt like a thousand knives being dragged across his back; he kicked them off and laid them back across Isobel. There was only one thing left to do.

He closed his eyes and sobbed.

* * *

No one saw him leave the imperial palace after Isobel's heart stopped beating against his hand six hours later.

Well, no one except the doctor, who'd ignored him as usual, and Owin, Isobel's oldest brother. The crown prince had been pacing in the sitting room for hours, and Chase had shoved him straight into the doorframe when he'd bolted from her rooms. He'd pay for that eventually, like he'd paid for the rest of his sins, but he and Owin had been close once. Maybe he'd escape punishment for his rash action—for surely Owin himself was in too much grief himself over Isobel to worry about it.

But it didn't matter. Owin hadn't followed him out—he was probably much too busy making arrangements for his sister since Chase had temporarily abdicated that responsibility to whoever would take it. No one else had shadowed him either, and there was something strange about that. The emperor should have sent guardsmen after him, or worse, ISC, but the streets of Rebet were dark and strangely empty.

He glanced up at the sky, starved for the stars for the first time in years, but saw only a rust-colored cloud in the distance. The wind he'd heard earlier had been an approaching dust storm, and he'd been off-world too long to remember what the beginning of one felt and looked like. Finally some luck. People wouldn't come out for another few hours, wouldn't see him stumbling down the street in bloodstained ISC dress pants and an old undershirt he'd found in Isobel's closet. And if they did, he decided he didn't much care.

Even so, he needed to find shelter. The coffee shops and authorized public houses that lined the main roads were popular for waiting out the storms that occasionally swept through the Maelor Valley, but he couldn't be seen in any of those. Not looking like this. A cathedral, maybe. No. His guilt—his sins—would be too painful there.

Enough wavering. You need to get inside.

Chase looked up and down the street. Emperor Devan II Park was nearby, its entrance within sight, and it would shield him from the storm. Did he dare? Marc had always loved it, and it would bring back painful memories, but there weren't any other choices.

Unlike the parks he'd become used to on Asria, the green space didn't look like anything other than cracked mud from the street where he stood. But underneath? The architects had done their job, and the park was as much an oasis as anything else on the planet. The creek at the foundation of the structure ran dry some seasons, but as he descended the stairs that led to the bottom, he could hear it rushing through the stone columns that held up the faux-sand ceiling.

It was surprising no one else was down here, especially since the howling wind had picked up, and a light mist of sand swirled around the more open areas of the park. Chase remembered it as a bustling place, full of children happily screaming and businessmen carving out small bits of stolen peace, but it was certainly empty now. Was it a holiday? Were people not hiding out in the coffee houses and public houses but celebrating at home or praying in the cathedrals? He'd been gone too long to know. He'd been gone too long to remember anything, really. Who he had been . . . who he was supposed to be.

The iron steps down the curved path clanged, the sound vibrating through the park. It could be a local seeking refuge from the dust storm like him, but . . . he yanked his pistol up without thinking. Grieving or not, he was ISC, and some things were instinctual. And if someone had followed him, especially one of the emperor's men—

"Gareth, put down the gun."

Chase squinted at the voice. At the single figure making its way toward him across the diminutive stone bridge, hands out to his side, shrouded in a thin fog of sand that had made its way below. The man was a hair taller than himself, but stooped now, as if the owner had had almost as bad of a night as he had. The immaculately cut suit—well, very few in Rebet would be out in a sandstorm dressed like they were about to meet a group of high-ranking council ministers. Especially when the newcomer had been wearing nothing so formal a few hours earlier.

Owin.

"Your Highness." Chase nearly breathed the words as he holstered the weapon. "You'll get yourself shot, sneaking up on people like that." Owin was lucky his reflexes were dull from grief. No, *he* was lucky. No matter how much the emperor wanted to punish him by making him live, he'd never survive accidentally shooting a senior member of the imperial family. "How did you—"

"Followed you. You weren't all that subtle when you left." Owin rubbed his arm where it had hit the doorframe. "I wanted to make sure you were all right."

"You're a terrible liar." No one in the palace was missing him, not today. Owin had more important things to do than hunt down his wayward brother-in-law.

Former brother-in-law now.

The pain in his chest became almost unbearable; pacing became impossible.

"It's no lie, though I admit it's not the only reason. We have some things to discuss."

"What things?"

Owin shook his head. "First things first. You're not planning on offing yourself, are you?"

It hadn't crossed his mind, but now that the prince mentioned it . . . what else was there to live for? Suicide could be honorable. He wouldn't be a danger to anyone any longer. He'd see Marc. And Isobel.

Maybe. The Holy One would have to forgive him for that to happen, and some sins were unforgivable, weren't they? He'd certainly been punished enough for them in this life—why not in the next as well?

Still, it was an appealing idea.

"Would you stop me if I was?" he asked.

"I'd make sure ISC did. One shout from me and they'd be here before you bled out." The words were humorous, his tone was not. "You're answerable to them, Colonel, whether you like it or not."

Did Owin know about the truth serum? His new orders to Asria? What else? Chase sank down against the trunk of the palm tree and ran his hands across his face.

"He killed Marc." Hot tears welled up again. How was there any water left in his body? "Right in front of me. As nothing more than punishment for a mistake I made. His own grandchild. Owin, I—"

His voice cracked. He hadn't called the crown prince by his name in over thirty years, not since they were children together.

"So I heard. What are you going to do about it?"

Chase chuckled mirthlessly. "You're a bad interrogator as well as a bad liar, Your Highness."

"Perhaps." Owin sank to the bench next to the tree and crossed his arms. "But the question—a rather valid one, I might add —stands."

"I'm not going to do anything about it." What else did Owin expect him to say? He might be grieving, and he might want to die, but he'd decide when and how. "Did Lient send you to ask me that? Or did—" He couldn't say the emperor's title. "Did he?"

"No one sent me. Believe it or not, I don't condone his actions."

"While I appreciate the sentiment, you know that doesn't matter."

"Hmm." Owin rubbed his chin. "What if it did?"

What did that—

Chase jerked his head up and stared at Owin. "Careful. As you made sure to remind me not two minutes ago, I still answer to ISC. I still serve the emperor, Your Highness."

Owin didn't flinch, just rested immaculately groomed nails against his cheek. "You'd turn me in for treason, brother? Tonight, of all times?"

Brother.

They stared at each other, then Chase blew out a deep breath.

"No. Not tonight." Probably not ever. Haedera didn't need the rest of Owin's brothers contending for their father's position. Hereditary position or not, things got messy when siblings were involved. Haederans liked order—there was no sense in disrupting that stability for no reason.

"Besides, serving the emperor is secondary to preserving the empire, if you've forgotten," Owin said.

"Really, sir, I don't need a lecture on loyalty and duty right now. When the storm settles, I'm headed to HQ to pick up my new orders." *Like nothing has happened.* "You can rest assured my loyalty to the empire is fully intact, and you can tell him that if he asks."

"I'm not lecturing, and I'm not reporting back to him. Simply reminding you of your duty, since you've had a rough few days."

"Fine. Serving the emperor is secondary to preserving the

empire," Chase repeated like he was twenty years younger. It was one of the tenets learned in initial ISC training and quickly forgotten, thanks to His Majesty's reputation as an authoritarian terror. Chase had forgotten it himself, and he knew the emperor better than most other officers. But the empire couldn't execute you as easily and quickly as its men could, and that at least was something worth saving. "So what?"

"So I hear the Commonwealth got their hands on a Shrike. With the new verium propulsion system. And that it's your fault."

Chase put his head in his hands. Did everyone know of his mistake and humiliation? Owin had the ear of the senior defense councilor, so of course he did. He'd probably heard before the emperor.

"Yeah," he said. "They did. And it is."

He hadn't known Avery would pick those handcuffs—the ones he'd told Linden not to worry about. Or that she'd be desperate enough and skilled enough to think of stealing a fighter to escape *Aurora*. Or that she'd be able to outrun half a squadron of *Aurora*'s fighters by disappearing into hyperspace. No one could have predicted any of that. *No one.*

Desperation makes us do a lot of strange things. You should have known.

"And once they figure out how to use it, how long do you think this advance of my father's will last? How much mercy do you imagine they'll grant us when they have the military strength to rival ours?"

Chase sucked in a breath. Owin wasn't skirting treason now—he was sticking his foot over the line and seeing if anyone shot at him. He had an obligation. Even the crown prince couldn't be speaking like this.

"You're proposing treason to save the empire," Chase said. "That's some impressive rationalization, Your Highness."

He glanced up through the crack, but the wind was howling. Owin's security team—and they were far enough away that he couldn't identify them as individuals, only as dark figures in the distance—couldn't be allowed to hear anything they were saying.

"Sure, they're up there," Owin said. "They think I'm informing the distraught Earl of Windhaven that his wife is dead. My father's dangerous, and you know it," he added without hesitation.

"What do you really want, Your Highness?" The headache building behind his eyes didn't allow for the mental interpretation of Owin's remarks. *Just come out with it.*

"I'll tell you what I don't want." Owin glanced around the empty park, then raised his eyebrows. "I don't want Iythea. Or Thaopra. Or Hanides. Or Asria. Or any of the rest of them. Never have, never will."

He stood and grinned down at Chase.

"I want the throne."

CHAPTER THIRTY-FIVE

It had taken months of anxious living in the hills outside Cadena before the knocks on her front door ceased to be frightening. Asria was a Haederan protectorate, true, and unease ran rampant across the planet these days, but the knocks were never the Imperial Haederan Army Katryn had feared since Iythea. No, most of the time it was a random Imperial Security officer from the local base stopping by for a routine check. Their visits were a hated reminder of Rhys and the war, but their regular presence kept all but the most curious neighbors away, and that was fine with Katryn. A reputation as a Haederan sympathizer—or person of interest—was better than people constantly dropping in.

Today her visitor was neither an inquisitive neighbor nor an unfamiliar Haederan officer from the garrison. Colonel Chase stood on her doorstep in a pressed ISC uniform, hands behind his back. On the surface, he appeared as polished as when he'd left Asria with Rhys, but the dark circles under his eyes and flash of gray at his temple told another story—he'd aged twenty years in the months since she'd last seen him. Silently, he followed her inside, through the house, and onto the back patio that overlooked the distant mountains. The view was the only thing that gave her peace these days.

Well. Not quite the only thing.

Chase took a deep breath and sank into one of the wooden chairs that pointed toward the mountains. Katryn had insisted on two. The decision had seemed foolishly hopeful when they'd first shown her to the cozy house in the hills, and even more foolish now that Chase was back from Haedera. Alone. She sat next to him, Grace fast asleep in her arms, and waited for the end.

"It's over," he said, looking not at her but out at the snow-capped peaks. "I'm sorry."

Her throat closed up, and for a few minutes, she couldn't speak. Why had she thought Rhys might be waiting down the road? Of course he wasn't on Asria. Of course he was dead, buried as a traitor on Haedera, perhaps with the rest of his family next to him. The thought of the sisters he'd loved so much being executed along with him was enough to make her sick.

"I'd assumed any good news would have come long before now," she finally said. "I wasn't hoping for anything different with your arrival."

Chase didn't look at her, didn't even turn his stare from the distant view. "You're lying," he said. "Not that I'd have expected anything else from you or any other sane person. There's nothing wrong with clinging to hope, no matter how slim the thread is. Only sometimes the thread snaps." He pulled a small folded note from his pocket and handed it over. "For you. I'm sorry it's been opened. All his communications had to be monitored. By me," he added hurriedly. "This one only by me."

The paper, especially around the broken seal, was fragile between her fingers, like unfolding it the wrong way would rip it. Katryn set it on the arm of her chair, though all she wanted to do was tear into it and read the words over and over.

"And his sisters?" she asked.

Chase met her eyes. "Devastated, I would assume."

Her stomach unknotted enough so she could breathe easily. Devastated was terrible, yes, but devastated meant alive. She nodded in relief.

The smallest curve of his mouth confirmed her optimistic assumption. He swung his knees toward her, his gaze landing on Grace.

"May I?"

Dare she trust him with the most precious thing she had left? With a quick prayer to the winds, she passed Grace over, and he kissed the top of her head, almost reverently.

"You are beautiful, Grace Alexandra Linden," he said. "Your father would be so proud." He shot Katryn a self-conscious look. "I trust you're not offended by my Haederan sensibilities if I say I hope she has freckles."

"I suppose we'll find out in a few years." It wasn't as horrifying a prospect as she'd have once assumed. "You have children, Colonel?" He looked far too comfortable holding a baby to not have any of his own.

Grace grunted in her sleep, and Katryn jerked toward her. Chase simply shifted her against his chest and rubbed her back until she grew silent.

"Twins," he said, closing his eyes. His voice grew soft. "I can't remember what they looked like when they were this young. I only have vague memories of holding them like this." He gave Katryn a strangled laugh. "I suppose that's no surprise. I was exhausted back then."

He looked exhausted now—but then, long-haul space travel did that to people.

"You must miss them when you're off-world," she said.

Or maybe he didn't. Except for Rhys, Imperial Security Command officers didn't have souls. That was what her new neighbors said, anyway. If Chase's people didn't quit stopping in, they'd soon begin to say the same thing about her.

"Very much so." Chase gave her an impression of a smile, though it didn't do anything for the dark circles under his eyes. "I have something to tell you, if you're willing to hear me out to the end . . . and if you allow me to hold this little one while I talk."

Katryn shrugged. He seemed to be the type to tell her whatever he wanted—whether she wanted to hear it or not.

"I take it that's a yes?" Chase leaned back in his chair and crossed a foot over his knee. "Rhys and I had quite a bit of time to talk on the way to Haedera, both officially and off the record."

He narrowed his eyes at her, like he was debating what to say next. "He lied to you about what happened to your brother. It wasn't suicide—your brother lunged for his gun and Rhys shot him in self-defense. I wasn't there, but I read the report. The rather detailed report, I might add. I can't say for certain what really happened that night, but I have to believe the official account. Major Feye was"—he sighed—"a rather high-level source for us. The most valuable Rhys had ever handled. There's no way he walked into that hangar intending to kill your brother."

A cold shiver worked its way down her body, despite the heat of the day. "Why did he lie?"

"I asked him about that discrepancy. It seems he didn't want to burden you with the knowledge of what had really happened, not right then. Right or wrong, he lied to protect you from a truth that may have broken you in that moment."

He nudged Grace a little farther up, over his shoulder, and she settled her soft cheek against his neck. "Doctor Holt, I don't know if he ever said as much out loud, but I do believe he loved you— even if he shouldn't have. Even if he didn't know it himself when he said goodbye."

"He killed my brother." She couldn't cry in front of this man like she'd done with Rhys, but she was growing closer and closer to that by the second. "He used him, and he used me. He . . . you . . . your empire . . . you are the enemy of everything I've ever known and believed in." One only had to look around Asria—at the Haederan soldiers who were all over this little part of the valley, at the fear in her neighbors' eyes—to know that. It was only grief and foolishness and misplaced trust that permitted her to confess this kind of Haederan-dictated treason to an ISC officer. "How can you say he loved me?"

Chase was silent for a long time.

"War is chaotic," he said. "It's messy. It always has been and always will be, and some of the best people don't make it through. And split-second decisions are never easy when your life is at stake. Believe me, Rhys paid for his quick decision. I think if he'd had an hour or so to ponder it, he'd have decided on a different course of action that morning—but he didn't have that kind of time. I try not to fault my people for difficult decisions, even when they result in death."

Was she supposed to believe that? He hadn't even answered her question.

"And that leaves me with what? A daughter without a father and a traitor brother?"

He kissed Grace's head. "Every child deserves to know their father, but she has a few dozen men at that garrison over there watching out for her. And she has you. Somehow, I think the two of you will make it just fine."

"And Xan?"

"Your brother," he said carefully, "died trying to save an Asrian citizen and Commonwealth intelligence operative from certain capture. Whatever crimes against the Commonwealth that he might have committed under extreme duress prior to that . . . it might ease your mind to know that he seemed to have changed his mind in the end. I am almost certain the consequences of that choice will be felt throughout the quadrant for years to come."

"Good consequences?"

"Only the Holy One knows." Grace began to stir, and he handed her over, then stood and stretched. "I suppose we'll find out eventually. Sooner rather than later if I have any say in it."

"I hope so." What else was there to say?

"So now what?" he asked.

Katryn bit her lip and gazed at the mountains. "I don't know. When she's a little older, I suppose I'll find something to do. There must be a need for engineers on Asria somewhere. If the Haederans allow me."

Her cheeks grew red. Even on Asria in the middle of an occupation, even with the soldiers, it was sometimes too easy to forget who the enemy was. Maybe Rhys had blurred those lines forever for her.

Chase reached in his pocket and held out a small card. "When you're ready, she's waiting for your call. There's no rush."

Her eyes lighted on the title first: Bella Martell, Executive Chairman of Cadena Dynamics. Even she'd heard of them—their work with novel metallic space structures was legendary across the quadrant. Katryn gasped at Chase, wide-eyed. Were more innocent people answerable to the Haederans—to ISC!—because of what Xan had done? It was intolerable. Occupation or not, she was still Zarcronian.

"Did you—did you threaten her into offering me a job?"

He burst out laughing as she stammered the question, his eyes dancing with the first real happiness he'd shown since he'd arrived. Katryn pulled Grace against her chest, but the infant didn't so much as stir at the noise.

"Of course I didn't threaten her," he said, choking down the remainder of a chuckle. "I only told her about your work, which yes, you've got me there. I may have done a little investigation on you and handed it over to her. She looked about as stunned to hear you were on Asria as you do right now."

After Iythea, the idea of anyone respecting her and her work was daunting. Daunting, and yet it gave her a relief so heavy that she wanted to cry. And if Chase hadn't coerced anyone . . . Yes, she would make the call in a few weeks.

"Then I appreciate it. What about you? Now, I mean," she added hastily, setting the card next to Rhys's note.

Chase smiled. "I'm expected back in Cadena tonight. I've got an early flight to Emot tomorrow. But first I'm going to make you dinner. And then we're going to stare at these mountains while you eat . . . and I'll tell Grace everything she needs to know about her father."

EPILOGUE

Emot wasn't nearly as bad as Avery had once said. She hated the place, though she'd never been able to give him a better reason than *I just prefer Cadena and Asria.* There had to be a story there, because, on the surface, Chase saw nothing wrong with the small planet. It was cooler than Asria on average, yes, but after his short time on Haedera, the chill and almost constant rain didn't bother him as much as it should—as it had when he'd first arrived on Asria. Neither did that disloyal thought, and the idea of not missing home as much as before was perhaps more disturbing than anything else.

Chase returned the sentry's salute and headed south across what looked to be a parade field but was probably reserved space to build more barracks—the Imperial Haederan Navy was certainly settling in. He took the long way to the commandant's office, and he risked running into Merritt Parker out here in this open stretch of meadow, but he needed to stretch his legs after the long shuttle flight from Asria. If Parker saw him, he saw him—for even Parker, as furious as he would be if he'd found out what'd happened to Avery, wouldn't chance an assault on an ISC officer in the middle of a prison camp. Not even if said ISC officer had promised him one thing and defaulted on that promise . . . or so he hoped. And if he was at all honest with himself, his next move skirted treason. It was something he would put off as long as he could.

As if what he was planning was anything compared to what he'd overlooked on Haedera. Owin had never struck him as the treasonous sort, not that mild and easygoing boy he'd known so long ago, but things changed, didn't they? And now . . . well, Owin had better know what he was doing. This plan of his could end badly for everyone—or it could be the chance for peace the quadrant needed.

It could be the chance for peace *he* needed.

The commandant's office came into view over a low rise, a flat-topped brown building on the far southwest side of the camp, right inside the shielding net that contained the three-square-kilo-meter facility. The reminder, right out the window, of being trapped day after day would wear on his nerves—that was part of the reason he hated space work—but maybe Admiral Treton didn't care. He got to leave the camp every evening, after all, back to the garrison on the other side of the river where a luxurious suite of rooms awaited him.

His long walk, relaxing though it'd been, had made him late; Chase slipped inside the front door without a word to the guards pacing outside. Treton was waiting down the hall outside the building's sole conference room, but he didn't look angry at the delay. No, curiosity about his ISC visitor overshadowed any of his anger toward Chase's tardiness. Too bad he'd never find out.

"He's inside, Colonel," Treton said as he approached. "But I'm not entirely certain . . ." His forehead creased. "I want it on the record that I haven't had any trouble with him since he arrived. None at all. I can't imagine ISC has much interest in him."

Ah, yes. Treton was afraid he was going to create a scene, terrify everyone else at the camp, and ruin morale—as much as one could ruin morale in a place where everyone was miserable to begin with. Instead of telling the admiral to mind his own business thirty seconds after arriving, Chase murmured his understanding and thanks and pushed open the door.

If the admiral had looked perplexed about what was going on, Lieutenant Colonel Stev Kanmar looked absolutely mystified as he sprang to his feet—though his confusion was tempered with an undercurrent of worry. Well, if Treton had told him an Imperial Security Command officer was here to visit, that made sense. What else had the admiral implied? Kanmar was probably reliving his past few months on Emot in his mind, trying to decide if he'd made any missteps that might have brought attention to him. He was grateful the man hadn't had a stroke.

"You," Kanmar said, recognition flickering across his face. "You were on the transport when they moved me from Alcaris. What—"

He narrowed his eyes, an unusual light green, like Avery's. In fact, he could be a distant cousin of hers, with the same delicate nose and strange Cadena accent, though he wasn't from anywhere near the capital. That made Kanmar a descendent of the Asrian aristocratic class, his family demoted to commoners after their bitter civil war hundreds of years ago. On Haedera the man would have likely had some sort of title, but the fates hadn't been as kind to him on Asria.

Or maybe they had. Kanmar had children back home, after all, and they were still alive.

Chase glanced at Treton, hovering in the doorway. Even if he shut the door in the admiral's face, they wouldn't get any privacy in this conference room with him out there.

"Let's go for a walk before it starts raining again," he said to Kanmar. "It's too nice to sit inside today, don't you think?"

Kanmar didn't argue, and neither did Treton, though Chase could feel the admiral's curious gaze on his back as they walked outside. *You can stare at me like that all you want, but I'm not going to tell you.* He led Kanmar away from the shielding field toward the barracks in the distance. It was almost a kilometer before he spoke.

"Royal Asrian Defense Forces Space Operations, right? Captured at Alcaris on 21 Cael of last year?"

"I'm sure you've read my file, sir." Kanmar didn't look at him, just kicked at the red clay as they walked.

Confrontational from the start. Wonderful—perhaps it was because he'd used the Haederan calendar. That'd been a novice mistake, but remembering the local calendar of yet another conquered planet was the last thing on his mind right now. Well, it didn't matter. He'd wear Kanmar down, and quickly. All he had to do was mention Avery's name.

"Is it better here than Alcaris?" Chase asked. It was a polite reminder, if not necessarily a polite question.

Kanmar shrugged, though a little of his hostility faded as their muddy footsteps proceeded onward—he'd probably remembered who was responsible for him not being in Perrin's clandestine facility anymore.

"It's a prison camp," he said. "On Emot. It's not Asria, and it's not home. But—but yes. Of course it's better. And it seems I have you to thank for that—for whatever reason." His glower said he expected an answer quickly.

"Luck on your part, I suppose. You were in the wrong place at the right time when I walked in, and I was having a benevolent day." Chase grinned. It was mostly the truth. *No going back now.* "How would you like to get out completely? To go home to Tarragona?"

Kanmar shuffled his feet in that appalling red clay. It was all over this part of Emot—how did the locals stand it? Chase resisted the impulse to scrape his own feet against each other. He was going to have to clean his boots before he got back on the shuttle, because the pilots would never let him tarnish their precious craft with mud.

Spacers.

"Going home is all anyone wants, Colonel," Kanmar said, "but that's not going to happen anytime soon. The war's still on.

Things are bad on Asria. And you wouldn't have built this place if you didn't intend on using it for a good long while."

All that was true—for the most part.

"The navy built it," Chase said. "And I don't much care if they have enough prisoners to fill it or not." There wasn't much, if anything, he cared about since Marc's death. Certainly not what the navy was doing on Emot. "Anyway, they won't miss one man."

Kanmar stopped and faced him, silent, his arms crossed.

"There's an amnesty program starting in a few weeks," he went on. "Defense Forces officers who cooperated after the annexation—"

"Invasion, sir."

Chase managed to not roll his eyes.

"—and meet certain requirements can swear into the Imperial Haederan Navy and continue working. Space Operations officers won't have any trouble finding a position. Nothing classified or sensitive, of course, but it's something to do. It would get you into space. It requires a clean background, so no one in this camp is eligible, but if you're interested, I can make things happen."

Just like last time, he didn't add.

Kanmar looked him up and down and burst out laughing. Actually burst out laughing at him, standing there in that ghastly mud, wearing a tattered Defense Forces uniform. No, this was most certainly not Haedera. Didn't this man know who he was?

"Swear allegiance to your emperor to get out of here?" Kanmar's laughter came to a sudden stop. "You think they haven't suggested that before? You all made the same offer after you first annexed us, and I didn't take it then. What makes you think I'd do it for you now? Because you did me a favor? I'll rot here before I'll betray Asria like that. I'll go back to Alcaris before that happens. Every single officer in this place would tell you the same thing. You're wasting your time."

He turned on his heel, back toward Treton's office, likely the one person he thought could run Chase off.

Holy One, grant me patience. And wisdom. And . . .

And whatever else.

Courage?

"It's the only way that she'll ever rule Asria," Chase called after him.

Kanmar slid to a halt on the slick ground, gave his feet a long look, then turned, his face blank.

"Who?"

"You know who."

One icy raindrop hit his forehead. He didn't look up, just brushed it away and waited as his heart thumped against his chest.

"Is this a setup?" Kanmar wiped his hands on his pants and glanced furtively around, the first real sign of anxiety he'd shown. "Did someone put you up to this? Admiral Treton? General Perrin? Trying to catch me—is someone trying to get me sent back to Alcaris?"

"Trying to catch you doing what?" Chase asked. "You haven't done anything. On the other hand, I just confessed to treason." His hair was soaked now, and it was becoming more and more difficult to suppress a shiver, but he wasn't going to move. "I'm the one taking the risk here. You could waltz right back to Admiral Treton and . . . well, I'm sure you could get something you wanted for turning me in."

He watched Kanmar process that argument, growing colder and colder as the rain fell harder. Maybe Avery had been right about Emot—it was a wretched planet. He had to get out of here, and he needed to convince Kanmar of the same.

One more gentle shove . . .

"So how about it?" he asked. "You want to help Asria? You want to have a chance to kneel in front of her one day instead of fighting a losing battle from here? I'm giving you that chance right here, right now. But I need an answer in the next thirty seconds—and your promise that you won't breathe a word of this to anyone. You can walk out of here with me today, head back to Asria, and continue the war."

Kanmar stared at his feet. They were going to drown in the lake that was forming before he made a decision—but he hadn't walked away. As long as he was standing out in this deluge, as long as he was thinking, there was a chance he'd make the right one. Chase brushed the water from his shoulders and held his breath.

"We don't kneel to anyone on Asria anymore. Not even the queen." Kanmar rubbed the back of his neck, then looked up and smiled. "What do you want me to do?"

ACKNOWLEDGMENTS

I don't know if there's any novel that comes into being without a large group of people behind the scenes, and *Shattered Honor* is no exception. Massive thanks are due to Andy, Meghan, Beth, Hope, Katherine, Amanda, Bokerah, Becky, Christy, Amber, Christi, and the rest of the village for their feedback and unwavering support.

ABOUT THE AUTHOR

Anne Wheeler grew up with her nose in a book but earned two degrees in aviation before it occurred to her she was allowed to write her own. When not working, moving, or writing her next novel, she can be found planning her next escape to the desert—camera gear included. She currently lives in Georgia with her husband, son, and herd of cats.

For more information:
www.anne-wheeler.com

ALSO BY ANNE WHEELER

'Last Mission'

The Brightest Void

Vortex

Crownkeeper

Crownkeeper Novellas

Treason's Crown

War's Crown

Queen's Crown

Shadows of War

Asrian Skies

Unbroken Fire

Shattered Honor

Faded Embers

The Star Realm Saga

The Stars Wait Not

A House of Nebulas